Readers love *Spring Affair*
by B.G. THOMAS

I0614676

"This book is full of pain and hurt, but also hope and elation. He really hit it out of the park for me with this one."
—My Fiction Nook

"I enjoyed this book very much. The characters are engaging and the storytelling pulled me into their lives. I was pleased with the conclusion and I am happily looking forward to the next book in the series."
—Live Your Life, Buy the Book

"B.G. Thomas's special touch in dealing with… issues, his humor, and the way he lets the story play out make it a fascinating character study and a touching, gentle romance at the same time. Bravo!"
—Rainbow Book Reviews

"*Spring Affair* by B.G. Thomas is more than a simple love story. It is an exploration of all we can be and all that we push away in fear that we will never be the person others expect of us."
—Joyfully Jay

"I found this book well written. The main and secondary characters were interesting and realistic… I can't wait for the next book in the series."
—Hearts on Fire

"Overall, this story is all about letting go and living free. Free of guilt, free of lies, and most of all being free to be who you are. I highly recommend this for everyone."
—The Novel Approach

"This book is very full, and it is the sort of story you want to read when you need to be filled up."
—Prism Book Alliance

By B.G. THOMAS

All Alone in a Sea of Romance
All Snug
Anything Could Happen
Bianca's Plan
The Boy Who Came In From the Cold
Christmas Cole
Christmas Wish
Desert Crossing
Grumble Monkey and the Department Store Elf
Hound Dog and Bean
How Could Love Be Wrong?
It Had to Be You
Just Guys
Men of Steel (Dreamspinner Anthology)
Riding Double (Dreamspinner Anthology)
A Secret Valentine
Soul of the Mummy
Two Tickets to Paradise (Dreamspinner Anthology)

SEASONS OF LOVE
Spring Affair
Summer Lover

Published by DREAMSPINNER PRESS
http://www.dreamspinnerpress.com

Summer
Lover

B.G. Thomas

Dreamspinner Press

Published by
DREAMSPINNER PRESS

5032 Capital Circle SW, Suite 2, PMB# 279, Tallahassee, FL 32305-7886 USA
http://www.dreamspinnerpress.com/

Summer Lover
© 2014 B.G. Thomas.

Cover Art
© 2014 Paul Richmond.
http://www.paulrichmondstudio.com
Cover content is for illustrative purposes only and any person depicted on the cover is a model.

ISBN: 978-1-63216-132-1
Digital ISBN: 978-1-63216-133-8
Library of Congress Control Number: 2014940015
First Edition July 2014

Quote by James Broughton used with permission of Joel Singer, heir to the estate of James Broughton.
"Altar Of Love" words and music © 2007 Karen Drucker and David Ault. Used with permission.
"Open Road" words and music © 2003 Heather Thornton. Used with permission.
"Time to Shine" words and music © 2002 Heather Thornton. Used with permission.
"The Hoo Hoo Song" words and music © 2007 Lori Whalen, Celia, and The Trestle Foote Faerie, by Red Granite Goddess Music. Used with permission.

Printed in the United States of America
∞
This paper meets the requirements of
ANSI/NISO Z39.48-1992 (Permanence of Paper).

This one is for my Faerie Brothers at MMF and those not yet met all over the world. You hold my heart in your hands. May we all dare to dwell in beauty, balance, and delight.

I want to dedicate this book to two men who touched me and changed me more than words will ever be able to say: DeeDee Pfeiffer and JayBee Becker. You were my gurus and my guides. I will love you as long as I breathe.

Special thanks to Andi Byassee for all her work (I don't know what I would do without you!) and VJ Summers for her sharp eyes (you are a lifesaver!).

Summer passes and one remembers one's exuberance.

—Yoko Ono

I hate camping, but I love summer camp.

—Zooey Deschanel

Aaah, summer—that long anticipated stretch of lazy, lingering days, free of responsibility and rife with possibility. It's a time to hunt for insects, master handstands, practice swimming strokes, conquer trees, explore nooks and crannies, and make new friends.

—Darell Hammond

To every thing there is a season, and a time to every purpose under the heaven.

—Ecclesiastes 3:1, KJV

Listen   Brothers   Listen
The alarms are on fire
The oracles are strangled
Hear the pious vultures
condemning your existence
Hear the greedy warheads
calling for your death
Quick while there's time
Take heed Take heart
Claim your innocence
Proclaim your fellowship
Reach to each other
Connect one another
and hold

—James Broughton

from *Shaman Psalm*

CHAPTER ONE

IT WAS June seventh, and that made it the first Saturday of the month, and first Saturday meant it was Porch Night.

Scott Aberdeen rushed around the apartment seeing to last and final touches. Everything looked good. There wasn't even an old filter in the Mr. Coffee maker. He adjusted his Versace glasses and checked the time, then dashed to the bathroom and checked his hair one more time. It looked perfect. When he glanced down at the sink, he saw he had remembered—*excellent*—to put everything away. He knew if he hadn't, the guys would tease him. So what if he used a lot of product, both on his face and in his hair? The key to good skin was moisturize, moisturize, moisturize! The way to have nice hair was to take care of it, condition it, and make sure it was in style. He might not be all that much to look at, but he was going to have smooth skin long after they were all looking wrinkly!

He checked his hair one—*more*—time.

Flawless. And it should be for what he paid for a haircut!

If nature hadn't given one the looks it had given Asher, Sloan (*oh, Sloan!*), or even chubby little bear Wyatt, then one had to improvise. Why else had he bought Versace when they were only reading glasses? Well, dammit! If he was going to wear glasses, they would be the *best* glasses and not some cheap-ass Walmart or Dollar Store brand.

Scott went to the kitchen, opened the freezer, and checked the cocktails. He'd finally decided on margaritas—the frozen kind. They were easy and they were tasty, and he didn't like to spring new cocktail recipes on his friends. You never knew if a concoction was going to turn out all right or not, and he didn't want (or couldn't afford) to spend a lot on alcohol and have the outcome be less than spectacular. Not when it was for his closest friends, the members of the Fabulous Four.

Or as Wyatt liked to say, the *Fab*ulous Four.

There would be no cosmopolitans with pink sugar on the rims of the glasses tonight. No chocolate martinis. And no watermelon breezes with coconut milk.

Nope. Not happening. With the price he paid for a haircut—and his "fiends" would never stop giving him shit about that, either—there were times when Scott worried the utilities might be shut off. So the margarita buckets would have to do. They'd been on sale (Buy One, Get the Second Half Off!) and with some cheap tequila and water thrown in the container with the mix—voilà—

cocktails! Cheaper than the martinis and ten times as much to drink. Maybe twenty.

What was really cool was all you had to do once you mixed them was stick them in the freezer. Scott wasn't sure how they worked, but instead of freezing solid, they came out slushy-wonderful, and he didn't even have to get the blender out. They were perfect for a summer day, and even though it was only the seventh of June, the heat was coming, baby. It was going to be a scorcher of a summer if today was any indication.

Scott heard laughter, peeked out his balcony doors, and saw it was Sloan—his blazing red hair unmistakable (and—*oh!*—there was that familiar sharp ache in his chest at the sight of him). And there was Wyatt, of course—short, a tad thick in the middle, and just as unmistakable wearing a rainbow beanie, complete with propeller, and a matching striped tank top And jeeze! *Could* the two of them drive anywhere separately? Terra's Gate wasn't that big a town!

Scott went to the door of his apartment with a flash of guilt at the damned ten-dollar bucket margaritas (at least he had bought the second one) because, after all, this was about Sloan's promotion. Would it have hurt him to spring for a little more booze? He only had to host once every four months, after all. And this *was* about Sloan.

A dizzy little feeling rushed through Scott. Sloan!

Scott stood at the open door of his apartment and waited for the intercom to let him know to buzz his friends up. But there was nothing, and then he heard them below, laughing and coming up the stairs. Some asshole must have left the security door propped open. What the hell was the use of paying for safety measures if his fellow tenants were going to leave the door open? Anyone could come in! He would have to complain to management again.

Wyatt was saying "… and *damn*, girl! You should have seen him. *Hunka*-cola, mm-*hmm*," followed by Sloan's laughter, happy and musical (and why shouldn't he be happy?), and then they had both reached the halfway point in the staircase and were now coming around the bend.

And damn but he was in love with Sloan!

Sloan, who was gorgeous—with beautiful skin the color of thick white cream with about a thousand red freckles across his cheeks and his cute button nose. And, oh oh oh, that new-copper-penny hair! Not to mention his eyes…. Golden brown like graham crackers.

Sloan, who didn't have a single clue how Scott felt about him.

Sloan, who for a long time had carried a frigging torch for Asher—the Greek god of their little quartet—a man who didn't know what love was and didn't or wouldn't or just plain *couldn't* love Sloan back. Certainly not the way Scott loved Sloan. Loved him an ocean's worth that constantly threatened to burst through the docks Scott had set up to keep himself from drowning.

Sloan, who had finally gotten over Asher only to fall for Mr. Goddamned Perfect, a man who actually loved him back. The new love had even come equipped with a son for them to raise—a *gay* son—and now the three of them were one big happy gay family.

"Hey!" said Wyatt, finally noticing Scott standing at the top of the stairs. "What's up, buttercup?"

"What's the deal, banana peel?" Scott replied.

Sloan grinned up at Scott, his eyes squinting and those dimples appearing in his cheeks, the right one deeper as always. Scott's heart skipped a beat. He *felt* it. "Scott!"

"What's cookin', good-lookin'?" Scott said.

"Hey!" Wyatt pouted. "He's good-lookin' and I am a banana peel?"

"You sure eat enough of them," Scott answered.

"Well, that's certainly true," Wyatt said as he and Sloan reached the top of the stairs. "Hey. I got a joke for you...."

Of course he did.

"What goes 'Aaaaahhhhh?'"

"You when you're getting it up the butt?" Scott answered.

Wyatt put his hands on his hips—Scott noticed that his shirt said "Nobody Knows I'm Gay"—and glowered at Scott. "*Very* funny." Then his brows shot up and he grinned foolishly. "You know, I probably *do* make a noise like that."

"Gross." Scott wrinkled his nose. Imagining Wyatt getting fucked by his big-gutted and balding boyfriend had not been on the agenda.

"You're the one who said it," Wyatt reminded him.

"Forget it, then," Scott shot back. "Just tell me the answer to the joke."

"Maybe you should save it until Asher gets here," Sloan suggested.

"I *am* here," came a deep voice, and sure enough, here came Asher, looking like Apollo with dark blond hair (or was it light brown?), flashing blue-green eyes, and a body to make Channing Tatum turn green with envy. He even walked like some ancient god, set down on Earth to care for mere mortals. All Scott had to do was look at Asher to know why he had never stood a chance with Sloan. It wasn't the first time Scott had had that thought. It wasn't even the thousandth. Asher was beautiful. He was perfect. And Scott knew all *he* would ever be was plain as a brown paper grocery sack. *Ugly. That's what I am. Ugly!*

"Asher," Wyatt cried excitedly. "What goes 'Aaaaahhhhhh?'"

"I don't know," Asher replied and leaned against the top of the staircase handrail. He looked like he was posing for a fashion magazine. "What *does* go 'Aaaaahhhhhh?'"

"A sheep with no lips!" Wyatt burst into laughter.

They all joined him, even Scott (albeit reluctantly). It wasn't a *great* joke, but then Wyatt was just getting started.

CHAPTER TWO

ASHER BROUGHT champagne. Of course he did.

"How else can we celebrate Sloan's promotion," Asher asked and opened the bottle with a loud *pop!* He did this on the balcony, and the cork shot a remarkable distance and bounced off the roof of a car in the parking lot. The view from Scott's apartment was less than picturesque. "It's not Dom, but it's the thought that counts, huh?"

Everyone agreed, but to Scott it seemed as if Asher were saying he'd spared Sloan no thought at all.

And, no. The champagne certainly *wasn't* Dom. Cheap Asti all the way. And if Miller was the champagne of beers, then Asti was the beer of champagnes.

It wasn't even champagne! It was a sparkling wine. It had to come from the Champagne region of France, or it wasn't Champagne. This shit was probably no more than about ten, twelve bucks. The two buckets of margarita mix, even with the buy one, get one free price, was more expensive. Hell, the bottle of Sauza tequila cost more in all probability. But Asher would get the glory and Scott would barely be thanked at all. Why did he bother even trying to host these things?

Luckily, Scott had champagne glasses, *nice* ones he'd found along with a crystal ice bucket at an estate sale, for a steal. He'd looked them up online and to his glee discovered the ice bucket was vintage, made by Cartier. It even had the Cartier signature on the bottom and was worth two hundred dollars. And the glasses, also by Cartier, were worth over twice that. He almost felt guilty. *Almost.* He'd thought about selling them on eBay, but thankfully he hadn't. How fortuitous that decision (procrastination) was today.

So they drank to Sloan's promotion.

"Here's to you," said Asher.

"You deserve it, my friend," Scott said and felt so proud of him he almost teared up.

"Wise, kind, gentle, generous, sexy," Wyatt added. "But enough about me. Here's to you, Sloan!"

And sure enough, Sloan laughed—even though Scott wanted to pop Wyatt one. He elected to take a drink instead. Because dammit, Sloan did deserve it!

Sloan worked in a call center and had been miserable for at least the last year. Then one day he took a chance and told the owner of the company what he thought of the scripts the operators had to use when serving the customers. What he said was that they sucked. It was pretty ballsy, considering the man he was talking to was none other than Peter Wagner.

Peter Wagner was not only the richest man in town—with a huge mansion on the hill overlooking Terra's Gate—not only a man with a college, a park, and a street named after his family, but was one of the richest people in the country as well.

Luckily, Wagner admired Sloan's balls and gave him a chance to rewrite one of the company scripts. It had gone over like a go-go boy at a gay bar. Dozens of calls and letters came in praising the operators for how helpful they'd been. It was clear Sloan was the cause.

Scott had been thrilled for his friend. Sloan had been miserable because he'd been relegated to mediocrity, and Scott knew he was genius just waiting to be discovered.

That script led Sloan to be discovered.

Soon he was writing more, and as of this week, he'd been promoted. Now everything a call representative read off their computer screens went through Sloan first. Apparently, it hadn't sat well with his supervisor, but fortunately, his promotion made the woman his peer.

Sloan was in a terrific mood, but then why shouldn't he be? Not only had he moved up in life, but he had that new lover. A hot, gorgeous lover who didn't look anything like skinny, ugly Scott!

"I'm so in love, I'm giddy" he was saying. Asher nodded and Wyatt squealed like a schoolgirl.

"I knew it! I *knew* Mister Man was family. And I *knew* he wanted you to be his Mrs. Man."

Sloan is not *a Missus. He's a man!* Scott wanted to scream the words aloud, but of course he didn't.

"Besides," Wyatt continued. "Someone *that* hot should be required to play for our team."

Hot. *Hot!* Scott ground his teeth together.

First Sloan was in love with Asher (and not Scott!) and had pined for the man for three damned years. And damn damn damn, but Scott couldn't even hate Asher, because god and slut he might be—but he was also a good man (at least most of the time), even if he wasn't always a nice guy. The paradox was infuriating.

Not fair!

Then—finally—when Sloan got it into his fool head Asher was never going to love him back (not in the way Sloan wanted to be loved), he all but instantaneously found someone else. At first, the only reason Scott hadn't gone crazy was the fact that Sloan's new obsession was married and straight. But then it fucking turned out that the man was in fact gay. He split up with his wife and now he and Sloan were *together*. They were a couple!

Not fair!

Not fair not fair not fair!

Scott had loved Sloan forever, and he met that son of a bitching "straight" and he'd been snatched away quicker than beer turned into pee. Scott had known Sloan for better than ten years. He'd fallen in love with Sloan during the first week after they'd met, in a class (he couldn't remember which one—business something?) at Wagner U.

For *ten* years Scott had carried *his* torch. And now it looked like it had blown out forever.

"How is he in bed?" Wyatt was asking (of course he was).

"Wyatt!" Sloan laughed, throwing back his head, joy rolling out of him. Even Sloan's throat was beautiful—the skin the color of alabaster. And his mouth was so kissable. But the only kisses Scott had ever received from Sloan were the friendly kind. Those kisses gay friends always shared.

"Come on. Dish!" Wyatt was actually jumping up and down. "You don't have to tell me his dick size—"

"I don't *have* to tell you anything."

"—although I will remind you I *had* a chance to see it once in the gym shower, and you wouldn't goddamned let me!"

"Knowing you, Wyatt," Scott said, "you'll figure out a way to make that happen anyway."

"Unless I never let Max shower at the gym again," Sloan added.

"Oh, like *you* don't want to see his schlong, Scott!" Wyatt furrowed his brows at Scott.

In fact, he didn't. Not at all. He did not want to see what Max had, for surely it was much bigger than Scott's. He couldn't see what Max used when making love to Sloan. No!

"I can hope," Wyatt said.

"Jeeze," Asher said. "You would think you've never seen a dick before."

"Come on, Sloan. You can at least let me know if he knows what to do with it," Wyatt continued.

Sloan smiled happily. "Oh, he knows what to do with it!"

"That's good," Asher said. "A lot of times straight men are *so* damned boring in bed. They've been taught all their lives to be slow and quiet and gentle."

"Well, let's just say he was a quick study," Sloan said and drank the last sip of his champagne.

"Thank God."

"Took to it like a duck to water, actually," Sloan added.

"Good," Asher said. "Because all that stuff about men giving better blowjobs because they know what they like is pure bullshit. Straight men usually give the worst head *ever*. They hardly touch your dick with their lips, and you have to keep telling them to use their tongue. God! It's like they think if they don't really suck *on* it, then they're not gay. At least the few times I went down on a woman I got my face *in there*."

"Eww!" cried Wyatt. He clamped his hands over his ears.

"Faggot," Asher said. "A little pussy never hurt anyone. Just like a little cock never hurt anyone, either."

"Well, certainly not a *little* cock," said Wyatt with a giggle.

"Enough!" Scott exclaimed. "God, you guys!"

Maybe Max is just a rebound, Scott hoped and then hated himself for the thought. But he couldn't help it. *Maybe Max will realize he's straight after all and go back to his wifie, and I'll finally get my chance.*

Yeah, right. You'd be too afraid. Just like you've been too afraid to tell Sloan how you felt for ten years now.

But how could he have told Sloan?

I'm not nearly in their league. Not like Asher with his movie star looks. Or Max with his rugged, macho Wolverine thing going on. Not like Sloan, whose beauty wasn't macho but more magical, like something out of a book by Tolkien.

Even tubby little Wyatt is hotter than me.

Hell. Weren't bears the new black?

And I'm Spider Woman!

Isn't that what Wyatt liked to call him, even though it made him so mad he could bitch slap the doofus? But why shouldn't he have such a nickname? He was skinny. Skinny skinny skinny! He had almost no definition despite how hard he worked out. When he looked at himself in the mirror, he swore he saw his rib bones, though his friends said it wasn't true.

"You've got *some* pecs there," Wyatt had once said to him in the locker room after they'd worked out and then reached out and palmed his chest right there in front of everyone.

"Wyatt!" He'd jumped back. "Goddamn!"

"You know, for a guy who doesn't believe in God, you sure do use his name in vain a whole lot."

"And you've got some biceps," Asher had contributed. He squeezed Scott's upper arm. "Flex for me."

Scott did. Or tried.

"They're not *huge*, but you got 'em."

"And do you know what most men would do for your fat ratio?" Sloan asked. "What are you? Like, five percent body fat? Less?"

"Except for that butt!" Wyatt whistled. "You have a *great* butt." Wyatt reached for that too.

Scott danced out of the way. "No! No way, José. Don't you dare grab my ass."

A great butt....

He thought maybe it was true. At least he thought of it as his one "asset." He'd fuck a butt like his. Not that anyone ever gave him the chance. He rarely if ever got to top. When a man did want him, it was invariably for his ass.

Wasn't that how Garrett from Bangor, Maine, had happened? If that had even been his real name.

They had met through E-MaleConnect, and "Garrett" had started chatting with Scott after seeing pictures of his butt, his family jewels concealed by a jockstrap.

"Baby, if you've got it, you have got to flaunt it," Wyatt had said to him one day while coaching him on how to set up the "ideal" profile. Scott had actually—through some madness—allowed Wyatt to take the pictures.

"I don't understand why you won't pose naked for me. I've seen you naked like a thousand times!"

"You are *not* looking at my junk!"

(And he really did think of his genitals that way.)

"Like it's going to make me lose control and attack you or something? Goddess!" Then Wyatt had asked him if he had a jockstrap. Ha! Did he have a jockstrap?

"Sure," he said. "You know I do?"

"Anything but your boring white ones?"

Did he? If Wyatt only knew. And yet he'd worn a rather boring black Bike jockstrap that day. At least Wyatt had approved. "It's the perfect combination of naughty and nice," he'd informed Scott. "And boy, you really *do* have a nice ass."

"Please, Wyatt," Scott had said while his friend took pictures. "This is tough enough as it is."

"Okay, Sweetie. Sorry."

And that was the picture Scott had posted. He actually locked his face pics, because God—what if someone he knew saw he was posting his ass on a gay contact site?

Soon Garrett was sending him message after message, waxing poetic about how beautiful his "bottom" was. Garrett had a wife, was very unhappy, and beginning to realize he was a gay man trapped by marriage. He desperately wanted to meet Scott and to have sex with a man for the first time.

It had all gone to Scott's head, despite the fact that Garrett wasn't the first. For over a year, Scott had been having online romances, falling in love with pictures on his computer screen and fantasies of the men he chatted with.

When Garrett got him to unlock his face picture so he could see what Scott looked like—and Scott had been terrified to do so—instead of rejecting him, Garrett began to profess his undying love.

Scott was sure he was in love as well. Garrett had come to see him—it was supposed to be for four days—saying if the time was as magic as he knew it would be, he'd divorce his wife and move to Terra's Gate.

Well, needless to say that hadn't happened. Instead…

Heartache. Heartache once again.

What was wrong with him? He knew he wasn't "hot," but he wasn't the Medusa. He wasn't as unattractive as some men he *knew* were in relationships. Would he ever find someone who was right for him?

He had been on so many dates in his life, and the men never called again. Why? He was smart. *Really* smart. He had a decent job working in a law office, even if he wasn't the lawyer he'd dreamed of being. It was in desperation that he'd turned to online dating. Hell! Maybe he should ask Wyatt to work one of his spells for him. Ha! Like he would ever be *so* desperate he'd go against everything he believed. Spells. Goddesses. Witches! It was no better than his parents' church mumbo-jumbo.

"Hey, Wyatt," Scott said, trying to keep the sneer from his voice. "Isn't this the month you go to witchy camp?"

Wyatt glared at him. "It's *next* month. And I've asked you about a thousand times not to call it that."

Scott clenched his teeth. "Fine. But that's what it is, isn't it?"

"You've asked me this before, and no, that's *not* what it is. *Yes*, there are men who go who identify as being witches—"

Scott rolled his eyes.

"—and most of us follow an Earth-based religion—"

Scott rolled his eyes in the other direction. "'Earth-based religion.' What the hell is *that* supposed to mean?"

"The *old* religions," Wyatt said. "The way humans worshipped for thousands of years, before it became all about bowing down before some old bearded guy who sits on a big throne up there in the sky."

Scott had heard it before. He'd heard it *all* before. "You mean like Zeus?" *Old religions indeed!*

"Older than that," Wyatt said. "Back when we *knew* our connection with the Earth. That we're all part of the circle of life—"

"Like in *The Lion King*?" Scott asked.

Wyatt crossed his arms. "Yes. Like in *The Lion King*."

"So you worship Simba the Lion King?"

"No!"

"All right," Asher broke in. "No need to make fun."

Scott's eyes went wide. "*You're* telling *me* not to make fun?" He clutched at his chest. "It's the big one! You hear that, Elizabeth? I'm comin' home to you!"

"You guys!" Sloan burst into laughter. "Come on! Let's be nice."

Let's be nice!

Scott looked at Wyatt and saw hurt in those big brown eyes of his. His stomach clenched. *Shit!* "Sorry," he said.

"Huh?" Wyatt replied.

"I… I said I'm sorry. I can't help it. It's the whole religion thing. I never understood it."

Wyatt gave a single nod. He looked uncertain.

Shit. Making fun of Wyatt was like spanking a puppy. Asher deserved sarcasm. Wyatt really was a big teddy bear. A big old flamboyant teddy bear. "No. Really," Scott said. "I'm sorry." He meant it. He loved Wyatt. Dammit. "If that's what you're into, I suppose it's a lot better than hellfire and brimstone." And it was true.

"You know, Heartland really is about a lot more than religion," Wyatt said.

Scott nodded distractedly. Margaritas. He had to get them out of the refrigerator.

"Scott?"

He turned. Those eyes of Wyatt's, so dark they were almost black, were looking right at him. "Yes," he said, standing up. Margaritas. That was what they needed.

"A lot of guys go who don't believe in the old ways."

Old ways? Scott opened his mouth to say something, then was stopped by the look of pure sincerity on his friend's face. Wyatt really believed in that stuff. And it bothered Scott. A lot. How could an intelligent, rational man fall for that shit? Didn't Wyatt know the modern so-called pagan movement was pure bullshit? That it was all made up by some horny old codgers like Crowley and Gardner back at the turn of the century and through the 1950s as an excuse to get naked with women? That they'd just made up a religion, like L. Ron Hubbard made up Scientology or Joseph Smith made up Mormonism? Today people actually thought they were practicing some ancient religion with their rituals, standing around in circles with their junk out there for all to see while they chanted the witchy-woo-woo version of kumba-fucking-ya! But it was all fake. It was no more real than the Pope's brand of crap. Or the loud, confused, empty rhetoric his Baptist parents believed in. They'd tried to indoctrinate him, but he wasn't having it. He was too smart.

Not real! Not any of it.

But then Scott saw Sloan and Asher looking at him, the expressions on their faces. Sloan with this pleading look and Asher, eyebrow raised, his face saying "Scott is about to be an asshole again." And it just wasn't fair!

Scott sighed. *Shit.*

Didn't they know he just wanted them to see reality? Karl Marx said it best: religion was the opiate of the masses.

But fine! Tonight was about friendship.

So Scott swallowed the comments he wanted to make and simply asked them if they were ready for margaritas instead.

They were.

"Who wants salt?" At least he had a tin of fancy salt. He'd found it at the dollar store.

When Scott came back with the drinks—they were in thick, heavy glasses, the stems shaped like a saguaro cactus—his friends were still talking about Wyatt's camping trip. *Shit.*

"It does sound like it could be nice," Sloan was saying. "As long as I could wear one billion sun block. You know how I burn."

"Yeah, poor baby," Asher said and laid a hand on Sloan's shoulder. He gave it a squeeze. "I remember one time when your blisters had blisters."

"I had to take tea baths for a week! I had to call in sick for work."

"Well you didn't get burned when we went to Sanctuary," Wyatt said, referring to the day when the two of them headed out to the camp for the day on a Saturday. Scott had not been invited. He'd been a little bitter about that.

Of course, who could blame Wyatt? The place was holy to him, and Scott had to admit he would probably have made a comment or three that Wyatt wouldn't have appreciated. Scott had no filter; he knew it. A thought tumbled out of his mouth before he evaluated how people might react to his honesty. And that is what it was. Honesty. He was honest to a fault.

"You *poured* sun block on me!" Sloan said and started laughing in that delightful way of his.

Scott felt a burst of old jealousy. Imagine Wyatt getting to rub lotion all over Sloan's body. He was just thankful that, according to Wyatt, Sloan had been too shy to take off his shorts and go naked, which Wyatt had had no compunction about at all. Had the bear put sun block on Sloan's lovely round ass, Scott would have gone crazy. Surely Sloan wouldn't have let Wyatt anyway, right?

"Didn't we have fun?" Wyatt asked.

"It was nice," Sloan replied. He looked at Scott. "Peaceful. Quiet." He looked sad for a moment. "That was right before I found out about Mom's cancer."

"Is that why you haven't gone back with me?"

Sloan shrugged. "I don't know. Maybe." He took a drink of his margarita. "Hey, this is pretty good, Scott."

"Thanks," Scott said. Sloan was being polite. He'd served the frozen brand before.

"Yeah," Wyatt added. "Not bad."

And now Wyatt. Was everyone a better man that he was, Scott wondered.

"I hear your Camp Sanctuary is a pretty cruisy place," Asher said with a smile. "Maybe I should go out there for the day sometime."

"Asher, please!" Wyatt cried.

"Well, it's true, isn't it? I hear it's a great place to go and get some dick. And if everybody's naked, you know *just* what you're getting ahead of time, and *no* one has to buy *any*one a drink."

"But Asher! Sanctuary is supposed to be a *sacred* place, not a pickup joint."

"But I thought you said sex *was* sacred," Scott cut in. He couldn't help himself. "What's that thing you say? Something about pleasure being worship."

Wyatt sighed. "For behold, all acts of love and pleasure are my rituals."

"See? Fuck for the gods!" Scott said. "Maybe there is something to your religion. If I had been able to get it on with my youth pastor, maybe I'd still be going to church today."

Ah, Pastor Bob. He had had such a crush on Pastor Bob with his jet black hair—almost blue, like Superman's in the comic books—and steel gray eyes. Sadly, the man had never taken a hint, not even a strong one or two at church camp, although by luck, Scott had gotten to see him naked in the shower house late one night and marveled at his adult penis, surrounded by a thick thatch of that blue-black hair. (Scott had very suddenly realized he was that bad word he heard people say sometimes—"cocksucker"—and didn't care in the least).

"*Please* don't make fun," Wyatt said, and Scott closed his mouth with a snap. He'd done it again. Made fun of his friend. Wyatt was right. This wasn't teasing. It was worse. It was making fun. But Scott hated that anyone, especially his friends, could so delude themselves into thinking there was a "god," male or female. There weren't any ghosts either, holy or otherwise. There was here and there was now. That was it. Belief in something "more" was plain ignorant. Couldn't they see that? There had been more death, more wars, in the name of religion than anything else in history.

"Well," Sloan said, "whatever your camp is, you always come back from your camping trips so happy and refreshed—"

Of course. Sloan. The nice guy.

"—so I can imagine a week at a place like that would do wonders."

"Go with!" Wyatt exclaimed.

Sloan shook his head. "I can't. Not right now. Go on vacation barely a month after my promotion? I don't think that would be a good idea, do you? Shelia would jump on that with both booted feet. Maybe next year." He looked over at Scott. "What about you?"

Scott laughed. *Yeah, right!*

"I've tried to talk him into it," said Wyatt. "No go."

"'No go' is exactly right," Scott said. "I've told you before. I'm not using my vacation time to run around naked in the woods with my dingle dangling, especially when it can be a hundred degrees at the end of July."

"And *I* keep telling *you* that you don't *have* to run around naked. Out of a hundred and twenty-five, -fifty, men, only about five or six go nude."

"And the rest wear dresses," Scott snapped. *Shit.* There he went again. *Reel it in.*

"No! Well...." Wyatt sighed. "Some of us wear skirts. But most wear sarongs—"

"*Dresses*," Scott said before he could stop himself.

Wyatt shrugged. "Sarongs *aren't* dresses. But I guess they're only a step away from skirts. But see, it's all a part of the faerie thing—"

"Does anybody need more margaritas?" Scott asked. It was the quickest way to change the conversation. Because something magic really would have to happen to get him to go to Wyatt's witchy-woo-woo camp.

And there was no such thing as magic.

CHAPTER THREE

AS ALWAYS, Scott checked his e-mail before he went to bed. He was quite tipsy—fairly drunk, if he cared to admit it—and knew it was a mistake. Once, he'd ordered a T-shirt off of eBay or Amazon or something and had no memory of doing so. It was a stupid shirt, too. Another time his inhibitions had been low enough that he'd spent way too much money on an online auction for some product for his hair made of "all natural ingredients." He wound up hating the stuff.

But despite the fact that he knew better, he opened his e-mail anyway.

Oh! He had a Facebook notification that God had made a post. He had to see. Sure enough, the comedian with the handle that had offended so many people had posted something funny. Today's was a picture of Jesus with the caption "My Father says if I get 1 million likes, I can come back!" Hilarious! If there really was a God, then this was the kind Scott knew he could get into.

He had an e-mail from UnderDudes. Probably nothing he was interested in. The daily deal was almost always some stupid underwear, like an elephant with a "trunk" for you to stick your dick in. Who would wear something that stupid? But what the hell, the price was almost always right. So he checked and sure enough. Dumb. Today's special was gold lamé. Really? *Really?* Who would buy those? Who would *wear* them?

Wyatt would, of course, that's who. But that thought made him shudder. Not a pretty image.

There was something from his mother with the subject line "Jesus Can Do Anything."

Delete.

An e-mail that had something to do with a king of some foreign country he'd never heard of giving away millions of dollars. Nice if it were true!

Delete.

"Single Horny Girls Near You!!!!"

Delete.

A plea for a donation.

Delete.

Discount over-the-counter prescriptions.

Delete.

Buy Viagra and Cialis Online C-H-E-A-P!!!

Delete.

Something from E-MaleConnect.

Fuck.

Delete it!

Because look what happened last time!

Scott had been sure Garrett was finally the man who would love him. The e-mails had been so wonderful. He'd professed his love for Scott over and over. And his pictures! Such a hot man. His cock, perfection.

But then when Garrett had finally come to Terra's Gate to meet him, Scott hadn't recognized him at first. Then he realized Garrett had done what had been done since the beginning of "online." No. Since long before. Since ads in the back of magazines—*imagine meeting that way!*—or mail-order brides. Garrett had sent a picture that was at least ten years old.

Over dinner at Jasper's—a *very* nice restaurant—Garrett's looks no longer seemed to matter. It was his heart that was important, right? What was on the inside? Especially as he kept telling Scott how handsome and sexy he was. The words had thrilled Scott.

So he'd invited Garrett back to his apartment and Garrett had fucked him as if it were the last time he'd ever fuck in his life. It had been intense, partially because Scott really didn't care all that much for bottoming. But since he used his ass to entice men into his life in the first place, what could he do but let the man fuck him? But it was more than that. Garrett had been wild. Not at all the sweet, gentle lover Scott had imagined he would be. And then, while Scott dozed off afterward, Garrett got up and left....

Left the state.

Left the frigging Midwest!

Went home to Bangor, Maine.

The plan had been for them to spend four days together. Four days of romance. Scott didn't get four hours. Worse, Garrett told Scott to leave him the fuck alone. That there wasn't a chance in hell he was leaving his wife, and "Christ on a cruise missile, don't you fucking know that?" Then he let Scott know he was throwing the phone he'd gotten from Walmart for twenty bucks in the garbage.

Twenty bucks. Garrett had had him—bareback!—for twenty bucks. A hundred and twenty if you counted dinner (that last hadn't been cheap. Scott had paid a male escort who charged more than that. Twice as much, actually.).

Garrett had gotten a deal.

So Scott knew better than to open the e-mail. Garrett had not been the first to lie to Scott, get him to believe, then hurt him.

He knew better.

Scott opened it anyway.

"Dear Allen," the e-mail began (because he'd used his middle name in his profile to keep anyone who knew him from guessing it was his).

Dear Allen,
My name is Daniel, and after reading your enchanting profile,
I HAD to contact you. I could not believe it! It was wondrous.

Wondrous? Scott read on.

I guess I should tell you about myself since my profile says
almost nothing. First though, I must be honest. I am older than the
age group you prefer. I tell you this up front and forthwith. In my
first draft of this missive, I waited until the end and almost sent it to
you. But then I found I could not. It felt somehow like a lie and
what could be more wrong?

Lie? Honest? What the hell? And just how old *was* this guy? Scott toggled
over to Lookin4Heart's profile. Well one thing was true. The profile said almost
nothing. Daniel, which may or may not be his name. Male. Smoker: No. Drinker:
No. That was about it. *Hmmm….* Certainly not the near novel he himself had
created for his own profile. A romance novel at that, with lots of stuff like
"looking for my soul mate" and "you don't have to be perfect."

I am forty-one years old. That makes me ten years your senior
and therefore I can only hope that you are still reading and not
reaching out to delete my letter even now.

Forty-one? That wasn't so bad, although not so very long ago it would
have seemed ancient. For a minute Scott had been afraid the guy was sixty, or
seventy or something like that. It had happened before. Once, this man had sent
him a picture of a muscle stud who could have been a porn star. Someone in at
least his late fifties had shown up and he'd been fat. *Big.* The seams in the back
of his black dress pants were showing and looked ready to burst.
Why do you even care? This guy can be nothing but trouble. Scott tried to
think about the string (the host) of disappointments and heartache, but curiosity
won over. Hey. He knew couples who had found each other on the Internet. And
besides, E-MaleConnect had testimonials. Videos too. Gay versions of those
eHarmony commercials on TV.
And you honestly think those are real?
They could be.
In fact, Scott needed to believe they were real. Couldn't they get in trouble
for falsely representing themselves?
Yeah, like anyone cares about a faggot dating service!

So now, if you are still reading, and I so hope that you are, here is my story.

I come from very religious stock. I married when I was a young man—

Oh, fuck me! Religion? Religion again? And he's another fucking married man!

Scott almost hit the delete button right then, but something—desperation? hope? a silly romantic soul?—made him read on.

I come from very religious stock. I married when I was a young man and had three children in quick succession, the youngest of which is eighteen and ready now to leave the nest and fly off to college, he did very well in school and has, for all intents and purposes, a free ride.

My life has been good. All except for the fact that I have had a secret that until now, with you, I have kept. I have always desired other men. There! I did it! I've never typed those words before. My God, my heart is pounding!

And for some reason, Scott's heart was pounding as well. The words on his laptop screen had him now. He couldn't stop reading if he really *had* wanted to.

I tried to deny it, Allen. I tried to fight it, but these desires have only grown throughout the years and I have come to see that these are needs that I feel and not wanton yearnings.

I began, in earnest and in secret, to research the seven scriptures in the Bible that speak about homosexuality. To my surprise I found that many theologians and historians shed new light on the subject. I discovered that there was a bias in the way the verses had been translated and that perhaps God was not against men loving other men after all.

Shit. Why does he even care what the Bible says? In all that research, didn't he find that the Bible was nothing but a collection written by ancient, ignorant men who were trying to understand the universe, and the only way they could was by blaming it all on gods and magic?

What a relief this was to my soul! Because I knew what I was feeling was not a "vile affection" and it was more than some lascivious cravings. I felt a love for other men! I saw how unspoiled my feelings were. The Platonic-Socratic view was that only the love between men could be truly equal. Yes! That is what I have always felt!

But then, dear Allen, something happened that not only tore my family asunder—

Asunder? Scott asked himself. *Really? Asunder?* Scott kept reading.

But then, dear Allen, something happened that not only tore my family asunder but rocked my entire church as well. It was revealed that my pastor and my wife were having an affair and it appears that it had been going on for years with none of us the wiser. In retrospect I should have known something. My wife had stopped pressuring me to do my husbandly duty right after her third pregnancy and she took the job as church secretary. I never wondered why and I suppose it had a lot to do with a certain relief I had felt over the matter.

Nonetheless, I cannot tell you how all this affected me. My marriage had been the center of my life, and I have read that some prisoners are completely lost when their time has been served. I was set free, but my life had been turned upside-down! I kept asking God, "Why? Why?"

There was no answer. Just as there had been no answer in all the years when I inquired, no begged, God to tell me why I had been created with the wish to "lieth with a male as one lieth with a woman."

Was He perhaps some cruel trickster? Some dark Lord, laughing up there on His throne in heaven over the plights of simple mortals? Was He like a boy who pulls the wings off flies, then drops them into the jaws of a Venus flytrap? Was He having fun at our expense? And my wife! Not once did I cheat on her. Not once, albeit I had the opportunities. I was true! I was faithful! How could God have allowed this to happen?

And there was also, of course, our pastor, tasked to watch
over his sheep, and standing in that pulpit for years lying!

And then, Allen, I knew! I knew!

There is no God!

Scott sat back in his chair, eyes wide, astonished. *This man*, he thought.
This poor man! Pouring out his heart to me! To me!
What was it in his bio that made this man open up to him?

How could there be a God? No! Of course not! And the more
I thought of it, the more ridiculous it all seemed. How ironic to
quote the Bible with, "O foolish people, and without understanding;
which have eyes, and see not; which have ears, and hear not!"

No God!

Of course not!

And the knowledge set me free, Allen. I am a man whose
shackles and chains have fallen away. I am no longer a slave to a
heartless and evil god.

Scott could hardly keep still. He was squirming in his seat. He wanted to
leap to his feet and cheer.

Yes! No God was right. Finally, an intelligent gay man—and from
Daniel's language Scott knew he had to be intelligent—who didn't believe in
God! He was convinced half the reason his dates never worked out was that
almost all gay men were obsessed with one religion or another. Why, nearly
every gay man he knew—except for his three best friends—lived in terror that he
might one day be going to hell because of something he couldn't do anything
about. Being homosexual. Even his friends believed in something kooky. Ghosts.
Reincarnation. Goddesses.

But not this man who had found him on a gay dating site.

And so at last I found this gay man's dating site, E-
MaleConnect. What a name! But at least it seems real. Men looking
for more than just sex. I want sex! I have waited a lifetime for sex
with a man. But I want, I need, more. I had discovered it in my

secretive years and knew this was the place. At last, trembling in anticipation, I made my first profile! It took me days! Once I was done I began looking and, oh, so many! So many men! So many like me. Like me?

Like me! I said it again! Men like me!

And my heart went out to them. Men. Looking for the love of other men.

And that is how I found you. Oh, Allen! What a profile you have! Your words went straight to my heart. It is like I know you, yet of course we have not met. But then I was confused by what seems a dichotomy. I was confused about the pictures you chose to place at your profile. Your words say one thing, but your photographs say something else.

Scott found he was blushing. *Shit.*

Of course the guy would be confused.

I posted pictures of my ass!

Pictures of his ass framed by the straps of several different athletic supporters attached to a profile that claimed he was looking for love. How to explain that to a man who had been conservatively religious and married his whole life? It did seem like the two didn't go together.

That's because they don't and you know it.

But hadn't those pictures gotten him attention? Hadn't Wyatt said he needed to flaunt his best features? That surely wasn't his face!

Sure. Attention. Men who want to fuck you. Guys who make false promises. But has even one of them given you something more? Why would they? There wasn't even a picture of his torso, like so many others posted. He was too ashamed of a body he could only consider skinny. The man in the e-mail was right. He was presenting himself as nothing but an ass to fuck!

But then dear Allen—

And that name—Allen—being used over and over again. It felt wrong. Even though it was his middle name, it felt like a lie.

—it occurred to me that while I have abandoned my God it did not mean that there was not any wisdom in the Bible. And don't those teachings—God or no God—say that we should judge not. Lest we be judged? Who am I to pass any kind of verdict when I know you not? There may be some reason why you do not show your face. Maybe you are a public figure (although I hope not a pastor or priest).

Hell no, not a pastor or *priest!*

Maybe you have scars or burns or some other disfigurement. My imagination flies, I cannot help myself.

No. No scars, Scott thought to himself. *I'm just plainer than white bread.*

I cannot even say anything because, one, I have not presented a picture of my own face—

No. But you didn't post a picture of your ass or cock like almost everyone else on this "looking for love" site!

—and two (and I hope I do not doom my chance of meeting you by admitting this), your bottom is one of the most lovely I have ever beheld! Is it all right to use the word "bottom?" I know you are a man and not some little boy, but "ass" seems wrong somehow and "buttocks" is too scientific. Too cold.

I daresay your bottom rivals that of Michelangelo's David.

Scott blushed again. Grinned. Really? Michelangelo's David may have a pretty tiny dick, but his ass was fine!

Despite that, it is your words to which I keep returning. So many men, myself included, have left so much blank in their profiles, so much to wonder about. And despite the fact that this site presents itself as one for men looking for love, it is obvious that most are hunting for something that springs from a far baser nature. Something far more transitory. You seem so different. You seem sincere, real, and best of all, intelligent. I keep thinking that you are just the type of man I want to meet.

But I have gone on forever. I should sign off now. I hope that you are still reading this and that I have not "weirded you out" as my daughter Naomi would say. I hope that you will write me. I wish that I may have discourse with you.

Please consider me?

Sincerely and with best wishes,
Daniel Witherspoon

Scott sat back in his chair. He didn't know what to do. He was surprised. Everything about the situation had surprised him nearly sober. Nearly sober. He was still tipsy enough that he wasn't sure how to react. How to think this through.

First of all there was the sheer length of Daniel's message. Scott was used to messages that said something like "nice ass. I think I want 2 fuk u. stats?"

He would send messages back when they were at least a little less like a response from a Criagslist sex ad and ask them questions about themselves, trying to see if they were dating material and not just a means to get off. He figured even if the odds were against him, surely there would come a day when the statistics said he'd find someone nice. But usually, he was lucky if they answered more than one of his questions, often with one or two word answers and more often than not with Internet slang and abbreviations, rarely spelled correctly, with no punctuation or capital letters.

Daniel, on the other hand, had practically written him a novel. And the contents! The mysterious man seemed so *real*. Garrett paled in comparison. Yes, Daniel had been married, but he wasn't any longer. No little woman he was promising to leave when the time was right (a time that would never come). So no worries there.

Daniel had grown children, but two were already off at college and the third was ready to leave the nest. The man was older, but not that much older. Scott had read a book once called *The Male Couple*, and the authors suggested that when there was at least ten years difference in the age of the partners, the two men were far more likely to have an enduring relationship.

Oh! Daniel didn't believe in God. Happy day! Huge plus. No religious guilt. No fear of hell or worries about whether he was going to heaven because he was gay.

And Daniel thought Scott's ass—his "bottom"—rivaled the famous statue of David.

Would he be disappointed to find out that Scott's dick was about the same size as well?

He's not going to see my dick. I'm done with Internet men. Done! I've been hurt too many times.

But what if....

No!

But it wouldn't hurt to exchange a few e-mails. What could that hurt? Really? What?

"... your bottom is one of the most lovely I have ever beheld."

Scott closed his eyes, his stomach flipping hard. God. Was Daniel being sincere? Was he nothing but a "bottom" to the man? Was Daniel just one more man who wanted to fuck his ass?

Could he have any to blame but himself if Daniel was, Scott realized. His pictures on the site were of nothing but his ass—a site he'd joined to find love.

Someone to save him from his obsession with Sloan.

Then—whether it was because of all the margaritas he'd drunk or something more—Scott made a split decision. He changed his profile. He completely deleted the pictures—didn't even lock them. He uploaded one of the only pictures he actually liked of himself. Sloan had taken it. The smile had been because he was looking at Sloan, very much in love with him that autumn day. Wouldn't it be ironic if a picture of him in love with a man helped him find the love of another? And why not?

Scott saved the changes. Looked over his profile again very quickly and decided not to change one verbose word of it.

He checked Daniel's profile. As warned, it didn't say much. To his disappointment he saw the man lived in Los Angles, but he supposed anything closer or more convenient would be asking for too much.

What Daniel's profile did say seemed promising, especially if he read between the lines....

Fool yourself, you mean.

But he thought what the fuck, anyway, and did it. He wrote to Daniel. Signed it Scott and admitted Allen was his middle name and damn Daniel if he didn't understand.

Two days later they talked on the phone. The next day they Skyped with their cameras on, and Scott saw that while the man looked like he could be older than forty-one, he wasn't bad-looking. The conversations turned out to be delightful. Scott's heart swelled, even though he knew he was probably doing it to himself again and setting himself up for a fall.

The next day flowers arrived, and he was thrilled beyond his own understanding. Scott wasn't really all that into flowers—that was more Sloan's purview—oh, and now *Max's* as well since he was helping Sloan with the weeding and watering and....

No. Forget Sloan—*like he could!*

Two days later more flowers—these red roses!—and they'd been talking every night since, and even though they had almost nothing in common, he felt happy when he had his Daniel time.

Could this be it?

Could it?

Too soon! Too soon to know anything.

A week and a half later, he was flying to LA.

CHAPTER FOUR

CEDAR CARRINGTON—known as The Jockster to his faerie brothers—was ready. The stretch of road was perfect. He'd driven it earlier, checked it out, found it to be—like the baby bear's bed—*just* right.

There was hardly anything on this road: lots of trees, fields, a few houses—and those belonged to farmers. At this time of evening, farmers were asleep. Cedar doubted he'd see so much as a kitchen light through a window in the darkness when he made his ride.

No cops either. He was sure of it. Or pretty sure, anyway, and he was usually right about such things. Cedar got feelings.

Boy, a cop sure would be surprised to see him, huh? He'd get a ticket for sure, and that wasn't counting the speed. Might very well get arrested. Hell! Might? With country folk? That's what *would* happen.

Then he'd call his mother. If he didn't decide just to chill in a cell for a few days.

But that wasn't going to happen. He wouldn't be calling his mother, either, at least not because he was in trouble again. At least his troubles were usually little ones.

The bike was a good one, a custom built, steel-blue Harley-Davidson FLHX Street Glide, and perfect for his needs. He didn't like the real loud ones—all that "loud pipes save lives" was bullshit as far as he was concerned. He liked to pass through the night without bothering anyone. Loud was for kids.

Cedar was beginning to tingle. He was excited. The full moon was rising over the trees, and that was perfect too. He wanted to run without even his headlamp, not even the purple lights he'd had installed in the undercarriage—and yes (oh, yes!), he knew it was stupid. Dangerous as fucking hell. He had to have the kill switch added because you couldn't buy a bike anymore where you could turn off the lamp once you started the thing up—but that had been something his father had been able to take care of. Cedar's mother would be furious if she knew (but she'd understand, he suspected, what with her lyrics about midnight winds and full moons and night birds taking flight). But he had to ride without the lights; it was part of it all. He would be shadow and darkness himself. A wind passing in the night.

No helmet either. Goggles only. He'd swallowed a bug once, but hell, that was protein. A bug in the eye, though? That sucked. Could blind you too, especially when you were really flying. He wanted to ride with the wind in his hair, even if it was cut high and tight with only a few inches on top at most. That wind felt marvelous. Almost as wild as the wind on his bare skin.

Now!

Now or never!

Cedar scrambled out of his clothes—few clothes to be sure on such a warm night: shorts, tennis shoes and socks, sleeveless T-shirt—and put them in the hard-shell saddlebag. He stood under the trees at the end of the long drive with a farm at one end and the highway at the other. He was naked now, except for his jockstrap, and he wanted to shout like Tarzan at the rush of it all.

Cedar didn't ride naked. No, the thrill, the kink, for him was the jock. He filled it well without looking obscene. All modesty aside he knew he looked good. Cedar was not one for pretending otherwise. He also knew he had little to do with his looks except that he took care of himself, exercised, ate right. Nature had been kind to him, and he thanked Her dearly. And his parents had something to do with it too, both good-looking even now in their sixties. Cedar knew his appearance got him what he wanted: a job, favors, getting out of trouble, and, of course, sex.

When it came to sex, he liked both women and men, although he preferred men. He lived to bottom, and while a woman could wear a strap-on and wear one well (he should know!), there was something about plastic or rubber that just couldn't compare with a living cock, no matter the quality of the toy. To actually have the person you were with *inside* you, rather than an alternative.

As far as love went, he'd felt for both, and yet…

There was something about the brotherhood of men. Especially *queer* men, no matter their sexual preference. And hadn't he learned that even men who thought of themselves as heterosexual could have queer spirit?

Now, Cedar climbed onto his Harley, and already he was thrumming. It was a sexual feeling, no doubt, his ass bare and spread over the leather seat, and all that rumbling power between his legs. Of course it was sexual! No one could deny it and not be lying. It was sex with a machine if you were wearing jeans and leather chaps. But bare skin against the bike? His most private self, tight against the seat? Gods! As long as you were careful not to burn the shit out of your legs, of course. And the vibration of the bike? It was like getting fucked and fucking at the same time.

He was getting hard already.

Cedar revved the engine and took off like a shot, the wheels throwing back dirt and dust and gravel. In seconds he was going eighty miles an hour down the county road, the night flying past him!

He was king of the world is what he was, and he wasn't Jack Dawson either. No! This was power he was astride and not Rose-fucking-DeWitt Bukater.

Oh, he was hard! Hard like the steel frame of his bike and hot as its tail pipe. And Cedar was dripping now, leaking like a son of a bitch into the stretched fabric pouch. Tonight's jockstrap was a black one, made by Nasty Pig because he was feeling *so* nasty.

Only two cars passed him, and he grinned at them through their windshields, and if they had time to register what they'd seen, he knew not, for he was far ahead and they were far behind.

He was a rocket. A comet. He was a force of nature. And when he finally reached the sign that let him know he should turn off, it was with reluctance that he did so.

Cedar switched his headlight on only long enough to make sure he saw the drive he'd scoped out earlier and didn't fly into a ditch. The moonlight was just bright enough that he could pull into the woods, stop his bike, and reach into his jock to grab his erection. He barely needed to stroke himself and he was shouting out in release as a powerful orgasm ripped through him. He drenched both himself and the fuel tank, his whole body rocking as he came. He nearly toppled the bike, and it was by some miracle that he didn't burn his leg on the tail pipe after all. Cedar finally dropped the kickstand, half climbed, half tumbled from his seat, and rolled into the moss and grass beneath the branches of a huge oak tree.

"Yes!" he shouted up to the tree and the stars and the moon.

This was how it felt to be alive.

CEDAR SPENT the night a few miles down the road in his small dome tent—supposedly a two-man tent, but only if they were both extremely comfortable with their masculinity and willing to get *very* close. Or that's exactly what they wanted. Cedar simply pulled into the woods, set up the meager shelter, didn't even light a fire. It was a very nice night, so who needed it? There was something nice about being without it. Closer to nature, the only light the light of the moon.

He was packing up the next morning when a young boy showed up with a big dog. Luckily, Cedar was dressed in jeans and a Dr. Who 50th Anniversary T-shirt instead of his night-riding outfit from the previous evening.

Cedar assured the boy he was leaving, and the boy let him know the dog was harmless. But it was a big black and gold German shepherd, and dogs didn't usually like "the Jockster," and so with a hello and a good-bye, he was on his bike and away.

Cedar stopped at a small town about half an hour later and found an old-fashioned diner. He hoped for some cheap breakfast. Small towns often had them. Say, a half order of biscuits and gravy (Morning Special!! Only $1.99!!) would work, and luckily, Cedar had the metabolism of a kid. He didn't need much, and when he did eat, he didn't gain an ounce.

Sure enough, it was "Two Eggs and Your Choice of Sausage or Bacon Only $2.99." He wished it was a little cheaper; his cash was growing short and he needed the two hundred hidden in a pocket of his boots. He was saving that, oh yes.

He sat in the corner where a young girl, *maybe* eighteen, was serving, instead of the side with the more matronly and round woman. He'd no sooner sat down when Young Girl came up to him and asked him if he wanted some coffee. Hell, yes! he wanted coffee.

"Hello darlin'," he said in his most charming voice. She was quite cute, hair like golden wheat and eyes the color of cornflowers. He smiled at her and asked for the special, and when she brought it for him, he asked if they needed any dishes washed.

"Do you not have any money, mister?" she asked.

"Oh, I do! I have money," he assured her. He pulled out a five to show her he did indeed have enough for breakfast and coffee, if only a modest tip at best. "But that *is* just about all I *do* have and I'd like to eat past this mornin'."

"I'll ask," she said and darned if she didn't blush. She turned and then surprised him by shouting, "Ma? You have any work for this boy?"

Boy? He hadn't been a "boy" in a *long* time. At least not in the way she meant.

The other waitress—the matronly one—turned from her table. *God, she's the mother.*

Placing one hand on her ample hip, she strolled over to them holding a coffee pot in the other and scrutinized him suspiciously as the daughter explained that he did have enough to pay his check.

Mom's eyes studied him all the more, and he just smiled as sweetly as he could and batted his long lashes.

"Well," she said finally. "We had quite a breakfast rush this morning, and Darlene's out having a baby…. We got a bushel of dishes back there. Let's see how you do with those and we'll see how it goes from there."

With a "Thank you ever so much, ma'am," Cedar headed through the metal bat doors into the kitchen. He'd washed many a dish in his life. He didn't mind. In fact, he found it rather Zen. A meditation of sorts. Grab the plate, dip it in the soapy sink, run the dishrag over its surface several times until it was clean, dip it in the rinse sink, place it the stack. One, two, three….

That morning turned into the day, which became several days, and then by week's end, he was trusted enough that he was sleeping on a cot in the office (if you could call it that) instead of his little tent and had charmed his way into the hearts of Doris (the mother) and Charlotte (the daughter, named after her grandmother). He kept a certain distance, though. Charlotte had gotten a crush on him fast, and he had no intention of going there. Not that he wasn't tempted. He was. Charlotte (*never* Charlie) was adorable and sweet and obviously wanted him to be her first. But he was smart enough to know that a shotgun wedding could follow and settling down was not in his game plan, not even one day when he was sixty or ninety or a hundred and two.

Not *ever* again.

The next Friday he took them both to the movies. He bought a huge bag of popcorn for them, along with three drinks. He insisted on paying; it was the least he could do. Besides, in Little Town, USA where he was taking a pause—a furlough, so to speak—the movie house wasn't very big, the movie was months old, and the tickets laughably cheap. Even the concession stand was a bargain; Cedar didn't spend twenty dollars on the three of them, total.

How much had he spent to see *Avatar*? Had it been at least fifteen dollars? For one seat. And that was five years ago.

With three meals a day and no room and board, he was doing fine, and now he knew he wouldn't have to worry about using his mother's credit card or the two hundred he was saving.

Cedar did break down and take Charlotte on a few rides on his bike, but only when her mother knew they'd be back in no more than an hour. He pretended not to catch the implications of one of Charlotte's comments like "You know there's a really nice watering hole down the creek a-ways and it sure would be a nice way to cool off from all this heat."

"I'm really deathly allergic to poison ivy and poison oak. I don't like walking in the woods…." It was a lie, but it was better than hurting her feelings. The truth was, a) Cedar had no plans of ever giving up his gypsy life. He loved it too much. He didn't want to make a home of "Little Town." Or Chicago or Palm Springs or Paris, France for that matter. And b) he'd seen a movie once, at least a decade ago, an animated film that was surprisingly adult, and it had left an echo in his brain he couldn't forget. A traveler, like him, has sex with a young woman, who winds up getting pregnant. He never knows because he hits the road. Year later he meets a young man, an orphan, and comes to realize the youth is his son. Cedar had cried. All his life that boy had grown up without knowing his father. And while Cedar hadn't spent more than a year total with his own father, the man claimed him at least. Cedar saw his father, almost stranger that he was, every couple of years. He'd seen him this last Christmas and taken his gifts, like his new bike, and why not? If Laird Addington couldn't give him love, why not stuff? The boy in the movie hadn't even had that.

Cedar knew he couldn't do that. He didn't want kids of his own, and he sure wouldn't help bring one into the world and then abandon it. He wouldn't—couldn't. He'd get a vasectomy, but he hadn't found a doctor who would do one. They'd insisted he was too young and he'd regret it later in life. Shit.

So he made sure he was rarely, if ever, totally alone with Charlotte. He didn't want to take any chances.

He didn't get involved with the guy who pumped gas (Yes! Actually pumped gas for you in this day and age) at the local Texaco either, although he was as hot as fuck and obviously wanted Cedar bad. The man—Elijah, of all things—had even cut his hair to look like Cedar's, which had only made Cedar let his own grow to a seminormal style. For him, at least.

No, in a town like this, if you farted at breakfast everyone knew and was talking about it by lunch. If he'd taken gas-station man to bed, chances are everyone would figure it out, and that meant wagging tongues (they already talked about Elijah), and as much as Doris liked him, Cedar suspected he'd be jobless faster than the famous Roadrunner disappeared in a little cloud of dust if she heard something about that. She was already upset by all the states passing gay marriage. Imagine her finding out her "boy" was bi?

Despite all that, Cedar liked the little town. He liked Doris and he liked Charlotte and being able to see a movie for two bucks—lousy sound system or not. He liked the lazy days of unfolding summer and working at the diner and the fact that Doris trusted him there at night. In fact, she had reached the point where she'd offered him the back bedroom in her house for twenty bucks a week, but then there was the increasingly amorous Charlotte to worry about, so he told her he really needed to save the money, but thank you. He liked watching *Hollywood Game Night*, hosted by Jane Lynch, in the evenings with the two of them despite the bad reception (and funny that Doris didn't know Lynch was a lesbian, and he sure wasn't telling her).

He did chores around the house, mowed the lawn, fixed the garbage disposal, changed the oil and spark plugs on their rusty brown 1974 Chevy Impala.

It might have gone on that way right up until the last ten days of July, but then two things happened.

The first was that he had sex with Elijah, the gas-station guy (even though he *knew* better). Cedar had gone skinny-dipping at Charlotte's fabled watering hole (who knew June could be so hot?), and he looked up and saw Elijah standing at the bank. Elijah stepped out of his clothes and waded in, his rigid erection pointing ahead of him like a divining rod. He was just as sexy naked as Cedar had imagined in the middle of a number of horny nights, fist wrapped around his cock.

And shit, what was Cedar to do?

It was good sex too, damned good, and it had been months since he'd been laid, and he just couldn't resist. Elijah was not only a good kisser, but he knew quite a few other ways to use those lips. As a matter of fact, they had sex several times that hot afternoon, cooling off (and cleaning up) in the creek between rounds. It turned out Elijah was a hell of a good fuck.

Then, as evening approached, *just* as Cedar had feared, Elijah turned all sweet and cuddly and asked him if he should go ahead and come out, even though it was such a small (tiny) town. After all, now that Cedar was around, they could stand up to anyone, right?

Shit!

Hadn't he known something like this could happen? Hadn't he just *known?*

He'd managed to break away, said he had things to do back at the diner. He didn't want to hurt the guy's feelings. He wasn't a total cad after all. But the look. The look on Elijah's face. The suspicion. "You used me," that look said and fuck. It was true, wasn't it?

Except Elijah had used him as well. He was a gay man living in a little town with almost no ability to connect sexually or emotionally with another man. Hadn't they brought each other enough today? They'd had a human connection. They'd had great sex. Wasn't that enough?

Then that very night, Cedar awoke to Charlotte climbing on top of him on the cot in the diner's office. *Oh, for God's sake*, he thought as she bent to kiss him. "Charlotte!" He pushed her back, more or less gently. "What are you doing?" Even in the dark he could see she still had her skirt on, but not her blouse, and her bra gleamed whitely in the soft light from the hall. He yanked his hand away when he became aware of it there between her breasts.

"What do you *think* I'm doing," she asked and tried to kiss him again.

"Well you're not doing that!" He wiggled into a sitting position and, taking her by the upper arms, pushed her back again. Neither was easy. She didn't weigh all that much, but she was straddling him on a cot and was resting most of that weight on her feet. What made matters worse was that he was naked, of course. He always slept naked (or in a jockstrap), but thank the gods he could feel she still had her panties on. He was hard (even worse) because he'd been dreaming about watering holes and a certain gas-station attendant, and he was damn grateful that that thin layer of cotton had kept her from taking the situation further.

"Why not?"

And how to answer that question? Make up something? Tell her he had a disease?

You could tell her the truth. Not easy. But Cedar believed in truth more than anything else. Not only to thine self, but to everyone.

"Don't you think we've waited long enough?" she continued and ran her fingers down his chest and tummy and...

He grabbed her hand. "No, Charlotte."

"But I love you Cedar—"

Oh shit, oh crap!

"—and I can tell you have feelings for me."

She tried to reach down between his legs, but he made sure she didn't succeed. "Charlotte! What would your mother say?"

"She doesn't have to know."

"Of *course* she has to know, Charlotte. Now let me up."

"Please, Cedar."

Oh piss! "Charlotte. I *can't.*"

"Why, Cedar? I can tell you have feelings for me."

"Because.... Because, Charlotte. Because I don't feel what you feel." There. Shit. Said it. The truth.

Charlotte let out a little sigh. "Oh."

Shit. He had hurt her feelings, and that was the last thing he wanted to do. "I mean, Charlotte. I do like you. But—"

"But what?"

"But I think you want more than I can give you. You're not looking for a little roll on this cot." Hard-on totally gone now (thank the Goddess), Cedar finally managed to wiggle out from under her and stand up. "You want more. And I can't give you that."

"Why, Cedar. I thought.... I mean, I was beginning to think...."

"You want a husband, Charlotte. And I'm never going to be able to be that for you. You want someone who will marry you and have a passel of children with you, and I can't do that."

"You can't have kids?"

He sighed. Lie? No. He wouldn't do that even though sometimes lies hurt less than reality. "I'm a gypsy, Charlotte. I live on the road. I just rest here and there sometimes. Then I'm off again."

"Oh." That tiny sad sound again. "That sounds pretty lonely to me. Kind of sad."

"I'm happy, Charlotte." More or less.

"I.... I thought maybe.... That maybe you were thinking of settling here."

"Gods, no!" Shit. That came out stronger than he meant it to. "Charlotte. I can't settle down. I'll never settle down. Not again. Not ever again. I'll be on the road until I die."

"I see," she said quietly.

Cedar saw the dark pool of his jeans sticking out from under the cot and reached for them.

"All right, then. Fine. I still want to do it with you." She stood up and came to him. "Please, Cedar. Be my first."

Cedar sighed. "No, Charlotte. Not in this town. Think of it. Your future husband finding out you're not a virgin? You'll be a pariah."

"A what?"

"The whole town would talk about you. You'd never find a husband."

She snorted. "Husband! In *this* town? Have you seen my choices? Shit!"

Cedar's eyes went wide. Shit was the first "bad" word he'd heard her utter.

"The only other man I like at all doesn't even like girls!"

Cedar almost laughed. Would have if it wouldn't have been cruel. Oh, God. She liked Elijah? She could sure pick men, couldn't she?

"The men in this town are ugly or stupid or just plain trash. They think the most exciting thing there is in this world is hunting, four-wheeling, and drinking cheap beer with their buddies. I'll be trapped here forever if I marry one of them. *You're* the best I've ever met."

Gods. He sighed again. "Charlotte.... You could move."

She gave a second scoffing sound. "Leave Mama? Leave her alone with the diner? And go where?"

Cedar suddenly realized he was still naked and figured it was time to do something about that. Talking about sex or *not* having sex while he was nude was pretty stupid. He was just reaching for his jeans when he heard the bell over the front door of the diner jingle.

"Charlotte!" came Doris's loud shout. "Are you in here?"

"Oh, no! It's Mama!"

Quick as a shot—even before he pulled on his jeans—Cedar leapt forward and turned on the tiny TV in the corner of the room. He was in those jeans less than twenty seconds after that. "Get your top on—*now*," he hissed.

"Charlotte!"

"Doris?" Cedar called back as he yanked his T-shirt down over his head. "Is that you? We're back here."

"Cedar! She'll *kill* me!" She snatched up her blouse and began to try to get it on. He could see her face clearly now in the bluish glow from the television. Marilyn Monroe was playing a ukulele with a small group of women (along with Tony Curtis and Jack Lemmon *dressed* as women) on the snowy screen.

"No, she won't. We're just watching television. You were keeping me company." He stepped up to her and quickly helped her get her top buttoned. Just in time.

"What are you two doing back here?" and Doris was standing in the doorway. Luckily they were dressed.

"Watchin' TV, Mama."

She'll be buttoned wrong, Cedar worried. Or have her blouse on inside out. But no, it was right. Thank you!

"*Some Like It Hot*," Cedar said. "One of my favorites. Charlotte, didn't you leave a note for your mom?"

"*Oh*. Oh, no. I forgot, Mama. I'm sorry."

Doris looked back and forth between them, the suspicion clear on her face. But slowly her features relaxed. "For—for a minute there I thought maybe you two was up to something."

Charlotte plopped down on the cot. "Nothing, Mama. Nothing at *all*."

Doris studied her daughter. Spared Cedar another glance, then turned back to Charlotte. "Maybe you should come to the house."

She looked up and didn't mask the sadness on her face. It was clear as could be. She shrugged. "The movie isn't over."

"You can watch it at *the house*." Doris turned to Cedar. "Sorry, but what if someone saw her leavin' here in the middle a' the night? People talk."

Cedar nodded.

"If you two really want to watch this movie together you can do it at the house."

"That's okay. I'm tired, Doris. I was thinking about turning it off anyway." On the snowy screen Marilyn was now coming down the aisle of a train car, still playing her ukulele, and singing about being gay and reckless too.

Doris nodded. "Charlotte. You go get in the car."

Charlotte nodded. "Okay, Mama." She stood up. "'Night, Cedar," and started for the office door.

"Charlotte," he called to her.

She stopped and turned around.

"Charlotte. You can have anything you want. You just have to believe."

"What I want is you," said the look on her face.

"*Thing*, Charlotte. You can have any*thing*. Set it in your mind. Know it. Believe in it. Anything can happen if you believe."

She shook her head and walked out of the room.

When they heard the bell in the other room tinkling, Doris said, "You were only watching TV, right? You didn't take advantage of my girl. You wouldn't do that, would you, Cedar?"

"No, Doris. I wouldn't do that to her or to you."

"But she wanted to…."

Cedar shrugged. "I'm not the right man for her, Doris. I was telling her that I'm a gypsy. If it weren't for how hospitable you two have been, I would have moved on weeks ago. I have this thing that I do every year, and it's just less than a day from here, and so I was just biding my time."

Doris nodded. Was that relief in her eyes? "I thought so. I thought you was goin' leave."

Cedar nodded as well.

"I was hopin' maybe you'd stay. But you got too much of the road in you."

Cedar sighed. "Yes. And Charlotte needs someone who wants to stay and be her forever."

"Yes, she does, Cedar." She turned and started to leave, then stopped in the doorway. "I 'spect you'll be leavin' sooner than later, then? I mean. If you don't, then next time you might not be able to say no to my girl."

Cedar took a long, deep breath and then let it out quietly. "I suspect you might be right."

She took another step, then turned back. Came to him. Hugged him. "I'll miss you, Cedar. Charlotte's going to miss you more."

"I'll miss you both," he said sadly, realizing in that second that he would leave before the sun rose in the morning. Luckily, he had all his stuff here. Doris had actually brought him his laundry, what little there was of it, that morning.

"She'll get over it, though," Doris said, and Cedar heard the doubt in her voice.

"She will, Doris."

Doris nodded, and this time when she turned, she did leave.

The next morning, sun just peeking over the trees, Cedar was on his bike and on the road again.

He was sad.

But he couldn't deny that the road was welcoming him back.

CHAPTER FIVE

AS SCOTT stepped through the gate at the airport, his cell phone rang. It was Daniel, and that made him smile. Anxious, wasn't he? That was nice. Someone who really wanted to meet him.

"Hey, Daniel," he said, grinning.

"Hey, Scottie—"

Scottie? He'd kill anyone else who called him that, but from Daniel? It was cute. Scott's smile grew broader.

"—you here?"

"I just walked off the plane."

"Good. Guess what? I'm in the airport."

"What?" he asked surprised. The game plan had been for Scott to meet Daniel at the curb. LAX was monstrously big, and the days of friends and family meeting you at the gate were long gone.

"The more I thought about it, the more I hated the idea of you waiting like that, like you were some kind of…. Well, I'm not going to say it. I'm waiting for you right now. Head for baggage, all right, my dear?"

Dear? If Scott wasn't careful his smile would get so big his head would just open right up like one of the Canadian characters from *South Park*. Imagine. *Dear!*

It didn't take Scott long to find Daniel, even in the huge airport. Even though Daniel Witherspoon was a little… thicker than he'd looked on Skype—

(Wasn't the camera supposed to add pounds and not subtract away?)

—and he looked a little older too, graying at the temples, and Scott supposed the yellowish light from Daniel's bedside lamp must have concealed that as well.

But Daniel *did* have flowers (maybe it was a straight man thing?) and it was obvious these were *expensive* flowers. Clearly not something picked up at Quick Trip or Aldi.

On top of that, Scott hadn't even expected to see Daniel *inside* the airport because of the extremely off chance someone Daniel knew might see them together.

So when Daniel was standing there, huge bouquet held out in front of him and *almost* kissing him—and he might as well have; it was clear to deaf and blind people that this was a romantic meeting and not just two friends—Scott forgave both the pudge and the lack of Grecian Formula. There but for the grace of… well, *something*… go I.

"Oh, Scott," Daniel said, voice actually trembling. "You're even more beautiful in person."

Scott's heart jumped. *Beautiful? Me?* "You too," he replied, voice catching—and forgiving Daniel's clothes as well. A church secretary had been dressing him for years after all. A *cheating* church secretary. He could see Daniel had tried, and wasn't that worth some points? Clean, crisp white shirt, a tie (lackluster though it was), and while the slacks were probably ancient, Scott decided to pretend they weren't. In fact, weren't high-waisted pants making a fashion comeback due to Spike Jonze?

They headed out of the terminal and damn if it wasn't even hotter in Los Angeles than Kansas City. Wasn't there supposed to be a breeze off the ocean or something? But then it didn't look like they were all that close to the ocean. They made their way to Daniel's car—an S-10 Blazer—and the man went from barely talking at all to out-and-out babbling by the time they hit the highway. There wasn't a lot of traffic, and Scott looked around the inside of the SUV. Not new, probably a good ten years old, but it was clean—almost immaculate. Nothing tacky hanging from the rearview mirror. No discernable gewgaw on his key chain. He wondered what Daniel's house looked like. Surely a house, probably fairly big with three kids—that was, at least three bedrooms because the daughter would have her own, at least one more for the boys, then Daniel and the pastor-fucker in a third. If he still had the house because the kids were all in college now.

Three kids.

Could Daniel really be forty-one?

If he had been eighteen when the first was born, even nineteen…. Scott did the math in his head. Yes. Daniel could be forty-one. The gray meant nothing. Scott's parents had both started going gray in their thirties. *God! I hope I don't. I could go any day.* And so what about the slight gut? Middle-age spread it was called, and Daniel wasn't that much thicker than Wyatt, and what was Wyatt's excuse? Wyatt would say it was because he didn't prescribe to the idea that men had to be young and have a six-pack to be beautiful. Right! *Sure.* No, Wyatt had a gut because he couldn't stop cramming food into his pie hole and drinking sugary pink cocktails.

And while Daniel wasn't stylish, at least he didn't wear a rainbow beanie complete with propeller and a matching striped tank top with the words "Nobody Knows I'm Gay" emblazoned across the front of it.

So yes, Daniel could be forty-one, and yes, that made him a good thirteen years older than Scott. But Scott's dad had been a lot older than his mom and…

Scott's stomach clenched hard.

…best not to use them *as examples, huh?*

Forty-one?

He spared Daniel a look to see if he thought the man really could be… and saw him looking back at him expectantly. He kept looking.

"What?" Scott asked. Shit. He hadn't heard a word of what Daniel was talking about.

"I asked if you were hungry. There… there's this little place not far out of the way that I have been wanting to try. But… I must admit I've been too afraid." Daniel made an uncomfortable-sounding little laugh. "But with you, dear one, it would be different."

Why? "Why?" he asked. *What kind of place is it?* "What kind of place is it?"

"Pinocchio's?" Daniel said, making it sound like a question.

Scott shrugged. "I've never heard of it."

"Oh. I thought you might have. It's…. It's…." Daniel gripped the steering wheel. "It's a gay bar." His Adam's apple bobbed fiercely.

"Ah…. I…." Did Daniel think he knew every gay bar in the country? This was LA for goodness sake. He bit back a grin. Thought about the name of the place. Wondered what happened when you lied? "Sure," he said. "Let's go." Then he let the smile go. "Would this be your first time?"

Daniel was staring ahead, and Scott saw him grip the steering wheel again, clench his jaw. "Yes," he said quietly, then turned his head and gave Scott a weak little smile of his own. "It's not the only thing I want to do for the first time with you." He blushed.

Scott found his smile wasn't going away.

THE BAR was nice enough: not huge—not even as big as The Male Box back home—and not small. It was doing a surprisingly brisk business for an early Friday afternoon, but they did serve lunch, and it *was* LA after all. The Male Box might have half a dozen patrons by now, mostly of the dedicated alcoholic variety, who had arrived promptly at noon, opening time.

Pinocchio's had at least twenty customers, with two servers darting around the tables that occupied what looked like a smallish dance floor. *They probably put them away in the evenings*, Scott thought absently while trying to decide what to order.

The menu was mostly stuff like hamburgers, fries, and chicken tenders—standard fair for a sports bar and damn if there wasn't a baseball game playing on the big flat screen on the back wall.

Probably plays Nicki Minaj, Lady Gaga, and Beyoncé later tonight…. And Katy Perry. Roaring for all the gay boys.

Scott played it safe and ordered the patty melt with fries and a glass of beer. Hey! They've got Boulevard. You couldn't fuck up a patty melt too easily. Except for maybe the onions. Onions?

"Could you make that without the onions?" he asked, and the striking black man ("I'm Calvin, how are you sexy boys doing today?"), thin with beautifully styled hair, assured him with a wink that they surely could. Daniel ordered the burger with same and fries, but not the beer. He got a "cola" instead.

"Don't you want a drink?"

"I'm getting one."

"I mean with some happy in it." Scott grinned in a way he hoped made him look fun and, if not cute, at least reasonably attractive. "We are in a *bar.*"

"I take it that you mean alcohol?"

Scott nodded.

"I'm driving."

Hmmmm.... That was nice, responsible. "You can have *one* drink, can't you?" he asked, just as the waiter arrived and placed his beer in front of him.

"Well, Scott. I don't drink," Daniel said and took a sip of his cola.

Scott froze. "Not even a beer?"

Daniel shook his head and set his glass down.

"But they've got *Boulevard!*"

Daniel shrugged.

"Wine? A glass with dinner?"

"No."

"No?" The idea seemed as outrageous as dancing naked on the surface of the moon. Without a spacesuit. Then.... "Oh, I'm sorry." He blushed. *I am so stupid! A complete idiot.* "You *don't* drink. I'm so stupid."

"No, Scott. I'm not an alcoholic. I've just never drank. For most of my life, it was because of church—"

"But you don't go anymore," Scott said.

"Well.... *Actually,* I still do."

Scott looked at him agog.

Daniel shrugged. "I still like the music. The fellowship. Those people have been my friends and family as long as I can rememb—"

"Well, what the *hell* do they think about you coming out?" Scott asked, astonished.

"They don't know."

"But...." *They don't know?* "What if...?" Scott clenched his jaw. A voice was crying in his head. *Danger! Danger, Will Robinson! Danger!* "But I thought.... You're not going to make me your dirty secret, are you? What happens if we get involved?"

Daniel reached out and laid his hand on Scott's. "We *are* involved, dear one." Then he looked down at their hands, and his face showed just as much surprise as Scott felt.

He started to take it away, and Scott took it back before he could.

"Look around you, Daniel."

Daniel did. He swallowed hard.

"Look there." Scott indicated a table near them with a nod of his head. Two young men—they couldn't have been much older than eighteen—were kissing. Quite passionately.

Daniel gave a long, long sigh, then looked at Scott. "We'll cross that bridge when we get to it, Scott."

Daniel managed a small smile, and despite Scott's sudden anxiety, he relaxed. Daniel had a nice smile. In fact he really was a nice-looking man. He might not be Hollywood gorgeous, like Max, Sloan's new *boyfriend*, but he was starting to see Daniel had his own handsomeness. Like Clark Gregg or James Gandolfini—although Daniel wasn't nearly as fat as the *Sopranos* star.

"So you've never even *tried* beer?"

"No, Scott. I have not. I've never even been to a bar, heterosexual *or* homosexual."

Scott's eyes popped. He couldn't help it. *"Never?"*

"I've been in restaurants that had a bar. I haven't had any reason to do so, Scott. I didn't drink. If I wanted a soft drink or a coffee, I would go someplace like McDonald's or Starbucks. Think about it, sweet one. Let's say I had gone to a bar. For just a Coke. What if someone had seen me? Someone who knew me? Someone who went to my church and they told everyone?"

Scott opened his mouth to tell Daniel he thought it was unlikely such a person would say a word. After all, they would have had to explain why they were in the bar, wouldn't they? But the look on Daniel's face made him shut his mouth before he could say a word. There was a... desperation in Daniel's expression that was so sad!

"Do you think anyone would have believed that I hadn't had a sip of alcohol?"

Church. Fuck church. See what it did to a person? The guilt? "So why today?" Scott asked him. "And a gay bar?"

Daniel shrugged. "I'm nervous, I can tell you that. I find it hard not to look every time the door opens. I remember a few years ago a group of us went to some of the gay bars and passed out literature. Pamphlets that let sinners... I mean... told gay men they could change if they prayed." He laughed. "Of course, I know now that is absurd. I think I was hoping for the same."

The front door opened and sure enough, Daniel shot a glance that way.

"It would be quite the bad luck should such a group pick today to do such a thing, you know? And see me sitting here with you? Touching you?"

Scott clenched his teeth. Made himself relax. "I'd tell them you were trying to save me."

A sad smile took Daniel's mouth. "The voices whisper, Scott. Telling me I'm a sinner. That I am about to step through the gates of hell. That I'll burn for all eternity. That I should jump up and leave you sitting here and run to the church and pray for forgiveness."

A sneer threatened to take over Scott's face.

"But then I think, who would I talk to? Certainly not the pastor. He's run off with my wife! I know now there is no God. He was made up by men."

Yes, thought Scott. God was made in man's image and not the other way around.

"But when you get taught that stuff all your life? It gets its hooks in deep." Daniel glanced at the couple who were apparently done kissing for the time being but still sat so close to each other they could have been conjoined twins. "Like them. I was always taught, from childhood, such public displays of affection were distasteful. That it was for home, behind closed doors. Never even mind that they're two boys!"

Daniel laughed again, but the look in his eyes.... That.... Was it fear? Scott's stomach clenched. What this man had gone through. Was still going through. *I've got my hands full here. Can I even help him? Yes! Yes, I can. I can show him a way to get away from that religious shit. Help him see the light!*

"They tell you so much. The pastors. The teachers. The deacons. Have I mentioned I was a deacon?"

Scott wasn't sure just what the hell a deacon was, but he didn't say so.

"See the way they have the lighting so low in here? They teach us that the people who own bars do that so that the darkness can hide the deeds of sinners. That sinners like the shadows. They know they're doing wrong, and they're uncomfortable with that, and so they sin in the dark. Where they think they can't be seen."

There was a long pause. Finally, nervously, Scott said, "So what do *you* think of your first bar, then?"

Daniel looked around him once more. The boys were kissing again but this time not quite so robustly. He stared for a second and then turned back to Scott. "It's *exciting*." His cheeks turned pink, and his eyes sparkled like those of a child standing in line at Disneyland.

The thought made Scott smile again. It was so sweet. "I know something else exciting that you want to do for the first time." He raised his eyebrows in a way he hoped was sexy.

"I do too," Daniel said. "And if I am crossing over the threshold into hell, I want you to be the one to take me there."

The sex was good. All the way to his house, Daniel had babbled about how he hoped Scott didn't mind, but he was going to put him in his daughter's room. He didn't think they would see his son. He was away for the weekend with friends on a camping trip. Making the most of his last summer before going to college. But why take chances?

Did that mean he was going to be sleeping alone? Scott had wondered. As if reading his mind, Daniel asked if maybe it wouldn't be a bad idea for them to wait a night or two? Talk. Sit together. Cuddle, perchance. He'd never jumped into bed with anyone without dating. Actually, he'd only slept with one person, and that was his wife. They'd both been virgins the night they married.

Scott found the idea horrifying. What if they hadn't been compatible?

Then again, as if once more being privy to Scott's thoughts, Daniel shared that their first night had been a disaster. Neither he nor his young bride had any idea what they were doing. He hurt her. A lot. It was months before either of them began to derive any pleasure from the deed. They hadn't even tried a repeat until after some counseling. With the pastor! A flash of anger swept across Daniel's face at that, but it was gone just as fast.

But plans to wait for sex didn't last long. They'd been sitting on the couch, watching television (a movie called *Shelter*, one of Sloan's favorites—Scott had watched it with his friends a dozen-dozen times) and having—*oh my God!*—a bottle of wine. Apparently, alcohol was everything Daniel had been warned about because his reservations and resolve flew out the window. Soon they were kissing—Scott had actually had to teach him to kiss and did so carefully so as not to wound Daniel's sense of masculinity—and soon that kissing had led to more.

Scott had to teach Daniel a lot. The first time the man tried to give Scott oral sex, he couldn't help but think of one of Asher's frequent diatribes:

(*"Straight men usually give the worst head ever. They hardly touch your dick with their lips and you have to keep telling them to use their tongue. God! It's like they think if they don't really suck* on *it, then they're not gay."*)

So Scott showed him, and in no time Daniel had begged him to stop. "You'll make me…. You know…."

"Cum?"

Daniel nodded.

Scott gave him a naughty smile. "You're not that old. I bet I can make you cum more than once," he said and proceeded to continue his lesson on fellatio. It was a fun lesson too. Daniel didn't have a gym body in any sense of the word. He wasn't toned at all. But he had a beautiful cock, and Scott could see why he'd hurt his wife that first night. Something like Daniel's cock needed to come with instructions. And Daniel was right. He hadn't lasted another minute. But with another of Asher's tirades going off in his head…

(*"And the second they shoot off they get all frosty with guilt and head out of there like a rocket leaving you with blue balls!"*)

… he immediately started kissing Daniel and telling him what a man he was, and soon the man was grinning and trying out Scott's lessons. This time, despite his recent orgasm, he did much better. He made love to Scott and his cock as if it were what he'd waited all of his life to do.

Perhaps that wasn't so far off from the truth.

They finished the movie after the first round, and then after a pizza was delivered (Scott had been thrilled when Daniel answered the door in nothing but his robe and left the door standing wide open so the delivery driver could see Scott similarly dressed and sitting on the couch), they went to bed. This time Daniel rained kisses all over Scott's butt, even though he seemed not quite ready to rim him—years of being told assholes were nasty and dirty, no doubt—and Scott understood. He had always been too squeamish to do it, as well. Scott was sure he was going to have to bottom once again, but then Daniel shocked him by asking for the opposite.

"Are you sure?" Scott said. They'd only briefly talked about anal sex in their phone conversations, and there was a lot Scott hadn't told him. About how to clean himself. How it was best to practice with fingers and toys before attempting to dive into the deep end of the pool—so to speak.

"I'm very sure, Scott," Daniel said and surprised him again when he said he'd bought a copy of *The Joy of Gay Sex* online ("My heart pounding the whole time!") and read about the very things Scott hadn't time to tell him. He'd bought something to clean himself out with and even a couple of toys.

("The first one was way too big, so I had to go back, and I was so embarrassed and tried to tell the girl that it wasn't for me but she knew!")

"I am ready, Scott, my love—"

My love? Scott grinned happily. *Love?*

"I've practiced. I am so ready."

There had been the briefest disappointment on Daniel's part when Scott dug in his luggage to retrieve a condom. Daniel had wanted to know what it was like to have a man leave his seed inside him, and Scott had had to tell him that he'd made a stupid mistake and fallen for someone's lines (*Garrett, that fucker!*) and let the man take him bare. How he wasn't sure it was safe for him to fuck Daniel without a condom. Scott almost panicked. He was terrified that it had ruined the mood, ruined everything. But then Daniel had pulled him close and kissed him and whispered how sorry he was that anyone would hurt Scott.

Then Scott rolled Daniel over and the man had nearly gone out of his mind when Scott carefully fingered his anus. He cried out. He shouted. He sobbed in joy. "Never have I ever felt anything like this, my love!"

To Scott's relief, he hadn't seemed to cause Daniel but the briefest moment of pain or discomfort when he entered the man. Daniel was on his back so they could look into each other's eyes. The joy radiating from Daniel's eyes made it difficult not to reach orgasm as fast as Daniel had his first time. But Scott made it last, and to his delight, Daniel came without even touching himself, and Scott followed soon after.

They fell asleep, and the last thing Scott heard was Daniel telling him he loved him. He couldn't remember being so happy.

It didn't last long.

WHEN SCOTT woke up an unknown time later, he was alone—Daniel was not spooned up against him, Scott's arms no longer around him. He propped himself up on one elbow and tried to see, but it was dark, and the numerals from Daniel's clock were shining brightly red from the other side of the bed. Ten thirty. Hmmm…. Not that late.

"Daniel?" he called out. *He must be in the bathroom.*

He sat up in bed and swung his legs out the side, looked around, and sure enough, saw a bright strip of light below the closed bathroom door. "Daniel?" This time slightly louder.

Scott heard a moan. *What?*

He got to his feet and went to the bathroom door, heard another long moan. A groan, really. Then, was that a sob? Next, another long drawn-out moan. The sound frightened him.

"Daniel!" He tapped on the door, not too loudly at first. He didn't want to scare the man. But when the only reply was what sounded like weeping, he knocked harder. Then tried the door. It was locked. "Daniel!" Had he fallen? Was he okay? The fear filled Scott's head, crowding out other thoughts.

He pressed his ear to the door, and yes. It was crying he heard. Stopped only by more moans.

"Daniel!" he cried. "Open the door or I'm going to knock it down!" If he could. How ludicrous would it be if he just bounced off and dislocated his frigging shoulder or something?

More tears. But now it sounded more like blubbering. What the fuck? Now another deep and long drawn-out moaning. Like something from a bad movie.

"This is your last chance! Open the door or I am breaking it down!" he shouted and then made a mock slam against the door.

There was a metallic sound, and the door came open. What Scott saw made him gasp.

Daniel was standing there, a blanket wrapped around him, face blotched and red, tears running down his face. He looked like he was in agony! Were— were those scratches down his cheeks? "Daniel! What's wrong?" The words exploded out of Scott like a cannon ball.

Daniel fell to his knees, striking the tiles with a loud cracking sound. His hands went to his face, and damn! He clawed down from just under his eyes to his jowls. Then he slipped down farther, his chest against the floor and his face against the carpet of the threshold to the bedroom. He made a long, horrible sound. Like crooning. Like a woman crying for her child on death row in some bad old black and white movie. What the fuck? He stepped back in shock. What the hell was happening?

Scott went to his knees as well and reached out to Daniel, who flinched back and then did a creepy skitter backward. It reminded Scott of another kind of movie. A Japanese horror film, where the child ghost moves quickly across a ceiling or something.

"Nooooooo…." Daniel sat back up against the toilet. "Oh, God! Oh, sweet God! I'm doomed. I'm going to hell. I am going to burn in hell!"

Holy fucking shit! Burn in hell? Fuck me! Burn in hell? Daniel was frigging hysterical. The shock was replaced by anger, and he stepped forward, swung his hand back, and slapped Daniel's face.

"Snap out of it!" Another damned movie. Cher slapping the holy shit out of Nicolas Cage in *Moonstruck*. Tippi Hedren slapping that crazy bitch in the diner in *The Birds*.

Daniel's head snapped back and clunked against the rim of the toilet although Scott had no idea he'd hit him hard enough for that.

And now Daniel was crying, face buried in his hands. This time it was "honest" tears. None of that movie shit. Not full-on hysteria but the weeping of a child who'd been spanked.

Scott squatted before him. "Daniel?" He reached out and touched the man's blanket-wrapped shoulder—in fact he looked like he was in some human-sized cocoon—and gave him a gentle shake, now embarrassed that he'd actually hit Daniel. He'd never hit anyone in his entire frigging life.

Daniel shook his head, wiped at his face, looked up. "It—It was a dream. It was a dream where…." He looked down again, voice catching.

"A dream?" Scott asked, confused.

Daniel nodded. "I was being taken to the throne of God, Scott. I was going to be sent to hell. For what I did tonight."

Scott sat down next to him, tried to pull him into a hug, tell him yes, it was just a dream.

Daniel wouldn't let him. "Oh, God forgive me," he whispered. He looked up. "Don't you see, Scott? I was wrong! There *is* a God. Just because my wife and pastor sinned doesn't mean there's no God!"

Oh, no. Oh, shit no….

"God wants me to know that. He sent that dream to me tonight. To let me know." He leaned forward. Took Scott by the shoulders and gave him a shake. "All sin is the same in the eyes of God. There is no difference between a little white lie and perjuring yourself in court so an innocent man goes to hell."

Oh no…. "Daniel," he said quietly, a strange despair rising up from the depths of him. *Please no. Please don't do this….* "Daniel. You had a bad dream."

Daniel nodded more vigorously. "Yes. I did, Scott. It was God. Scaring the hell out of me." He laughed. It was an ugly laugh. Crazy, even. "Hell. Out. Of. Me." He chuckled. Then he squeezed Scott's shoulders. "Oh, Scott. God was warning me. And….” His eyes went wide. “And I’m supposed to warn *you!* God wants me to save you too. We can’t do this! It *is* wrong!”

Scott shook his head. *No. No no no no…. He doesn’t believe in God. He wised up. He saw how stupid the whole God thing is!* He knew what was coming but asked anyway. “What’s wrong, Daniel?”

“Fornicating!”

Crap crap crap! Maybe he could reason with Daniel. Dreams could scare you bad. In the morning Daniel would see things more clearly. “You just had a dream, Daniel. Let me just get you back to bed—”

“No!” Daniel shouted and struggled in the blankets to stand up. “If a man also lie with mankind, as he lieth with a woman, both of them have committed an abomination: they shall surely be put to death!”

“No!” Scott stood up, anger blazing. Not again! Not that fucking religious bullshit *again!* “How can you call what we did tonight an abomination?” he yelled. “It was beautiful. It was wonderful!”

Daniel shook his head again, and it looked like he was slipping once more into hysteria. “No. It was *wrong!*”

“But, Daniel! *You* said it. You said it was beautiful. You said…. You said, ‘How can anyone believe that anything that feels so wonderful could be wrong?’”

“Of course it felt good!” Daniel was almost screeching now. “Sin *always* feels good! How else do you think that even Pastor York did what he did with my wife? He was a good man. But the evil of sex took him. He’s not the first. So many pastors fall into sexual immorality.” Daniel grabbed his hair and seemed not to notice his blanket falling and exposing his nudity to Scott. “It is the spirit of Jezebel drawing forth the lust of the flesh with her evil, seductive schemes.”

“What the hell is the spirit of Jezebel?” Scott asked, feeling as if his heart were being torn from his chest. This couldn’t be happening.

“Jezebel is a spirit of seduction, Scott! She woos us into sexual immorality. She comes to tempt us. Revelation 2:20 clearly reveals Jezebel and her sinister motives. ‘…thou sufferest that woman Jezebel, which calleth herself a prophetess, to teach and to seduce my servants to commit fornication…!’” Daniel pushed past Scott, yanking at his hair. “Pastor Jack Schaap. Bishop Eddie Long.”

What? Who were these people?

“The Rev. Michael Fugee fondling the genitals of a teenage boy. Pastor Jack Schaap was sentenced to twelve years in prison because of his sexual relationship with a teenager he was counseling. Bishop Eddie Long—having sex with teenage boys. Cardinal Keith O’Brien, Britain’s most senior Catholic cleric—sexual misconduct. Sex! Over and over and *over* again. And most of it? *Homosexual* sex!”

This list. This wasn’t new. This was something Daniel had been obsessing over.

"It's the end times, Scott! Don't you see? Satan is trying to capture every soul he can because he *knows* he doesn't have much time left."

End times. Shit. Scott shook his head. Crazy. Another crazy Christian. Thinking the end of the world is here. Didn't he know that people have thought it was the end times for two thousand years?

"Matthew 24:7. Jesus Christ warned of earthquakes as a sign of the end times. 'For nation shall rise against nation, and kingdom against kingdom: and there shall be famines, and pestilences, and earthquakes, in divers places.'"

Scott stiffened. He'd heard this before. Heard it all before. Many, many times.

"Scott. Think of it! Think of how many earthquakes there have been in the last few years. The earthquake that caused the tsunami that hit Thailand. The quake off the east coast of Honshu, Japan, that caused the nuclear meltdown. At least a thousand people killed in the earthquake in Turkey. The typhoon that just hit the Philippines last year. How about the volcanic eruption in Mount Pinatubo in the Philippines in 1991—it was the second largest eruption in the twentieth century. The eruption in Iceland in 2010. The volcanic eruption in Indonesia in February."

Daniel froze and his eyes went wide. "*Oh, my God.* Pestilences!" He spun around and came to Scott, reached out and cupped his face in his hand. "HIV! And I wanted you to… to… to lie with me as if I were a woman. Do you see? I was consumed. The spirit of Jezebel!"

Scott's anger turned to tears. They welled up in his eyes, and he backed up until he hit Daniel's dresser. Religion. Again. Made up by men to control other men. Love disguised as hate. A tear built up weight and rolled down Scott's cheek. Would he never escape this crap?

Gone. Family gone. Another man gone. And Daniel had seemed good. So good.

He wanted to tell Daniel to come to bed. Let Scott hold him. Let him feel his arms around him. That holding was real. *Touch* was real. People were real. Sex was real. Orgasms were real.

God was *not* real.

But it was too late.

Fuck God!

"Scott. Get on your knees with me. Pray. Pray for forgiveness. He will hear you! As long as you are still alive. Now. Before Judgment Day. It's not too late."

Scott shook his head. Too late.

He packed and called a taxi—asked the driver to take him to the airport.

Then changed his mind.

Fuck you, God, he thought.

He gave the driver a different address.

SCOTT HADN'T brought a very big bag on his trip. He was only supposed to be there four days. That included both travel days. The bag fit into the locker.

He took the towel the attendant gave him and left the locker room.

It was a Friday night. Just after midnight. The place was packed.

He entered a large lounge area where men sat around, most of them with towels, in lounge chairs, some leaning against a bar area buying—oh! Nothing alcoholic. *Fuck me.* But shit! So many of them were hot. Really hot. Did he even have a chance with his skinny body and his ribs showing?

Some of the men were fucking gods. They could be movie stars. Porn stars at least. Their muscles. Body builders. Olympic swimmers. Hairy. Smooth. Damn!

He went to the bar and got a Diet Coke and sipped at it, building the nerve to go deeper into the bathhouse. He couldn't have love. Why not sex? Give up on love. Fuck. And if he needed to bottom, fine. He had a great ass. Wyatt said it. Flaunt your assets.

Scott saw a hallway and took it. There were doors going down either side—door after door. Some open, men lying on cots—some on their bellies, asses sticking up in the air to make it clear what they wanted, others on their back stroking their cocks. He glanced in and when he saw one man who appealed, he paused, stood there in the doorway.

Please. Please want me. Invite me in.

The man glanced his way and glanced away. What did that mean? Did it mean to come on in or not? He didn't know. He'd never been to a bathhouse. Heart pounding, he leaned in just the smallest amount…

… and smooth guy shook his head, no.

Crash.

He crashed.

Damn! How could he crash over a fucking stranger?

Fuck you! There are a million men in here. You'll be sorry. I hope you get the clap.

Scott practically ran down the hall and found himself in a workout room, and shit if there weren't men actually working out. Who worked out at a bathhouse?

But those muscles. Oh, the flexing and the sweat, and oh, they looked like superheroes.

Crash.

And I look like a toothpick.

This was a mistake. A million men and no one would want him. Just fucked-up married men who would fuck him and then freak out and think the end of the world was coming. Or tell him to stop calling. Or meet their next-door married neighbor and turn him into a forever lover a month or two later.

There was a slight rush of bodies, and he found himself herded to a big room with lots and lots and lots of glass bricks and several huge hot tubs. Look! There was actually a spot for him to climb in. Between a big heavy bear guy and someone skinnier than him. And someone was paying skinny man lots of attention.

Climb in he did.

Bear guy was pretty heavy. He had big floppy man tits, but he turned and smiled at Scott, and he had a nice smile and good teeth. He started asking Scott about the game earlier that day, and Scott had no idea what he was talking about but pretended he did—took a chance it was about baseball, and thankfully, he was right. The guy *was* talking about baseball.

Then it seemed bear guy was wanting to hold a different kind of bat altogether, and Scott was surprised at how fast he got hard.

"Let's go to the steam room," bear guy said.

"Oh—okay."

Bear guy stood, not even trying to hide his hard-on, and stepped out of the tub, and Scott thought, *what the hell*, and followed him. If bear guy wasn't going to hide his rod, then why should he hide his? It wasn't the way Scott did things, but he was in LA. Who was going to know him?

And damn! Look at those assholes. Men who weren't at all interested in him saw that he was a grower and not a show-er, and *now* they were staring. Fuck all a' you!

He followed bear guy to a big glass door and in they went, and wow, the man did have a nice big round ass.

Be a bottom! Be a bottom! Be a bottom!

Sitting down Scott saw that bear guy had a pretty damned big belly. It had been hidden by the bubbling hot water in the tub. Big belly and man tits, and he knew the guy had a pretty big cock, but that belly was so big you couldn't tell when he was sitting.

Shit.

Did he run?

No!

Fuck You, God.

Sex. I'm an abomination. So go for it.

Scott strutted up to bear guy as sexy as he could, and just like that, the man was sucking his cock. He knew what he was doing too!

Oh, yeah. Oh, yeah! He let his head fall back while he relished those lips and that sucking mouth.

Scott heard the glass door swing open and looked up to give the entrant a confident look. A fuck-you, you're-too-late look and...

B.G. Thomas

It was Asher.

The color drained from Scott's face.

His stomach felt like it had fallen out and landed on the wet floor.

His erection vanished like a magician's rabbit.

Asher-fucking-Eisenberg.

Asher raised an eyebrow.

"Well fancy seeing you here," Asher said and strolled in like he owned the place. Asher looking like Apollo come to life. Asher with his huge cock swinging at half-mast in front of him like an elephant's trunk. He put his hands on his hips.

"Asher," Scott managed. "W-what are you doing h-here?"

"Commercial audition. Toothpaste." Asher smiled his perfect smile.

Bear guy sat back, yanking at Scott's dick. "What happened? What's wrong, dude?"

"Boy, if the gang could see you now," Asher said. "You are the *last* person I expected to see in a place like this!" He grinned.

Scott fled.

Crash.

CHAPTER SIX

CEDAR PULLED the bike into the long drive and made his way to the main gate. It was closed, of course. He couldn't really blame his mother. She'd kept it open until one morning when she'd come downstairs and found a fan in the kitchen making some fresh-squeezed orange juice for her. He'd been preparing to make pancakes as well. Blackberry. The man had scared her near to death, and luckily, a quick call to the police had taken care of matters. The fan didn't cause any trouble, just begged her to taste the juice. She only pretended to—with her past she knew the kinds of drugs some crazy person might have slipped into the concoction. After that incident, it was locked gates.

Cedar flipped open the security box next to the gate and typed in the code—or it was the code as long as his mother hadn't changed it, that is.

W-I-T-C-H.

It worked. With a metallic click, the great black iron gate began to swing back, and he revved his bike and shot through. The drive passed through some trees and then up and around, and there was the house. Two stories, stucco and natural stone, pillared front porch—it was a mansion is what it was. Not gigantic, he supposed. It was the grounds that made it ostentatious. The tennis court. The pool. The stables out back. Not the kind of house a normal kid grows up in. It would certainly have shocked Charlotte. The house was bigger than any building in the little town where she'd grown up.

Cedar pulled the bike up front and was just putting down the kickstand when the front door opened and his mother stepped out.

She was dazzling, naturally. It was like she really was a witch or goddess from one of her songs. He knew she was in her early sixties, but she could have easily have passed for a woman in her forties. Her hair was the carefully kept dark cloud around her head that it had always been, and yes, she was wearing her shawls and flowing skirts—blues today—as if she were standing on a stage and not the large front porch of his childhood home. He even looked to see if she was wearing a pair of her lace gloves, but no—not today.

"Cedar," she said, her voice a song. "What a nice surprise."

He climbed off the bike and went to her. They hugged, and it was a good hug. Not the perfunctory one his father always gave him—the hug of strangers or mild acquaintances. How could a man so free to spread his love far and wide be so parsimonious giving any to his son?

When she finally released him, she asked him in. "I was just getting ready for lunch. Join me and Angela on the patio?"

Angela? Which one was she?

He stepped into the house, and it was as stunning as usual—she'd hardly changed a thing. All white with pale pine floors and rugs, rugs, and carpets everywhere. Paintings on the walls—was that a Michael Whelan over the fireplace? Probably an original. A woman with a huge feathered mask. Exquisite, and so much his mother's taste.

He followed her through to the kitchen and oh, of course—Angela. His mother had produced one of her albums, and sadly, it hadn't done well.

"Cedar," Angela said. "What a surprise!" Echoes of his mother. But then weren't most of her followers? He still didn't know if the two of them were sleeping together. Cyan Carrington shared a lot with her son—but not everything. Sometimes he wondered if she'd had sex more than the one time she'd conceived him. "A mad week in Monaco with Laird" is what she called the event that brought about his creation. A week following the years where his parents had been nothing but bandmates—which of course had followed the six years they'd been naïve, dreaming lovers living hand to mouth in San Francisco when they were younger than Cedar was now. Those days were long past, though. Long past. He wasn't sure when the last time was his parents had seen each other face to face.

"It's nice to see you, Angela," he said.

She was standing at the large island counter with its granite surface, slicing cucumbers. Part of lunch? Was his mother a vegetarian this month? A vegan? Or was this just part of a salad? Who cared? It was food, and Cyan Carrington never ate anything that wasn't delicious. It had something to do with those starving SFO years. Could he blame her?

"Why don't you two head on back? I'll be there in a jiff," Angela suggested, and with a guiding wave of his mother's hand, he did as suggested.

The gardens were gorgeous. Roses. Roses everywhere. Roses of every size and color and description—some smaller than a baby's fist and some as large as saucers. They surrounded the mosaic-tiled patio, a goddess figure laid out amid fruit and more flowers. Magnificent. It probably cost as much as the pool he knew was just behind the hedges a hundred or so feet back. He liked that hedge. He could sun out there naked (or in a jock!) and not be quite so blatantly exposed to his mother or one of her guests. Not that she hadn't seen him naked. She had been sure to raise him without any shame for nakedness. Still. She *was* his mother, and he wasn't a kid anymore.

They sat at a glass-topped table with wrought iron chairs, under a canopy walled by dozens of sheers that flowed on the breeze. Tiny wind chimes provided music, and somewhere out of sight, another chime, huge, bonged like one from a Tibetan monastery.

"It's good to see you, my son. You're looking beautiful. Hair growing out. The sun has kissed it, if I'm right. Those streaks are no hair-color kit."

He chuckled. "All sun. No kits. I'm probably going to cut it again, though." He thought of Elijah copying his style and why he'd let it grow out in the first place.

"Shame. Right now I want to reach out and run my fingers through it. Your hair has always been so soft."

Cedar leaned over in his chair, tilting his head and offering his hair. She smiled her famous fairy tale smile, caught by countless paparazzi, and did just that.

"So soft, Cedar. I don't know where you got it. Not from me, and not from Laird."

"You're looking good too, Mother. You couldn't look any other way."

"I'll pay you for that later," she said, sapphire blue eyes twinkling.

"No need. You keep me comfortable."

"Not as comfortable as I wish you'd let me. You won't even let me find you a place to live. I know you like the road, but wouldn't it be nice to have a little condo somewhere you could make your home base? A place to light now and then? Someplace warm? Florida? How about in The City?"

The City. Meaning San Francisco. She would never stop loving San Francisco. "Maybe one day. Not today. I'll stay in the pool house a little while, if you don't mind."

Angela chose that moment to join them, carrying a serving platter with a decanter filled with a honey brown liquid and plates with sandwiches, sans crusts.

"That is, unless you have someone staying there?" He flashed Angela a look.

"No, dearest. That would be fine. Take it as long as you wish." No indication if she noticed his Angela implication.

Angela handed him a small plate with a sandwich, and a quick look showed him it was cucumbers and some kind of creamy spread. Cream cheese? The drink turned out to be tea. A taste proved it wasn't Lipton's. Something herbal, surely. It was delicious. And a bite told him the spread was probably a yogurt with feta. Again, delicious. Not something Doris would serve at her diner! He was sure the woman would be appalled. Where was the bacon? The grease?

"Will you be anywhere near St. Louis at the end of July?" his mother asked.

"I'll be at my retreat."

"Oh." A look of disappointment crossed her face. "Too bad. I'm doing a big benefit concert there. Thought you might want to come. Maybe join me for a song? You sure? It's a Saturday. July 26th."

"Mother, that is *the* Saturday night of the whole retreat."

"You could still come see me. St. Louis is only about, what? Two or three hours from where you'll be?"

"More like four," he said and took another bite of his own sandwich.

"With that souped-up thing you drove in here on?" She laughed in her high, musical way. "What is it, anyway?"

"Harley-Davidson. I had it custom built. Added an extra luggage rack on back and a passenger seat. Heated. Some cool purple lights and even a few strips of LEDS. I like it. Laird got it for me for Christmas." He rarely called his father by anything except his name.

"I bet that thing moves when you want it to," she said suggestively. "I bet you could get back to your men's thingie—" She snapped her fingers. "—in no time."

"Mom! That's the center night of the whole week! Saturday is *the* night to be there. I'm sorry. Besides, I can't get on stage with you—"

"You sing at that men's thingie," she protested. "Why *not* with me?"

Men's thingie! Men's "thingie"? "Mom! I'm not going to embarrass myself singing with you. Read about it in the papers the next day about how it was cute when I was a kid, but now that I'm grown and with a frog voice—"

"You do *not* have a frog voice. Your voice is lovely. I don't know why you won't let me produce an album for you."

Cedar burst into laughter and rolled his eyes.

"Tell him, Angela. Tell him what a nice voice he has."

Angela nodded and swallowed a bite of her cucumber sandwich. "You do, Cedar. A quite nice voice."

He shook his head. "Drop that one, both of you."

His mother sighed. "Okay."

They sat munching their food and sipping their tea.

"I can get you a beer, if you would like," Angela said.

"Maybe later. Thanks," he replied.

"So did you see your father for Christmas?" his mother asked suddenly.

He looked over at her and tried to read her expression. Whether the week he was conceived was madness or not, he knew she would always love Laird. Always. No matter what she claimed or how much she protested. Hell. She'd admitted as much on Oprah.

"Yes," he said.

"Was—was he in the States?"

He could see the look in her blue, blue eyes. A quiet desperation, perhaps? Words unsaid. Words won't-be-said? Love or not?

Cedar shook his head. "I actually made it to England." Gloucestershire, in fact.

He looked away, saw the country home in his head, the village around it, and those strange hedges he'd seen in movies his whole life. Someone had told him those walls of green could be hundreds of years old—even a thousand—and somehow that just didn't seem possible to his twenty-nine-year-old mind. Surely not. Did that even make sense? And the village—just like in all those shows he'd seen on BBC America. Like the one on that show he loved so much, *The Vicar of Dibley*.

The house wasn't as big as his mother's. It was, however, strikingly beautiful. And hell, it did have ten bedrooms! Lots and lots of red brick and peaked roofs and inside, huge beamed ceilings. It was maybe a hundred and fifty years old, with additions built later, including a recording studio. Nothing to sneer at.

Laird had been in that studio much of the week Cedar was there. Apparently, whatever his father was doing couldn't wait the few days Cedar was visiting, even though they hadn't seen each other in two years (or was it three?) But Laird did have one of his staff—a huge guy named Nigel—take Cedar into London for a couple of days, show him the sights. Turns out by the way Americans thought of it, London was quite close. Only about three hours. Once you got on the motorway, it was fast. He'd had his heart set on Liverpool. He had so wanted to see where the Beatles had come from. Turns out Liverpool wasn't *in* London, but was a city on the opposite side of the UK. He'd always thought it was like a suburb of Chicago, or something like that. Funny how one could be so ignorant of a country that was not one's own. Hell, a city in your own country! However, they did go see Abbey Road and walked across the Zebra Crossing from the famous album cover. He'd done it barefoot, even though it had been forty-four degrees. He had to do the math because that was seven degrees Celsius.

Nigel had even taken him to see *Les Misérables* at the Queen's Theatre. Cedar had wanted to see *We Will Rock You*, but the show was over. However, the man had made up for it when he'd been more than willing (apparently) to do a whole lot more and done it well back in their room at Park Plaza Westminster Bridge hotel, which sat across from the Houses of Parliament and Big Ben.

Man's last name was Benjamin, too. And he was big. The irony was too wonderful for words. He hadn't been too happy when Cedar told him to go sleep in his own room, though. Not at all.

But Cedar didn't spend the night with anyone.

Not anyone.

He wouldn't let a best friend share his bed for the night, let alone a sex partner, no matter how good he was in bed. That was one thing the karma did seem to consistently bring Cedar, though. Good sex partners and good sex. A bum fuck didn't seem to be in his cards. Maybe he'd done *some*thing really good for *some*one in a previous life!

"—right, Cedar?"

"Huh?" he said, jerking in his chair. He'd done it again. Faded away when someone was talking to him. He'd started do that in the last few months. He looked at his mother. "Shit. I'm sorry. I went to La-La Land." God! What the hell was wrong with him? He didn't do that to people. Especially not his mother. "I'm sorry, Mom. I was just thinking of—" Laird. And why they were strangers. *Why is he so distant? Is he ashamed of me?* "Why doesn't he want to be my father…?" And then he realized he'd said that last out loud.

He flashed his mother a glance and wondered how he must look—fought to try and make himself look normal.

Cedar saw the look in her big Disney eyes, and the emotions swimming there. A rare, totally unguarded, moment. Angela coughed and said she was going to go get them something else to drink.

"I'm sorry, Cedar. Your father…. He was always a free bird, you know? Like something he was always writing and singing about. Commitment was never his strong point. Not legal commitment, anyway. I guess he is more a great cat. He's loyal, but…."

Cedar shrugged. "Forget about it."

She laid a hand on his knee. "He does love you. He loves. Fiercely. But he's afraid of being trapped. Forever afraid of it. Had we not had—" She stopped and then continued. "—gotten married…" (and Cedar knew she had been going to say "had you") "… we might still be together."

Hell. Was that part of their own distance—him and his mother? Did she blame him somehow for her not being with Laird, even though they hadn't been together for some time when they'd had their affair in Monaco? Affair because she had been seeing someone (Cedar could never keep it straight who it was), and his father had been banging some famous model or other (he couldn't keep that straight either).

"You know, we're all going on tour next year." She made a sound that could almost be a laugh. "I bet he and I hook up again!" She waved her hand and looked away. "We always do…."

Just then Angela came back with a bottle of wine.

Maybe it was time to have a drink after all.

A FEW days later, Cedar was lying out by the pool. For his mother's sake, he was wearing a jockstrap—a white Timoteo with a red and white striped band—instead of sunbathing nude.

He was dozing when he became aware there was someone cleaning the pool. A very hot someone. *Well, day-um!*

Hardly a pool *boy* either. The guy was at least in his mid, if not late, twenties. Still cleaning pools at his age? He was tall, well built, and smooth as could be, just like Cedar liked them. Hair *could* be sexy, but for him this man was what it was all about. Like a Greek statue had come to life, but far better endowed than those tiny-dicked marble effigies. He was pushing a long pole back and forth, muscles in his arms and back and even legs flexing beautifully. The bathing suit was ridiculously concealing in other ways, though. Who's fucking bright idea was it to start the trend of trunks that came down practically to the knees? What idiot had somehow convinced the world that Speedos were out? How was the guy supposed to get a good tan in those things?

Cedar coughed to alert the man he was awake but had to do so louder before he took notice. He stopped with the big pole, which Cedar assumed was the pool vacuum. He had another pole Cedar would cheerfully let the guy manipulate.

"Hello," said the man.

Cedar sat up. "Hello to you."

"You must be Ms. Carrington's son."

Cedar stood and walked up to the man, holding out his hand. "Cedar."

The man took it. "Nice name. Of course, your mother is named Cyan. Guess it would have been a shame to give you a boring name. I'm a simple Sam."

"Doesn't look like there's anything simple about you, Sam."

Sam didn't say a word. Just looked at him. In the face. Dammit. He didn't check out the fact that all Cedar was wearing was a jockstrap. Sam's eyes didn't flicker down once. Piss. Of course, Cedar was the son of Sam's client. Maybe Sam was just being professional?

"Nice to meet you, Sam," Cedar said and gave a slight squeeze with his thumb, probably only the oldest gay signal since the cavemen.

Sam raised an eyebrow, gently pulled his hand away, and continued vacuuming. *He didn't even scope me out,* Cedar thought and then made it obvious he was doing just that to Sam. *Damn, he's built. What I can see.* What stupid trunks!

Sam vacuumed, seemingly oblivious.

"So, how long have you been doing this?" Cedar asked, trying to get the conversation going.

"About twenty minutes," Sam replied dryly.

"I mean, cleaning pools."

"Since I was in high school. Just summer work for extra cash back then. But after a while, when I realized I really liked it, my boss let me get more involved. After a couple years I became a partner and then bought him out when he retired. I don't get out in the field as much as I would like, but one of my boys called in sick, so here I am. Probably hungover is more like it. I don't mind, though."

"It's not… boring after a while?"

Sam stopped. "Nope. Relaxing. I can go into this nice trance when I'm alone."

Had there been an emphasis on "when I'm alone?"

"Works more muscles than you would think too. Helps keep me in good shape."

"Well! You are in good shape."

"Thank you, Cedar." Then nothing. No "You're in good shape too, Cedar"?

Shit.

"When you're done there, you want to sit and have a beer?"

Sam shook his head. "Nah. Too early in the day. I got more jobs to do."

"Sure you don't want to get out of the sun for a bit?" Cedar gave a bob of his head over his shoulder to indicate the pool house behind them. "I'm staying in there right now. We could sit and chat. Cool off a bit."

Sam stopped. He turned, squinting slightly in the sun. "You hitting on me, Cedar?"

Cedar smiled in his most mischievous way. "Nothing so strong as that. Not yet. Flirting. Is it working?"

Sam held up his left hand, wiggled his ring finger, which in fact did have a ring on it.

Shit. Married?

"I'm married, Cedar."

Cedar shrugged. *Never stopped a man from wanting me before.*

"Man or a woman?" Nice he could actually say that now with so many states passing gay marriage.

"Woman."

Really? "Really?"

One quick nod. "Really."

Cedar shrugged again. *Never stopped a man from wanting me before,* he thought again. "Course being married to a woman doesn't mean a thing, does it?"

"It does in my case. As nice-looking as you are, I'm just not into dudes. I appreciate the compliment, though." Sam went back to his work.

Well, shit. For some reason Cedar found the turn down strangely exasperating. Not that he always got his man, or his woman. And he had gotten laid just a week ago. But this guy was really hot and the whole situation was hot and… well, a pool boy? Who didn't fantasize about having a pool boy? People into boys, that was. Pool *men.* He wanted this guy. Was getting hard, even. And what other available guy was anywhere near around? "You could just sort of lay back, close your eyes, pretend—"

"I don't fuck around, Cedar. Really. Thanks, though." He stopped for a second. "I mean, I don't want her messing around on me. So how could I excuse messing around on her? How would you feel if a lover cheated on you, Cedar?"

Cedar shrugged. "I don't think I'll ever have a lover. I like the road. I like hooking up when I feel the need. But tying myself down? Nah."

Sam shrugged. "Excuse me for saying so, but that sounds a little shallow to me."

Shallow? Had Sam said he was shallow? "I'm not shallow. I just...." *I can't. Not after.... Not again. Fucking shit.* Sam was looking at him hard, and suddenly Cedar felt like a complete ass. *I'm being a damned predator here.* He took a step back. "Shit. I—I'm sorry."

It was Sam's turn to shrug. "No problem, man. Like I said, I appreciate the compliment. Just learn to take no for an answer." He began to vacuum again. "You don't get many of those though, do you?"

No, he thought. Then remembered Charlotte and the no he'd given her and how she'd felt about it. Weird to be on the other side, wasn't it? "Not really," he admitted. "Usually I'm the one being hit on, though."

Sam laughed. "I'm sure."

Cedar tried to think of what to say. He was suddenly feeling a little weird. *Shallow?* "I'm sorry."

"Don't be."

Cedar turned around and headed back to his lounger and wondered if he should just go inside. Suddenly, he was embarrassed he was bare assed. *God. Could I be a bigger jerk?*

"Nice ass, by the way."

Cedar jerked his head over his shoulder. Sam winked.

Somehow that made it a little better.

AT DINNER that night—something exceptionally delicious that turned out to have not one tiny bit of meat in it (maybe she was in one of her vegan stages?)—Cedar was worried his mother would slip in a little "The pool boy, Cedar? Really?"

But if she knew, if Sam had said anything, she wasn't saying. There wasn't even anything in her eyes.

She did ask him about love. Of course she did.

"No, Mother. No one."

"I worry about you, baby boy. You need someone."

Says the woman who has never been attached to anyone longer than a year (except Laird, of course). Hell, she'd gotten married last year for, what? Three months? And what a joke that had been to the media. He, on the other hand, knew the whole story, and it had been very painful and destroyed a friendship she'd had since high school.

"Don't worry." Now don't mention—

"It's just ever since Jul—"

"*Mother.*" He put as much force as he could into that one word without raising his voice, hoping upon hope that she would get it. The subject was verboten. Period. He looked at her. Beamed it. *Do. Not.*

Do. Not. Go. There. It was not something he wanted to talk about. Ever.

They stared at each other for what seemed like two or three years but was in fact what he knew to be only seconds. Then she nodded and asked him to pass the hollandaise sauce. Vegan hollandaise sauce? It sure was good, and how the heck had it been made without egg yolks and hell, even butter? Sometimes the ingenuity amazed him. Maybe he should get the recipe for HQMF?

Angela was chattering on about a new tune she'd gotten into her mind, along with a few lyrics, and soon he'd ceased to exist.

But no. That wasn't true. Every few minutes his mother's eyes would flash on him, and even though she wasn't always good at saying it, he could see the love in those eyes. Funny that she could write about it, but the words were hard for her to say.

Ironic, then, what she said next. "Do you have your guitar with?"

He looked at her in surprise. "Yeah."

"Play with me?" she asked.

"Now?" He looked over at Angela. Somehow, he wasn't comfortable with her—he wasn't sure why. There wasn't a damn thing wrong with Angela.

His memories went back to days when he was led out on stage, like Chastity Bono with Sonny and Cher, and the crowds sighing "Aaaaawwwwww," and how at first it had been fun and then boring and then he was just a robot.... But when he told his mother how he was starting to feel, she let him stop. She let him stop. She fought with Laird and she won, and she let Cedar stop. And now?

"Later," he whispered.

But later didn't come. Somehow the days passed and then it was time to leave.

CHAPTER SEVEN

THE FOURTH of July picnic promised to be incredible, but Scott's heart wasn't in it. Here they were, their blankets set out among a few hundred others on the back lawn of Peter Wagner's mansion home, and he couldn't get into it. What the hell was wrong with him? He was at *the* Peter Wagner's house! Well, his property anyway. Every year the millionaire (billionaire?) treated the town of Terra's Gate to a fireworks spectacular. It was better than the one Worlds of Fun displayed, which people from all over Kansas City lined up their cars along the highway to watch.

And yet a tiny town like Terra's Gate outdid a city many, many times its size.

Of course, Peter Wagner could afford it.

Scott had watched the fireworks for ten years now. He'd always enjoyed it. And this year, because of Sloan, he was a part of the big July 4th bash you could only attend by special invitation. A party that had more gay men than you could shake a dick at: men from all over the Midwest, all over the country.

"It's going to be so much fun," Sloan had told him the night before. "The Fourth at Peter Wagner's and then tomorrow is Porch Night. We don't want to skip Porch Night, right?"

No. Of course not.

"And so many men!" He'd given Scott a smiling look, his eyebrows bobbing. "I dare you not to meet some nice single man *there*."

Of course, while Sloan was giving this advice, his beloved Max was just inside the house watching television. The man couldn't even stay next door at his own house. It wasn't like the two men were officially living together yet.

And today the two of them were sitting together, Max—the gorgeous hunk—with his head in Sloan's lap, reading some book on Buddhism. They looked like the perfect fucking couple.

That was what was really wrong, wasn't it? When Scott would allow himself to think about it—the two of them, the perfect gay couple. He tried not to. Because when he did it was all he could think about. It was supposed to be Sloan and Scott! Not Sloan and Max, the stud, the college professor, and gay fucking husband of the year!

Look at them. Committed bliss. Dammit!

They looked like an ad from *Out* magazine—two beautiful men in love—advertising Bud Light or Atlantic cruises. Or maybe a Kindle Paperwhite? *See?*

Here I am cuddled up with another man, and I am reading my Kindle, and I can read it even though the sun is so bright today!

Scott wanted to puke.

You're jealous.

I'm not!

He was. Scott was frightfully, painfully jealous.

He had been in love with Sloan for a decade, and then Max showed up out of the goddamned blue, and—*wham!*—ten years' worth of fantasies and hopes smashed.

Max wasn't even frigging divorced yet! He was hardly out to anyone. And here he was with his head in Sloan's goddamned lap like the two of them had been a couple for years.

How *could* Scott "get into" this day? Watching the two of them? They'd start laughing at any moment and feeding each other little bites of this and that—a cracker with cheese or a piece of cantaloupe. *Oh*, and watching Max slather Sloan with sun block 1000 had been a treat, huh? Watching those big manly hands rubbing the white cream all over Sloan and Sloan giggling. "Max, that tickles!" and "Oh, but that feels good." *Puke!* Any minute "their" fourteen-year-old gay son would arrive with *his* boyfriend, completing the commercial for New Gay Today.

"So where is your kid, Max?" Scott said, leaving Sloan out of the equation and wanting to get the subject out in the open—to be warned when he would have to see a teenager who had already found love.

Jealous!

Not!

Jealous!

No, I'm not!

"Oh, he's in France. Paris."

France?

"With his mother. That was part of the agreement. He could stay here with us—" Max put an arm around Sloan and pulled him close (and wasn't that just as cute as shit?). "—as long as he spends the summers in France with his mother."

So what about his boyfriend?

"He wasn't too happy about having to spend three months away from Devin—his boyfriend—but they Skype all the time, and if it's meant to be, they can survive being apart for ninety days. He acts like it's ninety *years*. Teenagers!"

Oh? And how much do you like being away from Sloan—my Sloan—for nine hours while you're at work?

Max looked at Sloan in that way the two of them had been doing for weeks, like they were quite literally going to fall *into* each other's eyes, and then he said, "But then I can hardly stand being away from Sloan here long enough for us to both go to work. I guess maybe I should be a little more sympathetic."

"Oh, Max," Sloan said.

"I love you, babe."

"I love you too!"

And then they were kissing, naturally. Fuck. Scott looked away just in time to see Wyatt approaching.

Short, thick, chubby-cheeked (and shadow-jowled) Wyatt. Not hot. Not sexy. Not muscular. And he wasn't alone. He had his lover—of Scott forgot how many years—at his side. Of course, Howard was no model either. In fact Scott found him revolting. Shaved bald as a globe of the Earth, with a thick, dark, dirty-looking beard sans mustache, and a big Santa Claus belly—he was just gross! Howard had piggy little eyes and fleshy, round cheeks, and even his nose was plump. He was wearing a tank top with a Tom of Finland man on the front, and he was sweating already, his hairy chest all slicked down and wet, the flimsy top soaked down the front. And the two of them were just arriving. What would he look like by the end of the day? Scott could only hope the man was using deodorant. What really sucked a big one was that as fat has Howard was, he was also a muscle bear. Those weren't just man boobs on his chest. They were supported by heavy pecs that made Scott want to go mad with envy. Howard didn't even work out! He was showing off those muscles too, letting everyone see *he* didn't need to drag "no cooler." *He* could carry it. And who knew what all Wyatt had packed in the thing. Wyatt! Who was carrying a huge rainbow sun umbrella, wearing shorts *way* too short and a shirt with something written on the front. What was it?

He adjusted his Versace (reading) glasses, and as the bear couple arrived—Howard thunking the cooler down with a grunt and Wyatt stabbing his huge umbrella into the ground—Scott saw that the shirt declared "No Gag Reflex."

Scott shuddered.

He did *not* want to picture Wyatt demonstrating whether that slogan was true, especially with Howard.

Jealous. You're jealous.

Of them? Not hardly. Two tubbos that have only found a lover because nobody wants them?

Then the guilt hit again. Why did he think such things of one of his best friends? Wyatt might be a silly thing, but he was a friend. A good friend.

And yes, Wyatt had a lover. A lover he adored and had been with for a long time. Hell. As long as he'd known Sloan. Longer even. When he and Sloan had met Wyatt, the little bear was already coupled.

What the hell is wrong with me?

Why am I so bitchy today?

And why can't I find someone? Everyone's getting hitched!

Everyone but Asher. But then Asher didn't want to get with anyone. Not seriously. Not for more than a night. The only man who had ever succeeded in getting more than one night out of Asher was Sloan, and that had only been a weekend. Then he'd pined after their resident superstar for years.

Just like I've pined over Sloan....

But Sloan had only pined over Asher until he found Max.

Asher. Oh, dammit. Asher. Scott had avoided him like crazy since the great LA meet up. He was so embarrassed he could die. Horrified. He'd been sure Asher would bring it up. Get enough cocktails under his belt that he'd blurt it out. He sure had been hinting at something lately, hinting strongly enough that Sloan had discreetly asked Scott what was going on. "Nothing," he'd hissed, and thankfully, Sloan had dropped it. LA was the last thing Scott wanted to talk about.

Wyatt plopped down on one of the picnic blankets—he hadn't had to bring one; everyone had given their blankets to Sloan the night before, and he had arrived early and spread all four of them out in a big square to ensure they would all be together. He'd also opened, but not set up, a pop-up canopy tent. They were waiting for everyone to arrive so that together they could easily set it up. There were rules to this big shindig, and sun shelters were allowed as long as you took them down after sunset so they wouldn't block anyone's view of the fireworks.

Wyatt looked so happy he could burst. He was thrumming with excitement and babbling how he couldn't believe they were at *the* Peter Wagner's home.

Scott shook his head. Yes. It was cool. It was damned cool. But it wasn't like they would be dining at his table this evening, having caviar and pheasant under glass.

"Okay, guys," Wyatt announced. "I've got one of the best jokes *ever!*"

Oh, no, thought Scott and gave an inner groan.

"No, no!" Sloan waved his hands. "You have to wait until Asher gets here."

Scott wondered when Asher would show up. There was no telling. And with whom. Or even how many whoms. Hadn't he'd popped into a party once with two whoms? Redheads who looked like twins?

Oh, he hoped Asher didn't say anything about LA.

"I'm here," said Asher, and Scott jumped and twisted around, and sure enough, there he was, right on cue as usual. It was like all Sloan had to do was call his name and—*Bampf!*—there he was.

He wasn't alone, of course. Hanging on him was a kid who might be twenty-one and probably wasn't. He had a Kajagoogoo haircut, and it was bleached almost Andy Warhol white. He even looked a lot like the '80s group's lead singer. Young. An elf. Asher should be ashamed.

Wyatt only saw this as his opportunity to tell his joke.

"Okay! So this guy goes into a bar, orders ten shots of whiskey, and downs them, bam-bam-bam, one right after the other. Bartender says, 'What's up?' Guy answers, 'My youngest son just told me he's gay.'"

Howard took a Mike's Hard Lemonade out of the cooler, twisted it open, and handed it to Wyatt, who took it without even looking his lover's way. They were that polished. That much a couple. Scott sighed. Whatever he might say about Howard, Wyatt had someone. Someone he adored.

"Next day," Wyatt continued after a quick sip, "the guy goes *back* to the bar and orders fif*teen* shots of whiskey—downs them, bam-bam-bam, one right after the other. Bartender says, 'What's up now?' The guy answers, 'I just found out my *oldest* son is gay!'"

Howard pulled a Bud Light out of the cooler. Scott kept himself from rolling his eyes. Like he's watching his weight or something! *And how can he even drink that piss?*

"Next day the guy is back at the bar! He orders *twenty* shots of whiskey."

"And downs them, bam-bam-bam?" Kajagoogoo asked.

Wyatt nodded enthusiastically. "Bartender says, 'For Christ's sake, does no one in your family like pussy?'"

Wyatt grinned like the Cheshire cat. Leaned in. Nodded again. "'Yes!' sobs the guy. 'My *wife!*'" Wyatt exploded into laughter, and Kajagoogoo squealed. To be fair, it was one of Wyatt's better jokes, and Scott almost laughed. The rest did. Even poor newbie gay Max.

God. He *was* handsome, wasn't he? Scott didn't like hairy guys, didn't care for facial hair (and hated the new Adam Levine scruff-face thing Wyatt had going on lately), but boy, he *did* have to admit it. Max was an intensely attractive man. Not the movie star looks of Asher. No. More the Scruff.com kind of guy. But not *too* scruffy. Just right up to the line. And the fact that he was a teacher helped. He was smart. If Max had been interested in him instead of Sloan, he wouldn't have said no. Beard or not. At least his was trim and neat (the total opposite of Howard's). His eyes were beautiful too. Not as pretty as Sloan's honey brown eyes, but.... Scott suddenly saw the way the two of them were looking deeply into each other's faces, and, damn, who could resist either one?

Scott sighed.

Kajagoogoo meanwhile threw himself down next to Scott, and Scott flinched. What the hell? Asher, with a big canvas shopping bag, sat down right where he was supposed to. On *his* own blanket. Then he actually whistled at the kid and patted the ground next to him. "Come on," he chirped, as if talking to a dog. "Right here." Oh, and then worse—the kid got on hands and knees and scrambled over to Asher just like an eager pup.

"Who's your little friend?" Howard asked.

Of course he would, thought Scott. Damn. Look at the way he's staring at the kid!

"Everybody, this is Blue." Asher patted him on the head. "Blue, this is everybody."

Blue (*Blue?*) grinned happily and waved. "Hi-yee everybody! Nice to meet you."

And had Scott thought that Wyatt was wearing shorts that were way too short? Blue's shorts (*Blue?*) were like Daisy Dukes! Why... shit. One of the kid's balls had just popped out right as Scott watched! Smooth as a baby's bum. Shaved? Certainly not small, even though the kid was short. He didn't seem to realize what had happened, either.

I'm sure not telling him! Scott looked away, embarrassed. Then glanced back. He couldn't help it. *Letch!*

"And where did you come from, little Blue?" Howard asked.

Oh, get your tongue back in your mouth, Scott thought. Wanted to say it out loud, but didn't—for Wyatt's sake. He looked at Wyatt then and caught a look. An expression that was only there for a second. Hurt? Was it hurt?

"Oh, here, there, and everywhere." Blue giggled. "I get around."

I bet you do, thought Scott. *In fact I bet you get* passed *around.*

"Would you like something to drink, pretty boy?" Howard asked.

"Howard!" Scott barked before he could stop himself.

"What?" Howard asked.

"Well.... Is...." He looked at Blue, who was gazing up at him with eyes that belonged on a Disney cartoon character. "Maybe he's a little young—"

"I'm twenty-two!" Blue cried.

Scott stared at Blue agog. Twenty-two? He didn't look eighteen.

"We met at The Male Box," Asher said. "He asked me to buy him a beer...."

At that point, all Scott could do was shake his head. And if Wyatt had been bothered by the attention Howard was giving Blue, you couldn't tell now, Scott saw. Wyatt had thrown himself on his stomach, propped his chin in his palms, and began to chatter with the kid like they were a couple of high school girls.

And Asher? Asher dropped his hand and let it cup Blue's little round upturned ass possessively. Interesting. Possessive today, or more than that? Scott actually laughed out loud. More than today. *Right!*

Scott looked over at Sloan, and wow.... He guessed Sloan really was over Asher. He was too busy playing googly-eyes with Max to even notice.

So here I am again. Alone. Blue might be only a Fourth of July conquest, but everyone was paired up.

Typical. Just typical.

CHAPTER EIGHT

THE SUN had set and they were just taking the pop-up down. It had provided a day of shade from the blazing July sun. If June had been hot, today had it beat a long way. Scott was glad he paid the extra for the deodorant and antiperspirant he'd used. Everyone else was sweating like pigs. He? He was simply damp. And that cool little ChillMeTowel he'd found at the end of last summer was a wonderful discovery as it turned out. He didn't know how the damn thing worked, but work it did. Made of some kind of combination of polyester and nylon, all he had to do was get it wet and somehow the thing miraculously dropped thirty degrees below the average body temperature. He just rolled it up and put it around the back of his neck and shoulders, and perfect relief!

Howard had asked if he could try it, and Scott had politely turned him down. Imagine! His ChillMeTowel on that fat, hairy, nasty, sweaty neck! Scott's stomach twisted at the thought.

He could tell Wyatt was the envious one. It was usually the little bear of their foursome who found such cool things first. Not today. Too bad, so sad.

They were all buzzed good by now. They were stuffed as well. All of them had brought food to throw into the mix—ham, fried chicken from KFC, vegan pad thai, egg salad sandwiches, potato salad, coleslaw, cheese, several bags of chips, deviled eggs, a fruit salad ("Fruits for the fruits," Wyatt declared joyfully), brownies (some magic and some not), a cake with cherries, blueberries and bananas on top for a fun patriotic look, a jug of ice tea, sodas, and enough kinds of beer and cocktails to make any gay man proud. And Max brought "Earth-friendly" plates and flatware (along with the vegan dish). When gay men got together, the food was great.

"You know how you know if you're at a gay picnic?" Wyatt asked them all. When there was no answer—Scott bit the insides of his cheeks and didn't say, "Because *you're* there with a 'No Gag Reflex' T-shirt"—Wyatt giggled and said, "Because all the hot dogs taste like shit!"

Everyone groaned, and Asher threw a deviled egg at him. Blue laughed, of course—like a kid. *How old is he?* Scott couldn't help but speculate. The kid looked like he might be old enough to drink, even if it was only by the barest margin. But he acted way, way younger. Maybe they should card him? Scott didn't want to get arrested for contributing to the delinquency of a minor.

Blue climbed into Asher's lap and pushed him back so he was straddling him, giggled again, and leaned in to kiss Asher.

Did Asher know how old Blue was? Surely he'd asked. It was obvious there was going to be some wick dipping, and if Blue wasn't at least eighteen, there was also going to be a more serious delinquency contribution than the drinking of a Mike's Hard Lemonade!

Someone's cell phone rang. It was the theme from *Mission: Impossible*, so everyone knew it was Sloan's phone. He pulled it from a pocket, looked at the glowing little screen, and got a big smile on his face. "Oh! It's my friend Peni." He answered it. "Hey, buddy! How's it going?"

Peni? Scott wondered. *Who's Peni?* And was Peni a boy or a girl?

"Oh, good!" Sloan continued, obviously excited. "I'm so glad to hear it. We're off to the west. I'll have my friend Wyatt put his rainbow umbrella back up. It's huge. You can't miss it." He looked at Wyatt and nodded, and Wyatt staggered to his feet and tried to comply.

Right! Scott got up and helped his friend. Wyatt was way too drunk to do anything. Thank goodness Howard didn't let anybody drive his big truck. Wyatt was not in any condition to drive.

"Okay—it should be up any second. Call back if you can't see it, and I'll meet you by the fountain...." He nodded (as if this Peni person could see!) and signed off the phone. "My friend, Peni, from work is going to sit with us. You guys don't mind, do you? This isn't an official FF-only day, after all." He stood up and began looking around him.

"Who is Peni?" Scott asked.

Blue sat up, ceasing his kissing for a moment. "Pene?" Blue asked and burst into giggles. "Isn't that how you say penis in Italian? I think it's Italian. I think that's right. I know lots of ways to say penis!" He grinned. Wiggled on Asher's crotch. Asher moaned.

"Gross!" Scott wanted to shout.

"What's funny is that *is* how you say penis in most languages. Penis, that is, and not pene. Danish. Polish. Finish. German. Even Turkish."

How the hell did he know that? Scott shook his head. Blue had hardly shown the aptitude to know Spanish, let alone a host of other languages.

"Not that I *know* any of those languages—"

Ah, ha!

"—but if I wind up in another country I sure do want to know how to say dick!" He laughed. "Say dick! Oh, that's funny! But seriously, I do know lots of ways to say it. It's *verge* in French. I love that. Ver-ge!" He wiggled again. "And *bod* in Irish, and *titi* in Filipino, and *sambool* in Arabic and *rou bang* in Chinese, although that is more like cock. I think *ji ba* is the more polite Chinese word—"

Slowly everyone stopped what they were doing and stared at Blue.

What the fuck? Scott swore to himself,

"It's *jur jur* in Cantonese, I think, and *gogot* in Creole—whatever the fuck Creole is, something kind of Frenchie, I think—and *pinga* in Spanish—*can't* forget Spanish! It's *whalluper* in Scottish. *Whalluper*! I just *love* that. *Whalluper*! *Suck* my *whalluper*! And that's the *clean* versions! I know *lots* of naughty ways to say dick—"

Shut him up! Scott cried inwardly. *For God's sake! Someone shut him up.* He winced, realizing the word he'd just used. *I don't believe it. I just said, 'God's sake!' I'm going to kill that kid!*

"—like in Hindi it's *lavda*, and I guess that's supposed to be very vulgar. You can also use the word *toto*, which I love. Toto! Like Dorothy's dog, which is just perfect, don't you think? Did you know there are over twenty official languages in India? Like there is this one, I am pretty sure it is called Marathi or Maranatha or something like that, and their word for penis is *popat*, which means literally 'parrot' and I think that is *hysterical!* I can't tell you any of the others because the only reason I know that one, or two, I guess, is because I tricked with this hot Indian dude once, and he knew *popat* because his mother spoke Mar— Oh, but you know the more I think about it, I think that Maranatha was a word they used in my church when I was growing up, so maybe it is Marathi. It's *byxormen* in Swedish—which means 'trouser snake.' *Byxormen!* So funny! In Flemish you say *wiwi*, or *kraantje*, and guess what *that* means? Little faucet! And *ptak a vejce* is Czech for penis and testicles and that means bird and eggs, and *tippi* is the generally accepted Icelandic word, but that's just the beginning there! And *spaetzle* in German, just like the noodles, because—*duh!*—what do noodles remind you of? It's *pigyn* in Welsh, which basically just means cock, although I am not sure if that is *penis*-cock or *rooster*-cock—and it certainly *sounds* funny—and that isn't even *counting* the fun slang terms for penis in the UK, like pork sword or thirsty ferret or purple parsnip or my favorite, craning cyclops. Oh! And there is *pinto*. Oh God! It's *pinto* in Spain, which means 'small penis,' and that's why the Pinto car didn't sell well in—"

That's when Asher finally rolled Blue over in a quick move and planted a huge kiss on his mouth. There was mumbling for a second and something about *zayyin*, maybe, and a *dhanda* and finally, finally, he shut up and started kissing back.

Oh thank every nonexistent god ever made! Scott thought in relief. He didn't think Blue was *ever* going to shut up. He did figure Blue was probably going to get Asher's *shlang* (which Scott just so happened to know was a Yiddish word for dick) stuck in his mouth later tonight.

"Hey, Sloan!"

Scott looked up from his place on the blankets to see a beautiful dark man walk up.

"*Talofa*, Peni!" Sloan cried and jumped up and hugged the guy.

So Peni was a boy. Well, not a boy. A man. A pretty hot man.

"*O a mai oe?*" Sloan asked his friend, and just what the hell did that mean?

"*Manuia, fa'afetai,*" Pretty man answered. And: "*O a mai oe?*"

What the hell? Scott looked back and forth between the two of them. He was obviously missing something. Were they speaking in another language? More words for "penis"?

"I am doing great. Everybody, this is my friend from work, Peniamina, but just call him Peni."

"Yes, please," said Pretty Man—aka Peni.

"Peni, this is my boyfriend, Max."

Max jumped athletically to his feet and shook Peni's hand.

"Oh! Max!" Peni grinned, showing beautiful, perfect teeth that glowed in the dimming evening light against his dark skin. "I've heard *so* much about you!"

"Oh God," Max said, running his hands through his short dark brown hair. "Uh-oh."

"No, not 'uh-oh.' Well, at least not too much 'uh-oh.'" He winked at Sloan. "Wow. When you said he was gorgeous, you weren't kidding."

"Oh, come on," cried Max and dammit, was he blushing?

Puke! Scott wanted to puke.

"And you've met Wyatt, haven't you?"

"Yeah, we met at lunch one day."

Scott shook his head. *They did? Of course. Left out again. How come I don't know him?*

Pretty Man/Peni held out his hand to Wyatt and Wyatt, naturally, just threw open his arms and hugged him. Good old Wyatt.

Howard just sat higher and held out a hand, too, lazy or drunk to get up. And Howard was tall. Taller even than Asher.

"And this," Sloan said turning Scott's way, "is Scott—"

Peni's smile was back in a flash (not that it had gone away) and those teeth! Perfect. And those eyes. Like obsidian—stunningly deep and beautiful. He wasn't Spanish, nor Mexican.... Part African-American? Scott was stumped and—

"—only one of the *best* friends in my whole life. I don't know what I would have done without him sometimes."

Scott's mouth fell open and he quickly closed it. What? What did Sloan say?

Peni's smile changed. Sort of sad in a way. He looked deeply at Scott and gave him a nod. As he stepped forward to shake Scott's hand, he leaned in and said quietly, "Sloan has told me a lot about you too. It's an honor to meet you."

Scott reeled. Felt light-headed for a second. *What? Sloan said what?*

"And this," Sloan said, giving Asher a light kick in the hip, "is Asher. If he can stop playing suck-face, maybe he'll say hi."

There was a brief struggle of tangled limbs, and Asher rolled to his feet and held out a hand and...

Stopped.

For one instant, he turned to stone. Then he smiled. It started sweet, then turned sexy, then turned absolutely lascivious. "Well, *hellllll-o*, Peni."

Scott sighed. Good old Asher. Bulge in his pants from the hard-on kissing Kajagoogoo had given him and already coming on to Peni. *What a whore.*

Peni stepped back with a laugh and held up his hand in a "stop" gesture. "I've heard *all* about you too, Asher."

Asher placed his hand on his chest, a wounded look on his face. "What, me?" the look said. "What about me?" he asked.

Scott just shook his head again.

These are my friends.

"Why don't you sit down," Max said.

Asher moved over. "You can sit here," he said, folding himself down onto his blanket.

Blue gave him a sturdy look and cuddled close to him.

Peni glanced around and, seeing Scott was pretty much alone on his blanket, said, "Mind if I join you, Scott?"

Me? He wants to sit with me? "Yes!" he said. "I mean no. Please."

"Do you want something to drink, Peni?" Sloan asked.

"I don't know. What do you have? Something nonalcoholic?"

Wyatt shook his head. "We aren't allowed," he said.

"Not allowed?" Peni looked at him in confusion.

"We're gay and we're partying, and boring nonalcoholic stuff is not allowed."

Peni laughed. "Well, luckily, I have a few bottled waters in my backpack." Peni sat down and began to rummage through his bag and pulled out a bottled water.

Wyatt gasped. "Don't you know that fish fuck in that stuff?"

Peni pointed a long (sexy) finger (could fingers *be* sexy?) at Wyatt. "And I know all about you too, Wyatt, So watch it." Scott wasn't sure if he'd ever thought fingers could be sexy, but was there one thing about Peni that wasn't sexy? Especially that ass. Holy shit! You could set a cup of tea on that ass. With the saucer.

"You really can have something to drink," Scott said. "One won't hurt, will it?"

Peni gave a long sigh, looked at his water, looked around the circle of faces, looked at Sloan (who shrugged) and then said, "I—I don't know."

"I think we have a couple of these cute little bottles of wine," Wyatt said and got on his hands and knees. Sticking his chubby little butt in the air, he began to go through his big cooler.

"Oh, I can't drink a whole bottle," Peni said.

"Oh, no, girl. These are really small. Like one glass. And I mean a *teetotaler* glass. Ah! Eureka! Here it is!" He pulled out what was indeed a very small bottle of wine. "It's a moscato. Do you like sweet wine?"

"I—I don't know," Peni said. "I've never heard of a mass-caught-oh."

"Then you're in for a treat," Wyatt said and tried to open the bottle. "Dammit, it's wet. I can't get it."

"Oh, for Christ's sake," said Howard and took the little bottle and deftly opened it. He passed it over to Peni, who looked at it like it could be poison.

"It's not poison," Wyatt said. "Give it a try."

Peni gave a long smile, nodded, and took a sip. "Oh," he said. "Nice."

Interesting, thought Scott. Did Peni not drink? And if not, why? "Don't drink much?" he asked.

Peni shrugged. "Not until lately. I—I was raised Mormon. We aren't supposed to drink."

Oh fuck me. Religion. Again. Scott's interest in Peni plummeted.

"I—I think I'm giving it up—"

"Alcohol or Mormonism?" Asher asked.

"Being a Mormon," Peni said. "I mean, it is only a matter of time before I'm excommunicated anyway—"

"*Excommunicated?*" Scott asked with a gasp.

Peni sighed again. "Yeah. Mormons don't believe in the 'homosexual lifestyle.' I either have to be celibate or get married to a woman. No boy-boy sex."

"No boy-boy sex?" Wyatt asked. "Does that mean no man-man sex either?"

"Nope," Peni answered.

"That sucks," Wyatt replied sadly. "Or doesn't as the case may be." And then suddenly: "Oh! Oh!" Wyatt let out a long happy squeal. "Did I tell you? Howard and I got a pop-up."

"A what?" Scott asked, confused by the abrupt change of subject.

"A pop-up trailer! I am so excited I could just shit. We have named it the Rolling Brothel and I cannot *wait* to use it the first time."

Rolling brothel? Scott was disgusted.

"Wow," Sloan said. "You've been wanting one forever, haven't you?"

"Yes!" Wyatt was bobbing his head so excitedly he looked like one of those bobble-head toys. "For years we've updated one tent after another, but all I wanted—*we* wanted—was a pop-up. Howard likes to camp, and he likes to head to Sanctuary, and we've even gone to Cactus Canyon a few times, but he *hates* the loading and then the unloading and the setting up and all that shit—"

"That's because I *do* most of it," said Howard.

Wyatt shrugged and rolled his eyes and mouthed "Whatever" and then continued uninterrupted, "—and now that we have the pop-up, we can just keep most of our stuff in there year round. Keep it in the driveway, hook it up to the truck, drive out, crank it up, and violá! Instant salon!"

"Salon?" Peni asked.

"Yeah. We go to this campground called Sanctuary, and specifically, we go to this event called Heartland Queer Men's Festival—"

"Queer Men's Festival?" Peni said. "What's that?"

"It's a witchy-woo-woo week in the woods," Scott answered.

"*Dammit*, Scott," Wyatt snapped. "You know I fucking *hate* it when you call it that!"

Scott gave a shrug. "Sorry," he lied.

"You can be *such* a vagina!" Wyatt said.

Blue laughed. "You mean a *dick*, don't you?"

"No," Wyatt replied with his hands on his hips. "*Dicks* are wonderful things. Why would I call him that?"

"So you two got a camper?" Sloan said, artfully redirecting the conversation.

"Yes!" Wyatt crowed. "And the main reason was that Howard loves to camp and now we'll have everything in it already. Just head out and camp anytime we get a hair up our asses!"

Considering how hairy Howard was, that could be every day, thought Scott.

"But *specifically* for HQMF! It is ten days out in the woods in the middle of bumblefuck nowhere with anywhere from 95 to 150 gay men, and it is simply wonderful. And one of the funnest—"

Most fun!

"—things that happen are the salons in the evenings. Camp Sanctuary has this little plateau, and most everybody who doesn't use one of the cabins sets up their tents all around the perimeter. And a lot of us fix up our camps to be real fun, and we have themes and set up lights and stuff and have little cocktail parties or sing-alongs—"

Kumbaya, my goddess, kumbaya!

"—and drumming circles and herbal peace pipe gatherings—if you catch my drifterino—and generally just catch up with all the men we only get to see once a year. And this time we will have a pop-up and we can go *all* out, and we are going to have *the* coolest set-up on the plateau!"

"That many gay men?" Peni asked.

"It's incredible," Wyatt said. "Ask Sloan."

"You've been to a gay men's camp and never told me?" Peni turned to Sloan.

Sloan shook his head. "No. Not sure it's right for me. But I did go out to the camp where they hold it one day with Wyatt, and it is a wonderful, peaceful place."

"I've been trying to talk Scott into going for years—"

"And it's not happening," Scott said. "I am not spending my precious vacation time hanging out in the woods with a bunch of naked faeries—"

"Naked?" gasped Peni.

"No!" cried Wyatt. "Only a few of the guys go naked. Naturists. The rest of us wear at least a sarong. Sarongs are these pieces of—"

"Oh, I have dozens of sarongs," Peni said with a wave and another sip of wine. "Except my people call them lava-lavas."

"That's cool," Wyatt said.

"Your people?" Scott asked.

"I'm Samoan," Peni answered.

Ah. Samoan. That explained it, Scott thought. A lot of Samoans had immigrated to Independence, Missouri, because so many had converted to Mormonism.

"Anyway," Wyatt said. "Scott keeps calling it a witchy-woo-woo camp— even though he knows it pisses me off—"

"Which is *why* he calls it that," Asher explained.

"Not true!" exclaimed Scott. *Although it was, wasn't it?*

"—*and* what it *is* about is a bunch of men claiming their gay inner being, celebrating thousands of years of heritage, and rejoicing in our unity in the very midst of our diversity. We love and laugh and be together in brotherhood once a year for a little over a week, and my whole year revolves around it. Me and Howard both, right, Howard?"

Howard nodded dutifully, but Scott could see what he was really doing was staring at Peni. Asher too. For shit's sake. Peni was pretty, but he wasn't *that* pretty. And didn't the two of them *have* someone? He, Scott, was the only single guy here. *At least for tonight,* he thought, looking at Asher and his Super Glued-on paramour.

"It sounds interesting," Peni said.

"Maybe you should come," Wyatt said. "We'll watch out for you, won't we, Howard?"

Howard nodded, eyes still fixed on Peni. "Sure. Keep you right under our wings."

"Maybe…," Peni said. "I mean, witchy-woo-woo or not, from what I've heard, it's got to be better than what I grew up with."

"I understand the Mormons are pretty loving families," Asher said.

"Yeah," Peni replied wistfully.

"Here," said Wyatt. "Give me your cell number, and I'll send you the info."

"Oh." Peni paused, then gave a single nod. "Okay."

Scott couldn't believe it.

"As long as I wouldn't have to run around naked," Peni said.

"Most of us don't," Wyatt said. "I don't. Most of us do skinny-dip, though."

Peni considered it a moment, then smiled that perfect-toothed smile. "Well, hell. If everybody's doing it…. I guess I don't have anything to be ashamed of."

And there it was. That fast.

The image of a naked Peni wading out into a lake filled Scott's mind. He felt his cock flex. Dammit!

Suddenly, a high-pitched whistle filled the air.

Everyone looked up as a flaming rocket shot up into the night sky and…

… exploded in a mighty flower of red, white, and blue.

A cheer filled the air, and the rocket's glare had begun.

CHAPTER NINE

PETER WAGNER'S Fourth of July extravaganza didn't end with the fireworks display as most such celebrations did. In fact, it seemed the party had just begun.

Cue Ball, a sexy bald man known throughout gay and straight dance clubs in Kansas City as a DJ of no small talent, appeared on stage in a bright flash of lights and an explosion of confetti. The crowd went wild. He was in his gay attire, which was to say, not much at all. Music boomed from a bank of speakers, and the dance floor, set up next to Peter's magnificent fountain, blazed into life and seemed to be instantly filled with flailing bodies in various stages of undress.

Peter's Olympic-size swimming pool filled up again as well, the underwater lighting morphing slowly back and forth from Mediterranean blue to a deep purple. Torches were the only other lighting, and there were so many men, so many gay men, dancing and leaping into the pool, singing, laughing, swimming—and not a few of them nude. It was an orgy waiting to happen, as far as Scott could see.

Then to his amusement (and the protests of some of the revelers), Scott saw that wasn't the case after all. Security, which had been discreet all day (even ignoring the sweet smell of marijuana in the air and the only halfway discreet people passing the cause of said smell), suddenly appeared—seemingly from the woodwork (or hedges and rose bushes?)—and broke up any overly amorous activities. While skinny-dipping in the pool was permitted, apparently coupling was not. At least not the sexual kind. And that wasn't all. Scott overheard at least one reveler being escorted away from the party, slurringly assuring the big men that "*Nnnnooo….* I'm… n-not… wha-whatchamacallit… dunk… *drunk…* no! No *rrrrrrreallllleeeeeee….*"

"They're going to let him drive?" Scott asked Sloan.

"No," Sloan said with a shake of his head. "Peter Wagner rented buses to take people home, or to the local hotels if they don't live here in town."

That was interesting, Scott thought. Their host seemed to care just as much as his reputation said he did. Why, there were even people passing out condoms, and earlier that day there had been a tent where free rapid HIV testing was offered.

If Scott had been curious about the "great" Peter Wagner before, he was doubly curious now. And Sloan knew him! He wondered if there was a chance Sloan could introduce him. But he'd kept his eyes peeled all day and hadn't caught a glimpse of the billionaire. The thing was he wasn't sure if he would recognize the man or not. In real life people could look so different from the way they did in magazines or on TV. He'd once stood next to one of his favorite porn stars in a Kansas City bar, even chatted with him, for ten minutes before he'd realized who the man was. Only after they'd called the guy on stage to dance (strip) had Scott realized who he was. He'd been so short! So tiny! On Scott's laptop the guy had looked so... well... *huge*.

It turned out that Peniamina Faamausili—Peni's full name—was pretty damned popular that night, much to Scott's annoyance. After all, as far as he was concerned, Scott was the only truly eligible contender for Peni's attention in their little group that night. No one else had any business taking an interest in the beautiful Samoan man, let alone flirting with him.

After all, Howard (whose eyes had lit up like the impending fireworks when Peni had showed up) was married to Wyatt—even if not legally and only by means of some ludicrous ritual involving a calling forth of the nonexistent spirits of the four elements, a tying together of the wrists with a gold cord, and a "jumping of the broom." Even if the two of them weren't monogamous, Wyatt insisted there were rules guiding what was okay and what wasn't concerning their extramarital activities, although from the frequent hurt looks in the big, dark, expressive eyes of the Fabulous Four's bear, it appeared Howard wasn't following them. Of course, Scott had suspected that for a long time, and he thought it was only a matter of time before the relationship finally hit Defcon 1.

When it was Howard's turn to boogie with Peni on the coruscating dance floor, he was constantly reaching for the Samoan's ass with those ham-sized hands of his. If not for Peni's artful and near gymnastic avoidance of those mitts, there was no telling how much Howard would have man-handled those high, round butt cheeks. Luckily, Howard wasn't all that graceful, either with his moves on the floor or his gropes.

Sloan and Max, naturally, only had eyes for each other. Scott figured he could go into an epileptic fit and Max would just ask Sloan to pass that bag of potato chips, please. Watching the two of them dance was to die! Max danced just like a straight man, which was to say pretty badly. Scott only hoped the man fucked better than he discoed. Or no! Strike that. He hoped superhunk fucked just as badly. Maybe this google-eyed thing would be a flash in the pan!

Then it was Asher's turn, and he had a date for shit's sake! Blue might be a brainless little twink with the unfortunate gift of unending gab, but they *were* here together. Was Asher really flirting with Peni right in front of Blue? He left his little Kajagoogoo boy alone on the floor, and Howard took it as an opportunity to return to his original target. He shrugged and grabbed the kid and crushed him up against his big, sweaty body. It really, truly, was enough to make Scott want to vomit.

Asher was faster and more athletic than Howard and managed to snag Peni by the belt loops of his jeans and pull him close. Asher kept leaning in, obviously trying to kiss him, but Peni kept twisting his head to the side to avoid Asher's mouth. Asher used that as an excuse to say something into Peni's ear. Peni just laughed and somehow wiggled free and left the dance floor.

Great. Just when Scott had hoped to get his chance at a dance.

He built up the nerve to ask Peni anyway. Who knew when he'd have another chance with such a good-looking guy? When Peni declined, Scott felt his mood crash lower than it had been all day.

All day?

Hell!

Ever since he'd gotten back from Los Angeles.

But then to Scott's surprise, Peni asked him if he wanted to go for a walk instead.

Hell yes, he did! Scott hadn't been sure if Peni knew he existed.

They strolled off into the night, away from the dance floor and the pool and most of the partiers. Scott stuck his hands in his pockets and tried to think of something to say. He wasn't the best conversationalist. If he wasn't acting like he was in love with some stranger, he was more often than not insulting someone.

"Sorry about my friends," he finally said.

"What for?" Peni asked. "Most of them are pretty nice. I could use a little less attention from Wyatt's boyfriend…."

"*Tell* me about it," said Scott. "He's kind of gross. I don't know what Wyatt sees in him."

"He must have some good qualities," Peni returned. "Wyatt's awfully sweet, and I'm sure he'd have no trouble getting someone new if he wanted. Howard must give him something that he needs."

Wyatt? Sweet? Well, Scott supposed that was true. If you looked past the flamboyance. But not likely to have trouble finding a new boyfriend? Did Peni really think so? Scott had always assumed Wyatt hadn't dumped Howard because he was afraid he'd never find anyone else willing to put up with his eccentricities.

"Asher, on the other hand…. Jesus—*he's* the guy Sloan was in love with forever?"

"Tell me about *that* too!" Scott sighed. "Asher is a slut."

"But Sloan? He's awesome. He must see a quality in Asher that I didn't see tonight, right? I mean, Asher's your friend too."

Their walk was taking them past a long a hedge of rose bushes, the air fragrant with their sweet, heady scent, the only light a scattering of tiki torches like those around the pool.

"Yeah. Asher's all right. He's got some good qualities." Scott thought about his friend for a moment. He knew it was true. *Knew* it. "Trouble is," Scott confessed, "I'm too tipsy right now to remember any of them."

Peni laughed. Paused. Then grew more serious. "I think Sloan's a lot better off with Max, don't you think? Even with all the drama with him being married and all? I hope he doesn't think that Max has gotten over that and totally embraced 'the gay' yet. You can't deny who you are *that* long and change overnight. Max might still have a lot of baggage to deal with, and I hope Sloan's prepared for that…."

Scott nodded. He didn't know how to respond. The thing was he agreed. Sloan *did* need to be with someone who was *proud* of who he was.

Someone like me….

But Scott decided that discretion was the better part of valor. Peni worked with Sloan, and if Scott said the wrong thing, it *could* make its way back to his friend.

"Can I confess something to you?" Peni asked. He looked around as if someone might be listening.

Hmmmm…. "Sure," Scott said.

"Sloan?" Peni glanced over his shoulder. "I sort of had a crush on him."

Oh, for shit's sake! Somehow Scott stifled a groan. Of course. Of *course* he did. Who *didn't* want Sloan? *Except* Asher, who wanted every other man who ever lived. Scott ground his teeth in frustration. Took a deep breath. "Oh? You did?"

Peni looked around one more time, then stepped close to Scott and leaned in toward him. "I guess I still sort of do."

Scott's stomach sank. Why had he fantasized even for one *second* that Peni could ever, even possibly, have asked him to go for a walk because he was interested in him? A walk didn't mean dick! Literally.

"I'm pretty much over it. Over him. It was mostly a hero-worship thing, you know? Sloan is the first gay friend I've ever had."

"The first. Surely not. I bet you've had gay friends before, even if you didn't *know* they were gay."

"Maybe," Peni admitted. "But Sloan was the first out and proud gay guy I've ever been friends with."

And Sloan *was* out and proud. Ever since he got pushed out of the closet when he had sex with his fiancée's brother in college. Where Scott had met Sloan. In college, not in bed.

"I looked up to him. Not at first, though. At first he scared me."

Scott chuckled. "You were scared of *Sloan?*"

"When we met I was still pretending I wasn't gay, even to myself. And he *asked* me if I was gay—no—he just *assumed* it right off. He *saw*. He *knew*. And me? Mormon?"

Scott shook his head. Religion. Fucking religion.

"But bit by bit, I accepted it. Mostly. I have to tell you it took every bit of nerve I had to be here tonight. Sloan invited me to spend the day. I almost didn't come at all! I kept thinking, what if somebody *sees* me?"

"Well, if they're here," Scott said, "then they don't care that you're gay…." And hadn't he said that to someone else recently?

"That's what Sloan said! See! That's *exactly* what he said. But Scott.... What if someone saw me, *sees* me, and doesn't realize I'm not out. Not really. Not to my family, yet. My church. What if someone sees me tonight that I know from church. What if they assume I'm out and they tell people?" Scott tripped, caught himself.

Fuck!

Daniel's words echoed back at him: "What if someone had seen me? Someone who knew me? Someone who went to my church and they told everyone? Do you think anyone would have believed that I hadn't had a sip of alcohol?"

Religion!

"I could be excommunicated," Peni said.

"Well, aren't you going to be anyway, eventually?" Scott snapped and immediately regretted it.

Peni shrugged. "Unless I leave first. But I'm not ready, you know? Not yet. It's going to kill my family. Mom? It's hard to imagine what she's going to say. Do. I close my eyes at night when I go to bed, and I see a big hysterical scene. A rending of garments, tearing of flesh, covering her hair with ashes. Falling down on her knees. Wailing and all that...."

"Shit," Scott said with a gasp.

Fucking religion!

Peni nodded. Neither talked for a moment. A long moment.

"I'm sorry," Peni finally said. "We're supposed to be having fun, and here I am dumping this crap on you."

"N-no," Scott said. "It-It's okay."

They stopped when Scott saw a convenient bench, and he motioned toward it, an offer to sit. Peni took him up on it.

There was another long silence, and Scott found himself totally lost. He had no idea what to say.

Peni broke the silence. "I love my family, Scott. I love them with *all* my heart. It scares me to death to think about going through life without them. My mom and dad, they laid the entire moral foundation for my life. I'm not even talking the Mormon thing. I mean the values I live my life by. And I have brothers and sisters. I hear people complain about their families. Not me."

"How many brothers and sisters do you have?"

"Two brothers, two sisters."

"Gosh." What would that be like? Scott thought it sounded like chaos.

"What about you?"

Scott shook his head. "None. I'm an only child. It's a big part of why my parents don't talk to me. The gay thing. I'm supposed to carry on the family name, and *that* isn't happening. They're Baptists." He shook his head again. "They're crazy is what they fucking are. Always talking about the end of the world and how if I don't repent I'll go to hell when Jesus comes again. So I said,

'So why do you want me to have kids, then? If it's all going to end soon?' They didn't appreciate it."

"I imagine not." Another pause. "I guess Baptists and Mormons aren't that different."

"That's not what my family would say," Scott replied. "They think Mormons are more evil than Muslims."

"And my family thinks an angel told John Smith that all the existing churches are wrong and that the Book of Mormon is the correct doctrine to restore God's church."

"It's hard to argue with people who *know* they're right," Scott said. "I don't try anymore." Which wasn't quite true, though, was it? He did it all the time. He rammed it down people's throats, didn't he?

"No brothers or sisters," Peni said, artfully changing the subject. "Gosh. I can't even imagine. We're all so close. It's like we're a part of each other, connected, like a jigsaw puzzle."

"Then surely," Scott said, "they already know."

Peni looked at him. His eyes were so dark, especially in this light. Scott couldn't tell where his pupils ended and his irises began. "Maybe," Peni whispered. "Maybe they do."

"Good evening, gentlemen." The voice came as a surprise, and Scott looked up to see a tall, distinguished-looking gentleman with silver hair walking toward them, carrying a cane. His stride was graceful and his bearing straight. He didn't look like he needed a cane. He was wearing khaki slacks and a white open-collared shirt that both looked so light they could have been spun from air. A thick gold chain around the man's neck glittered in the torchlight.

"Good evening," Scott replied.

Peni didn't say anything.

"Taking a break from the hustle and bustle?" the man asked. "Far from the madding crowd's ignoble strife?"

"I'm sorry?" Scott asked.

"Or is this perhaps an amorous rendezvous that I am interrupting?"

Peni leapt to his feet, eyes wide. "Nothing like that!"

"I daresay that an interruption does not stop two determined individuals," the man replied and laughed. He had an unusual accent, melodious and not quite definable. A bit like British, but there was more.

Peni shook his head no. "We're just talking...."

Scott gave Peni a hard look. He almost seemed afraid....

("But Scott.... What if someone saw me, sees me, and doesn't realize I'm not out. Not really. Not to my family yet. My church. What if someone sees me tonight that I know from church. What if they assume I'm out and they tell people?")

Was this guy someone from Peni's church? He didn't think this old dude was security, did he? Ready to throw them out?

Scott stood and moved closer to Peni. "Relax," he quietly assured Peni. "It's all right."

"Ah!" The man grinned; it was impossible to tell his age. His eyes seemed immortal, but the lines around them told another story. His smile threw everything off. "Ah!" he repeated. "Were you two perhaps about to partake of the ganja?"

"Heavens no!" Peni all but cried.

"Alas, then. I mayhap would have asked for a hit. One would have been enough as I rarely partake these days. It makes me sleepy. Or silly. Silly-*er*. Or worse! Flirty! And I doubt there is a young man here who would welcome advances from an old man such as myself. A Scotch man am I."

"You're not old," Peni protested.

The man laughed so hard he had to lean on his cane. "And now thou dost lie, and lies should not be launched from such lovely lips, young man."

Is this guy for real? Scott wondered.

"Oh, to be young again and discovering oneself in this brave new world.... But then again, I have no regrets and would change very little." He smiled, stood up straight again. "*Talosia o lo'o e fiafia i lenei afiafi manaia.*"

Scott looked at the tall man in confusion. What had he said? He glanced at Peni and saw that his eyes had gone wide in surprise.

"Yes," Peni replied, the delight obvious in his voice. "*O lo'o fiafia.*"

Well, apparently Peni understood the strange nonsense the old guy had uttered. Was he speaking Samoan?

"*Ua fai sia vevela. A ea?*"

Peni shrugged. "It's not too bad. Especially now that the sun's set. *Na fa'afefea ona e iloa fa'asamoa?*"

"Why, I know Samoan because I live in Kansas City, young man. I'm a businessman. I employ a great many people of many different ethnic origins. And there are a great many Samoans living in Kansas City. How neglectful would I be if I did not learn as much as possible about such a great people?"

Who the fuck is this dude? Scott wondered. He looked at Peni, saw the slump that had been in his shoulders was gone. Peni was standing taller. Pride was beaming from his face.

"Th-thank you, Mr. Wagner—"

Wagner? Scott's eyes flew wide in surprise. *Holy shit!*

"—thank you, so much."

This is Peter Wagner? Holy shit!

"Please forgive me, son. I know your face, but not your name—or perhaps I did and in my decrepitude it has fled my mind. But—"

Decrepitude? As far as Scott could see, "decrepitude" was not a word he would use to describe this man. And despite the fact that Peter Wagner wasn't a young man, and despite his slight frame, Scott could see the great man also had a respectably built chest. This was not a frail man!

"—don't you work for me? Is it at Horrell & Howes?"

Peni looked at Peter Wagner agog. "I—Ye-Yes! I do."

Peter Wagner stepped forward, and held out his hand. "And your name?"

"Peniamina—"

"Ah! Benjamin, isn't it?"

"Yes!" Peni exclaimed. "But people call me Peni…. I can't believe you recognize me. All I do is answer phones all day!"

"*All?* All you do is *answer* phones? My dear lad, you are my ears and my voice with every phone call that you answer. Every customer you help, you are representing me. I pray that you don't feel that all you do is 'answer phones.' You… help… people. And by helping them, you help *me.*"

Scott could hardly believe what he was hearing. Did the man really feel that way? Damn. Maybe he was working at the wrong place. But no. There wasn't a thing wrong with the law office where he worked. But damn!

"And you, young man," Peter Wagner said, turning to Scott. "I've seen you around too. Baily, Cranston, and Watch, isn't it?"

Scott's mouth fell open.

"I own that too."

"How do you know I work there?" Scott stammered. "We've never even met—"

"I make it my duty to know not only about people, but to know *persons.* And I think I will make it my business to get to know the both of you. What is your name?" Peter held out his hand.

"Scott. Aberdeen." Peni elbowed him and he took Peter's hand.

"It is a pleasure, Scott Aberdeen." He turned to Peni. "Peniamina."

"Mr. Wagner," they chorused in response.

"Please. Peter. Mr. Wagner is the bastard that fathered me. And on that note, I must bid you adieu. Or in your case, Peni, *tofa soifua.*" He turned and began to walk away, swinging his cane like a dancer from a Broadway show.

"*Tofa soifua*, Mr. Wagner!"

"Peter! And *la maua le fiafia!*"

"*La maua le fiafia*, Peter!"

Scott turned to Peni. "What did he say?"

"He told us to have fun." Peni grinned. "So you wanna? Have fun?"

Scott's heart sped up. "S-sure."

Peni's grin widened. "Then let's go!"

CHAPTER TEN

"FUN" TURNED out to be something different than Scott's imagination had called into existence. So what else was new?

Fun turned out to be returning to the blankets and the rest of the Fabulous Four.

And joy of joys, Wyatt was talking about his witchy-woo-woo camp again. One thing Scott could say, though, was that he resisted calling it that.

Barely.

"I can't believe it's just a few weeks away," Wyatt cried. "We're going to have so much fun! Me and Howard are actually setting up a few days early to make sure we get one of the best spots. I—we—want to be near the top of the steps, but not *right* at the top of the steps, because some people get up way early in the mornings—doing yoga and shit—"

"What's wrong with yoga?" Max asked.

"—and we *will* be up late, girlfriends, let me tell you! Late, late, *late!*" Wyatt was squirming he was so excited. "But that's not the best part—I mean it *is* a good part, a *great* part—but we can party any time. There is this *wild* party at Sanctuary on Labor Day weekend. No, for Festival I like being with my faerie brothers. There is nothing like it on earth. They rejuvenate me. They make it possible to live in the real world the rest of the year. My whole year revolves around Queer Fest—"

"Queer Fest?" said Blue, his big eyes wide and curious.

Wyatt turned to him and nodded. "Yup. *Queer* Festival."

"I like the word 'queer,'" Blue said in an almost reverent tone. "Most people hate it. They say it's like the N-word, like 'faggot.' But I *know* I'm queer."

Wyatt's face turned radiant. "Yes!"

Asher looked at his playmate, eyebrow raised, a half smirk on his face. "What the shit are you two talking about?"

Wyatt turned to Asher. "Gays are forgetting who we are, Asher. Gay is becoming okay because we're becoming homogenized, no pun intended. Gay marriage, gay churches, even the Pope—an *enemy*—is suddenly telling people not to judge us. But don't you see? The world is saying that 'homo' is okay as long as we act just like *them*. Find a man, get married, adopt two point five kids, buy a house with a white picket fence. We're okay—*as long* as we don't wear pink and don't kiss in public. And as long as we're monogamous. And you know why they want that? Because they're *jealous*. Especially the men. They don't want to be married to *one* woman or only have sex with *one* woman for the rest of their lives! Men aren't *supposed* to be monogamous!"

"Well, I can swing with that part," Asher said. "I just don't know about this fairy shit...."

Scott narrowed his eyes. God. He had heard this all before. Next would be the witchy stuff. He turned to make a comment to Peni but found his new friend had dropped to his knees and crawled to Wyatt.

"You really don't mind if Howard is with other guys?" Peni asked. "Don't you want someone who is all yours?"

Wyatt turned his head to glance at his lover, then back at Peni. "We can't own people, Peni. Slavery is illegal." He leaned back against his big bear of a husband. "Howard and I are together because we *want* to be together. If he wants to fuck somebody else, how can I say I love him if I don't let him be a man? I don't love him as long as he acts a certain way. I love *him* for who he is."

Shit! Does he really believe this? Scott wondered. *Or is he just trying to convince himself.* Because while Scott didn't know whether monogamy was actually possible, he knew it was what *he* wanted. He wanted someone to love *him*. Not him and everyone else. Wanting someone to be monogamous wasn't "owning."

"I don't know, Wyatt...," Peni said.

"But doesn't your own religion allow men to have multiple wives?" Wyatt asked.

Peni sat back on his haunches. "Not anymore. We don't do that anymo—"

"That's *only* because Mormons have done the same thing fags are doing. Conforming. Forgetting who they are so that the 'moral majority' will accept them. Well, screw that."

Peni shook his head. "Wyatt, when I finally do this—finally come out, finally find a man—I don't know if *I* want to share either...."

Wyatt leaned forward. "Okay. Whatever. But don't conform. When you come out, don't let 'them' tell you what kind of gay man you have to be. We're *not* like them. We're *not* the same. We're different. We're *special*."

"Special," Peni said, his voice cracking. "Wh-what do you mean?"

Scott shook his head. Shit! Was Peni listening to this?

"Peni, we've been around for thousands of years. There were times when we were *celebrated* for being different. We were the ones who walked between worlds. We were shamans, priests, priestesses. The Roman emperor Hephaestion had his male lover Antinous deified and had an entire city built in his name. Their love was respected the world over, and men worshipped a *queer* god. Why, Christopher Penczak—only the *most* awesome gay witch *ever*—"

And there it is. Witch! Scott clenched his fists, trying to keep his mouth shut. *Let him talk, let him talk....*

"—says that Ganesha, possibly only the *most* popular of all the Hindu gods, was linked to homo worship and anal sex...."

"Ganesha?" asked Sloan, leaning forward. "I've never heard that before."

Wyatt nodded enthusiastically. "Yup. The whole trunk thing—like the biggest dick *ever*. And Thoth too! The Egyptian god of magic and language and writing. There is evidence that many of his priests were gay. It's the whole butt sex thing again 'cause Thoth is the one with an ibis head and those critters stick their own beaks up their ass!"

"Get the hell out of here!" Scott finally said, unable to keep himself quite any longer.

"I am *dead* serious," Wyatt all but squealed, sitting up and gesturing madly with his hands. "Homo priests served the goddess Isis in ancient Egypt. Apollo did it with guys all the time too. And Zeus fucked the piss out of Ganymede. Pan chased shepherd boys like a bee after flowers. The Greeks believed victory was theirs because of the love between men." Wyatt was trembling with excitement, talking so fast that even Blue wasn't trying to interrupt him. "For *centuries* queer gods were honored and worshipped. Native Americans honored gay men. It is only *Christianity* that says gay men are evil."

Peni sat back, and *oh fuck me*, Scott couldn't believe the look on his face! "What about the Jews? They call us an abomination!"

"That's fucking true," Asher said with a snarl. "You should have heard what my grandfather used to say—"

"And Islam!" Scott interjected.

Wyatt waved at Scott as if he were an annoying insect. "All Abrahamic religions! *And....* Are you *really* trying to tell me that Jesus wasn't a big old fag?"

Scott gasped. He couldn't help it. He may have rejected the religion of his parents, but to call Jesus a fag?

"Yes," shouted Blue. "Yes!"

"I mean, come on! John, Jesus's 'beloved disciple.' Tell me, you *tell* me that Jesus wasn't schtupping John! Have you seen the picture of the Last Supper?"

What would Mama think about that? Scott wondered. She'd have a freaking heart attack—after she scratched Wyatt's face off, that is. And how fucking weird was it that the idea of Jesus 'schtupping' John had so offended him. What was *that* about?

Once again, Daniel's voice echoed back to him: "But you get taught that stuff all your life? It has its hooks in deep."

Scott closed his eyes—*Fuck!*—and then opened them wide again. "So what's your fucking point, Wyatt?" he growled and hated himself for it, and worse when he glanced at Peni.

I've done it again. The way Peni was looking at him. *Like there's something wrong with me.*

"My point, Scott, is that my 'witchy-woo-woo camp,' as you call it, is a place where gay men are celebrated. For ten days I get to be with gay men who celebrate not only the fact that they're gay, but celebrate gay spirit. Ten days on acres of beautiful land and all gay men. And yes, some wander around naked, revealing themselves to nature and the sun and the rain—walking proud! And yes, we gather in circles and we practice ancient ways. We claim our place in history! We claim our right to be spiritual beings. You *tell* me what's wrong with that?"

Scott stood before his friend—his *friends*—and a few strangers, shaking. Shaking because his mind was in chaos. Chaos because yes, as gay men they did have the right to stand up proud of who they were.

But dammit! Why did God have to get mixed up in it? What was it about people that they needed some made-up deity's approval? Whether it was Jehovah or Zeus or fucking elephant-headed Ganesha—it was all made up! Couldn't Wyatt see that? He looked at his friends. Saw the expression on Peni's face. *You don't need God's approval! There is no God!*

And because he knew, *knew*, if he said any of this, he would be seen as a fuckhead instead of the sole *sane* man here, Scott did the only thing he could. With a silent sob, he nodded, apologized for his behavior, and left.

AND TO his surprise, it was Peni who came after him.

"Scott! Wait up!"

He didn't. He couldn't. He was practically power walking to his car, but catch up Peni did.

"Scott! Didn't you hear me?" Peni asked, coming up beside him.

A sob escaped Scott, and he hated himself for that as well as for so many other things. He tripped and flailed his arms, and Peni caught his hand and kept him from falling to the ground. Another cry slipped out, and he jerked his hand away and started for his car again.

"Scott, please!" He ran ahead of Scott and blocked his way. "Please. Tell me. What's wrong?"

Scott stopped. Clenched his fists. Tried to get himself under control. Fought against the tears blurring his vision. "God. How can you believe in God? How can fucking *anyone* believe in God? Why are you all worried about God? Every time. Every. Time. It always comes down to *God!*"

Peni shook his head, and to Scott's surprise, he saw tears in his eyes as well. "Scott, over eighty percent of the people in the world believe in *some* kind of god. Why not you?"

"*Because*," Scott shouted, "it's the belief in God that keeps my parents from loving me. It's God that makes my mom and dad think I'm an abomination. Because *they* believe in *God*, they kicked me out of their lives. They hate me. They fucking *hate* me!"

And then he burst into tears.

CHAPTER ELEVEN

AT A very young age, Scott began to suspect he was smarter than his parents. Sure, so does almost every other child on the face of the Earth since time immemorial, but Scott's suspicion came more from observation than childish conceit.

When Scott looked back at his life, he thought this idea probably hit him around the fourth grade. He was already reading Mark Twain by that time and was discovering Edgar Rice Burroughs's Tarzan books, as well as the John Carter of Mars series. He was reading at least two grade levels above his classmates. He remembered that all this was happening the year he had a teacher named Mrs. Grant. One day she had looked down at him with dark eyes and said something like: "You don't have *any* milk money, Scott."

Scott had looked up at her in confusion. "What did you say, Mrs. Grant?"

"I was telling you that you don't have *any* milk money. *You* said that you don't have *no* milk money. That's incorrect."

"My mom and dad say it like that all the time."

Mrs. Grant let him know they were wrong. It had taken Scott a moment to fully comprehend what she was saying and that she wasn't being mean. She was trying to help. He didn't want to sound stupid. He didn't want to *be* stupid. So after that, he wasn't upset about being corrected. Mrs. Grant was *supposed* to correct him—*teach* him.

So imagine that! His parents, who had declared that he would respect them, were wrong.

And he believed it. After all, Mrs. Grant *was* a teacher. It was only later that he found he was often smarter than people twice his age—*even* teachers.

After that he began to see there were other ways he was smarter than his parents.

They were useless when it came to helping him with his spelling, especially his father. It was the same with math. He might as well ask his G.I. Joe to help him with fractions. Neither his mother nor father had a clue what the scientific method was. How evidence grows until it supports a hypothesis, and if there is enough evidence to support that hypothesis, then it moves to the next step: a theory.

These observations gave him enough evidence for his own hypothesis. If his parents didn't know how to speak right and didn't know that the Grand Canyon was made by erosion, then what else didn't they know? What else were they wrong about?

One of his developing theories was that there was no such thing as God. After all, he'd just discovered there was no such thing as Santa Claus. His parents had lied to him about that, letting him believe an old fat man could sail through the night carried by a sleigh drawn by flying reindeer—a man who had the power to deliver presents to every boy and girl in the whole world. The Easter Bunny wasn't real either. So why should he believe in another old man who sat on a big throne up in the clouds somewhere? Wasn't God just the ultimate Santa Claus, after all, rewarding and punishing according to some list that was going to supposedly be checked once (and twice?) on "Judgment Day?"

Scott decided to test his new theory. He decided to pray.

His aunt Eunice was dying. She had cancer, although he wasn't supposed to know that. His mother wasn't very good about keeping it a secret. She seemed to be more embarrassed than upset or worried that her sister was dying. It was years later before Scott discovered his aunt had suffered from uterine cancer, and his mother believed she got it from having sex before marriage. It was God's punishment for her "wicked" lifestyle. Scott knew none of that in those far-off days, but he did know his mother and aunt didn't get along.

Scott, on the other hand, adored his aunt. She told him funny stories. She smoked funny smelling cigarettes she made on her own with a marvelous little device that rolled what she called "wacky tobacky" in small pieces of paper to create something called a "J." She admitted it did smell a lot like a skunk, but she kind of liked that, and it made her *feel* better. He wanted her to feel better. Smoking the Js made it so she could eat, and it helped her forget she was sick. "Not a bad deal, kiddo," she told him.

Aunt Eunice also shot straight with him. Told him the truth. She was the one who had confirmed that there was no Santa Claus—he was made up by Big Companies who used him as a commercial scheme to make more money. Scott was able to see that. Didn't companies use the Trix rabbit and Captain Crunch to sell cereal? The silly rabbit and the captain didn't really exist. They were just cartoons. Santa Claus was like that. He was made up and used by parents to control their kids! If you're not a good boy, you won't get anything for Christmas.

Scott found all this information very powerful and not the least bit distressing.

Aunt Eunice also let him watch *Tales from the Crypt*, which his parents absolutely forbade. That made her aces in his book.

Aunt Eunice was the coolest. The idea of her dying was almost more than Scott could stand, but he could see her getting sicker and sicker.

He figured this was the best possible test of his theory about God. God was supposed to be all-powerful. If you prayed, and you were a good boy or girl (like with Santa Claus), God answered your prayers. So Scott prayed.

He prayed in the morning when he got up.

He prayed at night before he went to bed. He even got on his knees. His mother was delighted that she didn't have to remind or threaten him anymore, and he didn't tell her he was praying that God would make Aunt Eunice better. He had a feeling his mother wouldn't approve.

Two months later his aunt died.

A couple of weeks later his cat Garfield got sick. He didn't want to eat, and he threw up when he did. He stumbled about and slept even more than usual. Scott begged his parents to take Garfield to the vet, but they refused. "He's a cat," Scott's father said. "If he dies we'll get another one. People give them away all the time."

Finally, Scott held his cat in his arms and did nothing for two days but pray.

Garfield died anyway.

"I thought you said that God answered prayers!" Scott told his mother angrily.

"He does," she said. "And sometimes the answer is 'no.'"

No? he thought. *No?* How could God say no about his Aunt Eunice or a little orange cat with big green eyes?

The only way that could be, as far as Scott saw, would be if God were just as evil as the other guy who supposedly had cloven hooves and carried a pitchfork. But Scott thought the idea of the devil was even stupider than that of an old man in the clouds.

God was just like Santa Claus. People made him up to scare kids into being good.

He never prayed again, and nothing his mother did would make him. No. After Aunt Eunice and Garfield died, Scott had no more truck with God.

No god at all.

IT WAS no small surprise when Peni called him Monday evening. Sloan had given him Scott's phone number. And it sounded like he wanted to go on a date.

A date? After he had told Peni that he didn't believe in God?

After he'd cried and made a fool of himself in front of the man?

After the man had held him like he was a baby?

After he'd suddenly pushed Peni away and run away into the night?

It was more than Scott could believe.

They had dinner at Café Namasté, a vegan restaurant Peni liked. It wasn't a place Scott would have picked out, but he was surprised at how good the food was. He thought the owner might be gay as well. What's more, Peni didn't mention the whole crying thing, didn't mention his diatribe about God—hardly mentioned religion at all.

They decided to go to a movie that Friday. Actually drove into the city and saw *Dawn of the Planet of the Apes* and then went out for a few drinks at The Male Box afterward. Scott found he was having a very nice time, and he thought Peni was too.

But then Peni brought up Wyatt's witch camp, queer camp, whatever the fuck it was.

"I was thinking of going...," Peni said.

Scott's mouth fell open before he could stop it. "You're pulling my leg, right?"

Peni shook his head. "I think it might be nice," he said. "To get away from it all. For the peace and quiet. For the brotherhood. I could use all those things. And I like to go camping. My family owns all kinds of camping stuff."

Scott couldn't believe what he was hearing. "Have you been talking to Wyatt?"

Peni nodded. "We went out for lunch the other day—"

Lunch? They went out for lunch? For some reason that hurt Scott's feelings. He'd thought maybe he and Peni really were giving dating a try, but surely he wasn't dating Wyatt too, was he? Wyatt? So this wasn't a date after all....

"—and then I went to his place—"

His place? You went to his place? God! They hadn't had sex had they? Hadn't Peni said he wanted monogamy?

"—and watched these DVDs he had of the talent shows they have at his camp. Some of it was pretty funny. One guy read this essay by David Sedaris, and I laughed so hard I was crying. And this other guy with a big beard got all dressed up in this black dress and this huge string of pearls and lip-synced to this hysterical song about fairies in the garden. I laughed until my sides hurt! And I couldn't believe how talented some of them were. Especially the guys who sang. It made me wonder if maybe I might have the guts to get up there and do some traditional Samoan dancing. What do you think?"

"I—I think that if you want to go, you should. I'm surprised...."

"Why?" Peni asked and took a drink of his Coke, rum-free.

"You being Mormon and all. I just figured hanging out with a bunch of witches might be a little weird for you."

"Wyatt said a lot of men go who aren't into the witch stuff."

"I guess." Scott took a swig of his drink. *It* had rum in it.

"Why don't you go?"

Scott laughed. "I don't have a tent," he said, spitting out the first excuse he could think of.

"I already told you. I have all the camping gear you can think of. The tents aren't small, either. I think if my brothers and father can share one, there would be plenty of room for you and me."

Share a tent with Peni?

Hmmmm….

The image wasn't an unpleasant one.

But then he thought about the heat and the sweat and porta potties and loonies running around with their dicks hanging—*and shit! What if he saw Howard's?*—and it was all he could do to repress a shudder. "It's like I told Wyatt. I don't have enough vacation time. My boss already let me take time to go to LA. I only get two weeks. I don't want to use them all on something I don't know that I'll like."

"Oh." Scott couldn't believe how disappointed Peni looked. Damn. Did that mean Peni really wanted *him* to go?

"I'm sorry, Peni."

Peni shrugged. "I just thought it might be a way for us to get to know each other better, you know?"

Scott found his heart was speeding up. Peni wanted to get to know him better? Even after his hissy fit at Peter Wagner's Fourth of July party? Did that mean…?

"I think we could be really good friends. We both have had religion effect our lives so deeply—"

Scott groaned. Did Peni have to bring that up?

"—and I thought if we got away from that, maybe saw people who had a whole different view of God, people who think that God loves gay people—"

"Peni. I don't believe in God!" It was louder than he'd intended. *Dammit!*

"Then go with me just to camp? We can hike. Swim. Didn't Sloan tell me you liked to go swimming?"

"In a pool," Scott said. "Not in a lake. There are snakes in lakes!"

Peni laughed and rolled his eyes. "Oh, don't be a fag."

Scott looked at Peni agog and then burst into laughter. "Did you just call me a fag?"

Peni grinned. "No. I said *don't* be a fag." His grin got bigger. "Not that there's anything wrong with that."

Scott just shook his head. "You are crazy, Peni."

"My mom says that all the time. Now you'll tell me you'll go."

Scott sighed. "I told you, Peni. I don't have the vacation time."

Peni gave a single nod and got that sad look on his face again. "Okay."

And damn if Scott didn't feel guilty. Crazier was the fact that he was blowing off the chance to spend a lot of time with Peni. In a tent. Just the two of them. But damn! Did it have to be Wyatt's witch camp? "What if just you and I go some weekend?" he offered. "We could go to Smith Lake…."

Peni shook his head. "It's Wyatt's *witch* camp that I want to go to, Scott. I want to be with gay men. Wyatt's told me so much about it, and I really think I want to go. It all sounds fun. Even the dinners. Wyatt says the attendees make the meals. He said he's made some of his best friends preparing dinner. He makes it sound wonderful."

Scott sighed again. He saw Peni really wanted this. Peni wanted to go, and wanted Scott to go with him.

Damn! Ten days in the woods in hundred-degree weather? With a bunch of guys who called themselves faeries? Scott knew he had as little interest in going as Peni wanted to go. So what did he say?

"I'll—I'll tell you what. I'll ask at work. Maybe I could go for just a few days—"

Peni shrugged. "I guess that would be better than nothing. I'll have to be by myself until you get there, but—"

"You mean this, don't you? You're going. To the whole thing."

Peni nodded. "It's weird. But the more I think about it, the more I want to go. I think I am going to go home tonight and get online and pay for my membership."

Scott looked at Peni, stunned.

Peni shrugged.

"I.... I...." Damn! Should he go? Should he do it?

But the thing was, he really didn't have enough vacation time. Not after some of the ridiculous trips he'd already made this year. Trips to meet men. Fuck!

"I'll ask, Peni. But don't hold your breath, okay? All I can do is ask."

And the smile that spread across Peni's face outshone the sun.

SCOTT WAS on the phone doing some research for one of the lawyers when Mr. Cooper—another of the lawyers—stepped into his tiny office. He didn't leave. In fact, he shut the door and stood there. For some reason it made Scott nervous. What could this be about? Luckily, he was just finishing his call, and it was with great trepidation that he hung up the phone.

"Mr. Cooper?" he asked. "Can I help you?"

"Mind if I sit down?"

Scott shook his head. "Of course not. Please."

Mr. Cooper, a handsome man, began a few moments of inane chatter. Asking where Scott had gone to lunch, how his Fourth of July was, and finally segueing into his trip to Los Angeles. Scott answered the questions, baffled that one of his bosses was asking him such questions. Not that the man was indifferent or anything like that, but it wasn't often he seemed to want to just chat. Cooper was an up-and-comer with Baily, Cranston and Watch and didn't have time to blab.

And just how did he answer the last question?

"It was a disaster," he blurted before he even knew he was going to admit anything like the truth.

"Oh?" Cooper said. He leaned forward and rested his chin on an upturned palm.

He wanted more? What was he going to say? He flew off to meet a man he hardly knew because he thought the guy had given up God and was ready for love with another man? And that the guy freaked out, lost his mind, thought he was going to hell? "Religion," he muttered without realizing it.

"Religion?"

"He needed God instead of me...."

Mr. Cooper nodded. "Is that's what's been bothering you lately, Scott? Had the two of you been seeing each other for a while?"

Scott laughed. "For a while? No. Not hardly. We met online, and I flew out to meet him a few weeks later, like a putz."

"Oh." Mr. Cooper sat back. He gave Scott a long look.

Scott swallowed hard. "Is there something wrong, Mr. Cooper?"

"Wil," Mr. Cooper said.

"Will what?"

"Call me Wil, Scott."

Scott resisted the temptation to call him "Wil-Scott." Then thought better of it. What the hell? "Okay, Wil-Scott."

"Wil" laughed. But then his face grew more serious. "Scott. I wanted to talk to you."

Scott swallowed again. "About what?"

"Scott, there's been a difference in you lately. I've been watching it go on for a while now. And I've watched it grow worse. You used to be so... up. Then bit by bit... you've changed. Your work has started to suffer."

Scott's stomach dropped. "My work?"

"You're making mistakes."

His stomach fell onto the ground between his feet. "Mistakes?"

"And you don't make mistakes. You made a big one on one of Watch's cases. Luckily, he won it anyway. He was pretty pissed, I have to tell you."

It felt like Scott's heart had stopped. Oh, shit. Not good. Not good at all. "Am... am I fired?"

Wil shook his head. "No. Although I had to calm him down."

Scott shook his head, looked at Wil in confusion. In grateful confusion. "Y-you calmed him down?" He suddenly felt like puking.

"I pointed out how good you were at your job—a regular detective. That this is the first time you've made a mistake like—"

"Why, Mr. Cooper? Wil?"

"For lots of reasons, Scott. I like you. And if you really want to know the truth, it's because we're the only two gay men in this office, and we need to stick together. Things are a lot better for us these days, but it's still tough. And you've worked here so long. All people would do is ask why you don't work here anymore. I don't want that to happen to you."

Scott suddenly felt like crying.

"But you have to do something," Wil said.

Here goes. What was it? "What?" he asked.

"You're going to take a vacation." The tone in Wil's voice made it clear it was an order. "At least a week. Somewhere fun. Get away. Meet some men. Or fuck, I don't care. Go on a Buddhist retreat. Contemplate your belly button."

"W-what?" Scott was stunned. "You want me to—"

"I want you to get out of here. I want you to relax. I want you to do whatever you need to do so that you can start applying yourself again. It's important. It'll save your job. And it will save you."

"I…. I…."

"Do you hear me, Scott? Vacation. Make it two weeks. Not one fucking day less. As soon as possible…."

"B-but I had plans later on this year. I need my vacation for then—"

"We'll figure that out then. Now I need you to get out of here. *As soon as possible*. Starting tomorrow if you—"

"Tomorrow? But I have several things here that—"

"We'll get someone else to finish—"

"Excuse me, sir. No. I have to finish these. It's important. One of them concerns a gay man."

"The Hartford case?"

"Yes." The man's lover had died and they weren't married, and his lover's family was trying to take everything. They wouldn't even let him come to the funeral. A flock of religious fanatics and—

Wil Cooper sighed, narrowed his eyes, and then nodded. "Next week?"

And suddenly he saw Peni's face in his mind. The disappointment on his face. Him telling the lovely man he didn't have any vacation time. *Well, fuck me.*

Scott laughed. "Would the week after that be okay?"

Wil's eyes narrowed even more. "Do you have something in mind?"

Scott sighed. "I think so."

"Something fun?"

No. Not really. But how would Peni feel if he took time off and did something else? And what was he going to do? Go to Los Angles? "I don't know. But it is in the middle of nowhere. I'll be able to look at my belly button."

Wil smiled, and it was a nice smile. He really was a handsome guy. And it turned out he was even nicer than Scott had imagined. Wil Cooper had saved his job.

"Good." He stood up and walked the few steps to the door. He turned back. "Make your reservations today."

Jeeze. "Okay," he said. "Today."

After Wil Cooper left Scott's office, he found he could only sit there for ten minutes. This was crazy.

You don't have to go to witchy camp.

He thought of Peni's face again.

No. Aren't you done trying to please other men? Go someplace fun! San Francisco. Atlanta. Provincetown. Key-fucking-West.

Then he heard Peni's words. He couldn't help it.

"I just thought it might be a way for us to get to know each other better, you know?"

Shit.

With a shake of his head, Scott pulled out his cell phone. A few seconds later: "Hey, Peni. Guess what? I talked to my boss. He's given me the time off—"

Peni squealed so loud Scott had to pull his phone away from his ear.

SO THAT night, Peni at his side, Scott got online and went to the site. The Heartland Queer Men's Festival. At first all he got was a black screen, and then slowly, the sound of drumbeats crept out through his speakers. An image began to form of a colorful butterfly. Only… it wasn't a butterfly. Scott saw the body of the insect was actually the silhouette of a man, his arms spread and morphing into lovely painted wings.

"Oh, my gosh," said Peni. "It's a penis!"

"No it isn't, it's a man," Scott said, but then—oh!—he saw what Peni was talking about. The man's legs, held tight together and toes pointed, did look like a penis, with the lower wings of the butterfly making testicles. Wild.

"It's beautiful!" Peni said.

Scott looked up at his new friend. Beautiful? Well, he wasn't sure about beautiful. But it was clever, he supposed. When he turned back to the screen, the words Heartland Queer Men's Festival had shimmered across the screen, along with the warning that some of the images might not be work safe, and finally, "Click Here to Enter."

Scott clicked—and to his surprise realized he was sweating.

A series of pictures began to form across the screen: rotating images of nature, sunsets, a turtle, a rainbow flag, and men. Men of every shape, size, and description. They weren't wearing business suits. They wore colorful swatches of cloth tied around their waists; they waded bare assed into a lake; they danced around fires, wore drag (no!), climbed trees, hugged, kissed, and…

"Oh, look!" cried Peni pointing at a picture of a man with an Indian guru's long, thick beard and wearing a formal black gown and a string of pearls that fell nearly to the ground. "That's the guy I was telling you about! The one that sings about fairies in the garden!"

"I-I see," Scott said. "Ummm…. Do we need to bring a dress?" Scott had a horrible sinking feeling. *Is it too late to get out of this?*

Peni laughed. "I wasn't planning on it. Do you think I would look good in something like that?"

Scott looked at him in shock and saw Peni was laughing at him.

"Don't worry. I wasn't planning on taking a gown," Peni said. "But I am taking my entire collection of lava-lavas."

"Lava-lavas?"

"I told you. They're the Samoan version of sarongs?"

"You told me that?" Scott paused. "Oh, yeah. Of course you did." It had been when he was all adither about the whole thing in the first place on the Fourth of July.

More words began to form across the computer screen…

> HQMF was created in 1990 as a place for queer men to gather and build community and to demonstrate that there are many ways to be a man. It is a sanctuary that allows us to express and discover our manhood, whatever we discover that to be!
>
> It was inspired by, but not confined to, the Radical Faerie movement created in 1979 by Harry Hay, but through the years has grown and changed into its own creation. HQMF welcomes all men eighteen years and older of all sexual persuasions but is mostly attended by gay and bisexual men, as well as those who identify as queer-spirited.
>
> There is no one man in charge of this celebration; all men come together in joy and love, sharing in the organizing, decision-making and running of the event. It is an experiment in community, and each member is responsible for his actions, his part of the greater whole, and the success of HQMF.

"You have to admit," Peni said. "It sounds interesting."

Scott found he didn't have to admit any such thing. *An experiment in community? Finding out what it means to be a man? A place to discover our "manhood"? And there isn't even anyone in fucking charge? Oh, yeah. That sounds like a lot of fucking fun.*

But when he saw the enthusiasm in Peni's eyes, Scott gave an inner sigh, faked a happy smile, and turned back to his computer.

> To register for Heartland Queer Men's Festival, click
> on the TURTLE icon to the right and select a registration

according to your preference. You can either print out a
form, fill it out, and send it by snail mail to the registrar with
your full or partial payment to the address at the bottom of
this screen, or register right here, online.

Pre-registration with full or partial payment received
by June 1, 2014 gives you a $25 discount. So register early!
And it helps us plan for food and supplies. Help your faerie
brothers! An additional $25 coupon for first time participants
only can be found by clicking on the BUTTERFLY icon to
the right!

After receipt of your registration form, you will
receive further information including maps, a list of
suggested things to bring, and other details about HQMF.

OR

Just show up! We want you to join our brotherhood! If
you feel the calling, then heed that call!

Do Not Miss Out On Something That May Change
Your Life Forever!

Scott looked back up at Peni, who was grinning like a child. "Let's do it,"
he cried.

AND SO they did. Peni paid the required three-day fee online. "We can pay the
rest when we get there," Peni suggested. Scott shrugged, figured in for a penny,
in for a pound, and paid for the ten days. After all, Wilford Cooper had made it
clear he wanted Scott to go on vacation. And the more he explored the site, the
more he realized he didn't really have to participate if he didn't want to.

Sloan said Camp Sanctuary was a peaceful and restful place to go.

Best of all, he was tenting with the lovely Peni Faamausili. Who knew
what might happen on a beautiful summer night?

WHICH MADE it all the worse when, one week later, Peni called in a flood of
tears. His father had died in a car accident. Peni wasn't going to Heartland Queer
Men's Festival…

CHAPTER TWELVE

… WHICH WAS why Scott found himself sitting on the front stoop of his apartment building alone on a Tuesday morning—stomach in knots, feeling hurt and betrayed—waiting for Wyatt to show up.

If it had just been the death of Peni's father, he wouldn't have felt so bad—at least, that's what he told himself. But it was more than that.

"I should be at the funeral," he'd told Peni the previous night when his friend had generously dropped off a tent and other camping necessities. That's what Peni had called them. "Necessities." A hammock? Really? He had a tent. Why would he need a hammock? And an electric cooler? Scott didn't even know if he'd wind up getting access to electricity.

"Don't be ridiculous," Peni had said, his big dark beautiful eyes awash with red.

The fact that he'd been crying made Scott's heart ache. He wanted to take Peni in his arms and kiss those tears away.

"The funeral is on Saturday, Scott. The exact middle of Festival. Wyatt says it's the biggest day."

"I know," Scott had replied. "But I *should* be there for you."

There was a strange flicker in Peni's eyes, and then it was gone.

"I thought I'd imagined it," Scott muttered to himself.

No. You pretended you didn't see it. You didn't want *to see it.*

"Scott, I'm Samoan *and* Mormon. My father was a chief—"

A chief? Even now, the thought came back. Peni's father was a chief? What did that even mean?

"—so believe me, I'll have tons of shoulders to cry on."

Scott had nodded at that, distracted and wanting to say something—surprised at the abrupt *need* to say something. "Sure. But…. Well, you know…. I thought that *I* should be there for you." His heart had begun to race and suddenly the impulsive words were out of his mouth. "I *want* to *be* there for you, Peni." He had stepped forward, reached around behind Peni—

Oh shit, and Scott felt his face heat up from embarrassment at the memory.

—placed his hand on Peni's lower back and gently pulled him forward.

Scott closed his eyes. As if were he unable to see, he could make what had happened go away. *Why, why, why did I do it?*

Scott had closed his eyes and leaned into Peni, tilted his head for the—

"Scott," cried Peni, stepping back. "What are you doing?"

Scott's eyes flew open, and he saw the shock and surprise on Peni's face.

"I-I just thought…."

"Thought what?" Peni asked.

"I thought maybe *you*…."

"I what?"

"L-like me…." Scott had blushed then, but now—the next day, sitting on a step alone—his face blazed all the more from the pure humiliation of it all.

"I *do* like you. I…. *Oh!* Scott, I do like you. I… I just don't like you *that* way."

Scott had staggered back—like a fool, like a bad actress in a 1920s silent film—thinking, *Oh shit. Oh shit! Oh fuck…. I've done it again.* "N-no. Of course you don't," he said, his voice sounding robotic in his ears. And very far away.

Done it again! Acted impulsively. When had he even begun to think of Peni that way?

How could I have not *known? Don't I fucking "get feelings" for someone at a second's notice?*

"Scott…? Did I mislead you somehow?"

"I…. When…. When you wanted me to go to Festival with you. You wanted to *tent* together. We've been talking every day, emailing, t-texting. I just thought you meant…."

And then he'd simply died.

There was a honk and Scott let out a cry, and his eyes flew open and there was Wyatt's little red Mini Cooper, with a smiling, waving Wyatt behind the wheel.

Scott stood up, grabbed the heavy tent bag, turned and, "Holy shit, Wyatt!" Scratched across the right quarter panel of Wyatt's car was the word "*FAGGOT*"!

Wyatt rolled his eyes and said, "Yeah, yeah, I know."

"When the fuck did that happen?" Scott exclaimed.

Wyatt got out of the car and shrugged. "Sometime in the last few days?"

"Sometime in the last few days?" Scott was incredulous. "You don't know *when*?"

"It was probably Friday night. Me and Peni met up at The Male Box and got cocktailed—"

Scott jaw clenched. *The Male Box? What happened to, "What if someone sees me and talks about it at church?"* And Peni went out with Wyatt. Fuck. Why not? Weren't they all one big passel of "just friends"?

"—so I didn't notice. I mean, I don't get in on the passenger side. How would I have noticed?"

"Especially if you were 'cocktailed?'" Scott asked him.

"Espesh!" Wyatt returned. Wyatt looked down at the camping equipment lying around Scott's feet. "Well, look at you, girl! You even have an electric cooler. Hope you have a few extension cords there. You'll need electricity for that bad boy."

Scott was still staring at the word "FAGGOT." What if someone saw him in Wyatt's car? Why, the ugly word would even be on *his* side.

Wyatt turned to face the car with him. "Kind of fun, isn't it? Kind of like what happened to Brian's Jeep on *Queer as Fuck*. Howard had a cow when he saw it though. And a horse. A sheep too. I think maybe a goose."

"Well, I should hope so! Of course he did. How could he not?" And why was Wyatt fine with it? He didn't seem upset at all. He loved his little ten-year-old Mini. He'd even given it a name.

"Well, what's there to do about it?"

"But...."

"But what? It's time for Festival! It'll have to wait until I get back."

"But.... But what if someone sees us?"

"Look! If it's going to bother you that much, we can go in your car." Wyatt put his hands dramatically on his hips.

My car?

In his Lexus ES 350? His cream, 2007, only ninety thousand miles on it Lexus? With a two-mile gravel road begging to nick his paint job and nuts dropping out of trees and birds that flew in and out of cars? He'd heard the story of the cardinal pecking at its image in a car's side view mirror and then flying through the car to the other side and back again ad nauseum, shitting all the way!

"No! Your Mini's fine," Scott squeaked. "Just fine."

"I thought as much. Now let's get your shit in the car and get the hell out of Dodge so we can get Scott Aberdeen to Witchy-Woo-Woo Camp so he can run around naked through the woods letting his dingle dangle!"

And with that, they hit the road.

THEY STOPPED on the way—Walmart—to pick up a few needed supplies: two industrial extension cords (the orange kind), beer, a couple of Bucket-O-Ritas, some sun block, mosquito and tick spray, and a half-dozen other sundry items. Scott even picked up the new John Grisham.

"Do you think we need one of those snakebite kits?" Scott asked, remembering a story Wyatt had told him about copperheads and a camper who went by the nickname of Snake Bite.

"Honey-boo, if you do what Mama Wyatt told you to do, you won't get bit. Big thing to remember is not to go tromping around at night without a flashlight."

"No tromping," Scott echoed.

"When the flashlight hits the nasty buggers, their eyes shine like reflectors. You can't miss them."

The image made Scott shudder. Beady eyes shining in the dark. Like something from a horror movie. Ugh. "Use flashlight," he said.

"That's why we stocked up those little LED kind for you. They last for-frigging-ever." Wyatt gave him a wicked grin. "Oh! Unless you wanted that kit for something else."

"Huh? What else are you supposed to use them for?"

"Your nipples," Wyatt replied matter-of-factly, as if Scott were a child. "Don't tell me you haven't heard that before! They can be *intense!*" Wyatt sucked in a hissing breath. "But watch it if you've got chest hair. Girl!"

They were pulling off the highway, now, and onto a smaller road, only two lanes, one in either direction. In what seemed like an instant, they were surrounded by pure country, with country houses and small farms and a long row of science-fiction-big power lines running along their left.

Cows, thought Scott. *I've already seen cows.*

The further they drove, the more country it got, with the farms getting larger and more widespread, the houses farther apart.

"You're going to be glad you have those extension cords too, believe me. It's going to be hot as hell."

"*Going* to be?" As far as Scott was concerned, it already was as hot as that mythical place. It had already been in the lower 90s this morning when he was dragging all his stuff (Peni's stuff) downstairs.

"There's a few days that might top a hundred," Wyatt informed him cheerfully. "You'll decide sarongs aren't such a bad idea after all."

"I don't think so," Scott said doubtfully.

"Mark my words. Anyway, Howard and I are loaning you our old tent fan. The pop-up has its own."

"Well, thanks, Wyatt. But do you think I'll even get electricity? Didn't you say you have to get there early to get an outlet and guys have been arriving since Saturday? They might all be taken."

"Oh! We already got you one. We staked out a spot for you."

"Huh?" Already staked out a spot for him? Would it be so close that he couldn't sleep for Wyatt's "salon" and him and Howard getting it on late at night? Ugh….

"We laid a tarp down for you. Close to us but not *too* close. We figured you might be a little nervous totally on your own. So, close enough to have some neighbors, you know, but you can sleep at night if we get too noisy. Plus *I* won't have to listen to your moans and groans if *you* get lucky. Love you, Scott, but that's something I just can't hear, you know?"

Scott laughed. Wyatt didn't want to hear *him!* And like he had a chance of getting "lucky," anyway. Or that he even wanted to. "I think I've decided on celibacy." He thought of Peni, how he'd been imagining them cuddled together at night. And dammit. He was going to be sleeping *in* Peni's tent, only without him.

Wyatt pulled right around a steep turn, and now there were just rolling fields on either side. Was that beans? Soy beans?

Scott looked back at Wyatt, and it suddenly hit him what was different. "You shaved!"

"You're just noticing, Sherlock?"

"I thought the eleven o'clock shadow was your new thing."

"It is." Wyatt reached up and touched his face, flinched slightly as if startled somehow that his facial hair was gone. "But my beard grows so darned fast, I'm shaggy in a week."

Scott, who could skip shaving for weeks and barely have stubble on his chin, could only trust that Wyatt was telling the truth.

"So I figured if I shaved this morning, by the weekend I'll be looking *fabulous*. I just *hate* shaving at Festival!"

"I bet you still douche," Scott said.

Wyatt's eyes went wide. "Well of course, *monsieur*! We *must* be civilized. No one wants to dive in a nice, pretty butt and get a Hershey squirt!"

"Wyatt!" Scott both shuddered and laughed. "That's just gross!"

Wyatt shrugged. "Sometimes the truth is."

There was a pause.

"My number one piece of advice for Festival is *not* to make up your mind about *anything*," Wyatt said. "HQMF is *never* what you think it will be, even if you've been going for *years*. Every Festival is different. Let it *be* whatever it's going to be. I learned that a long time ago. And gods, Scott. No sex? That would be like going to Amsterdam and deciding you *won't* get high before you get there. All that marvelous stuff and you're not even going to think about trying some? Come on!"

"You trying to tell me getting laid is a certainty?"

They curved to the left and went through some trees before the country opened back up to more farmhouses.

"Nope. I'm just saying that you don't go to Amsterdam without leaving yourself open to possibilities. Same here. Let Festival weave its magic. You never know what's going to happen."

Magic. Yeah. *Rrriiiiiiiiight*.

Two horses were running across a field. Then they were passing a big gate with an arching cast-iron lettering that said, "Michael Kirk Horse Farm."

Remote. This place is so remote. How far from civilization are we? And where the hell *was* the nearest hospital if he *did* get bit by a snake?

"See all the weed?" Wyatt asked.

Scott shrugged. "I see tons of weeds." The roadside was full of vegetation on both sides, some of it cultivated and growing in rows, some just a mass of greenery.

"Not *weeds*, Scott. *Weed!* As in cannabis, reefer, Mary Jane, mary-jah-wanna."

"Say what?" Scott craned his neck around wildly, but he couldn't make out one kind of brush or shrubbery from any other it flew past them so quickly.

"Ditch weed, dumbass. I am sure many a roach has been flicked into the night along here. And if the partaker didn't clean his pot properly before rolling a J, then there is bound to be the occasional seed. I imagine getting high is probably the only thing that keeps a teenager from going insane in these parts."

"I thought you liked being in the middle of frigging nowhere."

"With a hundred other fags, sure. Not alone. Can you imagine growing up gay out here? Shit! My high school had a gay/straight alliance. I'm betting the high schools around here are caught in circa 1955."

"And the pot is just growing alongside the road?" Scott asked, completely surprised. "You're shitting me. How can you tell as fast as we're driving?"

Wyatt slowed the car until they were barely moving along at a crawl. He stopped by one particularly large bush growing out over a barbed-wire fence on Scott's side.

"Now look."

Scott squinted. "I can't tell."

"Then you wasted your money on those frigging Versaces, my friend. Look again."

Scott stuck his head out of the car window and then... the seven-fingered, palm-like, serrated leaves took form before his eyes. "Well shit. That *is* marijuana. Is it any good?"

"It's not good for wiping your ass," said Wyatt. "That's why it's called ditch weed." He started the car rolling again. A cow stared at them curiously with its big bovine eyes, chewing its cud.

"I'll be damned," said Scott.

"Don't worry. There'll be more spliff than you can shake your dick at once we get there."

Scott made a puffing noise. "You *know* I hardly ever get high. I *do* work for lawyers."

Wyatt laughed. "Seems to me that would be the reason *to* smoke. You have friends in high places who could get you off." He laughed again. "High places! Get it?"

"I don't know...." Scott mumbled.

"There you go again. Making up your mind before you get to Amsterdam."

Scott shrugged.

"Well then, just watch it if someone offers you a brownie. Make sure it's not a magic brownie."

"Magic? As in witchy-woo-woo?"

"You know exactly what I mean. The gan-*jah*!"

Scott suddenly remembered being with Peni when Peter Wagner approached them on the Fourth of July. He'd asked for ganja too, hadn't he? Was it getting to be *that* common these days?

"Oh! And speaking of waving your dick, I want to assure you—" They'd been slowing down and now pulled off to the right onto a gravel road. The infamous gravel road that surely would have put a ding in the perfect cream surface of Scott's baby Lexus. "—that there really isn't that much dick to see except at the beach. I was just giving you a hard time. And baby? We are on the last leg. We'll be there in a minute! Ya-hoo!"

Scott turned and looked back to see a huge plume of white dust billowing behind them like a pale version of the smoke left by the Wicked Witch of the West's broom in *The Wizard of Oz*. His head fell back on the headrest. Shit. This was it. The first day. What was he letting himself in for? Gleaming snake eyes in the dark? Magic brownies? Sarongs? Waving dicks?

His thoughts were interrupted as a motorcycle pulled around them—not that it had to go that fast, Wyatt was only going about 35, but still....

"Hey," Wyatt cried. "That was the Jockster."

"The who?"

"The Jockster. 'Cause he is *way* into jockstraps, and that's his choice of uniform for Festival. I can't even imagine how many jocks that man owns."

Jockstraps? Scott thought, sitting up straight. He couldn't see anything of course. The guy on the bike—"The Jockster"—had disappeared up ahead in his own cloud of dust. Scott willed himself to relax and glanced over to see if Wyatt had caught his reaction.

"He's one of the only naked guys you'll see, okay? And he covers his dick most of the time. But believe me, his *butt* is a thing of beauty. You won't mind seeing it."

"Whatever," Scott said, willing himself to sound disinterested. He settled back, only to realize Wyatt was slowing down even more.

"Here we go," Wyatt said and turned off the gravel road and into a tunnel of quiet green.

CHAPTER THIRTEEN

DESPITE HIMSELF, Scott couldn't help but let out a little gasp when the car came out of the trees. Ahead of them was a lovely rolling hilly area covered in green grass, the road climbing as it went. To his right, Scott saw more sunflowers than he'd seen in as long as he could remember. Maybe ever. They were quite simply stunning in their beauty and covered a long earthen wall of some kind. There were butterflies everywhere—small white ones as well as huge gold-and-black-striped tiger swallowtails, a favorite from his youth.

Wyatt pulled off the road to their left into a small grassy field, where a carport tent had been set up and two men sat behind a plastic dining table. A third was standing beside a motorcycle, pulling off his helmet. *Cute*, thought Scott. He looked again at the man, who was running his hand through a short Mohawk-like haircut. Correction. The guy was very cute. And wasn't really a Mohawk. Just longer on top—dark blond wavy—and almost skintight short on the sides. Scott normally wouldn't have liked the hairstyle, but it fit the guy in some way he couldn't put his finger on.

Then before his eyes, Wyatt and the three men seemed to go into a fit of ecstasy. They were shouting each other's names and hugging while Scott stood by in surprise. One of the men who had been sitting behind the table was wearing simply the largest hat Scott had ever seen—bright pink, with a brim as wide as a Hula Hoop.

But that wasn't what startled him. It was what happened when the man with the pink hat jumped to his feet and came running around the table.

He was nude.

Completely nude.

Naked as a jaybird. Nude as the day as he was born. Except for the hat. And also for the fact, Scott thought, that he was obviously a whole… lot… bigger. Pink Hat had quite simply the biggest dick Scott had ever seen in his life. It looked as thick as Scott's wrist, and it wasn't even hard!

"Rat Bastard!" Wyatt squealed. "When did you get here?"

"Late last night, girlfriend," said Big Dick and threw his arms around Wyatt, who was cheerfully hugging him back.

Now that Scott couldn't see Pink Hat's simply ginormous penis he was able—although with a slack jaw—to get a better look at the man. He had reddish hair, was very tall and very slim (he couldn't have weighed all that much more than Scott, and he was at least a head taller), with about a week's worth of beard and… well, a sweet ass. No doubt. A very sweet ass. For some reason Scott couldn't help but wonder if the guy was a top or a bottom, what with his enormous kielbasa and tight, round little ass. It would be a crying shame if he was just one or the other.

The second man behind the table, a handsome older man who looked to be in his middle to late fifties, his hair and beard going gray, was standing up now with a huge smile. He too had a hat, which was a little crazy—wide brimmed with small pompoms around its edge—but at least he wasn't naked. He was, however, wearing what looked like a woman's black and silver negligee. He hugged the guy from the motorcycle and, sure enough, was calling him Jockster. Scott couldn't help but wonder what he'd look like in his "uniform."

When the older gentleman was finished hugging motorcycle guy, he turned to Wyatt, who had just stepped back from Big Dick. "And just who is your friend, Little Bear?" he asked in a thick, and possibly exaggerated, Southern accent.

Scott found himself all but staring at Big Dick's big dick. He couldn't help it. It was almost freakishly large, although perfectly proportioned. It was actually quite lovely.

"Scott!"

He jerked his eyes away from the penis and looked over to Wyatt. "Sorry." He glanced over at the penis's owner and saw the man was looking at him, arms crossed over what turned out to be a well-built chest, a smirk on his face. Scott felt his face heat up and turned back to Wyatt.

"Scott, this is Lula Belle," Wyatt said with a wave to the man who was clothed (even if it was in woman's clothing).

"Howdy," said Lula Belle.

Lula Belle? Really? Lula Belle? Somehow Scott figured that wasn't the man's Christian name. "Ah, hello… Lu… Lu."

"And the gentleman with the substantial… hat… goes by the nom de plume 'Rat Bastard.'"

"R-Rat Bastard?"

Rat Bastard grinned and nodded.

"And this," Wyatt said, pointing to motorcycle guy, "is The Jockster."

Scott gulped as The Jockster stepped toward him and asked him if he hugged.

"Ah…. Sure," he said and then, despite his nervousness, felt a little thrill as the man hugged him. He smelled of dust and the road, and he felt good. Hard and compact and slim under that leather motorcycle jacket.

"Everyone? This is my friend, Scott."

Jockster stepped back. "Just Scott?"

Scott shrugged, then nodded. "Yeah. I don't understand this weird name thing."

"Honey, it's just a part of it," said Lula. "Faerie names."

"Faerie name?" Scott sighed. He glanced at the men, with gigantic pink hats and negligees and leather jackets—and then at his friend. Wyatt. *Little Bear? Fuck. What do I do?*

All four men were looking at him expectantly. *Hell. When in Rome?* "So I have to do that? Pick a… faerie name?"

"Nothing you have to do," said Jockster. "It's not for everybody. Lots of people go by their own names."

And only a few men go around naked, thought Scott, letting his eyes dart once more toward that prodigious phallus.

"Faerie names kind of find you," Lula Belle said.

"Find me?" Scott asked. *Riiiight.*

Lula smiled and went back round to the other side of the table. "You preregistered?" He opened a notebook.

"Yes," Scott said.

"Last name?"

"Aberdeen."

"Yup! Right here. I have all the newbies separate. Or our off-site registrar does, actually. He's fabulous. Got yours here too, Little Bear. And you, Jockster."

Lula Belle opened the notebook and took out forms and handed them over. "There are a couple of highlighted places for you to sign. I guess I don't need your car information since you're here with Wyatt. Little Bear? Don't forget to fill in car and make and all that shit…."

So Scott sat down and signed here and there, and then Lula Belle handed him a little booklet. "That has just about everything you could possibly need to know. You've seen most of it if you checked out the web site when you registered, but it's nice to have a copy to look at once you get here. Make sure you sign up for community service. Little Bear can show you all that.

Scott nodded. On the cover of his booklet, it said, "Welcome to Heartland Queer Men's Festival."

"I hope you have a wonderful time," Lula Belle said. He came back around the table and offered a hug.

Scott shrugged. He'd never been hugged by a man in women's nightwear. *When in Rome.* Scott gave the man a perfunctory hug and, when he turned, found Bastard standing there, eyebrows raised, arms held out slightly before him, a question on his face.

Hell. He shrugged again. *Rome.* And hugged the man.

"I'll see you guys at the top," Jockster said. "I *gotta* get out of these fucking clothes! I am suffocating. Thank the gods I'm here!" He let up a loud whoop and climbed onto his bike. Then he looked at Scott and said, "If you need a little tour, let me know." He grinned and winked and shot off up the hill in a little shower of gravel.

Scott's heart skipped in his chest.

"Damn, girl," Wyatt said. "He's never offered *me* a tour."

IT WAS when Scott was climbing in the car that he finally saw the tree. He wasn't sure how he'd missed it. It was huge—probably a good eighty feet tall and unbelievably big in circumference. "Shit," he said. "Wow." It stood in the clearing beyond the tent setup. "Wow."

"We call him Iggy," Wyatt said, and Scott couldn't help but hear the reverence in his tone.

"Iggy?"

"Well, Yggdrasil." Wyatt pronounced it *Ig-drah-sill*. "The world tree from Norse mythology."

"Not into mythology," Scott said. Except to get the lay of the land, know the enemy. Discover just one more laughable story someone had made up to explain why everything existed. One more rationalization to help them deal with the day death came a-knocking. Religion was all about fear.

He, for one, was not going to live in denial.

"Ragnarök. Not one of my favorites," Wyatt said. "The Universe comes to a big, bad, horrible ending. Everyone dies, even the good guys."

Scott made a farting noise.

"Yeah, exactly."

"But that is still a big fucking tree," Scott admitted.

"You don't know the half of it."

"What's that supposed to mean?" Scott asked.

Wyatt gave a half shrug. "Don't worry about it. Come on, let's set up your camp."

Ah, yes. Camp.

They wound around a big hill, and as they went, Scott saw the long earthen wall was actually a man-made dam and—wow—there was the infamous lake he'd heard so much about. He had to admit it was lovely. He could even make out a raft-like float of some kind and, yes, there were two men—naked—diving off of it. Along the length of the dam, which had a narrow road across its surface, were several dozen poles upon which strips of brightly colored cloth had been attached. Ah. *Six* colors. Alternating. A rainbow flag of sorts. He was never really into the rainbow flag, wasn't one to wear gay pride shirts or have rainbow bumper stickers. But it was pretty.

The road became quite steep and then leveled off at an area with several buildings. "That's the dining hall, shower house, stuff like that. I'll show you that later," Wyatt explained.

They turned left up another steep incline, but nothing like the first one. This took them past a number of cabins, the second of which was surrounded by dozens upon dozens of beautiful swatches of fabric hanging on a clothesline. And there, a hairy guy hanging up more. He was wearing one himself. He waved, and Scott waved back automatically.

"That's one of the guys who sells sarongs. They're cheap too. Like maybe twelve bucks. Some are more than that. I have expensive tastes and always seem to pick *the* one that's twenty bucks. But still cheap."

"Not interested," Scott said. "Give it up." He looked out the window as they passed several more of the little cabins set a bit farther back from the road. "Those look nice," Scott said. "Why don't we use one of those?"

"You can if you want. There's about six beds on each side. You'll have to share with people you don't know. I just figured, knowing you like I do, you'd want the privacy of a tent. We really did get you a good spot, Scott."

"Well, you're right about the privacy." He thought about sharing a room with five strangers, making do with who knew how little area he could claim for his own, not knowing if someone would be going through his shit, not even being able to jerk off. Well. From what he'd heard about "pagans," masturbating might not be a problem. But the idea of a group jerk-off didn't appeal to him.

He looked ahead of them. "This road is narrow," he said. "What the hell do you do if you meet someone coming down?

"It always works out somehow," said Wyatt. "See?" He pointed out the windshield. "There? And there? Spots where the road widens. It works out." They moved up, around a turn, and then they leveled out again. Wyatt took the car past a little grove, where Scott saw several people setting up shelters, including a pop-up camper. "They call this area Nemeton."

"It that your camper?" Scott asked.

"No, we're further on. People camp in different places. This is a little more private. We like to set up in the main area. Plus, electricity. There is only so far that *this* Little Bear is able to rough it. You'll see. Any second now…."

And then they came out into the bright sunshine and onto what looked like a plateau. Off to the left was a large pavilion, and as they passed it, Scott saw it included a big stage.

"That's where we have the Know Talent Show. With a *K*. Get it? *Know* talent. Not *no* talent?"

Scott thought about it a second. "Yeah. Okay. I get it." Was he supposed to be excited?

Then he saw it. The plateau went a lot further than he first thought. The pavilion had made it look like he'd seen it all. But no. Beyond the stage area, a large grassy plot spread out ahead of them, a big oval, surrounded by trees. And along that tree line were tents. Not a lot. But then this was only the first day. And it wasn't even noon yet. Men were walking around, some setting up tents, and thank you! Not one of them naked.... *Ooopps.* "Said that too fast," he muttered under his breath.

One old man, in his sixties or seventies, wearing nothing but a scarf on top of his head like a turban, was strolling along as casually as if he were going to a grocery store. The fabric, in a leopard-like pattern, flowed on the breeze behind him.

"That's Bobcat. And *he* is a nudist."

"And Rat Bastard isn't?"

"Sssshhhh.... How was *I* supposed to know he'd be doing registration? He *never* does registration. Oh! Change subject. Look! There it is. The Rolling Brothel."

Wyatt pulled the car off the gravel road and across the football-field-like area, heading to the far side, and a big pop-up camper. As they approached it, Scott could see there was a big sun shelter set up as well, with a picnic table under it, along with several chairs and a lounger. There was also a pole with a tapestry hanging from it with two big bear paws painted on its surface. Wyatt parked and ran over to hug Howard, who was coming out of the camper wearing nothing but a bright red tie-dyed sarong around his waist. On the huge man, it looked tiny, and Scott was seeing a lot more of Howard than he really wanted to.

Get used to it, Scott told himself. He got out of the car and headed for the camper and noticed the sun shelter had screen netting cinched to the poles that could be zipped up at night. That would be nice, he thought. Protection from mosquitoes.

Wyatt was still kissing Howard, and Scott tried not to get grossed out. Try as he might, though, it was pretty difficult. He just didn't like the man, and watching them suck face was enough to bring an image of them rolling around naked to his mind. It was not a pretty picture.

But then, at least Wyatt has someone who loves him, Scott thought. *Better than me. I can't keep someone longer than a weekend.*

"Hey, Scottie," Howard said, apparently finally done kissing Wyatt. "I was kind of expecting you last night."

"We didn't want to try and set up after dark," Wyatt explained. "And he didn't have a tent yet."

"I take it you've got it now?" Howard asked.

"Yes," Scott said. "In the car."

"Well, let's get to it. Gonna be hot as hell today, and we don't want to be setting up in the heat."

Scott nodded and went back to the car, and the three of them unloaded his things. He couldn't help but feel a little guilty. Here he'd thought those bad things about Wyatt's lover, yet he was helping set up Scott's camp.

"Good. You got extension cords," Howard said.

Boy! What is it with extension cords?

There was a surprising moment when Wyatt stripped out of his clothes in front of him and put on a sarong. Scott had seen Wyatt naked more than a few times at the gym, but he wasn't expecting him to get naked right out in the open. He *did* have a camper, after all.

On the other hand, he couldn't help but be a little envious of Wyatt's lack of self-consciousness. There he was, a good forty pounds overweight, and he didn't mind people seeing him naked. Scott knew there was no way he could do such a thing. He didn't want anyone to see him without his shirt on the beach, and he'd fuck a dog before he'd go skinny-dipping and let anyone see his little pathetic dick.

Yeah. He was jealous. To have such freedom.

In the end the tent went up fast, and Scott did like the place Wyatt had picked out for him. It was the equivalent of about four or five camp spaces north of "The Rolling Brothel" and set back under several big branches heavy with leaves. If it did rain, between the tarp they used under the tent and the trees, the chances Scott would wake up in a wet shelter were pretty low. If worse came to worst, there was the tarp Peni had loaned him. He could always hang it up over the tent.

And why the fuck was he worried about rain? There wasn't a drop predicted for the next ten days.

The extension cords were going to come in handy. They let him plug in both the cooler and the tent fan—and that fan was going to make a big difference. He nixed the idea of adding the strings of lights Wyatt gave him to the trees, but was forced to put them inside his tent. Wyatt refused to take them back. They were fun, though. Too gay, but fun. One was a string of colorful flip-flops and the other he hadn't really looked at yet. They were still in the box. They didn't even look like they'd been opened.

Scott was pleasantly surprised at the air mattress. He figured it would be like the shitty ones he'd grown up with, but Peni's? It was as thick as two standard mattresses and after making it up, it turned out to be shockingly comfortable. Wyatt's electric pump got it blown up in minutes. No trying to do it by mouth or some hand pump either. It was great. Sleeping wouldn't be as uncomfortable as he'd worried it would be. In some ways, things were looking up. Maybe this could be fun after all.

Scott had to admit one thing. Camp Sanctuary was gorgeous.

He did like to swim. Just because he wasn't going to do it nude didn't mean he couldn't swim.

And who knew? Once the sun set, maybe he could do it. There was going to be a new moon. That meant it would be dark.

Did he dare?

And there was going to be cocktails. What had Wyatt said about "salons"? Lots of cocktail parties? There was nothing wrong with cocktails!

Somewhere toward the end of the camp set up, Wyatt wandered off and made lunch. "First meal is tonight, so we need to eat something. Aren't you glad I got the chicken at Walmart?" Wyatt asked.

Bobcat showed up and shared some potato salad with them. "Hey, in this heat I don't trust it long in my cooler," he said. He was a nice guy. Naked, yes. But nice. Sweet, in fact. And once again, totally not at all self-conscious. He had to be sixty if he was a day. It was no porn-actor body he had. It sagged here and there, his penis was nothing to brag about, and he wore thick, very large glasses. But after a bit, Scott almost stopped thinking about the fact the guy was naked.

Scott offered one of his bags of chips, they had a few beers, and it was good.

It surprised Scott just how good it really was.

CHAPTER FOURTEEN

AROUND FIVE that evening everyone gathered for "First Circle," something that Wyatt insisted Scott attend. He'd conjured up all kinds of images from that movie *The Craft*—with someone calling the four directions and summoning the "Lord and Lady" with much knife waving (would he have to cut himself? There was no fucking way he was cutting himself) and chalice sharing. It turned out, though, that Circle wasn't anything witchy-woo-woo at all, but simply what its title implied. The attendees gathered together and sat around in a circle of chairs out under a large oak tree by the buildings on the camp's second level.

Scott looked around him, his nerves making his stomach twist in knots. To his vast relief, there were very few dresses and only a small percentage of the men were, in fact, nude. Rat Bastard, minus his prodigious hat if not his prodigious penis. Bobcat. And a beautiful blond with a mane of dreadlocks (there was a black sheltie puppy curled up asleep beneath his chair) and a man who seemed to be his partner—bald but very handsome and looking quite familiar. He had a dog as well, this one a red and brown furball, which he held in his arms like a baby.

To be fair, Scott found he didn't mind over much that the last two men were naked at all, as he considered using your imagination to picture someone nude overrated. He lived in the "Show-Me State" after all. He did find it hard not to stare at their crotches, though. After all, seeing naked men sitting around as casually as if they were gathered for a bingo night wasn't anything he was used to, and they did have *very* nice dicks. Hell. Rat Bastard did as well. It wasn't just its remarkable size. And to tell the truth, Scott could only hope he looked as good as Bobcat when he was that age.

So that was, what? Four naked men? Wyatt had told him while they were on their way to the evening event that the registrar had told him there were about thirty-five attendees who had arrived so far. That meant about ten percent were wearing nothing but their birthday suits. There were also not thirty-five men sitting around with him. A quick head count said twenty-one. Some of those were preparing dinner. That eliminated a few.

"And some just don't go to Circle," Wyatt explained. "You aren't *required* to go."

"Then why are you making *me* go?"

"I'm not *making* you do anything. But you'll meet people this way. See what Circle's about. Then you can make up your mind if you want to come back. I will tell you that it's a good idea. That way you know what's going on, you can ask questions, let people know anything you might need. Lots of stuff. Keeps you informed. People who miss out on stuff have no one to fucking blame but themselves if they don't show up. But the real blessing is that a lot of magical things happen in Circle."

Magical. Riiiiiight.

But it was such talk that had Scott expecting much pomp and witchy circumstance. Instead, it was a lot more laidback than that.

"Hey, everybody," Wyatt said, raising his voice. "Attention!"

The talking settled down except for a few men who made hissing noises.

How rude, Scott thought, looking over at his friend, who seemed oblivious to the insult.

"I'm Little Bear," said Wyatt.

Little Bear. Going to have *to get used to that*, Scott realized, and wasn't sure if he could.

"I'm going to be your facilitator this evening. Welcome to the first Circle of Festival!"

More hissing.

Really? Jeeze!

"Tell us a joke," someone shouted.

Oh no! You're asking *for one of Wyatt's jokes?*

Wyatt's face lit up, and his eyes sparkled with joy. "Okay! What do you call a dirty fairy?"

Chatter followed, but no one knew the answer.

"Stinkerbell," Wyatt (Little Bear) cried, and burst into laughter.

Luckily he wasn't the only one.

God, they're encouraging him! To be fair, it wasn't a bad joke, especially considering the company.

Wyatt was on cloud nine and looking like he would burst. "Okay! Okay! Now why don't we go around and everyone introduce yourself, say where you're from, and then tell us… tell us your favorite animal! I was going to ask that you tell us what you're hoping to get from Festival this year, but I thought about it all frippin' day and I couldn't think of an answer, so I could hardly ask you to do the same."

There was a ripple of laughter and a few hisses as well.

What's with the fucking hissing? Scott wondered.

"So I'll start," Wyatt said happily. "I'm Little Bear and I'm from Terra's Gate, Missouri and my favorite animal is a big ol' bear." He grinned adoringly at Howard and leaned over and kissed his shoulder and said, "Silly old bear."

More laughter. More hisses.

The hissing was starting to piss Scott off.

"Okay. We'll go widdershins."

Scott had no clue what "widdershins" meant, but when Howard spoke up next, he could only imagine it was faerie speak for counterclockwise.

"I'm Big Sir—"

Big Sir? Or was that Big Sur? One thing Scott did know and that was that he was going to perform cunnilingus before he called Wyatt's lover "sir."

"—and I'm from Terra's Gate, Missouri—"

(Howard pronounced it Missour-ah, much to Scott's annoyance. Didn't he know the fucking state was named after the Missour-E Native American tribe? There wasn't, nor had there *ever* been, a Missour-ah tribe!)

"—and my favorite animal is a *nasty pig*!" Then he snorted to make sure no one had missed the point. This prompted many hoots and a few hollers. It just made Scott want to vomit.

Next came Lula Belle, who was wearing biker shorts with silver piping and silver cowboy boots to match. He told them all in a fake Southern drawl that he was originally from Arkansas and that gerbils were his favorite animal. "Oh, no! That's someone else, isn't it? Make mine puppies, then."

A couple was next who went by the names Dolce and Gabbana. Dolce was tall and had a bouffant of blond hair with even lighter silvery highlights, and none of it looked quite real. Very eighties-Flock-of-Seagulls. Gabbana was shorter, darker, with deep black hair just beginning to gray at the temples. They fared from Rockford and likened themselves to a sea anemone and a clown fish—very different, but so lovingly together. Scott kept mum—as did everyone else—and didn't say anything about how he wasn't sure whether the anemone was an animal or a plant. There were too many "Aaawwwwwws" going on. Why spoil their schmaltzy moment?

Will I ever find a Dolce to my Gabbana? What Scott would give for a man to have a schmaltzy moment with?

It was Bobcat's turn after that and his animal, no surprise to Scott, was a bobcat. To Scott's relief, a Tony and then a George were next. He wasn't the only one without a "faerie" name! It was a load off his mind for sure, especially when he thought the whole name thing was stupid in the first place. But whether such nicknames were dumb or not, Scott didn't want to be the only one who went by his real one.

And then it was time for dreadlock-guy to talk, and Scott found himself leaning in to make sure he heard what the pretty man had to say.

"Hey, everybody. It's good to be back. I didn't think Festival would ever get here this year."

A lot of people agreed.

"I'm Hound Dog. Most people call me H.D. And I'm from everywhere. But, well, finally…. Well, the impossible happened. I've settled down in Kansas City." He turned and looked adoringly at the sexy bald man next to him while everyone in the circle let out calls of surprise and congratulations.

"I knew you could do it!" shouted Dolce.

"So now I'm from Kansas City.... Wow!" He smiled happily. "I'm *from* somewhere!"

More congratulations followed.

"And... and *anyone* who knows *me* knows my answer to the animal question. I love dogs. In fact, I like them more than most of the people in the world."

There were nods of assent and at least one person said he felt the same.

"Except you all, of course," he added as if it were an afterthought. "Oh! And this...." Hound Dog leaned down and reached under his chair to scratch under the chin of his sheltie, who looked up at his master's touch. "This is Rammstein." As soon as he sat back up, the little sheltie put his head back down between his paws and seemed to instantly go back to sleep. "Rammstein has had a very exciting day, and he is worn *out*."

"Tell me about it," someone said and once more there was laughter. There was a lot of laughter around here, Scott saw.

Now it was his companion's turn. "Hello... ah, everyone." He smiled and Scott immediately felt envious of the two. They must have it made, two such beautiful men. Probably not a problem in the world. They even had puppies! "I'm Bean—as in *coffee* bean. I'm from Kansas City, and I have to say—" He reached out and placed his hand on the blond's knee and gave it a squeeze. "—that my favorite animal is Hound Dog."

There was much hissing.

"This is Sarah Jane," Bean continued and turned the small dog in his arms around so she was facing the men. "She's bossy but sweet, and her yip is far worse than her bite."

Sarah Jane barked as if to confirm this information.

"She's not the only one!" Hound Dog poked Bean in the ribs.

Bean laughed and put his shaggy little dog on the ground, and she instantly spun around and started barking.

Suddenly a big blond man threw himself down in the grass and ran toward Sarah Jane on his hands and knees. "Arf! Arf!" he cried, and she twirled around, tail lashing like a metronome, and returned the man arf for arf. Big Guy shook his butt and barked out (literally), "Hey, Sarah Jane! I'm Sundog! Arf! Arf!"

Dogs were quite popular in this group it seemed.

Sarah Jane dashed forward and, seemingly without a twinge of fear, Sun Dog snatched her up and rolled in the grass, where she began to lick his face as if it were covered in honey. Hilarity ensued. "I'm from Madison, Wisconsin," he said, only half attempting to keep her from kissing him. "And *my* favorite animal is... well, *duh!*"

Scott found himself laughing with the others. He couldn't help himself. Sundog was fun, and when he shook that big round ass of his, the sarong he was wearing parted to reveal a set of really big balls. It was provocative, that's all there was to it.

Just as abruptly as Sundog had thrown himself into the ring, he jumped back to his feet, scooped up Sarah Jane—who seemed to be some sort of dachshund mix—and gave her back to Bean. "Sorry, I couldn't help myself. It's not my fault! I'm a big old *daaawg!*"

Bean looked up at him with a wide-eyed expression. "Ah…. That's okay. I…." He grinned. "I… I'm sorry guys. Not sure about any of this. It's my first festival. I'll jump in, don't worry—"

Scott knew just how the man felt!

"—so forgive me if I mess something up or do anything wrong."

Everyone assured him that he was fine, they'd take care of him, and that they loved virgins. "Oh! And coffee," Bean added. "I've brought coffee. I heard you guys have good coffee, but I brought some to share, and I know you'll love it, and if you can get your ass up early, I promise you a treat you will not forget!"

Scott's eyes went wide. *That's* how he knew Bean. It was the guy who owned the coffee shop The Shepherd's Bean. Holy shit! Scott didn't recognize the man without his clothes, but he would be lying if he said he'd never wondered what the man looked like naked. And now he was seeing him in the altogether and—well—*hubba-hubba!*

"I've got so many questions," Bean was saying. "Like what's with all the hissing?"

Scott's eyebrows shot up. *Yes! Thank you!*

"Anyone want to answer that?" Wyatt asked and looked out over the group.

"I will," said an older man whose age defied guessing on Scott's part. "It's more than one thing really." There was something about the man. He'd been so quiet, almost invisible, until he spoke up. But now? He seemed to almost radiate… something. Something as hard to nail down as his age. The man had to be in his fifties anyway, from the gray in his thick goatee and sideburns and the many lines around his eyes. But, oh, those eyes! So blue and bright and alive. They flashed like lightning.

"I first heard hissing used as approval in a number of communities I was connected to sometime in the late seventies, early eighties. At that time it was named the 'Blessing of the Snake Goddess.' She holds Queers and other Edge Walkers as sacred. Hissing brings her blessing to the Circle."

Snake Goddess? What the hell was the man saying, Scott wondered. *Edge Walkers? Sacred?* What the hell?

"I always thought," Sundog said, "that it's just less disruptive than clapping. Especially when we have one of our powerful vibes going in Circle."

"That too," said the older man.

"And you can still hear when someone throws out a witty tail ender," Sundog added.

This prompted more laughter, which seemed to be the order of the day.

It was food for thought. Scott didn't believe in snake goddesses any more than he believed in the Easter Bunny. But he'd think about it. He could see how the low hissing sound was quieter than clapping.

"Thank you, Donald," Wyatt said.

The man named Donald smiled radiantly.

"Who's next?"

"I'm Lorax," said a short stout bald man with an enormous reddish walrus mustache.

What's with all the bald men?

Of course, none of them were near as sexy as Bean….

"I'm from San Francisco, and my favorite animal is a duck-billed platypus. Did you know there are those who believe that they come from another planet?" He nodded. "You know, Chariots of the Gods and all that? Maybe some ancient astronaut accidentally left his Planet X version of a puppy on Earth a million years ago or so. It coulda happened!"

More laughter! Jeeze. There was a lot of that. Somehow Scott had imagined a more… religious mood for this thing. But except for the ludicrous notion that Earth had been visited by aliens long ago and left their dog at Rest Stop Earth, there hadn't been much mention of God. Except for the snakes, of course. *Don't forget to watch out for snakes!* He shuddered and saw gleaming eyes in the dark once more.

"I'm Knottie Scottie," replied the man to the right of Lorax. He was a nice-looking man. A little hairy for Scott's taste, he liked his men smooth, but he couldn't deny that "Knottie" was handsome. "I'm originally from Lawrence, Kansas—transplanted to Washington, D.C. My favorite animal would be my housecat, Dusty."

Pretty eyes, thought Scott. Very pretty in that tanned face. And hey! He had a great name.

Knottie was wearing a yellow sarong and a black leather bar vest with yellow piping. *Wonder what made him wear that color?* Scott suspected it wasn't Satan but a different reason altogether.

"I did have two cats." Knottie paused. "There was… Ashley. But she's gone now."

"Passed into the Summer Lands," Donald said, his voice calm and compassionate.

There were more sighs of sympathy all around the Circle, and the two men to either side of Knottie rested their hands on his back and knee.

"She died the day before Halloween. I was all prepared to have a great one, too—you all know how much I love Halloween. I had a great costume too!"

Murmurs of yes. They knew.

"But after that, I couldn't go out." His voice caught, and his two neighbors hugged him tight. Across the room a handsome older man with a Superman shirt was openly crying.

To his surprise, Scott found his own heart aching. Vivid memories of his own cat came back. Garfield's thick orange fur. The way he'd wake Scott in the mornings by bumping noses with him, purring loudly so that the first thing he saw were those huge green eyes, and...

"He's a cat," the voice of Scott's father echoed in his head. "If he dies we'll get another one. People give them away all the time."

An unexpected sob caught in Scott's throat.

Jeeze! Where had that come from? What was this about? What was going on? Scott looked around the group, saw the sympathy on their faces. Saw one man with tears running down his face.

Scott shook his head. Pulled back his tears.

What's going on?

The man next to Knottie, another older gentleman, pulled away long enough to say his name was Focus and he was from Kansas City and he liked the octopus. "Think of how many of you I could hug if I had eight arms...."

"And how many of us he could grope," declared Howard. "And claim someone else did it!"

And then.... Well, damn. *Then* it was Scott's turn. Suddenly his stomach clenched and sweat actually broke out across his forehead, and although his mouth opened, not a word came out. *Say something. Anything! Don't sit here looking like a dumb fuck.*

"Did you want to pass?" Wyatt asked him.

Then a hand fell gently on the middle of his back. Scott turned his head and found himself looking right into the most beautiful eyes he had ever seen. His heart gave a mighty lurch, and the world, his chair, the men, the heat of the day—gone! It was just like that scene on the beach in the movie *Jaws* when the camera did that weird trick, zoomed in on Roy Scheider's face.

Except this was The Jockster, and how Scott hadn't noticed the man had sat down next to him he didn't know. Fuck! The man... the man was beautiful! How hadn't he noticed *that* when they'd met at registration? That long, strong jaw, stubbled with a few days growth of beard, those unbearably high cheekbones, that noble nose, sweet full lips (what would it be like to kiss those lips?), and his dark blond hair—long and wavy on top, shaved almost skin close on the sides, all of it shining in the last of the evening sunlight and looking so soft it was all Scott could do not to reach out and touch it.

Those lips moved. "It's okay. Go ahead. We're all brothers here. Let us hear you."

The world started to slowly form around Scott again, and his heart began to beat once more—was racing, it seemed—and he glanced around the circle, seeing nothing but kindness in the eyes around him. The hand on his back began to move gently in a circular motion and why had he been so vain as to wear a stupid shirt—he'd be feeling that hand on his skin had he not been so afraid. For some fucking reason, he felt like crying.

What is this?

Scott opened his mouth to speak and this time the words came.

"I'm Scott. I'm from Terra's Gate too. Wyatt there…." He paused. "Little Bear. He's one of my best friends." A warmth filled Scott's chest, and he had to fight another unexpected urge to let out a sob. His eyes grew wet as he looked at his friend.

One of his *best* friends.

It was true.

"L-Little Bear has been trying to get me to come here for a long time and…. It all sounded so weird. It all *looks* so weird. I'm not into all that witchy-woo-woo stuff…." He snapped his mouth shut. *Oh shit! I did it!*

But a chuckling started all around, and he saw to his surprise that not one of them was offended.

Really?

"I'm sorry. If I fuck this up, just know I'm a pretty skeptical guy…."

"Tell me about it!" cried Wyatt. "I practically had to drag him here kicking and screaming."

Once more amusement among the men, and once more, not one bit of cruelty in it.

Who are these people?

Scott swallowed hard. "B-be patient with me. Fuck. I've been saying something to myself all day. When in Rome, right? I'll give this a try."

When the hissing started he knew not to worry. The snake thing was weird, but fuck. So what? "What isn't weird in life? Life is the fucking weirdest thing I know!"

He grinned and so did everyone else, and Scott quite suddenly felt he was with friends. And how could that be? It made no sense. How could a bunch of men dressed in sarongs and broom skirts and negligees and leather and, look—over there, was that a ball gown?—how could men such as these, strangers, *strange* strangers, make him feel this way?

"And what's your animal?" Wyatt asked.

Animal? Hell! *He* didn't know. He looked around at the circle of men and then he saw Knottie looking at him, giving him a nod.

It came to Scott then.

"D-do you mind if I say cat too?"

Knottie smiled through wet eyes and nodded again.

Scott didn't explain about Garfield. It was years ago, and he didn't want to try and compare that to the raw hurt he saw in Knottie's face. He just said, "Yes. A cat. That's my favorite."

That hand on his back gave him a gentle pat. He could feel the warmth of it through his shirt (nice), and then its owner spoke.

"I'm The Jockster—for obvious reasons." He stood up and shook his groin, barely contained by the fabric pouch, at the circle of men. Scott's eyes locked on the ass Wyatt had been telling him about only that morning.

Fuck me running, Scott thought and barely stopped himself from gaping. It was high and impossibly round and smooth as marble. It was perfect. He wanted to kiss it. If there were anything Scott could consider worshipping, it was Jockster's bottom. He could fall down on his knees before that ass and... and... was that...?

Yes! As Jockster did a slow turn, Scott saw that he was wearing a Jack Adams, a brand of jockstrap that Scott had been coveting for his collection. But it wasn't cheap—thirty dollars the last time he'd looked online—and keeping his electricity going had taken precedence. This one was a bright blue, with red stripes around the waistband. The thing was that it was pretty old school—a lot like a Bike, so why it was so expensive Scott didn't know. It was retro with a modern flair, with extra wide leg straps, and as simplistic as it was, Scott still wanted one. And today the one he wanted was on Jockster. Of course, the stirring in his shorts wasn't just about the jockstrap. Jockster and his "boys" filled it well, and while the pouch left little to the imagination, Scott would gladly let that imagination stop imagining if only he could see the real thing.

He glanced up that sweet, flat tummy, all but devoid of any hair Scott could see (did the Jockster shave?) to the thumb-like dent of his navel and up to a well-formed chest and quarter-sized nipples the color of caramels (and would they taste as sweet?) and up and up and then—Scott's face blazed red when he saw the object of his lust smirking down at him knowingly.

Jockster finished his turn, and it was only then that Scott heard the cheers and catcalls, and he guessed they were saying fuck off to the hissing, whether their cries were "disruptive" or not.

"I'm from nowhere and everywhere. I call the road my home."

He sat down gracefully and finished. "I like the hawk. I like its freedom, the way it glides on the wind, floating above the earth and then diving as fast as a lightning bolt the moment it wishes. That is freedom! It's why I ride my bike, because it's the closest to flying a man can get, except for maybe hang gliding, and I may yet do that one day. I think if I were to ever take another name, it would be Hawk. *Free* Hawk. But then I think about it, and hell, what can I say?" He slouched back and thrust his crotch to the end of the seat. "I am The Jockster."

Even Scott hissed.

Next was Bunny Penrith from Lawrence, Kansas, and his favorite animal was a rabbit (of course) because they were cute and cuddly. "They will also scream like mad if you try to mess with them and… they *really* like to *fuck!*"

Scott burst into laughter and hissed once more. It was silly doing it, but it was kind of fun, and then Bunny's lover was talking (how many lovers were there around here anyway?) and saying that he was Drake and that he liked frogs and it was because "they go everywhere, and they are used to both nourish and destroy life (because some people eat them, and you can poison people with them) and they have *really—long—tongues!*"

And that flowed to Daddy Dean from Madison, Wisconsin, who liked cocker spaniels and his lover Leadfoot, aka Sister Hateful Heinous Bitch, who liked turtles, and Shawnti Fey who liked snakes and Magnolia Thunderpussy who loved owls….

But by then, it was hard to hear anything. Scott could only feel Jockster's hand on his thigh.

CHAPTER FIFTEEN

DINNER WAS a rather simple affair. "It's the first meal," a man named Snowflake explained. He'd popped into the circle for a moment to let them know they were just getting the kitchen in order and weren't even sure how many men were eating for this one. He was a very tall man who filled a position at Festival called "Kitchen Queen," whatever that was. First meal, he explained, like the last one, was never a big production.

Which translated to, basically, sandwiches—no meat of any kind—and a salad.

"No cold cuts?" Scott asked. "That's easy enough. What we don't eat they can set out for lunch tomorrow."

Wyatt looked at him like he was a silly child.

"No meat here," Rat Bastard said, munching on a piece of zucchini. "Festival meals are all vegetarian."

"Huh?" Scott stared at Wyatt. "You don't think that's something you could have warned me about?"

Wyatt shrugged. "I didn't think about it," he said and popped a baby carrot in his mouth. "The food is really good here, don't worry about it. Just wait until you try the chicken fried steak—delicious! Although I do think they started baking it. The heat was just too much."

"How can you have chicken fried steak without steak?"

"Well...." Wyatt laughed happily. "It *is* tofu, but believe me, you'll love it. You won't believe it's not meat."

Scott shook his head. "I can't believe you didn't warn me. I would have made you stop at McDonald's this morning so I could have gotten a steak bagel."

"Relax," said Jockster, who was sitting next to Scott (something Scott was happy about). "There'll be a PETA Circle—at least one."

PETA? What the fuck? "People for the ethical treatment of animals?"

Everyone at the table laughed. "No," Rat Bastard replied. "People Eating Tasty Animals. Somebody will have squirreled away some ribs or something."

Scott sighed. *When in Rome*, he reminded himself. *When in Rome, when in Rome, when in Rome....* He looked down at his plate. Well, at least it was one hell of a salad. Every vegetable you could think of, even avocados, which weren't cheap and were one of his favorite things to eat. And fruit! Fruit, fruit, fruit! Oranges and apples and tangerines and bananas and kiwi and mangos and papayas. There was even a homemade dressing filled with fresh herbs that Scott admitted was "to die for."

"To live for," Jockster said (or was it *The* Jockster? Scott wasn't sure yet). "There is power in our words. Never say 'to die for.' There's no telling what you might manifest, so make sure you manifest something good."

Scott looked at him slightly baffled. "Do you really believe that *The Secret* bullshit?" he wanted to ask, but for Wyatt's sake didn't. And to be honest, for his own sake as well. He couldn't remember when a man had so magnetized him. It wasn't like Daniel, who Scott had deluded himself into believing he loved in the course of some online conversations.

(*Danger! Danger, Will Robinson! Danger!*)

or Garrett, the man before him…

… in whom, fucking dammit, Scott should have recognized the same danger.

Everything inside him had screamed for him to run the opposite direction, but he'd been so desperate for love he'd thrown away his common sense and believed that was what those men offered him.

Hadn't he *known* somehow that there was no future with those men?

Hadn't he *somehow* known?

Hadn't he known as if there were some impossible psychic "knower" who was warning him to stay away? Of course, Scott Aberdeen didn't believe in such Sylvia Brown bullshit. Didn't believe in an "inner knower." What he believed in was some kind of animal instinct. The way an antelope suddenly perks up, ears twitching, when a lion is near. That's what it was. Something from hundreds of thousands of years of evolution. There was nothing fucking psychic about it. That completely natural part of him (that wasn't crazy or schizophrenic) would warn him with a million years of evolutionary instinct to fight or run. He had ignored that warning over and over again because of his desperation to find validity in an outside source. He would tumble into the arms (or beds) of men he should steer clear of.

Or he would do some dumb-ass thing like hold a torch for Sloan McKenna, who had long ago made it clear the two of them would never be lovers.

Yet Scott held out hope.

Why?

What the fuck is wrong with me? Scott had wondered for years.

My parents. My frigged-up parents, who were waiting for the trumpet to blow and the world to end and for me to be cast into eternal torment! They'd dance a jig of joy on that day, the motherfuckers! He'd give his life for Sloan and they? They—who were his *parents!*—would be happy and pointing their fingers at him as they were led through the Pearly Gates and he was cast into the Lake of Fire.

A lake that didn't exist, but one he'd cannonball into before going into *any* Heaven that they desired or believed in.

And for fuck's sake, he thought, staring at his cheese and cucumber and tomato sandwich, *how did my thoughts get here?*

"I don't even like to say 'be careful,'" Jockster was saying.

"Really?" Wyatt asked. "Why not?"

"Well, look up the word 'careful.' It's full of anxiousness. Be attentive! Be diligent!"

Oh! Of course, I was thinking about why Jockster, who's real name I don't even know, is different from Garrett or Daniel.

"What's wrong with that?" asked Rat Bastard, who was once again wearing a *giant* hat, but one not so ostentatious as the last. It was a good thing, too, because there was a really big fan blowing nearby, and R.B. might have taken off like the Flying Nun had he chosen such an accoutrement.

"Because by the very nature of being diligent, you are *looking* for something bad to happen. Instead, say, 'Be safe.'"

"Doesn't it mean the same thing?" Scott asked—he who had walked out in the middle of Wyatt's joyful presentation of *The Secret* one Porch Night several years back. It had been a ridiculous film, suggesting that merely *thinking* something could bring it into existence. The idea was as stupid as thinking that when the Buddha was born he could talk and walk, and when he did so lotus blossoms burst up from the ground everywhere he took a step.

New Age mumbo-jumbo.

"Look," Jockster said. "It's all in the lens that you look at life through. When you say, 'Be *careful,*' you are actually *looking* for something *bad* to possibly happen. When you say, 'Be *safe,*' you are looking for something 'safe' to happen. See the difference?"

"Not really," said Scott, as Rat Bastard and Wyatt, and even frigging Howard, said they did.

"You really *are* cynical, aren't you," Jockster said, leaning over so close his lips touched Scott's ear.

"I think the word I used was 'skeptical,'" Scott said, turning. And now their lips were close enough they were practically kissing, and wow, there was a *zing!* that went right to his dick.

"Same thing," Jockster said, sitting back only the slightest bit.

"I don't think so," Scott said. "I think if you're going to use a different word than 'skeptical,' it should be 'practical.' Or 'realistic.' I don't believe in this witchy-woo-woo stuff. It's just as bad as the Baptist bullshit my parents believe in."

Jockster draped an arm around Scott and leaned on him. "Maybe."

"Maybe?" The confession startled him.

"Maybe," Jockster repeated. "But I will tell you one thing. If I'm delusional in my thinking? I'm betting I am happier than you are."

The words hit Scott like a punch to the gut.

He was so stunned, he was hurt. He put his sandwich down, suddenly not knowing if he wanted another bite.

Because he wasn't happy. He wasn't.

He couldn't remember a time when he was. At least for more than a few hours or a long weekend with some man he had convinced himself he was in love with.

Scott swallowed hard. Felt the bitterness rise again and threaten to blow away the happy-weird-woo-woo feeling Circle had given him. "Are you saying that it's better to live in delusion and be happy than to open your eyes and live in reality?"

"I think it depends," Jockster said. "Are *you* saying it is better to live in so-called reality and be depressed than it is to live in so-called delusion and be happy? I'm *very* happy, Scott. If I'm happy because I believe in something that isn't real, at least I'm happy. And really, in the end, does it matter if I have the power to manifest good in my life or not? If what I believe is bullshit, at least I'm *happy*. It doesn't matter if it is real or not. I have a good outlook on life. Haven't they proven that people with a positive outlook live longer than people who don't? Don't people who get a cancer diagnosis have a better chance to survive when they have a positive outlook on life? I am pretty frigging sure they've proven that. So if I'm wrong about my witchy-woo-woo stuff, at least I am living positively, and that, my new friend, is better than living negatively."

"But it is better to live in reality!" Scott objected. "I *would* rather be miserable and live in what's real than be happy by deluding myself. I would rather believe in *nothing* than believe the fuck-shit-crap my parents believe in!"

Talk at the table ceased, and Scott had another of those realizations that he was being an asshole.

"Well, I don't know what your parents believe in, and maybe you can tell me later this week. I don't want to hear about it now, though, because I am forming my entire mind-set for what I am about to experience over the next week, and it is *going* to be something *good*."

Scott looked over at Wyatt, who was nodding. "But didn't *you* say to never try and expect Festival to be *anything*, because it's going to *be* whatever it's *going* to be?"

"More or less," Wyatt confessed.

Scott turned back to Jockster (and damn, he was still so close!) "Do you really believe that you have the power to manifest what you want in life? That you can somehow alter reality?"

Jockster leaned in close. "I believe in fucking," he said.

Scott jolted upright.

"I believe that fucking is about the best thing there possibly is, and that people should do it whenever they possibly can. I believe that sometimes two people meet and they *know* that they should fuck. That the sex is going to be great. They know that they know that they *know*. I think that if there were ever a reason that it was okay to cheat on someone, then that would be the reason. When two people meet and *know* that the sex is going to be so goddamned hot that they would be fools to ignore it, then they had better do it. No matter what. Because that doesn't happen very often. It's rare. And when you don't do it, you regret it for the rest of your life."

Scott gulped.

"You ever have that happen, Scott? Knowing that you've just met someone that might not be Mr. Right, but he sure as shit is one hell of a Mr. Right Now?"

Scott gulped again, looked across the table, and saw to his surprise that the others were seemingly oblivious to what was happening. Except for maybe that sleazy skank Howard. God, the big oaf was sweating, even here with the fan blowing their napkins all over the place.

"Want to have some tea after dinner?" Jockster asked him.

"Tea?" *Tea? Tea?* Where the fuck had that come from?

"Yeah. I was invited, and I'm inviting you. Tea."

"I—I don't know," Scott said, more confused now than ever.

"It's simple. You answer either yes or you answer no. Scott, do you want to have tea with me later?"

"I want to do anything with you that you will let me," Scott said.

Jockster smiled a smile that sent a jolt straight to Scott's cock.

And he suddenly knew that if he had sex with Jockster, it would be different than with Garrett or Daniel or the near endless string of men before them. It *was* as if he somehow *knew* that with Jockster, it would be great. It would be the best sex he'd ever had.

And that even if it were a one-night stand (*please don't let it be a one-night stand*), it was going to be different from what had happened with all those other men.

Because Jockster wasn't promising anything. That was the first thing. This was pure... lust? Is that what it was? When Jockster looked at him that way, it was pure animal, with no promises or even pretending it was anything else.

No pretending he would leave a wife and sweep him off his feet.

No pretending they were in love.

No pretending at all.

Why was it that Scott had stopped believing in God and Santa Claus, but he could still believe a man's lies? Why could he believe a man would leave his wife and kids for him? The fact that he had believed Daniel's words made him far stupider than if he believed in Peter Cottontail or that the duck-billed platypus came from outer space!

Jockster said he believed in fucking.

And suddenly, that sounded like a pretty good thing to believe in.

Word came that tea was to be at Lorax's cabin at ten.

In the meantime, they cleaned up their dishes, and then Jockster convinced him to help clean up the kitchen. Snowflake was letting people know that no one had volunteered for clean-up duty.

"It'll be simple," Jockster said. "And it will get one of your community services out of the way and done with. They ask you do one for every two to three days you're here. And for us early people to do them early because most people start showing up on Thursday or Friday and leave Sunday. Leave those duties for them."

"Sure," Scott said.

To his surprise there was no more talk of manifesting reality or delusion or even fucking. It was jokes and a story about how Jockster had recently spent several weeks living in a small town, and how he'd gotten hit on by a small-town gay man, as well as the daughter of a diner owner. Cleanup was pretty easy with a sink only half-filled with dishes and counters and the dining room tables to wipe down. He and Jockster had it done in half an hour.

Then Jockster helped him find his way back to his tent and told him he'd look for him later.

CHAPTER SIXTEEN

WYATT INSISTED that Scott go to the Welcoming Ritual (he could *hear* the capital letters in those two words in his friend's voice), even though it wasn't anything that sounded appealing to him in the least. Somehow, Scott had lucked out and "First Circle" hadn't been the wand waving, J.R.R. Tolkien, Dungeons and Dragons affair he'd imagined. But anything *called* a ritual promised to be just what he'd wanted to avoid.

"Besides," Scott told his friend as they wandered across the plateau, flashlights beaming out ahead of them in the growing dark, "I told Jockster I was joining him for tea."

Wyatt shot him a look. "Really? *You?*"

Scott shrugged, carefully keeping his flashlight on the lookout for gleaming eyes. He wasn't even for sure what he was looking for. Wyatt had said something about a copperhead's eyes shining like reflectors?

"You do know what that means, right? *Tea?*"

"What if he comes looking for me and I'm not there?" Scott grumbled.

"Howard will tell him where you are."

"How come Howard doesn't have to go, but I do?"

"Stop pouting," Wyatt said. "It'll be fun. And the guy leading the ritual is cute."

They reached the pavilion, and in the dark it loomed above them like some large warehouse building to which someone forgot to add the walls. It was fully a hundred feet long by fifty wide, with a ceiling a good fifteen feet high and all made of metal. He saw the stage down at one end, the one he'd seen when he and Wyatt had arrived at camp earlier in that day. There were dozens of tea lights set around on the ground, and up above there were what appeared to be thousands of green and red stars slowly dancing across the ceiling.

One of those laser show things, thought Scott. He'd seen them advertised somewhere; he just couldn't remember where. It was pretty cool, he had to admit.

Just as he was about to step up into the building, Wyatt held out a hand to stop him.

"All I ask, Scott, is that you be respectful, okay? I don't care if you think it's stupid—well, that's a lie, I do care—but just, please, keep your cynicism to yourself?"

It stung, even though Scott had to admit he probably deserved the comment. "So what do you want me to do?"

"Watch. Follow the leads of the others?"

"Fine."

"Wait! Wait up!"

They turned and saw someone running up to them (*the fool's not carrying a flashlight*), and Wyatt made a hushing noise.

"Sorry." It was Jockster!

Scott grinned and was grateful the dark hid the fact that his face had heated up. *No. Be careful! You don't even fucking know this guy's real name. Danger, Scott Aberdeen! Danger!*

Calm down.

But how did he? Scott had never felt so electrified by anyone before. Not even Sloan. With Sloan it had started with a high-school-like crush and had built into a movie star fan's daydream and finally an agony of unrequited love. And yes, oh yes, he did think Sloan was beautiful.

But it was completely different with Jockster. Scott was more than glad Wyatt hadn't talked him into wearing a sarong. The jockstrap-wearing man caused all kinds of things to happen to Scott's insides and had a distinct effect on a certain part of his outsides. If he'd been wearing one of those thin pieces of fabric tied around his waist and nothing else? Well, that certain part of his anatomy would be pointing the way ahead of him for all to see.

At least he'd know I'm not all that tiny. Scott had never been embarrassed about the size of his erection, just how small he was before he got hard.

From the shadows within the pavilion, a man of indeterminate age approached them. He was holding a pillar candle before him, and the flame shown upward onto his face, the mix of light and shadow giving him an ethereal look. Scott saw he was wearing trunk-style underwear, but he couldn't tell the brand, only that they were shiny silver and caught the candlelight (and made his basket look huge!).

"Good evening," said the man. "Welcome. Do you come as friend or foe?"

Friend or foe?

"I come as friend," said Wyatt.

"Do you come as brother or stranger?"

"I come as your brother," Wyatt answered.

"Then that ye cause no harm, enter freely in…."

The two men kissed each other on the cheek and with a nod to Scott, Wyatt entered the pavilion.

The man turned to Scott and a rush of nerves jangled through him. *Deep breath.*

Now that his eyes were growing accustomed to the lighting, he could see his apparent host had short dark hair, what seemed to be blue eyes, and a soft build. Not heavy at all, and not overly muscular. He did have a very nice chest, though. *Why, oh why, can't I have a chest like that?*

"Welcome," he said. "Do you come as friend or foe?"

"Friend," Scott said nervously. This was weird!

"Do you come as brother or stranger?"

"Ah… stranger?" Scott answered.

Jockster gave him a light elbow to the ribs and whispered, "Brother. Say brother."

"I mean brother," Scott said quickly. "I *meant* to say *brother.*"

"Then that ye cause no harm, enter freely in…."

He kissed Scott's cheek and Scott found himself giving a perfunctory one back.

Weird. This is really weird!

Wyatt and another man Scott wasn't sure he'd met yet were sitting on sarongs just a few feet away to the right. Scott headed toward him and halted when his friend held out his hand in an upraised—stop—signal. Wyatt made a circular motion with his fingers toward the candles. Scott looked.

Huh? He looked back.

Wyatt made the motion again. This time Scott got it. He was apparently supposed to walk *around* the circle. So he did, slowly, following the candles, trying to be respectful—his feet crunching in the pea gravel that was scattered out on the ground. He *had* to go slowly, or he would have made a hell of a lot of noise, and it was clear this was not to be a noisy affair. He walked the circumference and then was grateful Wyatt had loaned him a sarong (which he'd chosen to wear over his shoulders and not around his waist) because it gave him something to sit on. He spread it out and sat down next to his friend. A moment later Jockster joined him, sitting close enough that their knees touched.

Scott felt a rush of goose bumps.

Oh, for shit's sake, you're twenty-nine years old. Act like it!

Over the next ten minutes, men began to arrive. First, the guy Scott had noticed crying when Knottie told the story about his cat. He was wearing a black T-shirt with a silver Superman *S* on the front and black shorts. Then Lorax. Next were Dolce and Gabbana. Next a small guy with his hair tied up in a bundle on top of his head and a long beard that made him look like some Indian guru or ascetic. He was followed by an older man with silver hair and a mustache.

When their host finally sat down, not only had the circle filled in, but a second had formed as well. That seemed to please him.

"Greetings, my brothers," he said. "I'm so happy so *many* of you joined us tonight. For those of you who don't know me, my name is Dale."

Dale. How nice. Not Dolce or Gabbana. Not Hound Dog or Bean or Magnolia Thunderpussy or Flaming Faerie. Just plain old "Dale." That made Scott happy. Surprised him, though. Surely someone heading a ritual with candles and asking if you were friend or foe would have had a faerie name? Thankfully, the answer was no, and Scott found himself relaxing into the moment.

Then found out the man *did* have a faerie name after all....

"Although some people *do* call me He Who Looks Good in Underwear...."

At least the name fit.

"I had to miss most of Festival last year because it was my dad's eightieth birthday and well, that was something I was obligated to go to. No. I *wanted* to go. It wasn't an obligation. But I'm back and so glad to be with you.

"I thought we'd start things off by going 'round the circle and having us say our name and then share, *if* you feel like it, something about your year and perhaps something you hope to experience this year at Festival. I thought we could compare our answers again on closing night.

"So, I'll start. Like I said, I'm dale—with a small *d*. I think capital letters in a name are so pretentious—at least for me. And what I hope to do this Festival is cry."

Scott's breath caught. *Cry?*

"Festival is the only place year-round *where* I cry," Dale explained. "I never cry out loud anywhere else." He nodded to the man on his left.

And so it went, similar to the Circle earlier in the evening. Scott found out that the guy with the hairy chest who sold sarongs called himself Gentle Ben, the man with the silver hair went by the name Silvercrow, appropriately, and the gentleman (who turned out to have the most wonderful laugh) with the Superman shirt was named Super Jim. Also appropriate. Fun too. Scott found himself instantly warming to the man. Scott discovered that people had come to Festival for a lot of reasons, but number one were those hoping for healing—physically and emotionally. It had been a tough year, it seemed. As everyone shared, he found that one man was dealing with the death of his lover, another was clean and sober from crack for six months (there was much hissing), another had found out he had HIV. There were those dealing with stress—with their jobs, a family that couldn't deal with a coming out, and a married gentleman trying to decide if he *should* finally come out to his wife and family.

There was joy as well, as Dolce was excited about a career opportunity and Lorax was considering moving halfway across the country. And Super Jim and Silvercrow were at Festival for their honeymoon! They had just gotten back from Iowa, where they had gotten legally married. Once more there was much hissing, and Scott surprised himself again when he found himself joining in.

What they all seemed to agree on was that they were wanting a week with their friends, a shoulder to cry on, a joke to make them laugh, a song to lift their spirits. To party and swim in the lake and to generally get away from the real world—a place that could be hell. None of what Scott was seeing and hearing was anything like what he'd expected, and he had a crazy urge to cry.

What is this?

When it came time for Jockster to speak, he declared that what he wanted most was to get laid. "A lot!"

And was that his knee pressing up against Scott's? He realized he was getting hard again. Sounded good to him, and he knew *just* the man to help Jockster out.

"Like you *ever* have any trouble getting laid," Rat Bastard cried.

Jockster spread his arms. "What can I say? The faerie love me. So get your spot on my dance card early!"

There was a funny little drop in Scott's stomach. These men were lining up for Jockster. Was the jockstrapped stud planning on being with more than one of them?

"Pencil me in for tomorrow night?" asked a man who'd identified himself as Ferret. Very skinny with a sparse mustache. Scott found himself disliking the man immediately.

Even I'm more attractive than that... ferret.

"You *know* I'll make time for *you*," Jockster said with a growl, and Scott's stomach dropped five feet. Was he going to have to get in line? He'd thought maybe something—some kind of spark—was going on between him and Jockster. Was that foolish wishful thinking? Was it just an accident their knees were touching the way they were? Had he imagined the flirting? Had he *once more* created something in his head that bore no resemblance to reality?

You were expecting maybe a marriage proposal?

Scott looked at the man, saw how gorgeous he was. Of course the men would be lining up for a chance. And why wouldn't Jockster want a little bit of everything he could get off the buffet? *I'd want the same thing if I was that fucking hot!*

"Oh!" Dolce held up his hand. "If Ferret fails to keep his appointment, then *ink* me and Gabbana in!"

Jockster grinned merrily. "A three-way! Been a long time since I've done one of those."

Scott's stomach sunk even further. When it was his turn to speak, he found he was at a total loss for words. Somehow he managed to get his name out and then said, "I-I don't know the rest. I don't know what to expect. So far *every* fucking thing has been *totally* different than what I thought it would be. I guess I need to follow Wy—Little Bear's advice and just let happen what's going to... to happen."

To his surprise everyone smiled and nodded and hissed. Scott looked at Jockster and saw he was looking back, eyebrows raised high and grinning like the Cheshire cat. "Can I pencil *you* in for tonight?" he asked.

Scott's heart leapt into his throat and a lightning bolt struck his cock. *Fuck yes*, he thought. He nodded quickly. *You can ink me in. You can chisel me in stone. Tattoo me in!*

Fuck, what an effect this man had on him. It was crazy!

And I guess if I'm going to be just one name on his dance card, it's better than not being on it at all! At least he wouldn't spend *every* night in *Peni's* tent alone.

After they all shared, Dale led them in a guided meditation, and Scott decided to go ahead and give it a try. Sloan had been waxing poetic on the practice—perfect Max had been teaching him—and of course he'd heard for years meditation was good for you. It increased immunity, lowered blood pressure, helped maintain emotional balance (and shit knew he needed that!) just to name a few. Science had proven that. If there was a religion Scott had any respect for, it was Buddhism, *true* Buddhism and not the Tibetan or Thai brand. Buddhism was a philosophy, didn't teach anything about a God or gods, and Scott found its precepts interesting, though certainly not enough to make him convert. But why not, he'd give the meditation a try.

Sadly, and try as he might, his thoughts were wandering too much. Between the fact that his ass was starting to hurt planted in the pea gravel, the rush of new experiences into his rather routine world, his attraction to Jockster (hell, the more or less permanent semi he had in his pants at the moment and most of the day for the man), and the fact that he was apparently going to have to make an appointment if he wanted in Jockster's bed, his mind was just too all over the place.

Once the meditation was done, they all stood and gathered in one circle, arms draped around each other's shoulders or placed companionably around waists, and they sang one of the strangest little songs Scott had ever heard.

> *Dear friends*
> *Queer friends*
> *Let me tell you how I am feeling*
> *You have given me such pleasure*
> *I love you so....*

The words confused him. It was more than the use of the word "queer," which still made him uncomfortable, but it was the way it so obviously moved the men around him. Many had tears flowing freely down their faces. And what the hell did it mean by, "given me such pleasure?" They weren't going to end this thing in an orgy, were they?

The song—same words—repeated perhaps a dozen or more times, turning into a round as it did…

> *Dear friends - Queer friends*
> *Let me tell you how I am feeling*
> *(Dear friends - Queer friends - Let me tell you how I am feeling…)*
> *You have given me such pleasure*

I love you so….

(You have given me such pleasure, I love you so….)

By the end, Scott had gone from merely moving his lips to singing along. The tune was simple but compelling, melodic but haunting, and the round style added layers he'd rarely heard without instruments to accompany the vocals. He still didn't get it, but it put him in a strange state he couldn't identify. Discomfort and peace at the same time.

Finally, the ritual was ended in a traveling kiss. Dale kissed Bobcat. Ferret kissed Silvercrow. Dolce in turn gave a long and sweet kiss to his Gabbana, who gave Lorax one with just a bit less gusto, who kissed Super Jim openly, who kissed Jockster.

Then it was Scott's turn.

Jockster's lips touched Scott's, and he wanted to plunge his tongue in the man's mouth, crush his erection against the jockstrap's mesh pouch, kiss him so hard that Jockster would want to throw his dance card away.

He also wanted to run away—across the plateau, down the steep steps the led to the camp's second level, on down the hill past the sunflower-covered dam, and past the registration gate to the gravel road beyond. Run all the way home.

Which was stupid. More than stupid.

So instead he took the lead he was given, as Wyatt had advised, and let those lips touch his and guide him to know what to do.

It was a gentle kiss, with only the slightest pressure. A shock went through Scott, a jolt, a wave that ran through his whole body. Jockster brought up a hand and touched Scott's cheek and took a step so their chests were touching (and was there any way the man couldn't feel Scott's hard-on?) and it was all Scott could do not to moan into his mouth. Then, as the kiss ended, there was only the tiniest touch of Jockster's tongue to Scott's lips as they parted. And when he opened his eyes, he saw the man looking at him, looking with those deep eyes, looking into Scott's own, the barest flicker of a smile at the left corner of Jockster's mouth. The world stopped for a moment, then came back when Jockster nodded and looked over Scott's shoulder.

Oh.

He had to kiss the next man.

And fuck. It was Ferret. How had he gotten there? Hadn't Wyatt been to his left? Ferret. Who was penciled in on Jockster's dance card for tomorrow night. Ferret who looked more like a weasel and—*dammit!*—ugly! Could he get away with biting the shit out of the man's lips? Of course not. And everyone was watching (most notably Jockster) and so somehow he gave the man a friendly kiss instead. Not long, not short, certainly *not* sexy, but he did fucking kiss him.

And then Ferret kissed Gentle Ben, and it went on till it got back to Dale and they all told each other that they loved one another and finally—*whoa!*—everyone howled like wolves.

After much hugging, Jockster pulled him aside. "Tea time," he said and Scott was being led off across the grassy plateau.

CHAPTER SEVENTEEN

TEA, JUST like everything else so far, turned out to be nothing like Scott had imagined it might. With all the talk of rituals, he'd been wondering if it might be something akin to the Japanese tea tradition, with kneeling and quietude and the careful making of green tea.

Instead, it was a bunch of dudes sitting around Lorax's side of one of the cabins, passing around more than one joint. It wasn't a very big room either. The way the small beds were set around the walls, and one down the center, it was a tad crowded if not comfy. Scott realized that while these men looked quite happy with the accommodations, he would have hated it like he would have hated striding through the law offices where he worked totally naked—which was to say he wouldn't have liked it one bit.

Lorax was cutting up an extremely green vegetable of some sort, and Rat Bastard was taking what looked like shriveled, dried dog turds and pulverizing them in a coffee grinder.

"Want some?" Jockster asked, holding out a piece of slimy-looking green stuff about four inches long and thick as his thumb.

"What is it?" It wasn't zucchini. It was too green for that. It was the color of kiwi, but of course, no kiwi could be cut in a shape like this, and there were no seeds.

"Cactus," Jockster said.

"Cactus?" Scott asked.

"You know. Cactus. San Pedro in this case. It's nice and trippy. Easy. Not too crazy."

"Ah...." Scott looked down at the thing in Jockster's palm dubiously. It almost looked like a big green caterpillar. Uck. Eat it? "I don't know," he said. "I've never tripped before." A shimmer of fear passed through him. He'd read about Native Americans and peyote and the shit Shamans saw while on that stuff. Turning into flaming geckos or soaring eagles, and he just wasn't ready for that kind of thing.

"Look," Jockster said. "I know you don't know me, but I'd like to get to know you. There's something crackling between us, don't you think?"

Scott's eyes widened and he swallowed hard. Jockster *did* feel it then? *It's not just me?*

"We're gonna be here for ten days. You think I want to face you for the next week if I fuck up your whole Festival on the first night? You think I want to mess up a possibly beautiful relationship?"

Relationship?

Danger! Danger, Scott Aberdeen!

How many men had said something like that to get him into bed and then dumped his ass as soon as they'd had it?

But damn. Jockster was so….

Different? You don't fucking know this guy! What if he's some kind of drug addict?

"I'm not a druggie," Jockster said as if reading his mind. He placed his free hand on Scott's knee (zing!) and Scott's heart jumped a beat.

Fuck!

"My parents were, though. Fuck, were they. My mom once said that there was a time in her life where she never went anywhere without a gram of coke in her boot. That's *not* me. She made sure of that. She raised me telling me the dangers of drugs, and she knew them. She wasn't some Southern Baptist hick speaking out her butt about a world she didn't know a thing about. I *know* what chemicals can do. *This* is all natural. Lorax grew it in a pot on his own patio. It's not addictive. I only do it a few times a year, and my mom has it growing in her frigging garden! It'll give you a mild happiness. The lights will be prettier. The breeze will feel so nice on the hair on your arm." Jockster ran the back of his hand with the cactus lightly up Scott's arm, and Scott shivered. "The cicadas will sound louder, clearer. And I am only going to let you have one little piece."

Scott looked at that thing in Jockster's hand. Green. Wet. "I don't know."

Jockster nodded. "It's okay." He smiled and squeezed Scott's knee. "I'm sorry."

"Then I'll take it," said skinny Ferret who was just stepping into the cabin.

Fuck you will, thought Scott and snatched it from Jockster's hand and stuck it into his mouth before he could think about it. It tasted a lot like it looked, slimy and reminding him of cucumber that was just starting to turn bad. Alkaline.

"Here," said Jockster and held a piece of apple up to Scott's mouth. He opened it and let the man feed him, those fingers just grazing his lips. "Eat that quick."

So he did, and the tartness of the Granny Smith instantly wiped the alum-like feeling out of his mouth. He looked and Jockster was smiling at him and then inexplicably leaned in and gave him one of those tiny little kisses. Scott's heart nearly stopped.

Ferret meanwhile sat on the small bed across from him. It was a narrow bed. They all were. Not even as wide as twins. It was probably part of what happened next. When the thin man folded himself Indian-style, it spread his tiny version of a sarong completely, and the second biggest dick Scott had ever seen in person was revealed to all. It had to be a good seven or more inches long soft, and it draped itself over low-hanging, hairless balls the size of lemons.

Oh, for fuck's sake, thought Scott. *No wonder Jockster wants him.* He felt a sudden urge to cry. There was no way he could compete with that!

"Did you bring the water?" Lorax asked Ferret.

"I wasn't sure you were ready. It's steaming in the kitchen."

"Well, by the time you get there and back, we'll be ready," Lorax said. "Get your skinny ass back there and get it. Pronto."

Ferret did just that, and as he left, Scott saw the man's ass was no bigger than two halves of a cantaloupe and not that shapely.

He could fucking compete with that, though! He gritted his teeth, sat up, and wondered when the lights were going to start getting prettier.

It was then he noticed that Rat Bastard was taking the servings of ground dog turds and was putting them into a French press. "You guys aren't going to drink dog shit, are you?"

"Huh?" Jockster looked to see what Scott was looking at and laughed. "It's 'shrooms."

"Sha-rooms?"

"Mushrooms. Psilocybin."

Scott's eyes flew open. "You do those too? On top of the cactus?"

Jockster smiled. "Oh, yes!"

Scott suddenly felt uncomfortable. "Aren't mushrooms what were in that movie *Altered States*?"

Jockster laughed. Let his head fall back and laughed, and oh, *damnshitfuck*, he even had a sexy neck! How did you have a sexy neck?

"Yes, I guess they were. But these aren't from Mexico, and I don't know if even my mom would have done those at the height of her druggie period. And I promise these will *not* transform you into an ape."

"I—I—ah...."

"Make way! Make way!" It was Ferret, and he was back, holding a big teapot which was still giving a half-hearted (quarter-hearted?) attempt at a whistle. "Man with boiling water!"

"Just in time," said Rat Bastard as he turned what was apparently the last of the ground mushrooms into the French Press. "Here."

Ferret put the kettle down, and Rat Bastard poured and then pressed.

"Oh, fuck," Scott said.

"Don't do anything you don't want to. Stick with the cactus if you want."

"You're going to do them, though," Scott said, his heart racing.

"I sure as fuck am. I get these once every couple years *if* I'm lucky."

"And we were lucky," said Lorax. "Put me back a nice penny or three. It's been a couple years, though, and I wanted to share. If I don't, I'll be doing them for weeks and once or twice a year is *more* than enough."

Scott gulped and watched as Lorax began to set out coffee cups. "Do we have enough?"

Scott looked around the room. Lorax. Rat Bastard. *Ferret*. Jockster. Himself. The guy with the normal name—Tony? George? Oh, wow. And two guys he hadn't met yet. A sexy older man with lavender hair and a black man—his hair white as snow. Scott saw it wasn't natural, though. He couldn't have been older than twenty, twenty-one. That made, "Eight?" he said aloud. But that was only if he did them. Mushroom tea. Shit.

Scott looked at Jockster. Gulped.

"It's okay, sweetie. Don't do a damned thing you don't want to. Lorax, make it seven."

Something indefinable rose up inside Scott. He leaned in close to Lorax. "I-I kind of want to. But I'm scared." And he was. But….

"I don't want you to anything you don't want to," Jockster said.

Lorax began to pour the grayish fluid into the coffee cups.

"Lorax?"

"Yeah," Lorax said as he was about to pour the seventh cup.

"Make it six," he said. "I'm going to take Scott swimming."

"No," Scott broke in. "Eight. Make it eight."

When in Rome, after all.

And let Festival be…

… whatever Festival should be.

The last two cups were filled.

Before Scott drank, Jockster gave a little cry. "Bastard, do you have any of the Godiva mix?"

"You know I fuckin' do. I'm addicted."

"Get it for me."

"You're going to have to go into town and get me some more."

"I don't have to. I'll get someone else to. You know someone will make a town run."

"All right, goddammit." Rat Bastard went over to the other side of the cabin and came back a few minutes later with a can with a plastic lid. He handed it to Jockster.

Jockster opened it. "You're not allergic to chocolate, are you?" he asked Scott.

"No." What was Jockster up to?

"That shit can be pretty nasty. And you want part of the pulp. It tastes like dead opossum ass."

"I kind of like it," said Ferret.

"You? You like kimchi."

Ferret shrugged.

Jockster took out a big spoon and doled out a few dips of powdered chocolate into Scott's mug before adding a couple to his own. "Anyone else?"

"Oh, fuck it," said Bastard. "Give here."

Ferret declined, but everyone else decided to join in on the chocolaty goodness. It worked. It was good. The concoction didn't taste anything like ass, either opossum or any other kind. Not that Scott had tried more than one kind in his life, not counting ham or rump roast, that is. But the "tea" was good. There was a slight weird aftertaste and his stomach did seem to object to the pulpy last bits in the bottom of the mug, but besides that, there was no problem. It tasted like hot chocolate.

"Now what?" Scott asked.

"Now we go swimming," Jockster said.

CHAPTER EIGHTEEN

ONCE SCOTT knew he had his flashlight, he followed Jockster out of the cabin and down the long path until they reached the main buildings. Then it was down the steep hill and across the dam. It curved around, and the quarter moon reflected in the surface of a lake that looked like black obsidian.

"We're not really going swimming, are we?" Scott asked.

"Sure we are," Jockster replied.

"But… we don't know what's out there," Scott said.

"What do you think's out there? The Loch Ness Monster?"

"I don't know. Snakes. Snapping turtles?" The idea of wading out into that dark water spooked Scott a little. Who knew what really was out there?

They came around a short bend and through a copse of trees and began to hear talking. "Hey, good," Jockster said. "We're not alone."

As much as Scott liked the idea of being alone with the man, people made what they were about to do seem a little less scary. Less Chrissy swimming in *Jaws* while her drunk date collapsed on the beach.

They came out of the trees and saw shadows as at least a couple of men started a fire not far from the road. As Scott and Jockster came closer, the kindling flared into life, and suddenly, they could see there were twice that number, at least, crouched around the fire. One of them was Super Jim. That was good. He liked Super Jim.

By the time they joined the men, most of them had sat down on some logs that were laid around the fire, and he saw Knottie feeding the building flames with pieces of wood of different sizes, including a couple of small logs.

"Okay, what does this one come from," said Super Jim and began singing.

Seconds later the men chorused out, "My Fair Lady," and they joined in singing about how they all could have danced all night.

"Come on," Jockster said, and to Scott's surprise, the man took his hand and led him up to the fire.

Up close Scott could see that besides Knottie and Super Jim, Bobcat and Lula Belle were there (although it took a few seconds to recognize the latter in shorts and a T-shirt), as well as Hound Dog and Bean. In fact, the little dachshund mix suddenly gave a startled jump when she saw them and started barking like all the fiends of hell had arrived. It was hard not to laugh. Bean scooped her up, and if she were a cat, her hair would have been on end.

Bean did laugh. "She didn't see you," Bean said. "She doesn't get startled easy. I think she's embarrassed."

"She thinks she's a German shepherd," Hound Dog explained.

"Cerberus," added Bean. "Guardian of the underworld."

"It's okay, Sweetie," Scott said and slowly reached out a hand for her to sniff. She gave him one or two more suspicious little yips and then yielded happily when he started to scratch her head. "Think she'll let me hold her?"

"I daresay she will," Bean said, "Be warned, however, she will never let you stop paying attention to her if I hand her over."

"That's okay," Scott said happily. He was a cat man, but he loved any small animal, especially once he knew it wouldn't bite. Besides, he didn't want Jockster to think he was a coward. He took the little dog, who immediately snuggled up to him and tucked her head under his chin. "Awwwww." Oh, she really was a big baby! "Look, Jockster!" He turned to his sexy companion. "Want to pet her?"

Jockster had taken a step back, though. Not what Scott had expected. There was a wary look on his face. *Is he afraid of her?* he wondered.

"Let's go swimming," Jockster said, not stepping any closer.

Interesting.

"I'll join you boys," said Lula Belle.

"Me too," said Super Jim.

"What about the show tunes?" Bobcat objected.

"I won't be long," said Super Jim.

"Me either," drawled Lula Belle. "My delicate nature won't long be able to stand the chill."

Scott watched as the men began to make their way to the water, and he could see they were shedding their clothes on a small bench at the lake's edge.

Shit.

Shit, shit, shit.

"Come on," called Jockster. "Hurry up!"

Reluctantly Scott handed the little dog over to her owner and followed the men. He could just make out three bare butts from the light of the small fire.

Shit.

He didn't want to strip in front of the men. He didn't want Jockster to see how small he was. Especially now that he'd seen how hung Ferret was. With the light behind him, would it be enough to throw him into silhouette? He briefly considered going in with his shorts, but he had his wallet and who knew what else in his pockets, and he could lose anything in this darkness, even with his flashlight.

Sighing, he slipped off his shorts, and then thinking, *Fuck it*, pulled his shirt off, kicked off his tennis shoes, put his glasses carefully in one of them, and then put everything in a small pile before wading in after the men.

The water was perfect.

He didn't realize just how perfect until he was about waist deep, and by the time he had joined the others, he felt the most wondrous feeling wash over him. It was as if the water was actually welcoming him into its embrace. It really *was* perfect. Not too cold. Not too warm. Refreshing without being chilling.

What an incredible feeling.

He was naked.

Naked in the water.

Of course, he'd been naked in the bathtub, but he'd never ever gone skinny-dipping and *wow oh wow oh wow* did it feel remarkable!

"Oh—oh, my!" he cried.

"You okay, baby?" Jockster asked, coming to him.

"This—this water! It's incredible."

Jockster laughed. "Welcome to Serenity Lake."

Scott giggled. He couldn't believe it. He giggled? When had he giggled last? "It feels so good on my dick," he whispered.

Jockster got closer, their bodies all but touching. "Yes," he said quietly.

"I can't believe how it *feels*," Scott said, a sense of awe coming over him.

"What?" Jockster asked, getting even closer.

"The water. On my skin. God!" He giggled again. "I can feel it on my asshole!"

"Oh my!" Lula Belle cooed.

Scott blushed and then started laughing again. It was so funny! He ran his hands down over his body. "I can't believe it! I just can't believe it!" He wanted to shout because the water felt so good. He touched his nipples, then ran his hands down his sides and back over his ass.

"Haven't you ever gone skinny-dipping before?" Jockster asked him.

"I was a good Baptist boy," Scott said. "And then a big prude. No. When would I have *ever* had a chance to go swimming naked? You don't think any of the guys in school wanted me—the big old faggot—joining them when they had their parties in high school, do you?"

"Well, that's too bad," Jockster said. "I would have invited you."

"You didn't even go to my school!" Scott said and for some reason that sounded funny, too, and once more the laughter took over him.

"You like it?" Jockster asked him.

"I love it! I can't stop touching myself." He blushed again. He couldn't believe the shit he was saying.

"Sounds fun," said Jockster and took him into his arms. "Can I touch you?"

"Oh, yes!" Scott gasped and Jockster ran hands and thrumming fingers down his back and over his ass—clutched his cheeks and pulled him in tight. Scott could feel Jockster's cock against his own. It felt good. It all felt good. Was this what Wyatt was always talking about? Even Sloan had liked this lake. This wasn't magic, was it? *Naaaaaahhh!* No such thing as magic.

Then Jockster was kissing him.

This time he didn't hesitate to use tongue.

Oh God, Scott thought, and kissed him back.

There were sparks. Blue ones. Blue and purple, and they whirled around inside his head, and soon he couldn't breathe, and he threw back his head and cried out into the night and let Jockster lick and kiss and suck at his neck and god-god-god-god it felt so *goooooooood!*

He felt his cock growing and stretching out, and Jockster's too, and they were sliding up against each other. Scott wanted to cum it felt so good. For a second he thought he might. Why had he never felt like this? So alive!

Scott opened his eyes. The moon, God! It was so bright! So blue and silver and shimmery, and it was almost like he could see craters, but of course he couldn't, could he? You only saw that when the moon was full and there would be no full moon this Festival. In fact there was going to be a new moon, wasn't there? He thrust his cock against Jockster's and found he couldn't remember what he'd just been thinking about and didn't care. He pushed his chest against Jockster's and let their hard nipples tease each other.

"Look!" Jockster cried and pointed and…

Oh! A shooting star! Wow! He actually saw it go from white to blue to red and thought he might have heard it pop. "Make a wish."

"I already made mine," Jockster said and kissed him again.

It was categorically the most incredible kiss Scott had ever experienced. It was like his whole body had become a kiss. It was like it was more than Jockster's body and mouth against him, that tongue *inside* him—it was like they were fusing somehow and like *Jockster* himself had somehow entered him, become part of him. That tongue felt so amazing against his own, the two wrestling together, and even Jockster's teeth felt like—like—like he didn't *know* what!

"You want to fuck me?" he asked suddenly. He wanted Jockster to fuck him. Right now. He let his legs wrap around the slim man, the water easily supporting his weight.

"Oh, my luck. You're a bottom…," Jockster whispered in his ear and then sucked on his lobe.

"Y-you're not a top?" Scott asked. Every man he met was a top. He could count on the fingers of one hand the times he'd gotten the glory of fucking a man. They all wanted to fuck him.

Jockster shrugged. "I like it all. But I love to get fucked. It seems that every man I meet wants me to top them. I show my ass whenever I can. Why doesn't anyone want it? I think I've got a great ass."

"Oh—my—fucking—God!" cried Scott. "I would fucking—love—to—fuck—your—sweet-set-a-tea-cup-on-it ass!" He burst into joyous laughter.

"Oh girls!" said Super Jim. "Get a room. Or a tent. Or a cabin. Or run out there in the woods. But I am not ready for this. Okay. That's a lie. I am. But I can't see in this dark!"

Scott blushed again but was shocked he wasn't more embarrassed. Suddenly, he had to know the answer to a question. "So I take it your name is Jim. How did you get to be *Super* Jim?"

"Well, it's Gem, not Jim. You know, like a crystal? Not like James. It's Super *Gem!*"

"Oh!" And wasn't that cool? Wasn't that just wondrous? He loved it. "It's your faerie name!"

"Why yes, dear."

"I want a faerie name!"

"Give it time, dear boy. I am sure one will come to you. And I mean that. A name will find you. Just wait."

It was then, as the men found themselves forming into a little circle (although Scott was still half-hanging on to Jockster), that it happened. Super Jim was just beginning to tell them about getting married when something swam into the circle. Someone on the beach had moved just right so the firelight reached them, and a big warm brown eye caught the light, and Scott would have screamed if Lula Belle hadn't first. It was the scream of a twelve-year-old girl at a horror movie, when Jason Voorhees cut off the head of a girl's boyfriend just as they were fucking. It was a scream that went into the subsonic, and surely, Sarah Jane on the beach could hear. As if confirming this, the little dog began to bark, followed by a second dog. At least, it sounded like a second dog.

And the animal that had started this? With its furry head the size of a big dog's? It seemed almost to roll its eyes, and then it swam on.

Lula Belle, meanwhile, was moving faster than Scott's eyes could follow. There seemed to be trails streaming behind the man as he screamed again and splashed and thrashed, and it was almost like he was walking on the water.

Super Gem (Gem, not Jim) exploded into laughter.

"It's just a muskrat," Jockster cried and almost shouted he was laughing so hard, and Scott joined him and oh—it—was—*so*—funny! Funny despite the fact that the creature that had seemed to come out of nowhere had scared him too, and maybe that is what made it all the more funny. He'd pissed, it had scared him so much, but it was Lula Belle who had screamed first and all but teleported out of the water.

Scott couldn't remember the last time he'd felt so good.

The water. The man next to him. The night! The color of the moon and oh, look look look at the stars! He looked at Jockster, who said nothing, only finished laughing. So he said it again, but still nothing.

Oh! I'm not saying it, he thought. *I'm thinking it.* "Look at the stars," he said. He pointed and let his arm go up and up and up, and it seemed his arm was a mile or two miles or a hundred miles long, and maybe he could take one of those chips of diamond right out of the sky and give it to the man next to him.

"Feeling good?" Jockster asked.

"Oh, yes," Scott said. "Ever so."

"Let's go make sure Lula Belle is okay. Can you get out okay?"

"Why, of course I can. Why couldn't I? Shouldn't I? Whatever?" He shook his head. What a silly question.

Jockster took his hand and led him to the shore, and for a minute he shivered. A breeze had come up, but oh, it felt good. It was warm and it was good and they walked to the fire and as they did, Scott couldn't believe the sight. The fire! It wasn't just orange and red (but *oh oh oh* it *was* orange and red and *yellow* too) but it was also blue and purple, and he couldn't help but wonder if one of the logs Knottie had added to the flames was those kind that were supposed to make the fire turn all kinds of wonderful colors. There seemed to be dancing figures in the flames. Slim men with wings. Dancing.

Lula Belle had her—*his!*—hands on his hips and was staring daggers at them. "What *are* you laughing at?"

That only got them laughing again, and Jockster told the men at the fire, who had been starting their rendition of "Tonight" from *West Side Story*.

"It was just a muskrat," Jockster said.

"Well how was *I* supposed to know that? It could have been anything!"

"The Loch Ness Monster," cried Scott, and they fell on each other in great heaving guffaws.

It was only then that Scott realized he was naked and that Jockster and everyone had seen him. How could they *not* in the brightness of the flames? The water, thankfully, had not shrunk him too much, but fuck, now Jockster had seen him, and he didn't come close to comparing with Ferret and—*Oh my*, he thought. He still had half an erection at least, and there were people staring and—gosh—it looked like they liked what they saw.

"Let's go to your tent," Jockster whispered, and Scott turned and kissed him hard and told him that was one of the best suggestions he'd heard in his—entire—fucking—life!

CHAPTER NINETEEN

SOMETHING HAD happened to the steps.

Scott knew there were quite a few of them—

(and some echoing memory—Wyatt's voice—was saying something about how the old steps were made of rocks and blocks of stone and wound back and forth up to the top of the plateau, and "if you think you were afraid of snakes, trust me you were very afraid in those days," and these wooden steps were ever so much better)

—but now? Why, something had happened while they were at the beach. There were more steps now. At least twice as many. As many as three times!

How could that be?

Had someone come in and built more while they were swimming—

(and singing. Hadn't he joined the men on the beach singing? Hadn't he led them in the five hundred, twenty-five thousand, six hundred minutes from *Rent*—but no! How could that be? Jockster had grabbed his hand and said it was time to go to the tent.)

—and now there were so many more steps to climb and—*fuck me running*—look at all those steps!

"There must be a fucking billion of them!"

(*Wait. Hadn't they started singing "The Time Warp?" Yes! But then Jockster had grabbed his hand and told him that it was "... time to get you some coffee!"*)

"No, baby, not a billion. Sixty. Although sometimes it seems like it."

"There are more! Just look!" Scott pointed, and he could, and he could *see* there were more! They went and went and went and went.

"Baby...."

Scott turned to look at Jockster. Baby. He liked Jockster calling him "baby." That was important, right? He grinned, tried to kiss the man, and kissed thin air instead. Tried again. Got his chin. "Stop moving," he said.

"Baby?"

"What?" he said.

"You're tripping balls."

"What?" What did he say? Tripping balls? He didn't even know what that meant. He looked down at the ground. "I don't see any balls?" Wait! He had pants on. When had he put his pants on?

"Why don't we take a shower?"

"Can't," Scott informed him.

"Why is that?" Jockster asked.

Because you'll see how little my dick is, and you won't want me anymore.

"Oh, baby." Jockster pulled him close. "You have a very nice dick."

Scott's eyes went wide in horror. Had he said that out loud? "But Ferret's is so much bigger?"

"It's *too* big," Jockster said and then took him into the shower house. He helped Scott undress, and Scott tried to hide his cock and balls, and Jockster brushed his hands away and led him into the water—

(when had he turned the showers on?)

—and wow oh wow the water was so pretty! Someone had strung pink and purple and blue Christmas lights along the ceiling, they were the only lights that were on, and the water shimmered in pastels and crystals and wow oh wow it was *so* beautiful.

He turned and saw Jockster and oh, *he* was so lovely. The water was crashing down on him and splashing up in a fine mist, and the lights were shining through them and the steam and everything was so shimmery. He *looked* at Jockster and, yes, he *was* lovely. Long and slim and his body was so muscular—like a runner's or a gymnast's—his pecs high and round and his tummy a washboard of muscles leading down to the dark blond bush of his cock—and oh! That cock! It was beautiful. It was *beautiful.*

Suddenly, he remembered Pastor Bob. Oh, he had had *such* a crush on that man! So handsome with his Superman hair (even that little lock in front) and his steel gray eyes. He remembered seeing him naked in the shower house at church camp and being in awe of his penis, surrounded by all that blue-black hair, and wondering if he would ever look like that. How at that exact instant he had known he was a cocksucker even though it was five or more years before he ever got to do it. How he wanted to suck Jockster right now.

Scott started to laugh and found tears in his eyes at the same time. "I'm tripping," he said and Jockster agreed.

"Tripping balls."

"I *like* tripping balls!" Scott said happily and it was true. He did. He liked it. A lot. "Can you see?" he asked, pointing into the mist of the water beating around their shoulders and filling their lashes. Then he leaned in and kissed Jockster again and had he *ever-ever-ever* felt a kiss like this? It was fucking *ah-may-zing!* "Want to fuck now?" he asked Jockster.

Jockster smiled and wow! That smile! There were valleys and mountains in that smile and his teeth. Jockster's teeth were purple. "Not now. Let's get clean first."

"Yes!" he cried and took the soap that came from somewhere, he wasn't sure where, and ran it all *over* his body and paid particular attention to his ass because men always wanted to fuck him, and that is what Jockster would want, and *oh-oh-oh* that felt *good!* And *wait!* Jockster was the one who wanted to be fucked!

"Well hot damn!" Scott said.

"What?" Jockster asked and kissed him.

"You want *me* to fuck *you!*" And suddenly he wanted to cry. He was going to top. He was going to fuck Jockster. He was going to top. He was going to get to *top!*

"Yes, baby. I want you to fuck me. But first let's get cleaned up."

That sounded good, but first he *had* to tell Jockster something. "Don't you think the water is pretty? I've never *seen* such pretty water!"

"It's very pretty," Jockster said and pulled him into a kiss and then pushed Scott into the water and rinsed all that soap off.

"My asshole is tingling. It almost burns," Scott said because, well, damn it was true, wasn't it? His asshole *was* tingling!

"It's the Dr. Bronner's Peppermint soap," Jockster said.

"What?"

"Never mind, I'll tell you later."

Then the shower was off and Jockster was drying him, and he was using the towel on his little dick and didn't seem to mind. "My dick's not too small?" *Please don't say yes*, he thought and wanted to cry.

Jockster took him in his arms. "You have a beautiful cock," he said.

And then they kissed again and oh, it was such a nice kiss.

They dried and dressed and look! Jockster was wearing a Pump jockstrap, and damn, it was so pretty. The pouch was black with blue piping or stitching or something and the band was so-so-so blue. It seemed to shimmer, and the black words "PUMP!" seemed to be in a deep, dark pit.... How cool was that? What kind of jockstrap was that? How was it doing that? Was it a trick?

Then he realized what was going on.

"I'm tripping balls," Scott said.

"You sure are," Jockster said, and there was that smile again, and it was such a pretty smile.

When they were dry, Jockster led Scott to the kitchen, and there was Bean, and he was just making a pot of coffee, and how perfectly convenient was that? "It's like kismet or karma or one of those *k* words," he told Jockster.

"Yup."

"I gotta go potty," Scott said and had no idea why the fuck he said it. Well, except it was true. He did.

Jockster took him to the bathroom off to the side of the dining area, but not before Scott snatched up a cookie that was laid out in a huge baking pan and took a bite, and it positively *was* the *best* cookie he had *ever* had in his *entire* fucking life!

Jockster got him to the bathroom and asked him if he needed any help, and what kind of question was that? For God's sake. Help going potty! He knew how to potty. He somehow dropped his pants and Jockster closed the door—wasn't that nice of him? He was *such* a *nice* man!—and Scott dropped his pants and sat down and peed for about a billion or so years and looked at a small photocopied flier taped to the wooden wall in front of him.

It appeared to be about a masturbation workshop.

Wow....

A masturbation workshop?

Really?

The font on the flier looked like something out of a fifties sci-fi movie—*The Day the Earth Stood Still* perhaps—and wow oh wow! The letter seemed to be floating maybe an inch or two in front of Scott's eyes, while the rest of the flier looked to be at least five or ten feet away. It couldn't be that much because Scott could reach out and touch it. But it *looked* that far away. And the wood. "Look at the wood," he shouted. "Jockster! Jockster!"

The door opened a crack. "You okay?"

"Look!" he cried and pointed and his finger bonked off the wall and how the hell had that happened? It was at least five feet away. How could he be touching it?

Jockster came in the bathroom and asked if he was done, and he said yes, he had peed and he was all done, just like a good boy. He pointed at the wall again and told him that some of the grains in the wood looked like they were just a few inches from his face and some looked like they could be miles away.

Jockster looked and told him it looked *just* like that and helped him get his shorts up.

Then they had some coffee.

Slowly but surely, the world seemed to shimmer and warp and wave just a little less. Not a lot. But some. And fuck me running, was the coffee good. Wait. Hadn't Bean said he wouldn't make coffee until the morning? Was it morning?

After the coffee Jockster took him to the steps, and it wasn't morning. It was still night and he didn't see any copperheads, and then they were going up the steps and it took a long, long, long time because there kept being *more* steps no matter how many they climbed. They just kept going! Somehow they made it to the top, and then they were off to his tent, and Jockster was helping him into his bed, and then he knew nothing more.

CHAPTER TWENTY

CEDAR, AKA "The Jockster," felt a little guilty for making Scott sleep alone, and for a minute, for more even, he considered—wrestled with the idea—of breaking his rule. But no. The thought near brought on a panic attack. No. No sleeping together.

Not for love or money.

Not for tea or sympathy.

Not for gods or country.

Cuddling was one thing. It was fun. He wanted to cuddle with Scott. He'd wanted to take Scott to his hammock and suck his cock and make him explode and then cuddle.

Then for some reason, he'd suddenly realized he didn't want to have sex for the first time with Scott while the man wasn't perfectly cognizant. How good could the sex be?

Of course, it wasn't like he wasn't going to get a lot of sex this week. One bum fuck didn't mean there wouldn't be any good sex.

But… it was more than that.

To his surprise, Cedar found that…. What?

He felt responsible for Scott for one thing. Maybe he shouldn't have allowed the guy to do the hallucinogens.

No.

No. Scott was an adult. Scott could do whatever he wanted to do. He had tried to talk Scott out of it.

But no.

How was Scott *supposed* to say no? Somehow as Cedar had thought about it this morning, he saw that Scott had been put in a situation he probably hadn't been in before. A peer pressure kind of thing. Especially after Ferret.

Gods. Why didn't I see it? Cedar thought with a groan. This was why he avoided people like Scott. And Elijah and Charlotte. Responsibility. He had enough responsibility. He didn't need to take on anyone else. That's why guys like Ferret were perfect. There was affection and connection and fun. But that was it. More than a pickup, but nothing serious. It was like a boyfriend of sorts he only saw one night a year—*and* Ferret respected one of Cedar's *only* rules.

No spending the night.

No waking up all spooned up together.

Never.

Ever.

The thing is Scott would want more than that. Cedar should have known that the second they started talking. It was in those pretty eyes of his. The vulnerability.

Gods! Is that what I'm attracted to?

But gods damn, that kiss! Cedar couldn't even remember the last time a kiss had been like that....

Oh. Oh, but he could. He knew exactly when the last time had been.

And that's what concerned him.

He liked Scott. He liked Scott a lot. It worried him how much. He hardly knew the man—didn't even know his last name.

But there was something about Scott. He was like a lost sheep that needed to be found and helped back to the flock. Somehow, in some way, Scott had pulled himself away from the world. Away from people. Cedar understood. What had that pool boy, Sam, called him? Shallow? But it wasn't true. Cedar wasn't shallow. Not wanting a lover didn't make him shallow. He liked connections. He just didn't want any permanent ones. Now friends—that was something he wanted. Scott could be a good friend. He imagined Scott needed the same thing. In fact, he further suspected Little Bear might be Scott's only friend in the world.

Piss.

Cedar saw he needed to make sure Scott understood. Now.

Before it went any further.

Scott wasn't going to want one night. At the very least, Scott would want him to be his summer lover. At the *very* least. To be real, he was probably the kind who wanted a lot more.

So explain it. Be a man; let him down and break it to him easy. Do this right. Beneath that prickly, cynical mask he wears, there's a nice guy . A good man. Help him see that about himself. Treat him how you would want to be treated. Show him what good friends *the two of you can be.*

Isn't that what Scott really *needed anyway? A friend?*

CEDAR KNEW he needed to check up on Scott.

Fuck!

What if the guy had gotten sick? What if he'd thrown up and strangled in his own....

No!

Do *not* go there!

Scott's tent wasn't that far, just across the way.

Cedar made his way across the plateau. He could see Big Sir and Little Bear were up—and making breakfast, of course. Big Sir wasn't going to go without meat. Cedar could smell the bacon. Why come to Festival if you weren't even going to pay lip service to the Festival ways?

"Hey, Jockster." Little Bear waved as he got closer.

"Hey, Bear," Cedar said, still heading to Scott's tent.

"You want some breakfast?"

"Nah…. I'll get something down below. Granola maybe. Going to check on Scott."

Little Bear smiled that cute, huge, dimpled smile of his. "That's nice."

Cedar nodded and kept going. He was feeling a little panicky and how fucking dumb was that? Scott was going to be just fine. Hell, he might have even gone down already.

He ducked under the huge branch that guarded Scott's tent—it was a really nice tent. Kind of surprised him. Scott hadn't really seemed like the camping kind of guy. He wouldn't have expected him to have such a nice setup. On the other hand, Scott had expensive tastes. Cedar knew those glasses of Scott's weren't from Walmart or Costco. They looked designer.

"Scott," he called out.

Nothing to knock on, of course. He walked up to the zippered door. All the windows were zipped shut. Gods, it must be a greenhouse in there!

"Scott?"

He heard something.

"Scott! Are you okay in there?"

"Y-yeah…. Damn…. Jock—Hol—hold on."

Stumbling. Something falling over.

Then the zipper….

"Jockster…." And there was Scott, naked and looking so vulnerable Cedar just wanted to leap through the door and kiss him and….

Gods.

This was crazy.

But then Scott was covering his dick with his hands, and Cedar couldn't help but laugh. "I've seen it, Scott. No use in hiding it."

"But…." Scott blushed and looked away.

"But what?" Cedar asked.

Scott turned and his sweet little ass came into view, and gods, Cedar realized he wouldn't have any trouble topping that!

"I can't find my glasses. And I can't read without them. What if they're broken?"

"Stop! Don't move." Cedar unzipped the tent door further, stepped in, and looked around… "There. I see them." He stepped past Scott, reached down, and pulled them out from under some covers; he'd seen just the arm sticking out. He handed them over. "There you are, Sweet Pea." *Gods. Cutesy pet names? This had to stop!*

"Thanks," Scott said and put them on top of his head. "I really can't read *shit* without them."

They stood looking at each other, and then Cedar saw Scott cover himself again. He stepped forward and took Scott's hands away.

"Don't," Cedar said.

"I'm so fucking small," Scott whispered.

Cedar shook his head. "No, you're not."

"I fucking *saw* Ferret," cried Scott. "I'm nothing like him!"

"You think *that's* normal?" Cedar stepped closer, placed Scott's hand on his hips, placed his own hands on Scott's, then let them sweep around back and to the top of that amazing butt.

"N-no."

Scott actually looked like he might cry. What the hell was that about? "Then what's the problem?"

"Why would you want me when you can have *him?*"

Cedar smiled. He couldn't help it. "Well, first of all, you are a whole lot cuter than him."

Scott's mouth dropped. "I am?"

"Yes."

Scott shook his head. "I'm plain."

"No." *How can you even think that?* He kissed Scott on the nose, pulled him closer. "No, you're not."

Scott made a strange little strangled sound and Cedar's heart swelled.

"I think you're as cute as can be. And you have a *very* sexy cock. And remember. I've felt that thing hard. You're not small."

"I am when I'm soft."

"Well, when the rubber hits the road, soft is not what matters, right?"

Scott's eyes seemed to grow. He made a little half shrug.

Cedar kissed him. No tongue. Not yet. That could lead other places (nice places), but the inside of the tent really was like a hothouse. He pulled back.

"Want to get something to eat?"

"I—I don't know. My stomach is a little queasy."

"Yeah. That's the 'shrooms. It can happen. But I think you need to try. Maybe some granola?"

"Maybe," Scott said. "And my mouth tastes like shit."

"We can take care of that too."

Scott gave him a half smile. "Okay."

Cedar stepped back and watched as Scott dressed. He was a very slim man. But there were muscles on that frame. Very nice muscles. And such a cute flat belly, and his little treasure trail was so hot, and that fluffy brown bush looked so soft it was all he could do not to touch it. And Scott really did have a nice cock. Not huge. A few inches, but Cedar knew for a fact that it got a whole lot bigger. Nice balls too. Shaved?

Scott climbed into some shorts, nearly fell, and Cedar kept him upright (although he wanted to push him back onto that big air mattress and have his way with him), and watching him dress, Cedar saw what nice big beautiful hands Scott had. Nice feet too. Perfect nails. He bit his tongue to keep from laughing. Did Scott get mani- and pedicures? He bet he did.

When Scott was dressed, Cedar took his hand and they stepped out of the tent, and he reminded Scott to zip it up. "Snakes," he explained, and the look of total horror that came over Scott's face was almost comical. Then before Scott could close the tent, Cedar quickly told him to wait. He went back inside and started unzipping all the windows. "We've gotta let a breeze through here. I've heard it will make it to a hundred degrees today."

"Someone will see all my stuff. What if they take something?"

Cedar smiled. "Not here, baby. Not at Festival. Not going to happen. I have never known men I could trust so much. You could probably leave anything but hundred dollar bills lying out on your bed and no one would take anything."

"Really?" The look on Scott's face—astonishment.

"Yup. You've come to a whole new world, Scott. And if you really do let go, you aren't going to believe what's in store for you."

LITTLE BEAR offered them some breakfast on their way, and the green look that came over Scott's face would have made Cedar laugh if he hadn't known it would hurt Scott's feelings. He needed to work on this boy. Toughen him up.

No, that softness is part of what makes him so damned appealing.

They took the steps slowly—and hey, down was always easier—stopped at the halfway point, sat down, and looked out into the trees.

"It really is beautiful," Scott said.

"You haven't seen *any*thing," Cedar said.

After a few minutes, they went on down to the second level—where the camp buildings were—and Scott went into the communal bathhouse and brushed his teeth.

"If you have a little bag of some kind, I would just leave all your toiletries down here so you don't have to keep lugging them around. Leave a towel, anything you want."

"But what if someone tak—oh. You say no one will take anything."

"And shit, if someone uses your toothpaste, so what? Someone else will lend you some of theirs if you run out."

"B-but I use Luster."

"Huh?"

"Luster White 7 with fluoride."

Cedar shook his head, confused.

"It's the most advanced toothpaste I could find. All the benefits of nature and science. It's a whitening toothpaste. A leader in brushing and it promotes whiter teeth, like *twice* the whitening of the leading brand, and with the oral health benefits—"

Cedar burst into laughter. "You sound like a commercial. Are you in advertising?"

Scott shook his head. "I'm a glorified legal secretary."

"Maybe you should change jobs."

Scott laughed and grinned, and it was such a cute smile. "Maybe. You know anyone who's looking?"

"Who knows?" *I could always have Mom put her feelers out—wait, what am I doing? Helping this guy find a job? What the hell?* "Look, no one is going to take your fucking toothpaste. I promise. And if they do, I'll get you some more."

"It's pretty expensive. Like nearly twenty dollars. You can't find it at—"

"Twenty dollars?" Cedar couldn't help but chuckle.

"It's got *twice* the whitening of the leading brand—"

"—and all kinds of *oral* health benefits. Yeah. I know. Let's get something to eat."

SCOTT WAS able to keep the granola down. Luckily, there were plenty of bowls in the pantry because Scott had left his dishes in the tent. Cedar had figured he would have left them on the shelves set aside for that, but—

"You were afraid someone would take them?"

Scott had blushed. "I didn't know."

"You'll know for tonight."

Scott nodded.

They'd missed the pancakes. You had to strike early for those. And it looked like lunch wasn't far away, but it was going to be baby spinach salad with citrus dressing and sandwiches again, and neither of them had a hankering for that.

"Let's go to the beach," Cedar said.

"You like the beach, don't you?" Scott asked.

"I do. A lot. 'Sides, I want to work on my tan. My ass is too white."

"I like it." Scott blushed again, and that made Cedar snicker.

"You are *so* fucking cute."

There was that look of disbelief on Scott's face again. Damn. "Has someone called you ugly or something?" Cedar asked. "Someone I can go beat the shit out of?"

"No," Scott replied, then looked away. "But I have eyes. I can *see* most people are so much *better* looking than me. My friends.... Asher is a fucking god. And Sloan...."

Scott's breath caught, and Cedar couldn't help but be intrigued. Interesting. He would have to find out who this Sloan was.

"Sloan is so damned beautiful. And Wyatt... I guess I mean Little Bear. Even he is *so* much better looking than me."

Cedar shrugged. "He's cute I guess. But you're much more my type." Sloan. Asher. It was nice to know that Scott had more than one friend. "Little Bear is just a little round for my taste. And hairy. Do you wax or something too?"

"No." Scott shook his head. "I shaved my pits for a while, but not anymore. And I shave my—" He turned pink.

"Your balls?"

Scott turned even redder. "Yes," he whispered.

"You have really nice balls," Cedar said, leaning in, letting his lips touch Scott's ear, loving the way the man trembled when he did.

Scott giggled. "I like your jockstrap. Full Kit Gear." Now he was whispering in Cedar's ear. "I have one just like it. I like the blue. Blue must be your favorite color."

"You've got a jock like mine?" Cedar asked, surprised.

"I've got a whole *lot* of jocks."

Cedar pulled back, astonished, and saw Scott was blushing furiously.

"Nobody knows," Scott said quietly.

"*I* do," Cedar said and grinned wickedly.

"*Now* you do."

Cedar was intrigued. *Very* intrigued. "What do you have with you?"

"Just a Bike." Scott looked away.

"How come?"

"'Cause nobody knows!"

Gods, and had Scott just turned an even brighter shade of red?

"I want to see you in it." Cedar found he was getting hard at the very thought of it. And his outfit wouldn't hide that. Not for a minute. Not with the super soft fabric the pouch was made of.

"Maybe later," Scott said. "In my tent."

"It's a date," Jockster growled. What a fine shocker this was. Seems Scott was a little more than he'd expected.

CHAPTER TWENTY-ONE

SCOTT AGREED to go to the beach, and they made their way back up the stairs once again. They got Scott's toiletries, two towels (one to leave in the bathhouse and one for the beach), and his dishes. Jockster ran off for a minute and came back with a quilted bag that looked a lot like what Scott thought of as a hippy purse over one shoulder.

They put his shaving kit—a Polo Ralph Lauren leather bag—on a shelf in the changing area of the shower house. He had to gulp to do it. The damned thing had cost him over a hundred and forty dollars.

The dishes were cheap. He and Wyatt had picked them up at Walmart. But still....

It felt weird leaving things just lying around.

The towel he left behind was Kassatex—forty dollars. What if someone used it?

But when he turned to Jockster, saw him standing there, hand on one hip looking so fucking hot in his black Full Kit Gear jock—with the wide blue leg bands and the matching thin blue line that went along the bottom of the waistband and the blue stitching down the front of the pouch, a soft pouch that cradled his cock and balls in such a fucking sexy way—well, suddenly his expensive towel and whether someone used it just didn't seem to matter.

"You ready?" Jockster asked.

Scott nodded.

"Then let's go."

So they made their way down the big grassy hill to the dam, and as they crossed, Scott could see there were a lot more men on the beach today, and even from the dam, he could see they were naked—to the last.

Piss.

There was no way on Earth he was stripping on that beach.

Was...

... no way!

He'd changed into his trunks for a reason.

When they got to the beach, Scott saw just about everyone he'd met so far. Bobcat and Dolce and his lover Gabbana, naked as jaybirds and sipping beers or something. Dolce's pubic hair was pretty dark considering he was supposed to be blond, lending evidence that Dolce wasn't a blond in the first place. Oh, and over there. Ferret (ugh!). Prancing around letting that third leg bounce from thigh to thigh (practically knee to knee—double ugh!). There was Lorax, sprawled back like he had a porn-star dick as well, but his belly was so big it was hard to see if he had anything. Over to the right was the black man with the white hair—had he caught the man's name? If so he didn't remember it. There was Knottie sitting with Gentle Ben and Sundog. Just beyond them were Bunny and Drake. And of course that wasn't even counting all the men in the water and up on the float. And, yes, all naked, without a concern in the world.

Oh, fuck! Wyatt and Howard were out there. Of course, he'd seen Wyatt in the shower room at the gym. Hundreds of times. But not Howard. Oh, fuck. Scott hadn't been prepared for that! A naked Howard with a big belly and a dick so thick Scott could see it from the beach. Oh, no!

A naked Howard was the very last thing he'd wanted to see. He looked away.

Oh, thank goodness he did. Because hot damn, here came Bean and Hound Dog from down past the beach, their canine companions loping along at their heels. Scott figured if he lived to be three hundred and ten, he wouldn't get tired of looking at those men naked. And it wasn't like they were all that hung. Just like normal men (although their penises were very nice).

A pretty boy with near white hair was coming up out of the water, and well, what do you know, it was Blue from the Fourth of July outing at Peter Wagner's, and damned if his bush wasn't as white as the hair on top of his head. Nice dick too.

Does everyone in the world have a nice dick but me? Scott wondered.

Jockster had said he had a nice dick…. But did he believe it? He wasn't even three inches soft. How could that be nice? *How?*

Jockster found them a spot in the grass off to the left of the beach, which Scott could see now had to have been manmade. Heck. The sand had pieces of seashell in it, and Scott doubted this lake was connected to the ocean, Pacific *or* Atlantic. They spread their beach towels—

("Cute," said Jockster, looking down at Scott's rainbow colored towel with the alligator on it.

"Thanks," he said. It was from Lacoste and he'd been thrilled to find it on sale for only forty dollars.)

—and then they settled down and Jockster asked him if he wanted some sun block on his back and shoulders. "You don't want to get fried on the first full day or you'll be miserable all week. Go in stages and build up for the brag-worthy tan by next week. Make 'em jealous in that office of yours."

"Sure," Scott said. Any excuse to have Jockster touching him.

And those hands felt good. Strong. A promise of things to come?

That was when Ferret chose to join them. "Can I get some of that too?" the skinny man with the taxi-with-its-doors-open ears asked.

"Sure," Jockster said.

Scott wanted to growl but smiled instead. It wasn't easy. "You wouldn't want to get fried on the first full day," he somehow managed to get out of his mouth.

He was so grateful to see that Jockster didn't spend nearly as much time spreading and massaging the suntan lotion onto Ferret. He was already going to have to deal with going to his tent alone tonight knowing what the two of them were up to. But to see the foreplay? That would have been too much.

"Want me to get you?" Ferret asked.

"No, that's okay. Scott's got me."

"Oh. Okay."

Scott could hear the disappointment in Ferret's voice. At first he wanted to smile. But then...

Then he really *heard* that tone. The *longing*.

It was something he could understand. He could almost feel sorry for the guy.

Almost.

Ferret was looking back and forth between Scott and Jockster. He sighed and stood up. Was he thrusting his crotch forward to show off that dick?

Jockster was looking too.

Dammit.

So Scott started rubbing in the suntan lotion. He made sure he did a good job too. Jockster laid down on his front, resting his head on his crossed arms, and Scott spread the pale lotion far and wide—neck, shoulders and back and sides, arms and hands, those long muscular legs, and even his feet—rubbing and kneading, massaging until Jockster's skin soaked it all up and the white was gone. He surely didn't forget that round ass, even let his fingers slide a bit down the top of his crack. Jockster didn't object, after all. It turned out to be all Scott could do not to run those fingers down a whole lot farther. Thank goodness for all the people around him—it's what kept him from getting tacky and going too far.

Just as he was finishing, Jockster whispered, "If there wasn't anyone around, I'd have you stick that finger somewhere special."

"Oh?" asked Scott, feeling truly playful for the first time in he didn't know how long. "Where would that be?" He stuck a finger in Jockster's ear. "Here?"

"No!" Jockster said into his arms with a huff.

"Here?" he said, reaching into Jockster's armpits and giving them a tickle.

"No!" Jockster giggled.

"How about—" Scott walked his fingers down Jockster's back, skipped them over the impossibly luscious and round upturned butt cheeks, down down down his legs and then more tickling in between those long, suckable-looking toes. "—here?"

Jockster curled up, laughing and begging Scott to stop. "I'm ticklish!" he cried and so Scott gave his ribs some of the same treatment. As the man wiggled under his assault, Scott couldn't help but notice the growing erection in that black pouch of his jock.

Suddenly, Jockster sat up and grabbed Scott and rolled over on top of him and gave him the same tickling attack. Scott laughed till he almost peed himself and beseeched Jockster to stop for that very reason.

"Come on," Jockster said and leapt to his feet. "Let's go swimming. It's hot as a motherfucker!"

"Wait! Your chest! Your face."

Jockster grinned and stood, hands on hips, and once more Scott applied the lotion, dropping to his knees when he needed to, and it was so damned sexy—like he was ready to give the man a blowjob (and wasn't he? Ready?).

Jockster slipped out of his jockstrap, let it fall at his feet. Scott's mouth fell open and he rocked back, sitting on his heels.

Suddenly the memory of seeing Jockster naked in the shimmering purple-blue rain of the showers last night filled his mind. And fuck. The man did have a *beautiful* cock. It was perfect. Not huge and not small (as he was), with balls hanging loose because of the sun's heat, covered in a light dusting of hair—again not too much, just right. His circumcision scar was flawless as well. Not the jagged or discolored mess of some men's, but a masterpiece of surgical skill. Why, it almost looked like he'd been born that way.

There was no way he was stripping in front of this man.

How can he be interested in me?

But….

But he's seen me naked. He told me he liked my cock. He said it was sexy. He said I have really nice balls.

Another memory from the mushroom-induced state came back….

"My dick's not too small?"

"You have a beautiful cock."

His heart raced.

"Now let's—go—swimming!" Jockster reached down and pulled him to his feet and reached for the tie of his trunks.

Scott shook his head. Pushed the hands away. "No. I'll go in like this."

Jockster sighed. "Scott…. Swim naked with me."

"I did. Last night."

A shooting star flashed through Scott's mind. Stars like blazing diamonds.

"Scott. Let the sun touch your naked skin. You won't believe how good it feels! Remember how the water felt on your body last night?"

"I was tripping." Another memory. "I was tripping *balls*. You got me *so* messed up last night." It was the first time he'd mentioned the mushrooms.

"I'm feeling funny about that. Like I pushed you—"

"You didn't push me."

"—pushed you into a situation where you felt you *had* to take the—"

"I'm glad I did them." There. He'd said it. Because he had liked the trip. It had been wild and crazy and beautiful. "I wouldn't want to do it very often…."

Jockster shook his head. "No. Me either. I usually only do them Tuesday night at Festival. And we didn't do them last year at all."

"So… okay then. We're good." And wow. He meant it. Wow.

"Now, let's go swimming."

Which led to another problem. "I don't want to swim naked."

There was a long pause.

"Okay." Jockster walked back to the towels. He squatted and rummaged through his hippie bag.

And pulled out a pair of shorts. Stepped into them. Held out his hand.

"Let's go swimming."

Scott couldn't believe it. "Why are you doing this?"

"Because you're not going to be the only one."

Scott's heart skipped a beat. He couldn't help but smile. "People are going to wonder what you're doing."

"Yes." Jockster took Scott's hand and led him to the water. Scott felt like he was being watched. When he looked around, he saw he was right. It wasn't just Jockster they were looking at.

Almost everyone was looking.

"What's everyone staring at?"

"What do you think?" Jockster answered as the water swallowed their knees.

Scott shrugged.

"You know, I've been watching you since we got to the beach."

"I've been watching you too," Scott said with a smile.

"You know what I saw?"

The water had reached their crotches. Another step and it wouldn't matter if he had pants on or not. "What?" asked Scott.

"I saw you checking out dick."

Scott jumped as if he'd been goosed. "Huh?" Had he been that obvious?

He had been—had been checking out dick.

Jockster didn't care, did he? He was going to be having sex with Ferret later after all. How could he care?

"Bean. The guy with the dreadlocks. The pretty boy with the bleached hair."

Scott blushed. The water was reaching their nipples, the buoyancy beginning to make him light-footed on the sandy bottom.

"You were even scoping out Big Sir!"

"I was *not!*"

Now they were beginning to tread water.

"Whatever," Jockster said. "The point is, you're a man. Men like to look. Everyone around here? They're men. They want to look. Now they *really* want to look because you're not letting them see you naked. Not letting them see you in a place where looking is what you get to do. *You* looked."

"I—I…." Fuck! What was Jockster saying?

"If you hadn't worn your trunks people would have hardly given you a second look. Just a quick curious glance. Now they're wondering if there's something wrong."

"Fuck me!" Scott said.

"I thought we already determined that you were going to be the one fucking *me*."

Scott looked around him again. Were people looking? Were they? *Wait.*

"You're the one going to get fucked?"

Jockster swam close and kissed him. Hard. Grabbed his cock through his trunks, and son of a bitch if he wasn't getting hard.

Jockster pulled back. "You're still worried your dick isn't big enough, aren't you?"

"No." *Yes.* "Yes."

Jockster sighed. "You are a silly boy."

"I've been told that before." Scott felt a funny little rush.

"I want you to see something," Jockster said.

"What?" Scott asked.

"Look up on the float. Right now."

"Huh?" Look at the float?

"Now. Hurry."

"I…. Ah. Okay." He turned and looked. Saw that Lorax was standing there right at the corner. "What?" What was Jockster wanting him to see?

"His dick," Jockster said into his ear.

"His dick?" And from this angle, looking up at the big naked man, Scott could see what he hadn't been able to before. Lorax's big belly was no longer hiding his penis. "What about it?"

"See how small it is?"

And, oh. He did. It wasn't big at all, was it?

"He's not the only one either, Scott."

Scott looked at him.

"Scott. These men? They gather together each year to love each other. They see past what the world looks at. The love here is so wonderful. Sure. We're all men. We have our faults. We aren't perfect. We bitch. We grumble.

But when the rubber hits the road, we will die for each other. No one is going to judge you by the size of your cock. Only by the size of your heart."

There was a catch in Scott's throat.

"W-what if my heart is all shriveled up?"

Jockster moved in. Kissed him again. "It's not. I'd know."

"I hope you're right."

Just then Lorax cannonballed into the water, splashing them both. When he came to the surface he was laughing.

"Asshole," Jockster told him, wiping his face.

"Things were looking entirely too serious," Lorax said.

And maybe he was right, thought Scott.

He looked at the shore. Looked up at the floating raft. Looked at the men all around him. Looked at Jockster.

He made a decision.

"Let's go to the beach."

"Already?" asked Jockster.

Scott nodded. "I need you to go with me, okay?"

Jockster gave a shrug. "Okay."

Halfway to the beach Scott turned to Jockster. "Help me."

"Help you what?"

"Get out of this thing."

"What thing?"

Scott's heart started to pound. "My bathing suit."

Jockster's eyes widened. "Y-you sure?"

"No. Help me anyway."

And so Jockster did. He grabbed Scott's dick on the way and gave it a few playful tugs. Then he kissed Scott once more, and there was no sparing the tongue.

When they climbed from the water Scott was *not* small. He wasn't pointing to the sky, but small he wasn't.

Funny thing?

No one was really looking. Not more than a glance.

"You were right," Scott said as they sat on their towels.

"What?" Jockster asked.

"People were staring because I was *wearing* something."

Jockster nodded. "Yup."

Hmmm..., thought Scott.

And then he lay out to catch some sun.

CHAPTER TWENTY-TWO

DINNER TURNED out to be something called "Caribbean Black Beans and Rice," with a wonderful festive fruit salad and a cold cucumber sauce. It was wonderful, although Scott thought by that point he would have eaten *anything*, including yet another salad. He worried for a brief moment what beans might do to a possibly romantic evening—especially when it would mean an enclosed tent—then remembered Ferret and thought the hell with it and had a second helping. He was starved.

After they ate, Jockster suggested they go for a walk to work off the food. Scott, who was pretty sure he'd take a rocket to the moon or a deep-sea submersible to the Titanic to spend time with Jockster, readily agreed. A part of him warned of danger. Scott could almost see the waving mechanical arms of the *Lost in Space* robot in his head. He knew he was doing it again. Falling almost instantly under the spell of a man he found attractive. He knew this behavior wasn't healthy. He didn't even know Jockster's real name.

But fuck. He couldn't help it; there was something different about Jockster from all the other men he'd ever met.

Oh really? Like what?

He didn't know what!

Scott only knew he wanted to spend every second he could get with the man—especially after Ferret stopped by their table with a "See you later tonight?" and gave Jockster the most pathetic look Scott had ever seen. What had made it worse was Jockster hadn't told the man, no.

They took a path that led past the cabins to the north of the dining hall and overlooked the road that wound up and around to the top of the plateau. Scott so badly wanted to ask Jockster if he really was going to spend the night with Ferret. The thing was he didn't want to hear that the answer was yes.

Maybe, he thought, if he just stayed glued to him, showing Jockster the best of the best of himself—the part that didn't bitch or complain or lecture, the part that wasn't so damned pessimistic—then maybe Jockster wouldn't *want* to be with Ferret.

But every time Scott thought of the skinny man's huge cock, he couldn't help but think there would be no way Jockster would want to pass up the opportunity to play with such a thing.

They began to pass several sarongs hanging alongside the path. A red one covered with flames. One that was dark blue with white Asian characters along the border. A tiger print....

Scott didn't really pay them much notice until they came around a bend and quite abruptly found themselves in a corridor of color. He stopped.

"Gosh."

Sarongs were hanging on clotheslines that had been strung from tree to tree along their way. He couldn't believe how beautiful it looked.

"It's pretty, isn't it?" Jockster asked him.

"I-It is," he admitted.

As they started back down the path, Scott saw the swatches of fabric were in literally every color of the rainbow and in seemingly innumerable patterns and designs. Some looked like paintings: a herd of horses, a white tiger with big golden eyes, a school of tropical fish swimming over a coral reef. Some of the sarongs were solid, ranging from pastels to rich, dark tones. There were prints in tribal and Celtic patterns. Some were brightly tie-dyed, as if they'd come through time from the 1960s, while others were more fancily done in thick complimentary strips or bold stars. Then there were the prints: turtles and dragonflies, fish and geckos, butterflies and fairies and even skulls. Some looked like textiles from the '20s or '30s—something you might expect to find draped over a great-grandmother's hallway table: flowers and feathers and fleur-de-lis.

The forest of color was a dazzling treat for the eyes, and Scott found himself wishing he had a camera; if he could capture this it would make for a stunning photograph.

He stopped at several, fingering the fabric and admiring the images. One was mostly black but depicted a rich multicolored Chinese dragon. "Wow," he said. "This one's *gorgeous*."

"Yeah," Jockster said. "Beautiful. Do you like dragons, then?"

Scott shrugged. "Not particularly. But I like *this* one." It was cool. What could he say? "What about you? Do you like it?"

"Well, yes. But not as a sarong."

Scott laughed. "Excuse me?"

"A pattern like this one? I think it's best as a tablecloth or a tapestry. Maybe to hang over a window. But when you wear something like this, you can't tell what the picture *is*. The image just becomes a jumble of color. Not that there's anything *wrong* with that."

Scott started. *Wear?* No. He *wasn't* going to wear a dress! He'd told Wyatt that. Put his foot down, even.

They strolled a little further down and Scott found himself stopping again. A sarong with huge peacock feathers had caught his attention. The print was nice—not like something stamped on it on some assembly line, but more like it had been painted by hand. The blues and purples and greens were so luxuriant. He reached out, pulled it close.

"People will see your cock if you wear that one," Jockster said.

"Huh?" Scott looked at him.

"See?" Jockster ran a hand under the fabric and pulled it up in front of their faces. "This one is *just* a little sheer. You can kind of see my hand if you really look. With you being so shy about those pretty privates of yours…. Well, if the sunlight hits right, they won't be so private if you wear this one."

Wear? Scott laughed again. "*I'm* not wearing one of these things. And I'm certainly not showing my junk."

"Stop that," Jockster snapped.

Scott jerked. *What?* "W— Stop what?"

"Stop calling your cock 'junk.'"

"It's just an expression," Scott said.

"One I don't care for. Don't *ever* call it 'junk.' It's not *junk.*"

Scott looked at Jockster, totally surprised. Astonished even. There was passion blazing on Jockster's face. He *meant* this. "I— Okay."

"Promise me." The serious look still possessed Jockster's face.

Gosh. Then, anything to get Jockster to smile again: "I promise."

It worked. The smile was back. "It would turn me on to see you wearing it though. A peek at your pretty dick."

Pretty? Scott blushed. "I—I'm not wearing a sarong." Wyatt would never let him hear the end of it.

"Why not? You'd look damned hot in one." Jockster nodded and gave him a naughty little grin, eyes sparkling. "Slim as you are? I mean—*woof!*"

Woof? Me? Scott blushed all the more.

A barking startled them, and they turned to see two men approaching, a dog running ahead of them. It looked like Bean's dog. One of them was the guy with the hairy chest Scott had seen hanging the sarongs when he and Wyatt arrived the day before. The other looked similar, but was thinner, younger, and had a full beard instead of just a goatee. "May I help you?" he said. He had very blue eyes. *Very* blue.

Scott shook his head. "Nah. Just looking."

"If you want to try one on," he said, "we've got a mirror." He pointed and sure enough, there was a full-length mirror leaning against the cabin. His friend—Gentle Ben?—waved and climbed the steps and went inside. The dog ran up after him and seemed surprised when she wasn't invited in. She flopped down with a huff on the top step and watched them.

"Isn't that Bean's dog?" Scott asked.

Blue-eyes nodded. "She seems to have made us her godparents."

"What do you think about this one?" Jockster asked and pointed to one that was tie-dyed bright yellow and orange and red.

"No!" Scott rolled his eyes. "I can*not* wear something like that. I might as well wear a fucking dress."

"It's not a dress," Jockster protested. "And you *would* look hot in it. Sexy."

Sexy? Scott looked at the sarong again.

"You know how much you liked being naked today?" Jockster asked him.

Scott turned to him, blushed, and let out a long sigh. It was true. Crazy. Insane! But he had. Soon after he'd lain back in the grass with Jockster, several guys had joined them. Scott was pretty sure they'd checked him out, but it wasn't obvious. And fuck, hadn't he checked them out? They'd played cards and had a good time. Soon he'd virtually forgotten he was naked. Except for the fact that it felt so good. The sun and the breeze coming off the lake on his bare skin. Scott would never have imagined such a thing happening to him.

"Yeah," he admitted. "But I can't just run around like that. Naked. Like Rat Bastard. I-I just can't."

"Which is why you need something like this. It's the next best thing to being naked."

Was it? He looked at Jockster. The expression on the man's face. "You *really* think I'd look good in something like this?"

Blue-eyes stepped up. "I think you'd look good in the green," he said and pointed to another of the tie-dyed swatches of fabric. This one, though, rather than looking like something that had somehow escaped from the sixties, was more subtle. Two shades of deep green, similar, but different enough that they complimented each other. Like moss in a forest matched with the color of the deep sea.

"I-I wouldn't even know how to wear it," Scott stammered.

"It's easy. I can show you." He unclipped a few clothespins and took the sarong down, then hesitated a moment. Scott wasn't sure why.

"You want to take those off?" Jockster asked, pointing to Scott's trunks.

Naked? "Right here?" *Out in the open?* Scott looked around him to see if there was anyone around.

Jockster nodded.

Fuck. He glanced at the guy holding the sarong.

"Don't worry about it," Blue-Eyes said. "Here." He stepped forward and started to wrap the big piece of fabric around Scott's waist.

"Wait," Scott said. Then summoning up his courage, he untied the string in his bathing suit and let it slip down his (*skinny!*) hips and to the ground.

Blue-eyes didn't blink. He just stepped in once more, whipped the sarong around Scott, and then tied it by two corners with a double knot. Then he stepped back and surveyed his handiwork.

For some reason Scott felt as if his heart might stop.

The man smiled. "It looks good. What do you think, Jockster?"

Scott turned to Jockster, feeling embarrassed. Then his breath caught when he saw the way Jockster was looking at him.

"You look *fucking... beautiful.*"

"I-I do?" Scott looked down at himself.

"Decide for yourself," said the salesman. He waved over to the mirror.

With great trepidation Scott stepped over to the mirror. What he saw startled him.

The man who looked back at him wasn't Scott.

Not *really*.

It were as if someone else was looking back at him. What Scott saw was a young man, wider at the shoulder than he'd ever noticed, narrow at the hips, looking impossibly tall, and draped in rich, lush green. The fabric rested at his hips, knotted on one side, and draped gracefully to his feet. There was a definite bulge in the front, making him look much bigger than he considered himself to be, and as he turned, he couldn't help but be caught up in the magic of how the material moved. The leg revealed at the side looked so long, and the peek it gave of his buttock was startlingly erotic. And his eyes…. They seemed to almost glow.

"Looks so good with your eyes," Jockster said with a sigh. "Gods…."

Scott's heart skipped a beat. He could feel it. He almost wanted to cry. He turned to Jockster.

"Let me buy it for you," Jockster said.

"I…. I…." Scott gulped. Looked at his reflection again. Tried to imagine walking around in public this way. "I-I don't know."

"Wear it for me?"

Jockster was looking at him in a way that made Scott's already skipping heart start to race. He couldn't quite decide what the look meant. But…. But *wow*.

Scott looked in the mirror once more and saw… why, it didn't look like a dress really, now did it? It *was* kind of sexy. Like… well, he couldn't quite put a finger on it. "Wyatt will tease the fuck out of me," he said, knowing it was true. *I will* never *hear the end of it*.

"Who?"

"*Wyatt*." He saw the look of confusion on Jockster's face, then realized why. "Little Bear," he said.

Jockster shrugged. "Let him. Who gives a shit?"

Scott laughed and Jockster joined in. Up on the porch, the little dog gave a bark as if she agreed.

Well, hell. Who *did* give a shit?

"Okay," Scott said and with a sigh felt… something let go inside.

WHEN THEY reached the top of the plateau, Jockster led them away from the direction Scott thought they'd be going—away from the pavilion and the camper's circle beyond. They soon arrived at a row of sheds and large metal shipping containers like the kind you saw on a train. They went to one of them, and Jockster began to open a combination lock.

"You know it?"

"Sure. They let me keep a box of my favorite stuff here. I don't use it any other time of year, being a gypsy like I am. I don't really have another place to keep it. Not that's convenient, that is."

Jockster opened the lock with a snap and pushed the creaking door outward with a metallic clang. They went in—and *fuck*, it was *stifling* hot inside. Jockster found what he was looking for quickly enough—a tub about three feet by two—and then he locked the door back again.

"Take a side," Jockster said, and they carried the tub back toward where most people had been setting up their camps. A lot more people had arrived since last night, and things were looking quite festive. There were tents of every color, another pop-up camper, a tepee of all things, plus several banners and a few flags—rainbow, bear, and even the blue and black of the leather community.

Right before they got to the big wide-open circular area, Jockster said, "This way," and they cut into the woods to their right. There was a doorway of sorts cut into the trees and an unlit tiki torch. "So you can find me at night," Jockster said with a wink as they passed it. A short path took them down into the cool shadows to a small camp. There was a little dome tent, a few chairs, a fire pit, a cooler, and a hammock.

"Here we go," Jockster said. "Let's set it down right here."

They put the tub down between the chairs, and Jockster sat down in one of them. "Sit?" he asked.

"Sure." Scott did so just as Jockster opened the tub and began to go through it. He brought out a fabric bag—another "hippie" bag—unzipped it, and started looking through whatever was inside. Then—"Ah ha! Here it is. I was worried there for a second."

He got to his feet and held out a big necklace of dangling green glass and gold metal. "Here."

Scott was surprised when Jockster went down on one knee and fastened it around his neck. *What the…?*

Jockster leaned back and his eyes went wide. "Oh, Scott. Stand up."

Scott shrugged and did as bid, and as soon as he did, Jockster gasped and let out a "Ye gods. *Fuck. Me.*"

"W-what," Scott asked, reaching up and touching the necklace tentatively.

"You looked like something that stepped right out of a fairy tale. An elf. A… *greenman.* Or from that movie *Pompeii.* Or *The 300.*"

"M-me?" *Get out of here!* But then it clicked. When he'd looked in the mirror. He'd been trying to put his finger on something. Now he knew. When he'd looked at his reflection, he'd been reminded of a movie with Brad Pitt and that stone cold fox Eric Bana. *Troy?* Yes.

Scott blushed. "No." *I don't look like that.*

But then Scott noticed a shifting and stretching in Jockster's jock.

Jockster growled. "I want to eat you up."

Scott felt his cock begin to stir and he knew that in a second his prediction of not being able to hide an erection in a sarong was going to become truth. "That can be arranged," Scott managed.

Before he knew it, Jockster was kissing him.

Scott thought for one instant he would die. Or cum. Or both. He could feel his cock stretching out to its full length, could feel the growing hardness of the jockstrap pressed up against him.

Sex. We're going to have sex, he thought as he opened his mouth to let Jockster's tongue enter. Oh, what a kiss!

And then—

"Hey guys!" came a happy and familiar voice,

Scott and Jockster jumped apart, and there, coming down the path, were Knottie and Wyatt.

"Ooops," said Knottie, staring down at the rise in the front of Scott's sarong. He gave Scott a wink. "*Sweet.*"

Scott blushed furiously and covered himself. It wasn't necessarily easy.

"Gosh," said Wyatt. "I mean—*gosh!*"

"Stop it!" cried Scott, sure the Earth was going to open up and swallow him whole at any second.

"Oh, not that," said Wyatt. "Except… well…. *Gosh*—I had no *idea!*"

"*Oh fuck!*" Scott felt his face blaze all the more.

"But damn, Scott. You look fucking *awesome!* I thought you said you'd never wear a sarong—"

"I made him," Jockster said, jumping in.

You didn't, thought Scott.

"I am *so* glad you did." Wyatt nodded enthusiastically. "He wouldn't listen to me. Said he wasn't going to wear a 'fucking dress.' But, fuck, Scott! You look so damned cool! Like something out of *Lord of the Rings*."

Really? "I don't look stupid?"

"Nope," said Wyatt. He walked around Scott. "Makes your ass look smokin' too!"

Scott felt the blush coming on again. Being told he was "smokin'" by Wyatt was not something he was ready for. It really was embarrassing.

"It sure does," said Jockster. "Makes a big pushy bottom like me want to take a walk on the wild side."

"Ah…." Knottie cleared his throat. "Anyone want to get high?"

CHAPTER TWENTY-THREE

CEDAR DECIDED it was a good time to take Scott on a tour of the Camper's Circle. It was Little Bear who had actually given him the idea.

"We're having a salon tonight," Little Bear had said, suddenly jumping up in the middle of their passing of the doobie. "I need to mix cocktails. Otherwise it'll be just beers if I leave Big Sir in charge."

The sun was just setting, and Cedar knew it would get dark fast when it dipped beneath the tree line, so he made sure Scott had his flashlight. He would have to help him put together a little bag to carry the essentials for camp life: his flashlight, sun block, sunglasses, mosquito repellant, some water, and a few other things. Be prepared, as the Boy Scouts liked to say.

He was getting a kick out of watching the way Scott was walking. Admit it or not, Scott liked the sarong. He was playing with it, pinching a bit of the fabric at his waist and letting it swirl around his ankles. And damn, the necklace did complete the outfit. Scott looked wonderful. It was all Cedar could do not to take him back to his tent at that very moment.

But no. Not yet.

Scott needed Festival more than fucking. Not that Cedar planned on Scott missing out on the fucking. Hell no!

They started at the top of the steps. He saw Punkin' wasn't at his tent, or he'd be lounged back in his little screened-in porch area. Music was playing, though…. Maybe he'd gotten lucky?

The next camp that was open for business was Little Bear's place, and he had quite a few people already. That was good. Little Bear could be fun. Now he just had to avoid Big Sir's hands. Cedar didn't mind being touched, but Sir had been known to cross the line.

Oh cool, he thought, spotting one of the guests. It was Donald. A perfect man for Scott to meet.

The camp was a great setup, with a huge screened sun shelter that allowed plenty of room for visitors and would keep mosquitoes at bay. A big Persian-style rug was spread out on the ground and Wyatt was making something in a large jug cooler. There were strings of party lights hung everywhere, most notably around the pop-up camper and the screened-in sunshade. Somehow the hosts had found bear lights, and how perfect was that? There were lots of hearts as well in red, pink, and white. Surely Valentine's Day lights, but they were perfect for Festival. Love.

Little Bear squealed when they arrived and begged Scott to come help him. "After all, we don't have Asher—bartender *par excellence*—to give his opinion."

"So you'll have to make do with me?" Scott asked.

"Yup! I'll have to deal with you. *Somehow* I'll deal with second best. Besides, you'll make a hot waitress in that outfit."

To Scott's credit, he didn't make any nasty comments. It looked to Cedar like Festival was already doing the man some good. It wasn't the first time Cedar had seen such a thing. As a matter of fact, he'd been told he'd been the same way.

Made sense. He'd come here the first time just six months after....

"Not bad," Scott was saying. "Not bad at all. This must be the biggest batch of mojitos I've ever seen, though. I mean, *damn*."

"Well, I had to serve more than four tonight."

"You've even got mint in here?"

"I got it from Hesperides Garden," Wyatt said and pointed. Of course it was getting a little dark to see anything. Cedar made a mental note to take Scott to see it in the morning.

"Hey, guys," Cedar said, walking over to the seated men. Most wore sarongs, but one was sprawled comfortably back in a chiffon ball gown. Comfortably? He must have been roasting!

"Hey, Jockster," came a chorus of replies.

"I don't know if you all know Scott," he said as Scott was passing drinks around. "But this is his first Festival." Of course that brought welcomes and even a few hugs. Scott looked a little flustered, but that was completely replaced by pleasure the minute people began to compliment him on his attire.

"I-I just got this today," he said, swirling the sarong about him. "Jockster got it for me. And loaned me the necklace."

"Doesn't he look *fab*-ulous!" cried Little Bear. "I could just cry. My Cinderella transformed. I am *so* proud."

"*Stop it*," said Scott.

"Well I would never guess you'd never been to a Festival," said Bobcat, who was nude—as usual—his sarong tied on his head instead of around his waist. "You are a true faerie!"

Cedar looked to see how Scott would react to the comment and saw him beam and blush at the same time.

Gods, Cedar wanted him.

Relax. You have all night. All week!

All week? Now that was a funny thought.

Cedar introduced Scott all around. Besides Big Sir and Little Bear (who Scott knew already), Donald, and Bobcat, along with the kid from the beach with the bleached white hair (whose name turned out to be Blue), The Little Bearded Girl from St. Louis was in attendance as well—sitting there looking like a young version of an Indian swami surrounded by his faithful followers. A small gray poodle was sleeping in his lap.

"Would you care to try this?" asked the guy in the ball gown. "I've got a lovely cucumber-infused vodka."

"Scott?" Cedar asked.

"Maybe in a bit." He held up a drink. "I'll be having one of Wy... *Little Bear's* mojitos."

"Fuck," said Cedar with a shrug. "I'll try one."

He took one of the few two chairs together, sat in one and swung around sideways and plopped his feet in the adjoining one, saving it. He wanted Scott next to him.

"We were just talking about the origins of the Radical Faerie," said Bobcat.

White-haired-kid nodded enthusiastically. "I've been learning all kinds of cool shit!"

"Watch that one," Scott whispered into Cedar's ear as he handed him a plastic cup. "He can talk the leg off a chair."

"I was just saying," said Donald, "that it amazes me how only Harry Hay is given credit for the creation of the Radical Faeries. He did come up with the name, but there were already strong communities forming under a variety of other designations: Iowa, Arkansas, Wisconsin, Illinois, Washington, et cetera. The Queer Spirit movements were not created by just one person or small group. They appeared spontaneously around the world at about the same time. It was a remarkable set of synchronicities! I strongly suspect that if not so many of us had died during the AIDS crisis, this bit of history would not have been so easily forgotten." He let out a long sigh.

"Who's Harry Hanes?" Scott asked.

"Hay, my dear," Donald said.

"He was an early gay rights activist," said Wyatt. "One of the very first. He did so much for gay people. Who knows where we would be today without him? He was gay and open about it when *being* open about it got you thrown into jail."

"He formed the Mattachine Society, the first continuous gay rights organization in the country," said Bobcat. "I met him once. He was amazing."

"He wasn't the first gay activist though," said the Little Bearded Girl in a soft, quiet voice that made everyone have to lean in to hear him. "Harry Hay is so frequently referred to as the founder of the modern gay rights movement, but I think Karl Heinrich Ulrichs may be more qualified to be called its founder."

"Excellent thought," said Donald.

"He may be the first person in the modern era to openly 'come out' and publicly speak against the judicial persecution of gay people," Little Bearded Girl continued. "And he did it in the *eighteen* sixties and not the *nineteen* fifties."

"Really?" asked Scott. "I've never heard of him."

"Of course not. People try and hide our history," said Donald.

"There are some people who ridicule his 'woman's soul born into a man's body' theory on homosexuality," Little Bearded Girl continued. "But he was *way* before his time in insisting we're 'born this way.' Everyone else in his time—even other gay thinkers—thought men were gay because of some sort of negative psychological cause."

"That's what my mama says," Blue cried.

"Watch out," said Scott, leaning in to Cedar. "No one else will be able to talk now."

"She says I'm gay because she was too strong and my dad was too weak and didn't give me a manly enough role model and—"

"I don't think it really matters, do you?" Bobcat cut in. "We are what we are, and I for one am thankful that I'm queer."

"There's that word again," said Scott, joining them now he was done helping Little Bear pass out cocktails. "'Queer.' I don't get it. I don't *like* it."

Cedar moved his feet out of the second chair and patted the arm. Scott sat down and then surprised him by taking his feet back in his lap and beginning to massage them. Cedar figured Scott would be way too germophobic to massage dirty feet. Point for Scott. No. Two points. What he was doing felt incredible. And to give him credit, he had massaged Cedar's feet at the beach too.

"Nonsense," said Bobcat. "'Queer' is a *wonderful* word. A beautiful word. It says whom we are on a historical level, stretching back to the dawn of history. We have always been 'those who walk between the worlds.' Like the shamans of the Native Americans. Throughout time we were respected, admired, *needed*. Gay men were thought to exist in between the solid world beneath our feet and the ethereal realm of the gods. There were whole priesthoods that dressed as women and performed their duties as priestesses. And everyone knew."

"You mean like drag queens?" Scott asked.

There was a polite chuckling all around. "Far more than that."

"I've been trying for years to tell Scott about this stuff," Wyatt said, sitting at Big Sir's feet.

"This cocktail *is* excellent, Little Bear," said Bobcat. "Refreshing."

"Well, drink up because there's tons more! Faerie goodness for all!"

"I don't get this whole faerie thing either," Scott said. "'Faerie names' and dressing up in women's hats and negligees and all that shit." He glanced down at his sarong, touched the necklace. Blushed.

"I think you do," said Donald. "Or you would if you let yourself. You look beautiful tonight. Pretty. Pretty and witty and gay. Enjoy being pretty."

Scott blushed even darker, and the fact that was noticeable was saying something now the sun *had* officially set. "But... I mean.... Why? Why the dresses? The faerie wings?"

"Harry didn't like the fact that we were being assimilated," Bobcat explained.

"Resistance is futile?" Scott said.

"Well...," said Cedar, joining in. *Do I do this?* Cedar wondered. *Yes.* "Harry was very upset with what he saw happening to the gay community. He said we were conforming to society so we would be accepted. He said we were playing society's games and denying who were are."

"Yes," said Bobcat. "He considered gays to be a cultural minority. That we had pulled an ugly green frog skin of heterosexual conformity upon us, and that's how we survived with a full set of teeth. The dresses? That was a symbol for rejecting conventionality. He said if we carry the skin of conformity over ourselves, then we're suppressing the beautiful prince or princess within us. That may be massacring what he said, but I think it's close. He was wary of us throwing away our unique attributes to curry favor with heterosexual society in order to gain their acceptance."

"Yes!" cried Blue and leapt to his feet. "Yes!" He blushed and sat back down. "It's just what I have always felt, is all."

"He didn't like the way he saw the gay community marginalizing drag queens and leather men," Wyatt added. "After all, it was dykes and queens that started the Stonewall riot that brought gay into the living rooms of America. Gave us something to rally 'round."

"I—I...," sputtered Scott. He took a breath. "I guess I can't deny that. But come on! Little Bearded Girl?" He held up a hand. "Sorry, no offense."

"None taken," said that very same Bearded Girl.

"And Lula Belle? Magnolia *Thunderpussy*? I would *never* be able to call myself something like that...."

"You said you wanted a faerie name last night," Cedar reminded him.

"I did? I don't remember." Then Scott smiled a little lopsided grin that made him look adorable and Cedar found once again he wanted to fuck Scott right then and there. And what would *that* do to Scott's sensibilities?

"You don't? You were getting pretty insistent."

"I was 'tripping balls.'"

Cedar couldn't help but laugh.

"We'll be having a Queer God Ritual sometime this week," said Donald and reached out and patted Scott's knee. "Maybe you'll join us? Just to see what it's all about?"

"Sometimes participation shows you far more than listening to a bunch of old queens ever could," Bobcat said.

"Umm.... I'll think about it," said Scott. He turned to Cedar and, while the conversation continued, leaned in again. "Do you believe in this stuff?" he asked quietly.

"What stuff?" Cedar replied.

"Queer gods?"

Cedar sat back. Thought about it. How to explain…? Then: "Well, yes. I do. If man can say God is male… *or* female… why can't God also be gay?"

Scott shook his head. "I don't believe in God," he said.

"You don't?" said Bobcat.

"Oh no," said Big Sir, getting to his feet and crossing over to a large cooler. "Now he's going to start his 'there is no God' lecture. Anyone want a beer?"

"No, I *don't* believe in God," Scott said with pride in his voice. "Religion is the opiate of the masses. Or something like that."

"'Religion is the opiate of the people,'" said Donald. "Karl Marx."

"Yeah," said Scott. "That. I don't believe in gods—queer, straight, or any other kind. Man created God in his own image to try and explain why volcanoes explode and the sun goes across the sky. God doesn't exist anymore than Santa Claus or the Tooth Fairy. It's time we grew up and figured that out. We have science now. We don't need gods anymore."

There was a pause.

"Fuck," he said. "I did it again, didn't I?"

"What, my dear?" asked Donald.

"Made an asshole of myself. I just can't help it. The whole religion thing. My parents haven't spoken to me in years. Ever since I came out to them. They kicked me out of their lives. Is that what 'Christ' would do? I thought he fucking hung out with tax collectors and prostitutes."

"He did." Bobcat leaned forward and rested his elbow on his knee and his chin in his upraised palm.

"Wait," said Scott. "*You* believe in Jesus?"

"I do."

"But… I just assumed…." Scott waved at the world around him. "Witchy-Woo-Woo Camp and all that…."

"You're here and you're not 'witchy-woo-woo,'" Bobcat said.

"Yeah. But I don't call myself a faerie and have a name like Lula Belle or Magnolia Thunderpussy."

Bobcat gave a little shrug. "I consider myself, amongst other things, a believer in the White Christ, although I would not call myself Christian. You have to understand, though, your parents? They aren't a representation of *all* Christians."

Scott gave a scoffing laugh. "Wake up and smell the coffee." He took another sip of his drink. "Or the mojitos in this case. Have you seen the shit that's going on? Senates passing bills to allow people to discriminate against gay people on religious grounds?"

"Yes. And I've seen people like Governor Jan Brewer, a *Republican* by the way, veto the bill from Arizona. Missouri Senator Wallingford's bill went nowhere."

"What about that lobbyist who was trying to keep gays from playing in the NLF?" Scott asked. "Or the NFL? Football. Whatever the hell it is. I don't watch sports."

"He was laughed at," said Bobcat. "You're talking about Jack Burkman. Numerous groups took a stand and announced publicly that they no longer support him. There are hateful and hate-filled people in the world who claim to be Christian. But remember it's the squeaky wheel that gets the attention. The 'God hates fags' psychos are the ones that make the news, but there are thousands of churches in thousands of towns and cities with millions of Christians who don't hate gays or believe they're going to burn in a lake of fire."

Cedar held his breath.

"Scott. I'm sorry your parents did what they did," Bobcat continued. "Mine didn't, though. And I came out over forty years ago in a town of 400 people. My parents were New Testament all the way. They believed God became human and did just what you said. Hung out with prostitutes, lawyers, and lepers."

Scott bit his lip. "I—I just can't believe in some 'all-powerful God' who watches over mankind and throws lightning bolts and temper tantrums when we don't perform the way he wants us to. If there *was* a God, he *made* me gay. Why would someone who keeps the planets circling the sun give a shit where I stick my dick?"

"No pun intended?" asked Donald.

They all burst into laughter.

"What God *indeed*," Donald said.

CHAPTER TWENTY-FOUR

"So JOCKSTER," Scott said quietly as they crossed the plateau. Jockster had someone named Domi Dearest (of all things) he wanted Scott to meet. But he couldn't let go of the thoughts churning in his head. He needed to know.

"Yes?"

"So you really believe all that stuff?" *Please say no.* It hurt him to think such a marvelous guy believed in such crazy stuff.

How do you know he's marvelous? You've known him two days. Not even that. He got you fucked up on mushrooms!

"Yes," Jockster said.

Shit, Scott cursed.

"Yes, I believe there was a Harry Hay."

"That's not what I meant," Scott snapped.

"Yeah. I know what you meant." Jockster came to a stop, and Scott almost ran right into him.

Scott could hear laughter up ahead and he wanted be a part of it. Meet this "Domi Dearest" that Jockster was so enthusiastic about. But he needed something else too. The trouble was, he wasn't sure just what. The truth was his head was awhirl with everything he'd heard over mojitos, and he didn't know what to think. Some of it....

He heard rather than saw Jockster take a deep breath. The sliver of a moon hadn't risen yet, and it was damned dark.

"I believe in a lot of it. What part do you mean specifically, Scott?"

Hell! What part didn't he mean? But he'd skip the faerie stuff. That had gotten interesting and bore thought. And hell—surprise, surprise—it felt kind of cool wearing a "dress." Not that he was planning on admitting it. Yet.

But the queer god stuff? Had Jockster been serious about that? "You really believe all that god stuff?" *Please say no!*

Jockster sighed. "I believe there's *something*, Scott. I've *felt* it. *Experienced it....*"

Piss! thought Scott. *Another deluded—*

"I *don't* believe in... what did you say? Some god who watches over mankind and throws temper tantrums and lightning bolts?"

"So a 'queer god'?" Scott asked incredulously. "That's what you believe? Or that stuff Wyatt believes in? A Lord and Lady?"

Cedar shrugged. "Why not?"

"Because it's *ridiculous!*" Scott wept. "If there *was* a 'God,' how could he sit up there and let us wage war on each other? What kind of God would allow babies to be born with AIDS? If God wants parents to kick their kids out of their lives, then I want fucking *nothing* to do with him!"

"It's in the still small voice," Cedar said.

"What the fuck?" Scott asked.

Cedar sighed again. "I *don't* think that God 'allows' anything like that to happen," Cedar said. "*We* allow it to happen. *We* wage war. *We* hurt each other. We kill. Rape. Steal. Lie. Cheat. *We* do those things."

"But why does He allow us to do that kind of shit?"

"Who?"

"*God!*"

"Are you cursing at me or are you asking me why God allows us to do the shit we do?"

"Both." Scott began to pace. "Fuck. I'm going to do it again. Act like an asshole! I don't know *how* I have *any* friends at all!"

"Maybe we should talk about this later?" Cedar offered.

Scott stopped. "No. Please. Tell me."

Cedar took a deep breath. "Let's sit down."

He led Scott over to one of the plateau's big fire pits. There was no bonfire tonight, but the benches were there and that's where they sat. Scott wished he could see Jockster's face better, and shining the flashlight in his face would be rude. But he wanted to see Jockster's expression.

"I think 'God' is something that is pretty much beyond comprehension," Jockster said finally. "Indescribable. That's why I never try. I think It—"

"'It'?" Scott asked. *It?*

"Well, surely God is not a 'he.' Or a 'she' for that matter. God doesn't have a penis, let alone a long white flowing beard. Or a vagina. And since there is no gender-neutral word in English, I use the word 'It.' And I *do* believe that whatever 'It' is, It created the Universe…."

"All that made the world in six days shit?" Scott scoffed. He rolled his eyes.

"Nah, nothing like that," Jockster said. "Maybe the 'Let there be light,' but it would have taken billions of years. Not six days. And It wouldn't have needed to rest afterward either. More like a 'Let there be a Big Bang'!"

"And there was a Big Bang?" Scott asked and gave a laugh. There were sudden images of Sheldon Cooper in his head.

Oh, fuck! Sheldon is an asshole! I'm not being Sheldon, am I?

Cedar nodded. "And then the Universe came into being."

"Goddammit!" Scott cursed.

"Scott…." Jockster reached out and touched Scott's hand. "Is it just the thing with your parents?"

"What thing?" he snapped.

"Your anger with God."

"What anger!" he snapped. "I'm not 'angry' with God."

"Aren't you?"

"How can I be mad at something I don't believe in?"

There was a long pause. Scott sat there, and the waiting was making him anxious. What was this fucking about? Shit! If only he hadn't had those hits of Knottie's pot. He was still feeling foggy. And Wyatt's mojitos. They'd been strong. *Shit. Shit piss fuck.*

"What did he do?"

"He who?" Scott all but screamed. He glanced quickly to his left—toward the camp of Domi Dearest. No. The laughter didn't stop. His outburst hadn't been heard. In fact, there was one laugh that rolled out in the most delightful way. It made him want to be there with them, and not here discussing God.

You started it. You asked Jockster if he believed.

I wanted him to say no.

Well, as the Rolling Stones used to say, "You can't always get what you want."

"God," Jockster suddenly said. "Did you not get something you wanted? A Teenage Mutant Ninja Turtle action figure for Christmas? A passing grade on some test in school? Some boy you liked? Did he not like you back? Maybe didn't want to be your friend anymore when you told him you liked boys? Maybe someone died?"

"Yes," Scott cried. "All those things!" He stifled a sob that had come up out of the dark and crushed it back. He would not cry! "I prayed. I prayed lots of times! I prayed even when I didn't believe in it anymore, and believe me, I figured out a long time ago it didn't work."

"Then why bother?"

Scott laughed. "Because the one thing I do agree with Christians on is that when a man feels on the brink of the abyss, even an atheist prays. It's how you deal with the hopelessness of it all."

"The hopelessness of 'what all'?" Jockster asked him.

"The... the...." He motioned to the sky, to the ground, to everything around him. "That my cat Garfield died! That my Aunt Eunice died of fucking cancer. That Sloan can't love me like I love him. That men use my ass and throw me aside. *Laugh* at me when I tell them I love them. That a boy I liked in high school would let me suck him off, but when I wanted a kiss, he punched me so hard I thought I was going to lose a tooth." Scott began to shake, and it was getting harder and harder not to cry. But if he did, he might never stop. He clenched his teeth. *Willed* the tears away. "When my parents found out what happened, they near lost their minds. Took me to church. Told the pastor. *Humiliated* me. Prayed over me and told me I was an abomination and they probably *would* have kicked me out then, but Pastor Bob told them I could repent and be saved and that's what I had to do! Repent of something I didn't even believe was wrong. And what did God do? God didn't do shit! So that's what you want me to believe in, Jockster?"

"Oh, Scott. Don't you see?" Jockster threw one leg over the other side of the bench and then pulled himself closer to Scott. "Right there is the problem! You're still believing in *their* God."

"They say that's the *only* God."

"It's not the God I believe in," Jockster said. "I believe in a God that is so much bigger than that. Your parents are trying to make God finite, and God is so much more than that. But none of us can understand God! You can't understand the infinite with a finite mind. How can we understand something that could think up the entire universe and then set it into motion?"

Scott shrugged. "I don't even know what the fuck you're trying to say!"

"Every day people are discovering new things about our planet, never mind the universe. A new bug, a new life form, new ideas on how the Earth came into existence. Or how old it is. Do you know there are over 10,000 species of birds alone? Ten *thousand!* I can't even conceive of that, let alone even try to understand what God is! There's something like a million kinds of insects! A *million!* And that's just *Earth.* There are trillions and trillions of planets, all with their own uniqueness. How many of those planets have some kind of life living on them? And if they have as much variety as we do here? Think of what it would take to create all that? To *think* it up? And this 'Thinker.' It would *have* to be immortal. And while I haven't weighed in on the omnipotent part, it *would* have to be omnipresent. So how—how could It be *anything* we could possibly understand?"

Scott opened his mouth to answer… and found he couldn't. What…? What was Jockster saying? Why… why….

"And you're right, Scott! It certainly *wouldn't* care *where* you stick your dick. It certainly wouldn't get angry about it. Because It *would* have made you gay. So why punish you for it? God wouldn't make us and then set up an obstacle course for us to run through to prove we're worthy. It *wouldn't* destroy cities or cause a flood or send us to hell if we didn't believe one certain particular way. That is *religion* speaking. Not spirituality. Man has made up rules about God. Fear-based rules. Because people are afraid. They're afraid of what comes next. They're afraid of damnation. They're afraid of dying."

"Yes!" said Scott. "So they made up religions. And they fight about who's right. Why, the pure fucking audacity that my parents think *their* religion is right and the Jews and the Muslims and the Hindus and the Buddhists are all wrong. Fuck! They think the Catholics are all going to hell, and we're not even talking about Jehovah's Witnesses or Mormons."

And suddenly he saw Peni in his mind. That beautiful, sexy man trapped in religion as well.

"But Scott! Bobcat was right. All Christians aren't like that. Just like gays aren't all the same. The media shows the extremes, never the norm. If there's a gay pride parade, they don't show the PFLAG float or the bowling teams or the Metropolitan Community Church or the Big Gay Band! They show the Man/Boy Love Association. They show the porn-star float. Then everyone watching TV thinks that's all we are. And it isn't. And those Christians trying to stop gay marriage or pass bills allowing people to discriminate against us? That's *not* all there is. More and more people are waking up. More and more people are starting to see us, and *God*, in a whole different way."

Scott began to tremble and a tear—*fucking damn that tear!*—slipped down his face. *Fuck! I'm going to cry. I don't want to cry.* "W-what are you saying? I'm confused…. Are you talking about being gay or being God?"

"Yes! Yes-yes-yes! I'm talking about it all. Because if God made the Universe out of Itself, then that's what *we're* made of! We're made of God. And God is perfect and that makes us perfect just the way we are—even with all our mistakes."

Scott shook his head. "I… I…." What was this man saying? It sounded crazy. "I don't understand…."

"Who fucking does?" Jockster asked. "We can't. We can't understand because we only see things from a limited viewpoint. We're *not* God…."

"But *you* just said we are!"

Jockster burst into laughter. "Yes. You're right. You caught me there." He jumped up onto the bench. Did a leap and a twirl. Jumped to the ground and spun around again. "Because I don't get it, Scott! It's a mystery. A great big huge wondrous mystery! And I love it! I love that I *don't* know and I might never, ever know!" He stopped twirling and spun back down onto the bench in front of Scott. Pulled him close so suddenly Scott's sarong opened wide and his bare cock was crushed up against Jockster's fabric-bound one. Jockster hugged Scott to him so their chests were touching, their tummies too. Scott's heart started to race.

"This is God, Scott. Not the rhetoric and dogma that your parents believe in. *This* is God. This is what I believe in. Love."

"L-love?" Scott asked.

Then Jockster was kissing him again and fuck if he didn't almost cum on the spot. His cock reared up and pressed up against Jockster's abs. Jockster began to thrust himself against Scott, and that made Scott thrust up against Jockster, and his cock was running with precum and making that washboard-like flesh all slippery and—oh oh oh!—it was so good and—*damn!* He *was* cumming! Shooting like he couldn't remember when, shooting all over Jockster's tummy and chest and his own as well. He felt his seed splashing his neck and the world began to whirl around him in pink and purple and blue, and he was sure he was going to pass out and then they had collapsed against each other. Scott could feel his heart slamming, and damn if he couldn't feel Jockster's reverberating against his own.

They sat there, resting against each other, for the longest time, breathing hard, letting those breaths slowly, slowly, calm.

"Damn," whispered Jockster.

"Damn," said Scott.

"Not exactly how I expected our first time to go...."

"I... I thought we were talking about God." Scott said.

Jockster laughed. "I think that just proved there is a God," he said. "Somebody *had* to come up with something that awesome."

And while Scott wasn't sure he could possibly agree, he couldn't help but wonder.

Because Jockster was giving him a lot to think about.

CHAPTER TWENTY-FIVE

JOCKSTER TOOK Scott back to his tent, but sadly, it wasn't to sleep. Instead it was to get something to clean themselves up because—

"We *are* a mess, aren't we?" Jockster said, laughing. He'd lit his mini tiki torch and Scott could see Jockster's pouch was soaked, even though it was black, and of course there was the cum all over both their chests. "*You* shoot a *load*, don't you Scott? I mean… *fuck!*" He threw back his head and laughed again. "And smell us. We *smell* like cum." He looked back into Scott's eyes, deep. "Want to go to Domi's just like this? Stinking of sex? All wet and nasty?" he growled.

Scott blushed. "Oh, Jockster. I couldn't. Please don't ask."

Jockster stepped close and took Scott in his arms again, rubbed his chest, which was growing tacky instead of wet, against Scott's. It was a good thing they both had smooth chests or they would have had an even bigger mess on their hands—one a mere towel wouldn't clean up.

"It would be hot. Strolling over there and plopping down and everyone figuring out what we'd been up to."

"Jockster… please don't ask," Scott said, still blushing.

"*He* likes the idea," Jockster said, pointing down at Scott's crotch, and when Scott looked down, sure enough, his cock was starting to rise.

And the idea *was* sexy and nasty and naughty but… "I can't," he said.

Jockster laughed evilly. "Okay." He stood back and then wiggled out of his wet jock and threw it over into his hammock. Then he turned and got down on his hands and knees and climbed half into his small tent.

He wiggled his ass, and Scott's cock rose up to full erection. He couldn't help it. The torchlight was landing just exactly right, and even by the subdued illumination, Scott could see that Jockster's hole was perfect and pink. Hell! Was it winking at him?

Jockster giggled again and backed out of his tent and stood up and climbed into a clean jockstrap.

"You're mean," Scott said.

Jockster whirled around. "Anticipation, buddy. And it's not like we didn't *just* have like the best orgasms *ever*. At least *I* did!"

Scott grinned. "Me too."

Jockster spread his arms wide, then swiveled his shoulders and ambled past Scott as if he were working a runway. He turned and walked back. Then he turned to face Scott again. "What do you think of this one?"

"It" made Scott's cock even harder. It was blazing white with the words PUMP! in deep black across the front of the waistband. The Canadian brand was one of Scott's favorites, even when it was such a simple style as the one Jockster was wearing. He had no idea why. They just turned him on to no end.

"Hot as fuck," Scott gasped.

Jockster growled again. "And later you can take it off."

Oh damn. Oh damn damn damn. *Later* he was going to fuck Jockster. *He*, Scott Aberdeen, was going to get to top!

"Do we have to wait?"

Jockster both nodded and leered at him at the same time. "Anticipation," he sang from that old familiar song. "Anticipaaaaation, is making you wait!"

He turned around, bent to pick up his bag, wiggled his ass again, and then stood back up. "Come on, we're going to Domi's!"

SO JOCKSTER took Scott to Domi Dearest's camp, and thankfully, there were just enough chairs left. Domi didn't even mind when they rearranged them (well, not *too* much) so the two of them could sit side by side (their knees pressed tightly together, silently making promises to each other of things to come). There was quite a crowd, but Jockster said that was pretty normal when it came to Domi. Their host was a gracious—"As long as you don't piss him off too much," Jockster whispered in Scott's ear and then giggled—and handsome man in his early fifties, and his camp was apparently the happenin' place to be. Even more than Wyatt's. There were a lot of people there—Dolce and Gabbana, along with Hound Dog and Bean (as well as Sarah Jane and Rammstein), Focus, Lorax, Rat Bastard, a sexy man Scott had yet to meet, and Gentle Ben and the blue-eyed man who had sold Scott his sarong. Scott wasn't too happy to see Ferret was there too, but at least he was on the opposite side of the cluster of partiers. And hopefully, he wouldn't have to worry about the man—especially now that they had had sex and Jockster had said they'd be having more before the night was over.

Greg, an amateur but ingenious bartender (he was pretty hot too—damn but there were a lot of hot men at a faerie festival!) was quite busy creating something called Aviation cocktails.

Oh! And wasn't it nice that his name was Greg? Scott cherished finding Festival attendees with normal names.

"You said you wanted a faerie name last night."

Isn't that what Jockster had said?

"What's an Aviation cocktail?" Scott asked, thinking about the weed and the mojitos he'd already had—followed quickly by the thought, *So? You're not driving, live a little!*

"It was really popular in the 1910s," Greg explained, handing over a clear plastic cup filled with a bluish mixture. At least it looked blue. It was hard to tell with the light from the chandelier (a tangled ball of multicolored round Christmas lights) hanging above. "Gin, maraschino liqueur, crème de violette, and lemon juice."

"Of course you know what *I* always say," said Domi. "*Nice* people don't drink *gin*."

"Well, nobody ever claimed I was nice," Scott said and tried the concoction. "Gosh!" He took another sip. "Wow! That's wonderful! My friend Asher would be envious. I've never tasted anything like it. I…. I don't know how to describe it."

"Floral," Greg said.

"Yes!" said Scott. "It tastes like flowers smell."

"It's the liqueur," Greg continued. "It's flavored with violets."

"Wow…," Scott said, awed. Who ever thought about a violet-flavored alcohol?

"Told you this would be fun," said Jockster.

"As fun as me fucking you?" Scott asked quietly, surprised at his own boldness.

"Hopefully not," Jockster said. "But we have lots of time for that."

It turned out the delightful laugh Scott had heard out on the plateau belonged to Domi, their host. He laughed a lot and told funny stories and was a pure delight to be around. As it happened, he liked camo. While Scott was sitting there, someone bequeathed Domi a pair of camo underwear. Apparently, Domi had a camo sarong, shoes, and a cooler, and even the dome they were sitting under came in the same pattern.

"The camo is so all those *people* I *don't* like can't find my tent," cried Domi.

Lula Belle showed up and, when asked if he wanted a cocktail, wondered if Greg could make him a Pink Lady.

"Sure," Greg said. "I think I've got some grenadine. Wait! No egg white, though…."

"Could you just jerk off in it, then?" Lula Belle replied, and there was a general chorus of laughter.

"See?" said Domi. "*Just* what I said. *Nice* girls don't drink *gin*."

"Seriously though, darlin'," Lula Belle said, "I'll take whatever y'all are having."

"Is 'y'all' a preposition?" someone asked (Scott wasn't sure who).

"No, y'all is a pronoun: second person plural nominative—and objective," said Dolce.

"Having been raised in Kansas," Gabbana added, "we just say 'you guys.' My friends in New York were particularly confused by this, as they thought it was gender specific, and the females kept feeling left out."

"It has always been my interpretation that 'y'all' is plural," Rat Bastard interjected, "but maybe that is the way it's used in Eastern North Carolina, so that is why I think of it as plural."

"Yes, plural," Lula Belle replied. "But when speaking of the larger group, such as in Circle, one then uses 'all y'all'—as in 'all y'all bitches can bite my ass.'"

"Oh, that Lula Belle!" cried Lorax. "Never can please him. He's always beggin' for something: 'Bite my ass. Play with my tits. Jiggle my nuts....'"

"Singular in the nuts!" Lula Belle cried and lifted his newest skirt to reveal that, yes, he had only one testicle.

The crowd burst into laughter and Scott just sat there stunned and wide-eyed.

"I think 'y'all' are just a bunch of *idiots!*" Domi was saying, and everyone laughed all the harder, including Domi. Apparently, he was just kidding on the idiot part, and Scott couldn't help but join in on the man's infectious laughter.

And wasn't that interesting? The hot guy whose name Scott didn't know had stepped in behind Domi and was massaging his shoulders. *Boyfriend?*

Domi patted his hand and asked for another Aviation cocktail, and Good-Looking turned to get it for him.

Hmmmmm..., thought Scott. *Very interesting!*

"Jockster," said Domi. "Any chance you'll play a song for us? You do have your guitar, don't you?"

Guitar? Song? What? Scott looked over at Jockster in surprise.

"Gods, Domi. I'm not sure...."

"Oh come on. Aurora was supposed to give us a little concert, but he wasn't feeling all that well. Personally, I think he's riding Borealis in that little ham-can trailer of theirs."

Domi's comment was followed by a general chorus of requests for Jockster to play: pleases and pretty pleases. Scott could only sit there and try not to look too stupid.

Jockster played?

"Okay," Jockster finally said. "One song. I'll be right back." He leaned over and gave Scott a little kiss. "*You* stay here. I'll just be a second."

Scott could only nod.

Play a song?

While Jockster was gone, Scott decided it would be a perfect moment to take a quick pee, so he slipped off into the darkness to relieve himself. The sarong certainly made it easier. The flow had just started when Ferret, of all people, stepped up next to him. Scott gulped. He wasn't happy about it. The slip of a moon had risen and there was just the tiniest bit of light, but it was enough to illuminate Ferret's ridiculously large penis when it sent out an arc of urine easily twice the distance of Scott's own.

Show off, thought Scott.

"You know you could loosen the leash a little, right?"

Ferret's words startled Scott. "Huh?"

"The leash? Share a little."

"Share a little of what?" Scott finished his business and self-consciously flipped the sarong closed.

"Jockster. I get that you've got him. But there's a whole fucking week, and he *did* say I could get with him tonight."

Scott turned to the man, eyes wide in surprise. "Excuse me?" *What the fuck?*

"You know Jockster gets with me every year, right?"

"No, I didn't," Scott said. *Fuck you.* "Maybe this isn't your year."

Ferret finished pissing and shook off his cock.

Could he even get that thing hard? Scott wondered. It was so big and Ferret was so skinny that surely a hard-on would cause a lack of blood to the brain and make him pass out.

"It would be if you'd back off. You *could* share."

"Why the fuck should I?" Scott asked, feeling foolishly possessive. Why should he share indeed?

"Because...." And then something strange happened. There was a little hitch in Ferret's voice. "A guy like you? So damned good-looking. You'll have no trouble getting all the sex you want. Me? All I got going for me is this!" He waved his cock at Scott. "I'm fucking *ugly*. But I fucking need held every now and then, you know?"

Scott's mouth gaped open. The words couldn't have shocked him more.

"I can see the way he's frigging looking at you. You got your hooks in him. Give me a night. One night." Scott heard a sob. Then a growl. "An hour. *Please!*" And then Ferret stomped back to Domi's salon.

Scott found his way back to the salon and fell more than sat in his chair. This was turning out to be a very unusual night. But then, hadn't things been weird since the second he'd arrived at Festival and a naked man with a huge pink hat and an even bigger cock greeted him at the front gate?

Just then, Jockster appeared from out of the darkness. He was carrying a guitar. A very lovely guitar. Jockster could play?

He gave Scott a look of what appeared to be embarrassment, sat down, struck a chord on his instrument, and began to make a few adjustments. Then he cleared his throat.... "Okay. *One* song. And I've been feeling very spiritual today, so I hope you like this." He looked over at Scott. "Tough if you don't." He winked.

"Now *that's* being spiritual," Focus said.

Jockster looked at Scott. "This is what I believe." He took a deep breath, paused, then began to play, his long fingers dancing across the strings. Scott got goose bumps at the sound.

Jockster could play?

Jockster could do more than play.

Jockster opened his mouth and began to sing in a beautiful clear voice that sent shivers up and down Scott's arms and back. He was stunned.

Jockster could sing…!

> *Lay it down, set it free.*
> *Let my heart rest and let it be.*
> *Lay it down, set it free.*
> *Lay it down on the altar of love.*
>
> *I was walking through the season of dark and lonely change.*
> *Where the world was on my shoulders,*
> *and my faith was rearranged.*
> *I knew I'd never be given more than I could bear.*
> *Spirit reassured me there was an answer to my prayer.*
>
> *If I lay it down, set it free.*
> *Let my heart rest and let it be.*
> *Lay it down, set it free.*
> *Lay it down on the altar of love….*

At first the lyrics to Jockster's song made Scott uncomfortable. Jockster wasn't saying "Jesus." He really wasn't even saying "God." But Scott couldn't help but hear echoes of a childhood of Baptist hymns. Yet… as he listened he heard the sincerity in Jockster's voice. Jockster *believed* this and Scott couldn't help but be stirred by the emotion in his words….

> *So every single moment I am left with the choice*
> *to stay in separation or listen to that Voice*
> *that beckons me to open and be grateful for every day.*
> *It simply reminds me that there can be another way.*
>
> *If I just lay it down, set it free.*
> *Let my heart rest and let it be.*
> *Lay it all down, set it all free.*
> *Lay it down on the altar of love.*

Set it free? Scott wondered. *Set it free.* Jockster's lyrics made it sound easy. *Easier said than done, Jockster.* Because it didn't feel that way. It felt like there was a wall of stone a mile thick separating him from laying down the burdens on his heart and on his mind.

> *Love is all there is,*
> *and love will lead the way...*
>
> *Lay it down, set it free.*
> *Let my heart rest and let it be.*
> *Lay it all down, set it all free.*
> *Lay it down on the altar of love.*
> *I'm gonna lay it on the altar of love...*

Jockster's voice faded away on the night breeze. There was a long silence.

Then the little group burst into applause.

Scott didn't know what to think.

But he was very surprised when he realized there were tears running down his face.

AS IT turned out, Scott got just a little too enthusiastic when it came to imbibing, though. By midnight he was slurring his words and dozing in his chair. Jockster finally decided to take Scott back to his own camp, where Scott gave him a sloppy kiss and invited him in.

"Maybe we should wait until tomorrow night."

"I don't wanna," Scott said. "I want you wight *now*."

Jockster turned on the light Scott had attached to the ceiling of the tent and helped him into bed. It was a good thing, too, because he barely made it, and the world started to spin as soon as he hit the mattress.

"Tomorrow," Jockster said.

"Then shpend the night. We can have morning shex."

Jockster jumped to his feet. "No!"

Scott looked up at him, startled. There was a blue-white glow around Jockster's head from the bright LED light.

Jockster sat back down on the edge of the mattress. "I mean, no," he said more softly.

"Did I shay shum-ting wrong?" Scott asked (or tried to ask), concerned.

Jockster shook his head, and now that he was sitting, Scott could see the strange, sad look on the man's face. "Nothing wrong. I just can't sleep with someone. Too many years sleeping alone, you know? I feel claustrophobic."

Scott pouted. Jockster couldn't sleep with him. Scott liked sleeping with a man. Holding him close. Spooning. Waking up in the morning. Not that he'd had many chances to do that.

Jockster leaned down and kissed him sweetly on the lips.

"I'll come get you in the morning." Jockster reached up for the light.

"Jockster?"

The beautiful man paused. "Yes?"

"Why didn't you tell me you could play?"

"You didn't know?"

Scott shook his head and the world wobbled. "N-no...."

Jockster gave him a beatific smile. "Good."

"Y-you really *do* believe in that God shtuff...."

"I believe in spirit, my sweet. Now good-night...."

Scott started to protest, but Jockster was already up and turning off the light. Scott's vision turned into traveling bursts of stars before his eyes, and then he heard the zipping of the tent and he tried to get up and ask Jockster to stay and then it was just easier to fall back and go to sleep.

CHAPTER TWENTY-SIX

FERRET WAS waiting for Cedar when he got back to his camp. He jumped up and smiled, proving what a lot of people didn't seem to know. Ferret—aka Wilmer something (Cedar wasn't sure he ever knew)—was not as unattractive as some people said. Yes, he was thin—very thin. Yes he had a very skinny neck, which made his Adam's apple look abnormally large. His eyes were quite big, and because of how slender he was, they appeared "buggie," much like Steve Buscemi's (but not quite Marty Feldman's). Yet all you had to do was *look* (and Cedar had done so) and it was clear that they were a stunning green, like jade and emeralds somehow worked and mixed together with malachite and green glass. Yes, he really was *very* thin, almost emaciated. But there was muscle "on them there bones," and his ass was a tiny thing ("I don't know how he doesn't fall in the toilet," said one vicious queen) but it was quite round (not nearly as flat as the vicious queen's). And there were those ears!

But most of all, Ferret was sweet.

And Cedar liked him. He really did.

Plus he was killer in bed. Those muscles knew how to drive a cock, and Cedar had been on the receiving end of Ferret's pistoning hips for several years now, and he had enjoyed every minute of it.

"I knew if I waited you'd show." Ferret said jumping to his feet.

"Ah, hey Ferret."

"I brought us a couple beers," Ferret replied eagerly. "Put them in your cooler."

"Not sure I should have one," Cedar said. "I've had a lot to drink tonight."

Ferret grinned like a schoolboy. "I don't *ever* remember you *ever* having too much of anything."

Which, of course, is why Ferret was here. And looking down at the considerable bulge in Ferret's sarong—which seemed to be rising a bit even as he looked—Cedar couldn't help but think the man was right. When did he ever have enough sex?

But….

Ferret stepped up to him and ran long fingers up Cedar's torso, ran the tips around his nipples. Cedar trembled. He loved having his nipples played with. "I've been waiting for you. The minute you went off with that guy, I thought, 'His dick ain't big enough for you.'"

"His dick is very nice," said Cedar, the words tumbling out before he'd even thought of them.

"But it ain't this one," Ferret said, a desperate tone in his voice.

Ah, Ferret. Don't you know how unattractive desperation is?

He looked up and saw the anxiety there in those huge green eyes. Eyes that some thought were ugly, but in which Cedar could only see the crystals of the earth.

Shit.

Ferret fell to his knees and pressed his face against the white Pump! jockstrap. Mouthed Cedar's cock through the fabric, breathed heat onto it, making it respond. Unconsciously, Cedar dropped a hand to the back of Ferret's head, getting a moan in response. Gods, Ferret knew how to suck dick too!

Ferret sat back, looked up, and sucked on several fingers, hinting at the blowjob to come. He leaned forward, sucking at Cedar's crotch again, and letting his hands roam around back, running them down Cedar's crack, finding the hole—and oh gods!—sticking one in ever so slightly. Out. In. Out. Deeper. A little deeper. And how much better would that cock feel? Yes, it would hurt like a motherfucker at first—it always did—but once they both got their stride?

Scott's face suddenly flashed to Cedar's mind out of the darkness.

It'll hurt him. It will hurt him bad.

He knows I was planning on being with Ferret tonight.

It will still hurt him.

If he finds out.

He'll find out.

"You can't tell Scott," he said, amazed that he'd said it. Amazed at the sound of his own voice. The... *wrongness* of it.

Dammit! I don't even fucking know *Scott! He's not my boyfriend. I don't know his fucking last name. There is* no *reason for me* not *to enjoy Ferret tonight.*

He looked down at the man, saw the anguish in those eyes.

He needs me!

Scott's face was still there.

I don't do "boyfriends!"

Ferret must have seen something in Cedar's eyes because that's when he pulled the front of the jock down and Cedar's cock sprang out like Jack from his box. A tenth of a second later, his entire erection—not the equal of Ferret's but no small thing either—vanished into the man's mouth, and Cedar threw his head back with a strangled cry.

What if Scott shows up? What if he walks in and sees this?

Maybe he needs to. Make sure he understands the boundaries.

"Stop!" he exclaimed and Ferret pulled back, questions in his eyes.

"I—I don't want to cum yet," Cedar said, struggling to understand something he hadn't expected to say.

Ferret stood and kissed him, hard. Gave him a kiss that had set him on fire in years past and now just made him want to push the man away.

Fuck!

I don't owe Scott anything.

Except maybe an explanation.

But he knows I was going to hook up with Ferret tonight!

Ferret will be here all fucking week.

So go to bed alone with this hard-on?

Yes! You've done it before.

Ferret stood up. "I want to fuck you," he said with a snarl. "I want to fuck you so hard you walk bowlegged tomorrow."

The idea was licentious and pornographic and made Cedar's cock throb all the harder.

Fuck!

Ferret took him by the hand and led him to the hammock, bent him over and dropped back to his knees and started rimming Cedar like few men ever had or knew how to.

Oh, damn. "Okay. Okay," he said.

He turned and saw Ferret's grinning face.

"You've got a condom?"

"You know I do!"

"Then get in the tent."

"That tiny thing?"

"Do it! And lay on your back. I'm gonna ride." At least he would be somehow in control.

Ferret fairly scrambled into the tent, and Cedar climbed in behind and then straddled Ferret's torso. He reached back, instantly found the colossal cock (he'd measured it once; just shy of twelve inches), and began to line it up with his spit-soaked hole.

But Scott's face was still there in his mind.

Dammit! What's going on? I hate this!

He tried to banish Scott's image, but try as he might, it didn't work.

The cock tip found its mark, started to nudge its way in…

"Dammit," Cedar cried and rolled off of Ferret.

"Wh-what's wrong?" Ferret said, his anguish filling the tent.

"I—I can't," Cedar said.

"Wh-what?"

"The beans," he lied (and he didn't like to lie, not even if it saved someone from being hurt). "I'm likes seconds from farting the worst farts on the planet—"

"I don't care!"

"I care," Cedar said. "*I* care!"

He grabbed Ferret's big hot cock, pulled off the condom, and began to jack Ferret quickly, trying to get him off as fast as he could.

"Jockster! *Please.*"

But Cedar ignored the pang in that voice and kept jacking, and he *did* know how to play with a cock, and before long Ferret was cumming, his ass arching off the air mattress. Then after a long moan, he fell back into the bedding.

"My God!" Ferret managed to say and then let out another deep groan.

There was a long pause, one that seemed to last for hours, even though Cedar knew it was only moments.

Then: "Do-do you want me to suck…."

"No," Cedar said. "No. That's okay."

"But I like—"

"Not tonight," Cedar all but barked. He climbed over Ferret and jostled out of the tent. It seemed so *close* in there. The air so hot. He couldn't breathe!

A moment later Ferret joined him and those eyes. Pain was in those eyes.

Now I've hurt him!

"I'm—I'm sorry," he said, looking away.

"N-no. It's okay. I get it," Ferret said quietly. "And I'll get lost. I know you don't like people to stick around after."

"Wait," Cedar said, trying to make it better. "We'll have those beers."

"Keep 'em," Ferret said. He turned and started walking away—stopped. "Wow. I never thought I would see the day."

"What?" Cedar said.

"Jockster. *The* Jockster. Hung up on someone." Ferret walked into the darkness.

"I'm *not* hung up on anyone."

Scott would wonder how Ferret could just walk off into the night without a flashlight.

Scott!

"Dammit!" he said aloud.

And then he plopped down and had both beers.

CHAPTER TWENTY-SEVEN

SCOTT ACTUALLY got up before Jockster, despite the heavy partying. He put on his sarong—*Jockster bought me this!*—decided to go for a walk, and found a group of men doing yoga on the stage in the pavilion. He stood and watched and when invited, shrugged and decided, what the hell (when in Rome!), and gave it a try. He couldn't do many of the moves, but the leader told him afterward if he showed up early the next morning, he would start him with some beginning moves.

"Thanks," said Scott, not sure if he had any intention of doing such a thing.

"I hear there's pancakes this morning," said Hound Dog, another of the men who'd been doing yoga that morning. Watching him doing the poses was part of what had stopped Scott dead in his tracks in the first place.

"I'll be making coffee," said an equally nude Bean. "A Kiboko peaberry from Tanzania. It's to die for."

"Live for," Scott said, not even knowing he'd done it, and tried not to look at Bean's crotch. God, if only the two of them had a porn video. He'd be first in line to buy a copy.

Bean laughed. "To live for is right! It's bright and juicy and sweet, like dried apricots and dark chocolate."

"Sounds wonderful," Scott said. He'd had Bean's coffee before, of course. He'd made special trips into the city just to go to The Shepherd's Bean, the man's café.

"See you downstairs?"

"Sure," Scott agreed. "I'll get Jockster."

But Jockster wasn't at his camp.

Maybe he was having pancakes?

Scott went down to the dining hall to find Jockster wasn't there. He wasn't showering either. Then he went back to the dining hall just in time to get a few of the last of the pancakes. They were big and fluffy and marvelous, and Bean's coffee was heaven.

The thought made him laugh. Heaven, indeed. If there was such a place, they'd serve Bean's coffee for sure. And who knew—he didn't, did he?—that there *wasn't* such a place? Was there any proof there wasn't?

He decided to shower after that and, hey, he didn't have to climb those steep stairs. His shaving kit and his towel were in the shower house after all.

I wonder where Jockster is...?

The shower was busy with men, and he stood there, watching for a second. He noticed the one small stall set off by itself. He hadn't seen it the other night. It had a curtain.

He was halfway to it when he checked out the showering men one more time. He didn't have the *smallest* dick.

And so what if I do? he thought. *Who cares? Jockster likes my dick! He thinks it's beautiful!*

For goodness sakes, you shower at the gym.

Of course, he had perfected the art of prepping himself a bit first so he wasn't too small when he took off his workout clothes.

Expensive workout clothes.

Shit. My version of a middle-aged man's little red Corvette? Am I that pathetic?

Jockster thinks I look good naked!

So with a shrug, he pulled off his sarong and, heart pounding, hung it on a hook outside the showers. He joined the men there, took the one showerhead that was left, and soon found himself laughing with the others. It felt good. Being with these men. What had he heard someone say—was it Wyatt?—that it was a brotherhood?

Scott had never had a brother. But if it was anything like this, this smiling and laughing and soaping each other's backs? It was nice. Really nice.

In fact it felt a lot like the Fabulous Four.

He didn't let anyone soap his back, and scolded himself after.

Why didn't you?

He'd seen one man soaping more than *just* another man's back. He'd seen a cock rise. His own had, and he'd gotten an appreciative glance, and he'd blushed, but it had felt nice, hadn't it? He also saw that he was accepted here. They acted like he'd been a part of their little group for years. There was no one judging him. No one seemed to be comparing him with anyone else.

He was just a part.

Included.

After that he thought, *What the hell? Go to the beach. Why not?*

But on the way Scott saw a group of men gathering at a table under the oak tree. He stopped and saw they were making necklaces. *Interesting.* And it seemed that Zebra the Baker (the very man who had made the delicious cookies the evening before) was sponsoring the little class, and was explaining that most of the materials they were using were things he'd found on the land. Big round hard seeds that reminded Scott somewhat of Milk Duds (these were from the Kentucky coffee tree), some smaller seeds (still big enough to string) that came from the Eucalyptus and looked a lot like tiny versions of the old-fashioned mines he'd seen in submarine movies, and a few other odd items. Some were beads Zebra had brought with him, beads he said would make a good centerpiece for their work, and he asked that they take no more than a few of those. There was a large blue-green one that appealed to Scott, and before he knew it, he'd joined them and was constructing a necklace.

"Well look here!" said Wyatt. Damn! How was Wyatt always catching him doing the very things he said he wouldn't do?

"Don't tell Asher," he hissed.

"I won't say a frigging word," Wyatt said and joined the group.

"Where's Howard?" Scott asked, not really caring about the answer.

"He went for a walk," Wyatt answered, picking through the objects on the table. "He likes to walk the land. Makes me happy. There's so much he doesn't participate in out here, but he loves the land."

"Isn't he a witch?" Scott asked, stringing one of the hazelnut-looking whatchamacallits, followed by one of the small tan thingamabobs. It balanced the whole feel, switching back and forth like that.

"Pagan," Wyatt said absently.

"Huh?"

"He considers himself pagan."

"What's the difference?" Scott added a few more of the smaller seeds. It was starting to look pretty cool if he did say so himself.

"You can be pagan and not be a witch. But if you're a witch, you pretty much have to be a pagan."

"I don't get it." Scott held up his necklace and examined it, not quite sure if it was done.

"You know, things fall under the umbrella." Wyatt was starting to add some beads to his own necklace, but Scott didn't think his friend's looked as good as the one he had created. "You can be Christian without being Catholic, but you can't be Catholic without being Christian."

"I see," Scott said, not sure if he understood at all.

"That's pretty good, Scott," said Zebra. "Have you done this before?"

"No," said Scott shaking his head.

"You've got a natural talent, then. Hold it against your neck. Let me see."

Scott brought the two ends of the string up behind his neck so they were touching.

"Yeah. Nice. But I suggest you add just a few more of the small ones on either end—give it a tad more length. Then I'll show you how to make the hook."

Scott grinned, pleased despite himself. He saw the necklace the teacher was wearing, and it was really quite lovely. So if he liked Scott's creation, that was really saying something. "Thanks," he said.

After he was finished, Scott decided to go for a walk. He'd find Jockster sooner or later. He took his new necklace back to the shower house first, though, so he wouldn't have to carry it around. He knew what would happen. He'd put it down absently and forget where he put it.

As he passed the last of the buildings, he realized he hadn't been inside that one yet. *I wonder what's in there?*

Curious, he decided to check it out.

It was a fairly long room with chairs running around the walls and several piles of the mattresses like the ones in the cabins piled in a corner. Just inside the door was a clothes rack stuffed with clothing. Women's clothing, it seemed, when he checked them out. He rolled his eyes but couldn't help but get a kick out of the men who pulled items off of hangers and held them against their bodies and asked each other how they looked. A short gold-sequined dress. A pink polka-dotted gown. Holy shit—a poodle skirt!

And it looked retro!

It was all Scott could do not to grab it. No No-no-no! Retro or not, he was *not* going to wear a skirt.

"I think you'd look hot in it," said the guy Scott remembered as having the "faerie" name of Leadfoot (aka Sister Hateful Heinous Bitch from Madison, Wisconsin).

"I don't think so!" Scott said, laughing. No way! Not happening!

Leadfoot darted forward and held it against Scott's waist. "Oh, *gggiiirrrl!* It's to die for on you!"

"To live for!" Scott said.

He did notice a bag, though. It was some kind of over-the-shoulder fabric thing that looked like it would hold a bowling ball, and the fabric was orange and brown and yellow gold. *Hmmmmm...*, he thought. Not too girlie. And the bags people were carrying around did make sense. There was all kinds of stuff he could put in it. His flashlight—that way it would always be on him. And sun block, of course. A towel. The necklace he'd just made. He wouldn't have to leave it in the shower house. He started to walk away and then, with a grin on his face, he snatched it off the rack and slung it over one shoulder. He wasn't sure if it went with his sarong, but at least it didn't clash too badly. He'd take it. Apparently anything there was fair game.

Then he noticed that at the far end of the room there were several tables set end to end, and a group of men were decorating them: hanging great lengths of shimmery fabric and tapestries from the drop-ceiling panels, draping more of the fabric on the tables and setting up all kinds of things on top of it. As he got closer he saw those things included statues, candles, crystals, pottery, and more, even pictures.

He saw Dolce was helping and stopped him. "What's all this?" he asked.

Dolce smiled. It was a different smile. Bittersweet, maybe? Scott wasn't sure.

"It's the Festival Altar. We set it up every year, usually earlier, but sometimes it takes a few days. We put things here that represent us—faeries, queer spirit, personal images for however we see God.... Sometimes people leave something they want to get rid of. They just lay it on the altar and trust that something magical will happen."

Something magical. *Right.*

"You're a part of us this week," Dolce said, reaching out and stroking Scott's cheek. "If there's something you want to leave here, whether to charge it with Festival energy to take home with you… or just to get rid of and leave behind forever, you're welcome…."

Oh. And then "something magical would happen"?

Scott shook his head. *No such thing as magic.* He didn't say it out loud though. He wasn't even sure why. Maybe it was in the tone in Dolce's voice. Maybe that sweet touch to his cheek. He looked back at the altar. "Who are the men in the pictures?" he asked, genuinely curious.

"Our ancestors," Dolce said.

"Ancestors?" They had ancestors?

"Brothers who are no longer with us."

No longer with…? Then it hit him. "You mean they…."

"Died," said Dolce.

"Oh." Scott gulped. Looked at the pictures. Some of the men were really young.

"H-how did…."

"Different ways" came the answer. "Isn't it interesting how people always ask how someone died? Does it matter?"

The comment stung for some reason. "I didn't mean to offend you."

Dolce smiled gently and reached out and dropped a hand on Scott's shoulder. "You didn't, brother."

Brother. There was that word again.

"Just a comment. I think it's because so many of us are afraid of dying." Dolce patted at his bouffant of highly piled and shellacked blond hair. "We want to know that we're still alive."

"You think so?" Scott asked. It was food for thought. In fact, the more he thought about it, the more it felt right. People were afraid of dying. It's why they made up places like heaven.

He paused for a moment. Felt a gentle little smile creep onto his face.

Because hadn't he decided there was no proof heaven *didn't* exist?

Dolce pointed to a picture of a redhead who couldn't have been older than thirty. "That's Coco Peru. He died of complications from AIDS. She was so sweet. A wonderful singer." Dolce sighed. "*Such* a voice. And funny. Oh, my God!" He pointed to another picture, this one of an older man. "Helen Heels. Wise. So wise. And he looked good in a miniskirt too."

"A miniskirt?" It was hard to imagine. "He looks so… rugged."

"Oh, he was. Strong like an frigging ox! And a *big* ol' bottom."

AIDS? Scott wondered.

As if reading his thoughts, Dolce shook his head. "Cancer. Fine one year and gone the next. It went through him like wildfire. Such a shock. Do you mind taking off your shoes?"

"Huh?" Scott asked. He hadn't registered that Dolce had changed the subject.

"Your shoes." Dolce pointed down, and Scott saw he was standing on a long straw mat, beautifully decorated with winding strings of purple and green. "We think of the rug as sacred. This is our altar, you know. Everyone is allowed to add to it. Leave something for the week. Help decorate it. Add pictures of loved ones. And taking off your shoes before stepping on the rug is a sign of respect."

"Oh," said Scott. "I—okay." He stepped to the side and kicked off his sandals. He'd often found such ideas of "sacred" to be as silly as thoughts of God. But this morning? This morning he found he really didn't want to offend. Not in any way. A strange peacefulness he didn't quite understand had settled over him. He felt nice and he found he didn't want it to go away. So what if he didn't believe the rug could be "sacred." Dolce did, right? And these men accepted him. Called him brother.

He paused. Thought about it more and for some reason, felt a hitch in his throat.

Is this place getting to me?

Stupid!

But when he went back to Dolce, he left his shoes behind.

Dolce pointed out more pictures. Anita Mann. Joe Gatton. Big Nancy Girl. Gary Root. Charlene Hart. Diamond Don. DeeDee Pfeiffer. JayBee. He knew not a one of them. But something happened inside of him. There was a stirring in his heart. A connection. He told himself it was stupid. *Fucking* stupid. But he couldn't help it. He wanted to cry.

In fact, he did.

Jockster's voice came back to him then.

> *Lay it down, set it free.*
> *Let my heart rest and let it be.*
> *Lay it down, set it free.*
> *Lay it down on the altar of love.*

He suddenly found himself stumbling outside the building and near collapsing onto a bench that was against the building. Scott found he was having a hard time breathing.

What's going on?

You're acting crazy!

He fought the tears. People would think he was insane.

He didn't know any of those men—those "ancestors."

Those men who were spoken of with such reverence.

Would anyone ever think of him that way?

"It's a fucking miracle I even have any friends," he muttered. Especially friends as good as Sloan and Wyatt and even fucking Asher.

"Oh God," he said and dropped his face into his hands.

A moment later someone sat next to him.

Fuck! Whoever it was would say something now. "Are you okay? Can I help you?"

But whoever it was didn't say a word. And when Scott finally looked up, the man turned out to be Wyatt.

No. Not Wyatt. *Little Bear*.

Little Bear smiled at him and then…

Then Scott cried. He didn't even know why. He leaned against Wyatt and cried on his shoulder, and the man who could have said anything—could have made fun of him in fact—said only three words.

"I love you."

To Scott's surprise, he said it back.

Then he asked Little Bear for a favor.

CHAPTER TWENTY-EIGHT

SCOTT STRODE down the steep hill wearing the new sarong Wyatt had helped him pick out. Well, he had known which one he wanted, but he wanted to make sure it looked okay. Wyatt had been very enthusiastic about his choice. It was the one with the peacock feather pattern in deep, luscious blues and greens. It went perfectly with the blue bead in his new necklace.

His new bag now had several items in it as well. He'd climbed the interminable wooden steps—not as impossible now that he wasn't tripping balls, but a challenge anyway—and retrieved a towel and a his little LED flashlight ("They last for-frigging-ever!"), bug spray, sun block, and even the John Grisham novel he'd forgotten all about.

As he walked across the dam, he passed the rainbow pennants on his way and found himself wishing once again he'd thought to bring a camera. It would make another great picture.

He swung his arms as he walked, loving the way the blue feathers and peacock eyes swirled around him and how the big blue bead on his necklace thumped against his chest in a most satisfactory way, and for a while, he pretended he was somewhere else, some*when* else—a thousand years ago, two thousand (three?)—and that he was in ancient Greece or someplace like that and that Jockster was the man whose face could launch a thousand ships.

It was fun to think about.

Scott also liked the way his new bag bounced against his hip and smiled as he realized he'd ensured it was on the opposite side from where he'd tied his sarong. He didn't want to cover up where the fabric parted to reveal his long legs and that flash of ass. What had Wyatt—*Little Bear*—said? "Baby, if you've got it, you have got to flaunt it!" Scott could almost hear his friend singing the ancient Donna Summer song even now.

Scott reached the beach and saw perhaps a dozen men. Several of them asked him to join them, and he chose to sit with Super Gem (not "Jim!") and Silvercrow and they told him all about their wedding.

It had gone splendidly, they explained. They'd gone to Iowa to get married, since their home state didn't yet recognize same-sex marriage. "We chose the town of Sydney," Gem said, "since it's the closest county to Festival where gay marriage *is* legal. Silvercrow called the courthouse ahead of time, and we were delighted to discover they were very welcoming." Gem smiled happily and oh, that smile! It made Scott's *heart* smile back.

"Oh, Scott!" Gem reached out and took Scott's hand. "The magistrate judge expressed his understanding of how important our marriage was to us, that we had traveled a great distance, and how special the day should be. We could have the ceremony in a dreary old office or he and his wife would meet us at a lovely state park nearby with a bluff overlooking the Missouri River. Can you believe it?" Gem laughed his wonderful laugh (and weren't there a lot of wonderful laughs here?) "We opted for the park, of course! And requested the necessary forms."

Gem sighed happily. "Then several days before Festival, we dropped our 'honeymoon cottage,'—that's our little trailer—at camp...." He laughed again. "Then it was off to Sydney! We were warmly greeted by the county officials and then, paperwork completed, we drove to the state park with some dear friends and the magistrate judge and his wife. They'd prepared a lovely ceremony especially for same sex couples that brought us all to tears."

Scott sighed, fighting back tears of his own. Would anything like that ever happen to him?

"There was none of that 'obey' stuff either. We were declared 'best friends who amazed each other' and 'partners in marriage.' Can you imagine?"

Scott found it hard to imagine indeed. And wonderful.

Don't cry!

But hell! Super Gem was. Why shouldn't he? No one would even blink, would they?

"We returned to our friend's home to celebrate, and the next day headed back to camp. And now it's our *honeymoon*, and it is going to be the most delightful days *ever*—surrounded by a hundred of our best friends in the world!"

A hundred best friends! Imagine! *Could I be one of your best friends, Super Gem?*

Scott surprised even himself when he hugged Gem and then turned and hugged Silvercrow as well. *If my friends could see me now*, thought Scott. They wouldn't believe it. *If I'm not careful, I am going to turn into as big a fag as Wyatt!*

Scott looked around him.

Men.

Men dozing in the sun on the grass or the raft in the lake, passing a joint or telling jokes or playing cards or, look over there. Dancing on a table.

I called this stupid!

Then, in a bolt of bravery, Scott untied the sarong and let it fall open. His penis was the smallest of the three of them but who gave a tin shit? They didn't seem to. He joined them when they went in the water, and here it was, maybe ten-thirty in the morning, and he was walking and swimming naked, and it felt good. Really good. He even took an inflatable raft—it was the blue one, he wasn't ready to grab a pink one—and saying "fuck it!" lay on it on his back.

Super Gem talked to him and asked him where he was from, and he was so sweet and gave Scott the most wonderful foot massage in the world.

"Should I make up a faerie name?" he asked.

"It will find you," said Super Gem. "You'll see."

When in Rome?

At some point Scott's new friend went swimming across the lake, and while it was no Lake Michigan, it did have to be at least four hundred feet across at that point, and Scott knew he wouldn't try it. Impressive.

Scott saw several men who had climbed on the big raft—the float—the very one where he had seen those naked men from far off when he'd first arrived at camp. Funny that it seemed like a week or so ago at least, but this was only—Hell! What day was it? Was it Thursday? Could that be right? Was it only the third day? Something weird had happened to time here. If it was only Thursday, then there was still a good week left before he had to go back to the real world.

It was true, wasn't it?

There was something—could he use the word?—"magic" about this place.

Fuck it!

He climbed up on to the raft and walked naked—yes, Jesus, Mary, Joseph, Ganesha, and Lord and Lady, *naked!*—across the wood surface until he found a free space and lay out in the sun. It felt wonderful. It felt free. Had he ever ever ever felt so free? Why, it was almost like when he was on that mushroom trip, but he wasn't. He was sober. Stone cold sober.

The only thing that could make it better would be if Jockster were here. They could spoon together naked—*naked!*—in front of everyone.

"Hey," said a sweet and gentle voice.

He opened his eyes, and it was as if he were in some sweet, sappy romantic movie. It was Jockster, looking down at him. Oh, those big beautiful eyes. Scott smiled and somehow he didn't remember when a smile felt so wonderful. "Hi," he said.

"How are you today?"

"I am *fab*-ulous," he said and meant it.

"You look so beautiful I want to make love with you right here in front of everyone."

"Okay," said Scott before he even knew he'd said it.

Wow. Did Jockster just blush?

"How about if I take you somewhere else instead?"

"Okay," said Scott. His cock flexed. Sex? *Oh!*

Jockster stood and dove into the water, and Scott rose and leapt in after him. They swam to the shore, and Scott did his best to stride up onto the beach without thinking about it. They went to his towel and Jockster gave him a strange look.

"What?" he said.

"I didn't recognize this as your spot."

"Oh?" Scott looked down. Well, maybe that made sense. There was nothing there Jockster *would* have recognized. He'd left his Lacoste towel up top. The sarong was his new one. Jockster didn't know about the bag. He looked at Jockster and grinned. He picked up the sarong and swirled it around him and tied it at his waist.

"Where did you get that?"

"From the sarong guys, of course. Well. Sort of. I mean I haven't paid for it, but Little Bear"—*Wow! I just called him Little Bear! Without having to think about it!*—"said it was okay for me to take one and pay for it when I ran into one of the guys who sell them. I was going to leave it, but Little Bear said *never* do that because it could sell, and they try to have only one of each sarong because what fag wants someone else wearing the same thing he's wearing and—"

Jockster burst into laughter and kissed him. Kissed him right there in front of everyone. Pulled him into his arms and kissed him and kissed him and kissed him. Never even gave him the slightest bit of tongue, but Scott couldn't remember being kissed like that even once in his life.

Of course he got a hard-on, and of course there was no way to hide it, and damn if Super Gem wasn't right there and giving him a friendly stare.

"I like the necklace. Where did you get it?"

"I made it," Scott said, reaching up and touching it. He felt a touch of pride. "You really like it?"

"I do."

They stood there awhile staring at each other, and Scott wanted to laugh and he wanted to cry and he wanted to twirl around and have his sarong swirl around him like a ballet dancer out of *Swan Lake*.

"Come on," said Jockster. "I want to take you to a very special place. Gods, I hope you think it's special too."

Scott took a deep breath. "Okay. Let's go."

Scott followed Jockster south past the beach and through a long grassy swath along the lake. Trees lined the way to the right, and here and there were a few tents and camping areas, including a big screened-in setup that seemed to be something other than a place to sleep. There was no tent near it, but inside was a table covered in crystals and several large wooden phalluses. *Another altar?* Scott wondered.

They went into a grove of trees where wind chimes hung in the branches, tinkling in a light breeze. Crystals hung there as well, and off to the left was a statue of a nude woman perched atop a pedestal. "They call this place Gaea's Haven," Jockster said. "It's sacred to those who find God in the feminine."

Scott nodded. Shrugged. Why not? Whatever floats your boat.

"Wow. Knock me down and pick me up. You didn't make fun."

"Huh?" Scott looked around him. It was such a lovely place. "Make fun?"

Jockster laughed. "Never mind." He took Scott's hand. "Come on."

A little further on there was an opening in the trees, and a path opened up that took them into the woods. They walked along, holding hands, down through a lovely corridor made by nature, with overreaching branches that sheltered them from the sun but sent occasional lances of light downward as if especially designed for their delight. The path wove to the right and then left until they came to something that stopped Scott in his steps.

Ahead was—well, what was it? A gate of sorts. Branches and thick vines had been bent down and up and around into a hoop, with the path running right through it. Innumerable strings of beads, crystals, chains, and medallions hung in clusters throughout the structure, creating something that looked... well... magical. There were more wind chimes, and everywhere, scattered all over the ground, were crystals and polished stones, coins and more medallions, and even plastic toys and tiny figurines. It was lovely. Like something from a fairy tale.

"Wow," said Scott.

Jockster grabbed him and pulled him into the gateway and kissed him hard, this time demanding entrance into his mouth. Their tongues intertwined, and Scott went hard again (not that he had gone completely soft) and crushed his cock against Jockster's. Today's jockstrap was a very sexy black Wolf brand complete with a silhouette of a wolf filled in with the American flag set in the middle of a very thick waist band. Jockster gave him a playful "*Gggrrrrrrr.*"

"I want you so bad," Scott said, his voice cracking like a schoolboy's.

"We're almost there," said Jockster. "Just a few more minutes."

Scott growled back. "We could do it here."

Jockster's brows shot up. "You'd be willing to fuck where someone might walk up on us?"

Scott gulped hard, trembled—and not all because of fear. There was excitement as well. "It would turn you on, wouldn't it?"

Was Jockster blushing?

"Y-yes. I think it would. It would be a sight. But…. Let's wait until we get to Green Man's Grove. It will be a perfect first time."

"Green Man's what?"

"You'll see," Jockster said, wiggling his crotch against Scott's. Then he pulled away and ran a few feet before heading down a second smaller path that broke off from the main one. "Come on," he called over his shoulder, and Scott had to force himself to move. He was transfixed by the sight of Jockster's perfect ass, the muscles flexing as he moved, stunningly framed by thin black leg straps and the thickest waistband he'd ever seen.

But he didn't want to be left behind, so he started after him.

The new path was more winding and first climbed, then dropped back down again until it quite suddenly opened into a small grassy area. Tall sunflowers, white daisies, and purple coneflowers grew along one side, and just up ahead was a knee-high circle of stones about twelve feet across and...

Jockster and Scott froze.

There was someone there. Three someones.

Three *fucking* someones.

And one of them was Howard.

Scott's mouth fell open in shock, and he found himself rooted to the spot, staring, not wanting to, but unable to look away.

Howard was fucking, and he was fucking hard. Fucking a young man who was sprawled back on a low stone table. A second man stood at the opposite end and was holding the young man's legs up, high and wide giving Howard easy access to the young man's ass. Scott couldn't see the face of the man being fucked because his head was hanging back off the edge of the table, his mouth being used by the third man. He saw a flash of white hair.

Fuck. Was that Blue?

"Take it!" Howard cried. "Take it, you goddamned bitch. Gonna *breed* you. Fill your sweet little ass with my cum. Fill you until you drip."

"Yeah," the second man was saying. "Gonna fill you from this end. Choke you with my jizz."

"Fucking little *slut*," Howard said, his big ass jiggling as he pounded into the young man. "Flirting with me—on the Fourth."

Shit! It *was* Blue.

"You wanted this *then!* You wanted it *bad*. But you... went off... with that asshole actor instead! Now *I* got *your* asshole. Gonna *breed* you, bitch—breed you *good!*"

Blue wasn't saying anything. Not that he could. But the sounds? Scott couldn't tell if he wanted what was happening or not. And he had no idea if he should say anything. He wanted to disappear, fall into a hole in the ground and just vanish.

"Let's get out of here." Jockster grabbed his hand with a hard yank, and without giving Scott much choice, pulled him back the way they had come. "Fuckwad Big Sir," he was mumbling. "That's a sacred place!"

"I—I...." Scott didn't know what to say. Any sexual excitement he felt had vanished at Howard's words and the sight of that thrusting ass. He couldn't help but wonder if Wyatt knew. His friend hadn't known where Howard was—thought he'd gone for a walk. They did have an open relationship, though, so....

"Son of a bitch!" Jockster cried, still dragging Scott behind.

Scott tripped on a root and would have gone down if not for Jockster's almost painful grip. It did cause Jockster to spin around though. "Gods!" Jockster said and reached out to steady him. "I'm sorry. It's just that...."

"I guess...," Scott managed to blurt. "I guess I'm confused. I mean—it's not something I ever wanted to see, but.... Ah. Weren't you taking me there to do the same thing?"

Jockster was breathing hard, shaking, mouth opening and shutting several time but without any words coming out. It wasn't something Scott expected to see in the man. He always seemed so composed.

Finally, he spoke. "Yes. I guess. Yes, it was. But...." He looked away, wiped at his eyes. "I don't know. I...." He cleared his throat, looked around, and sat down on a fallen log. "It was the way Big Sir was doing it. Just reaming that poor kid out. *Using* him...."

"We don't know that Blue didn't want it," Scott offered, not knowing if he was defending Wyatt's loathsome lover or not. Was it his place to say anything? And damn! Since when did he *not* judge? Wasn't judging his main mission in life?

Jockster sighed. "You're right."

"You said that place is supposed to be sacred?" Scott said.

"It is!" Jockster cried. "It is sacred and... fuck! Sacred to *men*. Sacred to male energy. And men *fuck*. So I don't know what's bothering me. But it is." His eyes went wide. "He said he was going to 'breed' Blue. That makes me wonder if he was wearing protection. And somehow with Big Sir, I don't know if fucking without a condom is such a good idea."

"W-why?" asked Scott, suddenly shaken. No condom? But hadn't Wyatt said that when they played with others, they *always* used condoms?

"I've heard Big Sir doesn't always play safe," said Jockster.

"W-what?" Scott sat down next to Jockster. "But...." But Wyatt said they always used condoms when they had sex with other men! "He doesn't always play safe?" he muttered. But Howard always fucked *Wyatt* bare. They didn't use condoms when they were alone together. Had Howard endangered Scott's friend? Hell. Was he endangering Blue even now? "What do we do?"

"What *can* we do?" Jockster let out a long sigh. "It's done. He's shot that boy full by now. Gods. Should I have said something? I mean, Blue acts like a boy, but he's not. He's an adult. He's letting Big Sir fuck him bare. If he even is bare. We don't know. Maybe it was just fantasy talking." Jockster jumped to his feet. "I fucking *hate* this!" He looked down at Scott. Shrugged. "Let's get out of here."

Scott and Jockster did not have sex that afternoon.

THEY WERE hanging out with Domi Dearest and his sexy (boy?) friend when they heard the bell ringing across the land.

"Will you go someplace with me?" Jockster asked.

"Where?" Scott asked.

"Heart Circle."

"I think we'll stay here," said Domi. "We're going to… ah… take a nap."

"I think that's our cue to vamoose," Scott said, laughing. Jockster was still looking at him though—waiting for an answer. *Another circle?* But he saw something else. Jockster wanted this. Scott sighed. "Okay."

Instead of sitting under the big oak tree, the Heart Circle was inside the big building Scott had investigated that morning. And a "Heart Circle" turned out to be a regular circle, but multiplied. Several times. It was a time of sharing. Lula Belle, today in shorts and a cowboy hat, was the Facilitator. As usual, the routine was to go around the circle and say your name. But this time, instead of telling everyone your favorite animal or movie or whatever, you were to express anything you needed to lay on the altar.

Oh no, thought Scott. He looked at Jockster and tried to beam his thoughts to the man. *Why? Why are you doing this to me?*

"Trust me," Jockster mouthed, then leaned in close and whispered, "I needed to turn the mood after what we saw."

"Oh fuck," was all Scott could say. He didn't want to think about that.

"I thought we could pass around the Festival Cloak," Lula Belle said. He stood up, kicked off his shoes, and approached the altar. There was a chair set in front, and draped over it was some kind of big crazy quilt. He carefully—*reverently*—Scott saw, picked it up and then swept it around his shoulders. Worn like that, Scott could see it was indeed a cloak. It had a high collar of gold and diamond-shaped pieces of fabric at the shoulders of deep, rich primary colors. "For those of you who don't know, this is our Ritual Cloak and it *is* this faerie brotherhood. There's a book on the altar that explains what it is all about, and I encourage each of you to come read it and feel free to hold the Cloak, touch it, absorb its spirit."

Scott gulped. Felt himself growing uncomfortable. He'd somehow avoided the witchy-woo-woo-stuff for the most part, but now here it was.

"The book explains what each piece means—right now I will just say that the gold collar symbolizes queer spirit and the shoulder pieces signify many of our core values and beliefs. The elements, mysteries, queer spirit…. Then as it goes down, the other pieces represent gay heritage, gay love, our founders, transformation, healing, compassion…. We are constantly adding to it. We add pieces for the changes that we are going through as a community. Pieces for those who have passed…."

Lula Belle closed it tight around him, shut his eyes, and trembled. When he opened them Scott saw his eyes were wet. "This piece, for instance," Lula Belle said, pointing to a lavender piece along the very edge—shiny and covered with sequins—"is for Helen Heels, who passed this year."

There were several stifled sobs around the room, and Scott saw that Super Gem was openly weeping.

"We love you, Helen Heels, and will never forget you."

"Or your hot ass," someone cried out, and there was a ripple of laughter.

Gosh, thought Scott and found for some reason he wanted to cry as well. And he didn't even know this man—this "Helen Heels"—who was remembered for his hot ass with a piece of purple sequined satin.

Would he ever have people crying and laughing for him one day? Scott wondered. How funny to be remembered for having a "hot ass." And Scott could see it was not in disrespect. These men... they *loved* Helen Heels?

Will anyone even show up to my funeral? Certainly not his parents.

Scott found he couldn't help but wish he had known some of these ancestors. Helen Heels. The others whose pictures he'd looked at and who were thought of with such veneration.

Lula Belle walked around the circle and shared things about his family. He got quite emotional.

Equally emotional was Gabbana, the man who had seemed so happy-go-lucky the last few days. "I've been diagnosed with cancer."

There was a gasp throughout the room.

"I've got a good chance," he said, smiling. "I'm going to beat this with Jerry—Dolce—at my side. And all of you." He nodded and Lula Belle draped the Cloak around his shoulders. "Thank you, my friend," Gabbana said, smile wavering. He cleared his throat. "Doc says I have like a seventy percent chance."

Oh shit. And hadn't Dolce just been telling Scott about Helen Heels this morning? And all the while his own partner had cancer? *Shit!*

"But dammit, I'm scared!" Gabbana said and dropped his face into his hands and let out a long sob. The men to either side of him put their arms over his shoulders and held him tightly.

Friends. True friends, Scott saw.

Then the handsome Silvercrow gave his version of getting married to Super Gem. Once more Scott felt his heart being stirred, and he began to lose his apprehension. He could almost forget that his turn was coming.

I can always pass....

Little Bear came next, and of course he was silly—never serious was Wyatt! "Okay, there was this gay couple, and they had been together for *twenty-five* years, and one was celebrating his sixtieth birthday! Well! Suddenly this faerie appears and tell them that because they had been such a loving and faithful couple for so many years, she would give them one wish each.

"Well, the one who was throwing the party said, 'We've blown all our money on parties and fancy things, and I've never gotten to travel. I wish we could see the world.' The little fairy waves her wand and—*poof!*—he had the tickets in his hand.

"So then it was the birthday boy's turn, and the son of a bitch says, 'Well, I'd like a lover who's thirty years younger than me.' So the wise little fairy waves her magic wand and—*poof!*—he was ninety!" Of course, Wyatt laughed the hardest, but that was okay. He did get laughs.

Wyatt then went on to tell everyone that he'd had a really good year and was madly in love and so very blessed and so happy he had a new pop-up camper and, "Please come by the Rolling Brothel whenever you see the party lights on and let's *par-tay!*"

Then he surprised Scott further when he said he was very grateful that "my dear friend Scott here has come to Festival. He's one of the best friends I've ever had. He can be a cantankerous ol' queen, but when you get to know him, you see he is a sweet and beautiful soul."

Scott was speechless. What did you say after that?

"Okay, I pass," Wyatt said and then, just as the Little Bearded Girl was about to share, Wyatt suddenly said, "Wait!"

There was a long pause.

"Look. I'm sorry. I'm not done." Wyatt took a deep breath. "Sorry Stephen," he said to the man who reminded Scott so much of an Indian swami. Wyatt looked out over the faces of the men around the room. "You know, everybody, I make it a life mission to be as positive as I can. To always look for the silver lining. But—"

Oh shit, thought Scott. *Please don't let this be about Howard and Blue!*

"—well...." Then to Scott's surprise, he saw that Wyatt... it looked like he was going to cry. His huge brown eyes were filling with tears and he said, "Right before I was to head out to Festival, Howard came in the house screaming about what had happened to my car. I didn't know what the fuck he was talking about, and that only pissed him off more. So we go outside and there—" Wyatt's voice caught. "Someone had scratched the word 'faggot' on my minicoop! I didn't know what to be more upset about. That I was called a faggot in this century or that they did it to my minicoop. I love that car. Goddammit! 'Faggot?' I just can't believe it. I've tried to laugh it off. I've been telling everybody it's like I'm Brian from *Queer as Fuck*, but... I...." His voice caught again and a tear rolled down his cheek. "*Faggot?* I told Howard it must have happened when I went to the bar, but you know what I think? I think it happened while I was at work. And that means one of my *customers* thinks so little of me that he would fuck with my car. They must *hate* me to do something like that." Wyatt shook his head. "Or worse. What if it was someone I work with? I feel so.... God! I feel...."

Wyatt let out a sob and Scott sat frozen. He didn't know what to do. He was stunned. Wyatt always seems so carefree and silly. Like nothing could get to him. At least not that way. Why else would he wear crazy T-shirts, many of which broadcast to the world that he was gay?

What do I do? He had this sudden compulsion to jump up and run to his friend—a compulsion that frankly stunned him. If there was one thing that Scott didn't believe in, it was making a scene. But to see Wyatt—*Wyatt* of all people—crying? Fuck! Had he ever seen Wyatt cry?

Go to him, said an inner voice he wasn't used to hearing. One he'd pretty much squashed down a long, long time ago. But if he got up.... What then? Everyone would stare. The men to Wyatt's left and right were hugging him. *I would look like a fool if I jump up and go over there!*

Fuck!

Suddenly Scott wanted to cry.

What is happening to me?

"I try to be a good man," Wyatt finally said. "I believe that what we give out to the Universe comes back to us. Wiccans say that it's the Rule of Three. Whatever energy you put out, whether it is positive or negative, comes back to you three times. The Christians? Isn't it sevenfold? Tenfold? Don't the teachings on Karma say it's a hundredfold?"

Wyatt let out another sob. "I do *good!*" His voice caught again. "Gods! Why would someone do that to me? I feel... fuck. I feel *raped!*"

Now it was all Scott could do not to cry. He looked at Jockster in desperation, and the beautiful man nodded. First to him. Then to Wyatt.

"Are you sure?" Scott whispered.

"I've never been surer."

So Scott stood. People turned and looked at him. He didn't like being looked at. He took a step. Froze. Looked at Jockster. Got a nod. He took the biggest breath of his life and went to his friend. His goofy, believes in crazy crap, wears stupid T-shirts, has a loathsome raping lover, drama queen *best* friend—

Better even than Sloan, isn't he? Admit it!

—got down on one knee and said, "I love you, Wyatt."

Because, goddammit, he did!

Wyatt looked at him in complete shock. Scott was almost ashamed at the degree and depth of shock he saw on Wyatt's face, and then his friend threw his arms around him and cried on his shoulder.

Scott suddenly remembered crying on Wyatt's shoulder.

And he pulled his friend even closer.

Wyatt gasped out a "Pass!" to the Little Bearded Girl, who spoke of, well, Scott wasn't sure of what. He was holding Wyatt. At some point he was urged to go back to his seat and kissed full on the mouth by his little bear friend and it was all he could do to make it back to his chair.

He got there just in time to hear Jockster speak up.

"So I went and saw my dad this last Christmas. I wasn't there much more than a week, and do you know he sent me into London? With a guy who works for him? I hadn't seen my dad in two years, and he couldn't take a week off. Spent almost the whole time in his recording studio."

Scott looked over at Jockster, numb. What? What did Jockster just say? Recording studio?

"So I go with—*Gods*, I don't even know what the guy was. Bodyguard? Go-fer? I never quite caught it. He took me to see *Les Misérables*, even though what I wanted to see was *We Will Rock You*, but I guess it wasn't showing anymore. I wanted to go to Liverpool, but apparently that was too big a pain in the ass. It wasn't, however, too big of a pain in the ass for this big huge guy to *fuck* me in the ass. Isn't that to die for?"

Scott almost said "live for" but knew it wasn't the time or place.

Had he been stunned by Wyatt being suddenly so vulnerable?

Now Jockster? Who seemed so magical himself? So perfect? So more-than-human?

"I want a *dad*," Jockster continued. "Is that so much to ask for? Just to call the old man up and say, 'Hey, you want to go for a fuckin' beer?' But I guess he's too busy singing something that no one wants to hear anymore?"

Sing? His dad sang?

Scott glanced around and most of the men were nodding. Nodding. Were they in on something Scott didn't know about?

"So it wasn't good. I don't know why he doesn't want me in his life. I know it's not the gay thing. He's as bisexual as David Bowie and Lindsay Lohan and—" He laughed. "—I guess my mom." Jockster laughed again. "My *mom!*" He laughed. "She wanted me to go to some benefit thing this weekend and sing with her! Like I'm a kid again! Like I'm Chastity Bono or something—although I should say Chaz if I am going to be politically correct, right?"

Scott's mouth wanted to fall open. It was only with the greatest effort that he kept it shut tight. What the fuck was going on? First Wyatt comes apart and now... now Jockster was talking about a dad and a mom that everyone seemed to know about? Were they famous or something?

But it was more than that!

It was Scott himself. Weird shit was going on. Lots of weird shit.

"I know a lot of you probably think, *boo-hoo*, The Jockster thinks he's got it *so* bad."

What? Why would anyone think that about Jockster?

Jockster shrugged. "Isn't it funny that people who live a normal life want something out of this world and exciting, and people who live, well, an *ab*normal life only want to be normal? You know, I read once, I don't know if this is true, that Sigourney Weaver's parents have these *boring* names, and they hated it. So when they had kids, they gave them all unique and interesting names... except for Sigourney! Turns out the kids didn't *like* their unique and interesting names, and so they named her Susan. *Susan!* And *she* grows up pissed that she has a normal name and her brothers and sisters have cool names, so she *changes* her name to Sigourney! Isn't that a hoot?

"Everybody? Count your blessings! Scott, it's your turn."

It was said so fast that Scott didn't realize at first that Jockster was done. He didn't know what to say. He was still too confused by everything he'd just heard. Things that didn't quite make sense.

His mouth was open to say *I think I'll pass*, when something else came out instead...

"Hey. I'm Scott. Just plain Scott. No faerie name for me. Although.... Well.... Okay, so my life has sucked. I've been stupidly in love with one of my best friends for about ten years and he just found Prince Charming. I have to watch them making lovey-dovey eyes at each other all the time, and I just want to scream. My friend never had a *clue*, not *one*, how I felt! Not one! He was too busy pining away for *another* friend of mine who felt for him about what Sloan feels for me. Nothing! So in some fucked-up, desperate desire to be loved, I've been meeting these guys online. Men who promise me the sun and the moon and the stars, and I believe them every time and I let them fuck me. Fuck *me!* And I am not even a *bottom!* I let them because I think maybe that will finally get someone to love me! But the minute they've had me, they vanish. Kaput. Gone!"

Scott sat back and watched this. He didn't know who this was who was talking. It couldn't be him, could it? He, who always made sure it was in his best clothes and with an expensive haircut that he faced the world? A guy who would *never* spill his guts in front of a bunch of witchy-woo-woos who were comfortable in chiffon and sequins?

"I don't really have many friends, just three, and I'm finally seeing how... well...." He looked around at the circle of faces, all listening intently, some nodding for him to go on. They were *listening*. Like they cared! "I guess I'm a bitter bitch, but for God's sake! Who wouldn't be? My parents.... They're very fundamentalist Baptists. They kicked me out the fucking door when I came out to them—kicked me out of their lives. Aren't Christians supposed to be loving? I mean, all that 'love the sinner and hate the sin' shit? Well, I haven't seen too much 'love' from people like my parents. It's because of them I decided that there is no fucking 'God.' No Santa Claus. No Tooth Fairy—unless someone with that faerie name shows up this weekend."

There was a scattering of laughter.

"And no ghosts or reincarnation or UFOs or Big Foot, and somehow I wind up *here!* At witchy-woo-woo camp!"

More chuckles.

"I wind up in a place where people believe in goddamn faeries. Or queer gods or... I don't know. And I want to tell you all that you're crazy. You're crazier than *they* are. The people who live out there in... what? The real world? But... in the last few days. I.... There's something about this place.... I'm starting to feel more *real* than I ever have in my life!"

Scott began to tremble. Had he said that? Had he really said that?

To his surprise he heard hisses. Saw smiles.

"Something *weird* is happening," he said, voice catching, "and I don't understand. I wasn't looking for this!"

He stopped.

Because something inside him said, "But maybe it was looking for you."

Preposterous.

Ridiculous!

What is happening to me?

And then there were arms around him. Holding him. Tight.

CHAPTER TWENTY-NINE

THAT EVENING, over coffee and cookies, sitting under the most magnificent stars Scott had ever seen in his life, Jockster came to him and whispered in his ear. "It's time," he said.

"Time?" Scott asked and looked up into eyes lit only by a few candles on the picnic table.

Jockster nodded, not saying a word. It took Scott a second—he was still caught up in the so-called Heart Circle, even though it had been hours ago. There had been a delicious dinner of spaghetti and "meat" sauce and only the best garlic bread ever he'd had in his life. But that had all been in a daze. He felt high. He felt almost tripping balls.

Then it hit Scott what Jockster was talking about.

Time! It was time!

Jockster smiled and held out his hand. Scott took it and was helped to his feet. "I've been getting ready," Jockster said.

"Getting ready?" Scott asked.

Jockster leaned in. "Getting *ready*." He glanced over at the shower house.

"Oh! Well, don't you want *me* to shower?"

Jockster pressed close again. "I didn't just wash on the *out*side."

Didn't what? Then he realized what Jockster meant, and Scott blushed. "Oh!"

"Let's go," Jockster said and took his hand and without another word—without saying goodbye to the men he'd been sitting with, laughing with, singing with—they started up the path that led to the north and through the hall of sarongs and past the north cabins. "I wanted to take you to Green Man's Grove…. But after what we stumbled on with Big Sir and—"

"*Uggg*," Scott groaned.

"Yeah." Jockster squeezed Scott's hand. "Never mind." He stopped, pulled Scott close and kissed him. "I wanted this to be special. So we're going someplace else."

Special? Scott's heart began to race. *Special?* A bolt of fear struck Scott's chest like an arrow to the heart. *Special.* He'd heard that before, hadn't he? More than once? Was this just another empty….

Jockster kissed him again, ever so lightly, with a mere touch of tongue to his lips, and then Scott didn't care about his worries anymore.

Jockster stepped back and then began leading him up the path. As they came around a bend, Scott saw a light off to their right, and soon it became apparent it was a tiki torch. It stood at an opening in the woods. As they approached, he could see that someone had tied a string of gold garland across the beginning of the path with a sign hanging from it.

"*Reserved by the Jockster,*" it read.

"Reserved?" Scott asked quietly, butterflies beginning to flutter in his stomach.

"Reserved," Jockster said. "I didn't want anyone to barge in on us." He ducked in under the garland and Scott followed. The path ahead of them was narrower than any Scott had seen this past week; there wasn't even room for them to walk side by side. But even though the night was very dark—the moon was just the tiniest sliver tonight—Jockster had lit the way with more torches, these smaller and only about a foot from the ground.

"Watch your sarong, baby. It's just perfectly made to burst into flames. I don't want to have to put you out. Not that way, at least."

Scott didn't say a word. He could only stare at the sight before him. Sure, he'd been seeing Jockster's butt for the last few days. But tonight he could only gasp at the beautiful way the flames illuminated that completely perfect ass. It was like poetry or something.

Scott was startled away from that view, though, when he saw two golden figures to the left and right—Egyptian statues, the mini torches making them gleam in the dark—their dark, lined eyes seeming to watch him as he passed.

Ten feet further on, two more statues, also Egyptian, but these of gods and not men, were perched on pedestals to either side of the path, like guards. Jockster reached out and touched them as he went and Scott somehow found himself doing the same.

Immediately after the figures, the path opened up into a huge round clearing. There was a short wall of stone built all around it. The big open space must have been at least twenty feet across, and yet one more statue loomed over them at the far end, looking down with the head of a bird.

But it was what was at its feet that took Scott's breath away.

Several blankets had been laid out, with pillows. They too were well lit with two tall torches. To the side was a flat stone holding a pillar candle and a bottle of wine and plastic cups.

"Sorry they aren't wine glasses," Jockster said.

"Oh, Jockster," Scott sighed.

"Cedar."

"I'm sorry?"

"My name. It's Cedar."

"I-I…." He was confused. Jockster had two faerie names? "Cedar?"

"It's pretty weird, huh? But that's my name. My *real* name. Considering my mother's name, it's no real surprise. I guess I should be happy she didn't name me Sunny Bebop or Dweezil."

Scott shook his head. He had no real idea what Jockster was talking about. "You say the strangest things."

"I just wanted you to know my real name before we make love," Jockster said.

"Make love?" Scott asked, heart pounding.

"Make love," Jockster—*Cedar*—said and kissed him.

They skipped the wine.

THE KISS began so gently, so softly, Scott could scarce feel the lips against his own, feel Cedar's big hand cupping his cheek. But then ever so slowly, they pressed harder, as if asking for permission. Scott gave it, and Cedar's kiss grew stronger, harder, and then his tongue was demanding entrance. Scott gave him that as well and oh, that tongue! Scott had never really enjoyed that before—it had seemed... unhygienic. But now? Oh, now it was sensuous, exciting, making Scott's entire body start to tingle and shiver. Cedar's arms came around him, pulled him tight up against his beautiful body, their flat bellies together, their chests seeming to interlock.

Scott's sarong-draped cock was pressing against Cedar's jock, and he could feel the pouch grow hard. Now Cedar was running his hands up and down Scott's back, and it was like little electric shocks flashed out across his skin everywhere Cedar touched. Scott copied the man, feeling those wonderful muscles under his hands. They felt so incredible. Everything about Cedar felt astounding.

Cedar! His name is Cedar. What a wonderful name. It's perfect.

Scott let his hands fall to Cedar's butt, holding those round globes of muscular perfection. He gripped them and pulled Cedar closer, and Cedar moaned in his mouth, gripped Scott's ass in turn, ground his hardness against Scott's. Oh, even Cedar's hands on his ass felt divine. Before—with *all* those other men—it had felt like an invasion. Now it felt so right.

Yes. Touch me anywhere you want!

Cedar let go of Scott's ass, and he almost cried out in protest, but there was a fumbling then, and he realized Cedar was trying to untie his sarong. No. Not trying. He'd succeeded, and now the silky fabric was sliding off Scott's body and even that felt good. If not for the way they were crushed up against each other, it would have fallen to his feet, and Scott wanted it to go away. Wanted nothing keeping all of him from pressing naked upon all of Cedar.

So he reached down and pulled and tugged and shoved at the jockstrap, and Cedar laughed and helped him, and then the sarong was falling, catching a moment on his erection, and the jock was slipping down around Cedar's ankles and—*oh! oh!*—their hard cocks were pressed tight alongside each other, and had anything ever felt so extraordinary? Scott heard more moaning and realized it was his own.

Now Cedar's hands were on his ass again and his fingers running down Scott's crack and—*Oh!*—touching him there, there in his most private place, and he knew if Cedar wanted to fuck him, he wouldn't hesitate to let him.

"Touch me there," Cedar whispered. "Please. I've wanted you to ever since you put that damned suntan lotion on me."

"What?" Then Scott laughed. The sun block, and yes, he'd wanted to take his oiled finger and press it up inside Cedar, and now he was being asked? He took Cedar's perfect ass cheeks into his hands, gripped them hard, let his fingertips creep slowly into that cleft, marveling at the heat there. He let those fingers travel down, down, slowly, stroking, Cedar moaning, and…. *There*. Oh, there it was. The tiny puckered entrance to Cedar's body. Scott let just the tip of his first finger touch, touch, play with the tiny folds, and Cedar arched against him and moaned all the more.

Somehow they made it down to the blankets, remarkably soft on the hard ground, and they rolled first one way, then slowly the other. Cedar was kissing his face and his neck, his ears and throat, and it was all Scott could do not to cry out into the night. He wrestled Cedar over onto his back and kissed the man's face the way Cedar had kissed his, and when he reached Cedar's Adam's apple and the hollow of his throat, Cedar *did* shout out.

Scott blushed and stopped and Cedar asked him what was wrong and Scott said, "They'll hear us."

Cedar grinned. It was a radiant, happy smile and he said, "Good. Let them. I want the world to hear. I want the queer ones to know what's going on. I want all our faerie brothers to know. I want the gods to bless us and bless this!" He rolled Scott over and pulled his hands up over his head and buried his face in Scott's armpit and licked and sucked and Scott couldn't help it—he shouted into the night. He didn't know about gods or queer ones, but if this was part of being a faerie, so be it. Wouldn't it be sexy if he were to hear the same thing?

Why not? Why the fuck not?

Now Cedar was sucking at his other armpit and damn! It was sexy too. Cedar was doing things Scott had never wanted to do and making his whole body come alive. Who knew your pits were so erogenous? He'd always thought people who did that were just fucking kinky. Now he wanted to try the same thing. They rolled again, and he placed his face in Cedar's armpit, and unlike Scott's own, there was almost no hair there at all. There was, however, a musky sweet scent—sweetly acrid—that Scott would not have expected, and when he pressed his lips against that place, they both let out sighs of pleasure. It was so warm and wet and the taste slightly tangy and ever so real, and soon he was sucking, harder and harder, Cedar's begging him for more, and for a moment Scott thought he might cum.

He treated the other armpit the same, pulling at the hair with his teeth and only being urged further on. He straddled Cedar and ran his hands up that marvelous, completely hairless torso and the swell of his chest and felt his mouth drawn down to Cedar's maroon nipples.

"Yes! Yes!" Cedar said, and the harder Scott sucked on them, the more Cedar's pleading cries rang out.

Now, oh so suddenly, Cedar was on top and kissing Scott again, and now kissing down, downward, sucking at Scott's nipples and knowing somehow that Scott didn't want his sucked quite so hard. Cedar did give them a playful bite or two, and Scott was surprised how he arched up to meet those sharp teeth. But Cedar did that for only an instant, and now he was going down, that slight beard stubble so exciting on Scott's skin, and going farther down, and then Scott heard a gasp.

"Fucking beautiful, Scott. So beautiful." And then Scott's cock was engulfed in the hot wetness of Cedar's mouth.

"*Fuck!*" Scott shouted, and his ass tried to come off the ground, and he desperately pressed himself even deeper in Cedar's mouth. Cedar didn't gag once, took Scott to the root, his tongue doing impossibly wonderful things, his bristled jaw flexing against Scott's balls.

Beautiful. He thinks my cock is beautiful.

Then—*oh no! I'm going to cum! Too soon!*

But Cedar stopped—stopped at *just* the right instant and was kissing Scott again and it was as if they were sharing their souls with that kiss.

They were grinding their hard cocks together, and Scott saw he was still too close, just that simple thrusting could send him over the edge, so he pulled back, and that was when he really saw Cedar's full erection for the first time. What had Cedar said? Beautiful? Yes. He'd never really thought of a cock as beautiful before either. But it was. Perfect and hard, the circumcision scar flawless, the balls heavy and completely hairless.

Slowly, ever so slowly, he lowered his face into those balls. The skin of Cedar's scrotum was like satin, and the musky scent nearly drove Scott mad with desire. He licked the soft folds and gingerly sucked one of Cedar's balls into his mouth, nursing it ever so carefully. It was just the right size, not too big to make it uncomfortable and big enough to fill his mouth just right. He let it slip from his mouth and took in the other, and Cedar rocked his head from side to side, groaning out his pleasure. Then Scott licked up the shaft—soft skin, hard shaft— and when he reached the summit, saw the pearl of precum. He licked it up without hesitation, and it was a sweet, salty joy across his taste buds. He took the column into his mouth, took it halfway easily, and then excitement and joy allowed him to take the entire length into his mouth and throat. Another first. He didn't gag once. He let his nose nestle into the thick, soft pubic bush and breathed in the smell of him—musk and spice—and oh, he wanted to taste Cedar's cum.

But he wanted to taste something else first.

He reached down and took Cedar by the back of the knees and lifted, spreading his legs, lifting more so the cleft of his cheeks spread wide and revealed Cedar's asshole. It was lovely. It was perfect and pink and Scott wanted to cry it was so damned exquisite.

Could he do this? He never had. He'd been too afraid, too prudish. Too afraid of germs. Too afraid of everything in life!

But now he saw he wanted nothing more.

He bent down and kissed it. It quivered under his lips and before he knew what he was doing, he was kissing it again and again, then licking the tiny folds, the moist clenched entrance into Cedar's body. It was nothing like Scott had expected. The more he licked the more the tiny folds relaxed, and Scott was nudging his tongue inside. Cedar tasted like new pennies. He smelled fresh and musky and manly, and soon Scott was feverishly rimming the man in a way he never thought he would.

"Oh-oh, Scott. I need you in me!"

Scott looked up through Cedar's parted legs and saw the desperation on Cedar's face. "There," Cedar said. "Next to the wine. There's a condom. *Now*, Scott. *Please.*"

Scott trembled. Cedar wanted him to fuck him. Wanted him to top. Scott had never wanted anything more in his life.

He lowered Cedar's legs and found the foil packet and ripped it open. He rolled it down his throbbing cock, fearful he would cum just doing that much. "Lube?" he asked.

"You have me wet enough. I can take you."

"I don't want to hurt you," Scott said. That was the last thing he wanted.

"It won't hurt but for just a second. That's part of it. To *know* you are in me. Please, Scott. I can't remember ever wanting someone to fuck me this badly."

Scott stifled a sob—now where had that come from?—and nodded. He looked down, but it was hard to see by the torchlight. And when he tried to feel, one of Cedar's legs fell to the side and…

Then Cedar was holding his legs wide and high by himself and damn, Scott felt that spot, not as tiny anymore, wet, opening to his touch. He lined his cock up with that hole, still seeming so small, and nudged forward. Again. He'd done this so few times. He felt like an awkward virgin.

"It's okay," Cedar said. He wiggled down closer and that pushed the head of Scott's cock through that tight ring.

"Oh!" they echoed at exactly the same time.

Scott looked down into those stunning eyes and slowly, he gave a push, a second, and slid into the hot depths of the enchanting man beneath him. Cedar swallowed him and Scott fell forward on top of him, burying himself to the hilt.

Cedar shouted, his eyes closed tightly.

"Are-are you okay? Did I hurt you?"

There was nothing but gasping in response for the longest moment and then Cedar pushed down, wrapped those long, muscular legs around his waist, and pulled closer, pulled him down into a kiss. "Fuck me, Scott. Please."

That is just what Scott did. Slow and long and gentle at first, them both making strangling noises, and Scott could scarcely believe the joy and pleasure he felt. Bit by bit, he began to build up speed, and Cedar was watching him now, when they weren't kissing, and even then Scott would open his eyes to see Cedar staring back.

The pleasure began to build and build, Scott could feel his balls pulling tight against the base of his shaft, and then he was exploding into Cedar, his vision going wild and crazy and full of purple and white and blue sparks. And stars. His orgasm went on in great rocking waves, one atop the last, building and building until he couldn't help but shout, "God!"

And as the pleasure finally crested, as it began to abate, he could only think it.

God.

From nowhere a second slam of pleasure began to hit him in shockwaves, and to his surprise, Cedar began to ejaculate himself. It shot out in a beautiful jet of white against Cedar's tanned skin and without knowing what he was doing, Scott bent and managed to capture the head of Cedar's cock in his mouth and took the next waves of Cedar's orgasm. It filled his mouth and he gulped it down greedily.

This is Cedar came a thought from deep inside him.

A third round of shockwaves hit then, and he slipped out of Cedar and collapsed on top of him and then they were kissing again, sharing a remnant of Cedar's seed. He felt he should roll off of the man but didn't have the strength, and those legs were still holding him, now locked under his buttocks.

"It's okay," whispered Cedar. "I want to feel you on me."

So he rested and then, he didn't know how, they were lying side by side, arms around each other, legs tangled, foreheads touching.

Somehow, Scott didn't say, *I love you.*

It took all his strength.

Because this moment was perfect. And the last thing he was going to do was ruin it.

Besides. He couldn't be in love.

Could he?

CEDAR TOOK Scott back to his camp and loaded him into bed and even got under the covers and cuddled with him. Scott knew Jockster—*Cedar*—wasn't going to sleep with him, but at least he was holding him until he fell asleep.

Cedar was a nice name. Yes, it was different. But it was a nice name.

And being held in Cedar's arms was nicer yet.

It didn't take Scott very long at all to fall asleep.

CHAPTER THIRTY

SCOTT WOKE the next morning to the sight of Cedar standing over his bed. He was awash in morning light. Cedar had unzipped the windows, and that meant anyone passing by could see them. Suddenly, Scott didn't care. He tossed the light sheet off his body and lay there naked, his cock hard with his morning erection, for anyone to see. But especially for Cedar to see.

Cedar's jockstrap was hella sexy today. A red CellBlock 13 Grappler with a mesh pouch that let Scott have a sexy peek at Cedar's cock. God! He could see it! He didn't know if he wanted anyone to see Cedar in something like that. But then he laughed. Was there a man at camp who hadn't seen Cedar naked on the beach? Let 'em see!

"So, do I have to worry?" Scott asked looking up at the sexy man.

"Worry?"

"The red. Are you going to want me to fist you?"

Cedar raised an eyebrow. "What if I said yes?"

Scott trembled. "I-I guess I would have to see if I could do it."

Cedar sat on the edge of the bed. "You really would."

Scott trembled again. Gulped. "I—I would if that is what you wanted."

Cedar dropped his head back and laughed. "Oh, Scott. You are something special, aren't you?"

"Me?" Scott swallowed hard. *Me?*

"Yes, you," Cedar said with a smile. He was gazing down at him in a way that Scott didn't ever remember anyone looking at him before. Like something from a movie. *Somewhere in Time*, maybe. *That's what love looks like*, he would think whenever he watched that movie.

Is it love? Scott wondered. He almost shook his head. Love seemed impossible. He'd learned not to trust in love. It didn't happen fast. When it happened fast it was lust, not love, no matter how good it felt.

But looking up at Cedar—if that was anything like what love looked like, Scott didn't know how he would bear it if it really came his way.

"You're going to get raped if you wear that in public," Scott said.

"You better walk close behind me then," Cedar said.

Cedar scrambled onto the bed and soon the jockstrap was on the ground.

This time it was Scott bottoming.

Neither of them complained.

"YOU KNOW," Scott said, after, holding Cedar close. "I've always felt I *had* to bottom. Guys always want my ass."

Cedar nodded. "Your ass is perfect."

Scott blushed. "It's—it's just that I like to top and… I mean… last night is one of the first times I ever topped in my life. And…." God. How did he say all this and not sound stupid?

"And I don't usually want to top," Cedar said. "But Scott…. With you I wanted to."

"So this won't be like, a problem?" Scott wondered aloud. He'd heard of the problems of "two bottoms don't make a top." What he hadn't heard was of a bottom wanting to top or a top finding out he liked bottoming.

"Actually I think it's going to be a great week," Cedar said. "I never liked topping so much in my entire life. Your ass, Scott. I mean, I'm sorry, but it was made for fucking."

"Yours too," said Scott.

"Then let's make sure neither of us is deprived of anything," observed Cedar.

Scott nodded, his heart skipping a beat. What about Cedar's dance card? What about Ferret?

"I just fucking hate the fact that we live in a time where we have to use condoms," Cedar said. "We come to a place like this, we run naked under the sun, we live like man was *supposed* to live, but when we make love we have to be separated by a piece of latex. I *hate* it. I didn't want to cum in that thing. I wanted to cum in *you*. And last night. I wanted you to cum *in* me."

Scott's heart started to speed up all the more. It would have been nice. To feel Cedar inside him, even after. To know that feeling was Cedar.

And I let that bastard Garrett fuck me! He wasn't worth it. And here is a man I want cumming in me and I can't. "Cedar… I need to tell you something."

"What, sweetness," Cedar asked and wiggled closer.

Would Cedar still think he was "sweetness" after this? "Ah. A few months ago. I—I let this married man…. I let him…. I let him bareback me."

Cedar took a breath. Nodded. "I see."

"He said he was going to leave his wife. That he was gay. And he lied. He just used the line to get me to let him have me bare. And I was so damned stupid. I let him. So. The thing is… I've been hoping I am negative. That he *was* married. But he lied about everything else, so maybe he does that to men all the time. I got tested, and it was neg, but they said it was too soon to know for sure and—"

Cedar stopped him with a kiss. "It's okay. I've slipped once or twice. Been a few years so I pretty much know I'm neg, but I understand. Sometimes our little head does the thinking for our big head. Our cocks want what they want. They want the real thing. It kills me that a man can't cum *in* me. I love that part."

Scott nodded. "Yeah. It makes me feel...."

"Closer?" Cedar asked.

"Yeah," Scott answered. "Closer."

There was a long pause. "I guess I need to tell you something too." He sat up and looked away.

Scott's stomach clenched. He took a breath. Cedar hadn't judged him. Could he judge Cedar? "Tell me."

There was an equally long pause. Then: "I fooled around with Ferret the other night."

Scott felt it like a soft punch to the gut. Shit. Ferret?

Cedar still didn't look at him. "It was the night we were at Domi's. You got drunk, and I got you in bed, and I went back to my camp...."

And Ferret was waiting for you.

"He was there, waiting. And he started, well, practically begging!"

Scott found Ferret's voice coming to him from out of a dark night...

"A guy like you? So damned good-looking. You'll have no trouble getting all the sex you want. Me?"

Ferret had said he was good-looking! Scott had never thought he was good-looking.

"All I've got is my big dick," Ferret had said then. "I'm fucking ugly. But I fucking need held every now and then, you know? Give me a night.... Please.... An hour. Please!"

"And... he was so desperate. He...."

"It's okay," Scott said, and downright dumbfounded himself in the process.

Cedar looked at him, eyes full of questions. "We.... He didn't fuck me. I just jerked him off and—"

"It's okay." *I don't want to know.* "Ferret needs held once in a while too." *And you and I hadn't had sex yet. And shit, we're* not *a couple. You can have sex with anyone here if you want!* "We're not married," Scott said, and his heart hurt. Which was stupid. *We're not married.*

Cedar's eyes got big. Wet? Were they wet? "I'm sorry. It was so fucked up."

"It-it's okay," Scott said again. And somehow he meant it. "I mean it."

Cedar sat there, staring at him for what felt like forever. Finally, he said, "You know, it's getting damned hot in your tent. Even with that fan. We should probably get out of here for a while."

"Shit!" said Scott, sitting bolt upright. Morning!

"What?"

"I totally fucking forgot. I was going to go do yoga this morning."

"You've got a week," said Cedar, getting up and climbing into his jockstrap, lifting a leg high to climb into it and flashing some pink at Scott.

"You're going to get me hard if you keep winking at me," Scott said. *I cannot believe I said that! This place is bringing out the naughty in me!*

Cedar leaned way over, reached back, spread his cheeks, and definitely winked at Scott.

"Oh, damn," Scott said and reached out and pulled Cedar to him, burying his face in the man's steamy crack. He nosed up and down it until he found Cedar's asshole and began tonguing it with gusto.

"No, no, no! Later!" Cedar shrugged away.

"Son of a bitch," Scott said. "And *fuck* you look *hot* in that. I wish I had brought some of mine. I don't give a fuck if Wyatt... *Little Bear*, figures out I have a major jock fetish."

"You can wear some of mine if you want," Cedar said with a leer.

"R-really?" Scott asked. His cock shifted. It sounded hot. "You wouldn't mind?"

"I think the idea is hot." He squatted and got close to Scott. "Want to wear a clean pair or a sweaty pair?"

"I want to wear *you.*"

"Later, bad boy. Let's go eat. I'm starved."

A HALF hour later, it was Cedar who came up with the idea.

"Want to go into town?" he asked.

Scott put down his spoon. "What?" he asked through a mouthful of granola.

"Would you want to go into the city?"

"I.... Why? I thought you said you don't like to leave the land once you get here. I'm sure I remember you saying that."

Cedar shrugged. "That's true. But we could get some of your jockstraps." He gave Scott a lascivious smile. "We could wear each other's."

Scott felt his cock shift under his sarong. "That would be hot. But I don't have a car."

"We could ride my bike."

"Really?"

"Sure. Why not? I had a passenger seat added. Might as well use it."

"It's a ways to Terra's Gate."

Cedar shrugged. "How much?"

"An hour or so."

"That's okay with me if it's okay with you. I'd like you to hold on to me that long. And besides, I still want to go into the city. That's another... what?"

"About an hour there too," Scott said. "We could skip my place if you want."

Cedar shook his head. "I don't want. I want to do both."

Scott thought about it a minute. "When would you want to be back?"

"The sooner we leave, the sooner we can get back," Cedar said and took a bite of his own cereal.

"Well…." Peni suddenly sprang to Scott's mind. And not so much Peni as Peni's father and the funeral he knew he was going to miss. And while he wasn't sure he wanted to go to a funeral, they could go to the wake. "Is there any way you'd be willing to let me pay my respects? A… friend of mine. The one who talked me into going to all this in the first place? Then loaned me the tent and stuff?"

"I didn't think you were much of a camper boy. Surprised me that you had so much nice gear."

"Well…. Peni had to bail because his dad died. He insisted I skip the funeral. We could run in for the wake, though. I think he might appreciate it."

Cedar raised an eyebrow. "You like this guy?"

Scott shrugged. "I thought I did. Now I think it was just desperation. I do that. A guy pays me the least bit of attention and I think I'm in love." Scott took a deep breath. *Is that what I'm doing with you?*

"I see," said Cedar, and Scott could *see* the unasked question in the air. He decided to ignore it.

"Okay," said Cedar. "When is it?"

"I'll find out."

Cedar nodded. "Okay. Then we can plan when to leave. Wait. I don't have shit to wear to a wake."

"I bet I have something you can fit into."

Cedar gave him a wicked grin. "I just bet you do."

CHAPTER THIRTY-ONE

THEY LEFT around two o'clock, both dressed in T-shirts and jeans, and both missing their camp clothes. Scott would never have thought it. *I enjoy wearing a dress*, he marveled.

Of course, a sarong wasn't a dress. More or less a towel, in a way. And didn't Peni say men and women in his family wore them all the time? In Samoa people wore them in public. Men did. Scott wondered if he should have bought Peni a sarong, but hell, was that the kind of thing you gave someone when their father died? Probably not.

Since the funeral and wake were going to be east of the city, they decided to head to Terra's Gate first. Traveling well out of any kind of rush hour, they got to Scott's apartment in under an hour. They would never have gotten there so fast in his car.

The ride had been exhilarating. Terrifying at first, especially once they got on the highway. But then it was a pure head rush. It was like flying. The next best thing, Cedar had told him.

Cedar. Funny. It was hard to think of the man as anything but "the Jockster," but Scott had made the transition easily enough.

It was nice clinging to Cedar. Letting his hands drift, clutching his strong chest and then traveling down for a handful of cock. Soon he was pressing his own cock against Cedar's lower back, and oh, the vibration of the bike while he was doing it made Scott want to cum.

They didn't stay at Scott's nearly as long as he'd hoped. They picked out perhaps a dozen jocks—all of which "the Jockster" appreciated to no end. He even told Scott he was envious of a few of them.

"I stole a couple," Scott admitted, turning bright red.

"Stole?"

Scott felt his face heat up all the more. "Not from a store…," he managed to get out.

"Where, then?" Cedar asked, eyebrows raised and a smirk on his face.

"Locker rooms," Scott said, thinking he might die of embarrassment. "Hot guys. There was this one muscle stud…. So damned sexy, and straight as hell. Even Asher couldn't get him into bed—"

"Who is this Asher you keep talking about?"

"—and when he showered he would leave these jocks on the bench that were so wet with sweat they were practically dripping," Scott continued, ignoring the question about Asher. "And one day—"

Cedar burst into laughter. "You took the gift the Universe was offering you...."

"I felt so guilty!" Scott practically squealed.

"But not so guilty you didn't do it again."

"Not so guilty I didn't do it again," Scott admitted.

Cedar hugged him tight. "Tell me you jacked off with it in your face later."

At that point Scott figured he could have fried an egg on his face it got so hot. It also made him horny. The jockstraps made him horny. Cedar trying on a pair or two (after finding a pair of slacks and a dress shirt of Scott's for the wake) made him more so. And the talk of the sweaty athlete's jockstrap made it all but unbearable.

Unfortunately, Cedar was having none of it.

"We don't have time," Cedar said.

"We've got plenty of time," Scott said. "The wake isn't for a few hours yet."

"We're going somewhere else first," Cedar said.

To Scott's shock, "somewhere else" was the free health clinic.

"You don't have to," Cedar said, pulling his bike out front and parking it. "I hope this doesn't piss you off. I made an appointment to get rapid testing. We'll know our results in a half hour."

Scott couldn't believe it. He looked up at the sign, heart leaping in his throat. "Wait. They don't do rapid testing on Fridays. The guy isn't even in."

"I talked them into it."

Scott looked at Cedar, stunned. "How the fuck did you do that?"

Cedar shrugged. "I have my ways."

"When did you do that?"

"While you were making calls to find out about the wake."

"Damn," Scott said. He looked back up at the white sign with the big black letters. Did he want to do this? *I'll know. Or be pretty sure at this point.*

"They won't let us do it together."

"I talked them into that too."

"What? But...."

Cedar shrugged, grinned, waggled his eyebrows.

"You have your ways?"

"I do."

Scott grinned despite the fact his stomach was doing nervous summersaults. "O-okay. I mean, if you were able to pull strings like that, then who am I to throw a wrench in the works?"

So they went in, and even the lady behind the desk was surprised when the two were admitted together.

"This is such an honor," said the older man who took the lances and pricked their fingertips in order to do the test.

An honor? What the fuck had Cedar told them?

The twenty-some minutes it took to get the results were the longest of Scott's life. He knew the odds were in his favor, but still. What if?

The agony was worth it.

He was negative.

The relief was monumental.

And Cedar was negative.

The relief was more somehow. Like maybe they could….

No. Don't go there. Do. Not. Go. There.

Danger! Danger, Scott Aberdeen!

Carpe diem.

Seize the day.

The day.

Then Scott began to laugh in utter joy.

He was negative!

And now he had his whole life ahead of him.

THE WAKE was a much bigger deal than Scott had imagined. He'd been to more than one, so he thought he knew what to expect. You went in, said you were sorry, walked past the body everyone said looked so natural (which was always a lie) and then you got the fuck out.

It turned out Samoan Mormon wakes were more than that. A whole lot more. It made Scott more than a little uncomfortable. There was praying and a message, and quite suddenly he was transported a decade or so back in time and was hearing—seeing—the pastor of his parent's church up there in the pulpit, preaching hellfire and brimstone and warning about the sins of rock and roll, adultery, lust (and yes, homosexuality!), and Scott felt himself break out into a sweat and his stomach started clenching so hard he was afraid he might vomit. He wanted to flee from the place, but how could he? And how would Peni feel if he did something like that? Wasn't Peni going through enough without Scott making a scene?

And then Cedar was ever so subtly taking his hand and holding it tight, and somehow he got through it. People began standing up to say something about the dead, and there was singing in Samoan.

"O le alofa tunoa ofoofogia ose leo ese le malie.

Ua faaolaina ai se agaga pei o au."

Scott was surprised when he recognized the melody. "That's 'Amazing Grace,'" he whispered to Cedar.

"So it is."

Finally, it was over, and Scott had a moment to give his condolences. Peni looked incredibly handsome in his suit, and Scott could see that the fact his father had died must have finally hit him. In the few days before Scott had left for Festival, Peni had remained remarkably composed. Now his eyes were swollen and red and wet.

It was surreal because Scott had no idea how he would react when his own father died. They weren't close. Hadn't been even before Scott came out. It was like his father didn't know what to make of him—treated him as if he were an alien or something. He'd never been overly physically abusive—Scott could hardly ever remember being spanked, for instance.

But sometimes there was abuse where the scars didn't show, at least physically. Imagine grieving so much over your father, he thought. Imagine *not* wanting to throw a damned party to celebrate!

But that wasn't the way it was with Peni. Whatever Scott might think of religion, he saw it had given Peni family. A good family. A family that loved him.

But would they love him if they knew he was gay?

Scott introduced Cedar, who told Peni his prayers were with him.

Prayers. Just what kind of prayers did Cedar make?

Peni seemed grateful Scott had showed up, told him he was silly for doing it, thanked him again with a fierce hug, then demanded he not stay for the funeral. "We have not yet begun to mourn," said Peni. He did spare Cedar an odd look, and then Scott one as well.

Scott couldn't help but blush.

Why? I didn't do anything wrong!

Scott did get a chance to introduce Cedar to Sloan and Max and even Asher (who had snuck in at the very end of the service—liquor on his breath), who all eyed Cedar suspiciously but were polite. Even Asher didn't make a comment, wicked or otherwise. Scott knew what they were thinking. *Ah, Scott has done it again. Thinks he's in love and he's going to get dumped and then he'll cry and....*

Well, fuck you, he thought.

I'm not in love, and so what if I do *have a massive crush on this hot guy who somehow thinks that* I'm *hot!*

"So Asher is the one you and Little Bear claim is some kind of god?" Cedar said on their way out. "I don't get it."

"How can you *not* get it?" Scott said. "He makes Matthew McConaughey look plain."

"*Not,*" said Cedar.

"Cedar! He's a *star!* Or he's going to be. He has *the* movie-star looks. He can get any man he wants. He gets *straight* men in his bed."

"He wouldn't get *me*," Cedar said. "For probably the same damned reason he gets most of the men he shoots for."

"What's that?" Scott asked, as Cedar climbed onto his motorcycle and handed Scott his helmet.

"That much confidence. Turns me off."

"Most people *like* confidence," Scott remarked. "Turns them on."

"But Asher is conceited. He takes it for granted he's going to get his man—"

How can you possibly know that in the two minutes you met him? Scott wondered, surprised by his instinct to defend the man.

"No thanks. I like my men a little more vulnerable." He gave Scott a look that made his knees turn to rubber, and then Cedar cocked his head to the side so he had access to give Scott a quick kiss despite the fact they'd put their helmets on. "Besides, you're better looking anyway."

Scott drew back in astonishment. "There is *no fucking way* that *I* am better looking than Asher Eisenberg."

Cedar gave that shrug Scott was beginning to see was characteristic of the man. "You like what you like." He touched Scott's chest, dropped his hand to Scott's hip, then reached up and cupped his cheek. "And I'll like what I like."

It was all Scott could do to climb back onto Cedar's bike.

CHAPTER THIRTY-TWO

THE HEARTLAND Queer Men's Festival Auction was a hoot. It began with an act that had Scott's jaw dropping to the floor.

A man dressed as a nun and going by the name of Sister Serena Sarong So-Right was wheeled out onto stage on a huge cross that was strapped to a dolly and pushed by a man dressed as a Roman centurion. Then, lip-syncing to Queen's classic "I Want to Break Free," the "nun" broke free of the cross and then—even Scott looked upward for a bolt of lightning to fall—dirty danced with a gorgeous young man wearing a loincloth, a crown of thorns, and looking just like Jesus. And it was a *filthy* dirty dance too, with mock blowjobs and butt fucking! Then, just when Scott thought it couldn't get worse, a group of line dancers came out on stage dressed as Muhammad, Buddha, Moses, Ganesha, and Pan. The house erupted into hysterics, and Scott literally fell off his chair laughing. To make matters worse, Sister Sarong So-Right then hosted a Dirty Jesus contest, with four men dressed as Jesus—their wigs mop heads dyed brown topped with cheap vine wreaths for crowns. The owners of the conservatively owned Hobby Lobby would have had a heart attack. The Jesuses then went through the crowd throughout the evening, asking for donations.

And the charity?

Why, it was Heartland Queer Men's Festival. It seemed that Festival turned no man away for lack of funds—and it wasn't a cheap festival either. So the auction covered scholarships and other unforeseen expenses.

Several more men showed up on stage to help with the auction, a few of them dressed as nuns, and besides the four Jesuses, there were hot men in jockstraps. Among them, to Scott's surprise, was Cedar. But then Scott had to laugh at himself for being surprised. After all, Festival Cedar *was* "The Jockster."

Cedar was wearing one of his most scandalous jocks too.

The men in jocks and naughty underwear were what was known as "runners," and when articles would come up in the auction that potential buyers wanted to see closer, the runners would "run" the items out among the audience, trying to get them to bid higher.

There were many hilarious items, including an inflatable man with a dildo penis, a basket with a "love kit" inside (including bath oils, massage oils, lube, condoms, and a butt plug), bad porn, and a clock that played Muslim prayers.

But there were also some pretty damned cool items, like a huge quilt constructed from jeans and made by Zebra the Baker. Seemed that Zebra was a man of many talents. There was also some original artwork, a beautiful and sexy needlepoint of a nude man (it looked like a painting from a distance), some impressionistic oils painted from different sites around camp (including the corridor of sarongs), a few very nice pieces of pottery, and a couple of sarongs hand dyed by Hound Dog. Scott even found himself bidding on the painting of the sarongs and the real ones made by Hound Dog but had to drop out when the price of all three of the items he was interested in rose pretty sky-high.

The evening went fast and furious and turned out to end, Scott learned, much faster than usual.

It seemed Donald had scheduled the previously mentioned Queer God Ritual for that very night. The Auction had been known to go late into the night, leaving everyone totally exhausted—but now there was an extra motivation to "get 'er done." Donald only made it to Festival once in a new moon. And hey! It was a new moon!

But….

Ritual.

Yeah. The very thing Scott had been determined to avoid. Something he said he would not attend for any reason at all. Of course, Scott had gone to "Heart Circle." Hadn't that been something that had far more meaning than he'd expected? Should he just rule things out?

And there was the fact that Cedar was not only going, but participating as well.

That was a horse of a different color….

CHAPTER THIRTY-THREE

THEY GATHERED outside the dining hall, Scott wearing his peacock sarong. Cedar was up top at the Camper's Circle, where the ritual was going to be performed, so Scott stood nervously under the oak tree with the others. Wyatt was gone too. Of course he was going to be a part of it.

"Queer God Ritual," Scott mumbled under his breath.

"I *know*," Blue said. "Isn't it exciting?"

Exciting was not the word Scott would have used. But Cedar *was* involved....

And when in Rome....

The bell began to ring. A thin man wearing tights patterned to make his entire lower body appear to be tattooed stepped into the circle of men. He held the most unusual flute Scott had ever seen. Shawnti Fey. That was his name. Scott found himself wanting to ask how the name came about. It was an interesting name....

A week ago I would have rolled my eyes.

"Brothers, faeries, faggots—"

Faggots? Scott's eyes widened in surprise.

"—queer ones, dreamers. It is time for the Queer God Ritual. We are going to climb the old steps tonight. Watch yourself. Watch your brothers. Be reverent. Be respectful. Remember this is High Ritual and deserving of respect."

Scott gulped. *This is important to Cedar*, he said to himself. *This is important to Cedar.*

Shawnti Fey began to play a haunting melody on his flute and to walk away from the dining hall. The men fell into a line behind him, and he took them a short way before entering a line of trees. When Scott got there, he saw something he had somehow missed before: a zig-zagging set of upward-climbing steps made of natural slabs of stone cut into the wooded hillside. He saw he had to be careful, even though the way was lit by candles and torches. As steep as the sixty wooden steps that led from the shower house and dining hall up to the upper plateau might be, these had the ability to be more treacherous. They were, however, beautiful, and the torchlight certainly set a fantastical mood.

As he climbed, he was quite surprised as he passed two nude men making love in a small hollow cut into the wall of earth. They were lying on a bed of shining fabric, surrounded by votive candles, and Scott couldn't help but be moved and aroused. It was an incredibly erotic sight, and he had to force himself to move on and not linger behind.

When they finally reached the plateau at the summit, Scott found Dolce and Gabbana waiting for them. They were whispering something to Drake, the man ahead of him in line. Scott couldn't catch what they were saying. Of course, that was probably the point. They were talking to Drake, after all, and this was some kind of sacred witchy-woo-woo, right?

Don't call it that came a voice from deep within Scott, and a shiver passed over his arms and back. He bit his lip and found his case of nerves had just doubled.

Drake moved on, and Scott saw it was his turn. Steeling himself, he stepped over to Dolce, who stood slightly in front of his lover. Dolce was holding a long bouquet of flowers—sunflowers and black-eyed Susans and purple coneflowers. He dipped them in a bowl of water at his feet, then gently sprinkled Scott's skin. He then leaned into Scott and said, "May the tears of the Queer Gods cleanse and heal you."

"Ah… thank you," Scott whispered back.

I sure as hell can use healing.

Scott saw he was done here and moved on to Gabbana. The dark man with the very black eyes reached out and placed his hands on Scott's shoulder and, like his mate, leaned in and quietly asked a question that startled him. "Are you a cocksucker?"

Scott drew back for just a second and saw the pure sincerity in the man's eyes.

Just go with it, Cedar had advised him earlier, reluctant to tell him too much of what was in store. *And be respectful.*

That seemed to be the advice of the day, didn't it?

Am I a cocksucker? It was the question his father had asked him. Yelled at him. Wasn't it one of the last things the man had ever said to him?

(*"Won't have no cocksucker living in my house!"*)

But as he looked into Gabbana's eyes, he suddenly knew what his answer was supposed to be. Gabbana wanted truth. Wasn't that what this whole Festival was about? What had Bobcat said? About Harry Hay being angry that so many gay men were assimilating themselves in order to be respected?

Scott saw that Gabbana was growing concerned. There were men waiting behind him. There was a Ritual waiting ahead of him.

Do it came the voice inside.

Scott nodded. "Yes," he said. "I am a cocksucker."

Curiously, there was no sting. Especially when Gabbana gave him a radiant smile in return. "Then enter into the joy of the Queer Gods!"

"T-thank you," Scott replied. What else was there to say? He stepped past the man and saw that a ring of torches had been set up in the very center of the Camper's Circle. The men who had arrived ahead of him were forming a ring before him, spreading blankets and towels and sarongs and sitting down, waiting.

A circle of cocksuckers, Scott realized. All of us. All of us men who love men. Or at the very least, love sucking cock. For some reason the thought made him smile. He was in a brotherhood of cocksuckers! The smile turned into a grin. What could be better than that?

In the middle of the group of men was a large pile of wood. Donald stood next to it, dressed in a long black skirt, his wrists adorned with many bracelets and his ears with large hooped rings.

Four men stood at equal distance from each other, and after a moment Scott saw it for what it was. They were standing at the compass points. *This is it. What I've made fun of Wyatt for years. The "calling of the corners." Can I do this?* But then Scott saw Cedar, and without another thought, he took the blanket he'd brought and laid it at the point nearest his lover.

Lover. I'm thinking of him as lover? Scott! What are you getting yourself in for?

Once everyone had climbed the steps and were standing evenly around the circle, Donald raised his hands above his head. Shawnti Fey's music came to a quiet finish.

"Good evening and welcome to the Queer God Ritual. This is a ritual for and about Queer men. If you do not identify as a Queer or Gay Man, now is the time for you to leave and to search for your own paths…."

Scott pulled in a long breath. Queer or gay. Well, he could go with the second. There was still a part of him that objected to the word "queer." He'd heard the word used in far too ugly a way far too many times to feel any other way.

Besides, how would Cedar feel if he left?

There was a pause, and once it became clear no one was leaving, Donald continued.

"This is a time of being together and of being alone," he said. "This is a time to meet the Queer Ones.

"Will you please join me in singing our sacred song, 'Purple God.' For those of you who do not know it, it is a simple song, but powerful, and I know you will easily pick it up. Please join us as you are moved to."

Song? He was going to have to sing? Cedar hadn't mentioned that.

And Donald broke out into song, and soon many voices joined him.

> *Purple God, Queer God,*
> *Green God, Fairy God,*
> *Golden God, Faggot God,*
> *Come be with us….*

Scott shivered as the words were repeated over and over and over again. The song became richer and more powerful as the men joined in and sang louder and louder.

Fairy god? Scott wondered. *Faggot god?* What did that mean? *Faggot? Really?*

> *Purple God, Queer God,*
> *Green God, Fairy God,*
> *Golden God, Faggot God,*
> *Come unto us!*

Finally, the singing began to fade off, and there was only silence.

Wyatt, who was standing to the north of the circle clad in flowing green, took a few steps inward, turned, and then faced outward. "Black Bull," he shouted out into the darkness. "Black Tulip, Queer Spirits of the North, come unto us. Element of Earth. Ground beneath our feet. Come to us!"

Scott felt another shiver. The words made him a little uncomfortable. But then that made sense, of course. Ritual by any other name was still ritual. And as much as he was coming to appreciate these men around him, he still didn't know if he could believe. It still seemed so strange to him.

But to his surprise, he found a wanting inside of him. A *wanting* to believe. It had been a very long time.

Then Bobcat stepped into the circle. Bobcat. Who had told Scott he was a believer in Jesus. How could he be participating in this?

No. He didn't say that. He said he was a believer in the "White Christ." He said he didn't think of himself as Christian.

Scott started to shake his head—stopped.

Respect.

He took a deep breath.

Respect. These men deserved at least that. *These men who have shown you nothing but love.*

Bobcat turned around. As usual, he was completely naked, except for a blue sarong tied onto his head—unashamed of his old man's body, his potbelly, his thin arms and legs.

Could I ever be so brave? Scott wondered.

"Golden Dragonfly," Bobcat called to the sky. "Goldenrod, Queer Spirits of the East. Come unto us. Element of Air. Breath in our lungs. Breath that gave us birth. Please! Come to us!"

Then it was Bunny Penrith's turn. He was wearing a double sarong, one a vivid red, the other a bright yellow. In his hand was a hammer, and he raised it to the sky. "Green Hummingbird, Green Lily, Queer Spirits of the South, come unto us! Element of Fire. Flame within our souls. Please! Come to us!"

And then Cedar—The Jockster—stepped into the circle. He was wearing his blue and red Jack Adams jockstrap and a beautiful necklace of blue around his neck. It was the first time Scott had seen him wear anything like it, and he found his hand reaching up to touch the necklace Cedar had given him.

Cedar turned and glanced down at him and smiled and then looked up into the night sky. "Purple Shark, Purple Rose, Queer Spirits of the West. Come unto us! Element of Water. Spirit of blood and spit and cum. Please, come to us!"

Scott's eyes widened in surprise. *Blood? Cum?*

Then the four of them, along with Donald, began to sing again....

Purple God, Queer God,
Green God, Fairy God,
Golden God, Faggot God,
We welcome You!

A silence settled over the circle. Donald stepped out of its center and began to slowly walk its circumference. When he had made one complete round, he began to speak. "Now is the time to begin our journey. Make yourself comfortable. You may wish to lie down or stay sitting up. It's up to you. You may wish to close your eyes or leave them open. It's up to you. Please make yourself comfortable."

Scott looked around to see that the men near him were doing exactly that. Some were sitting Indian style, hands folded meditatively in their laps. Some lay on their backs.

Do what you're most comfortable doing came that voice. It seemed like good advice, wherever it had come from. He decided to lie down and close his eyes. Then, if anyone thought he was doing this weirdly or wrong, he wouldn't know.

"When in Rome," he whispered to himself. "When in Rome do what the Romans do...."

And then to Scott's delight, he felt Cedar settling next to him, shoulders touching, Cedar's left foot lightly touching his right.

Thank you, Cedar, my love....

"We are here now," Donald continued, and from the way his voice grew softer, then louder, then softer, Scott guessed he was still walking the circle. "Hear the fire. Smell the water. Taste the air. Feel your body...."

And to Scott's surprise, he found himself doing exactly that. His hands had settled onto his chest and his fingers danced over his nipples, bringing them up hard and alive, then down his ribs, and his belly....

"Remember to breathe," Donald said, and it was good advice. Scott had almost forgotten.

"We are here *now*. Be *here* now. Root yourself in this now. *Feel* your toes. Feel your feet, feel your ankles, feel them relaxing."

A meditation, Scott realized. But he thought it was way different than any Max practiced. *When in Rome* came his voice once more—and then he felt Cedar's finger lightly caress his own.

All right, he thought. He did it. He focused on toes and feet and ankles. Felt them relax.

Don't force it, warned that voice. *Just do it*.

"Now feel your calves," Donald said, his voice growing more and more soothing. "Feel your knees, feel your thighs, feel them relaxing.

Silence.

"Feel your balls, feel your cock, feel them relaxing."

Scott smiled. If Cedar didn't stop touching his fingers the way he was, relaxing is not what his cock would be doing.

And then it occurred to him.

Here? Here before these faeries and their Queer Ones? A hard-on would be just fine. Perfect even. In fact, just the thought made his cock stir.

"Now feel your butt, feel it relaxing. Feel your asshole, feel it relaxing...."

Scott wanted to giggle. His asshole?

But then....

Why not?

He relaxed his tense butt cheeks. Willed them quietly to relax. Wiggled so they moved aside and his asshole was, indeed, all but touching the ground. Why not! Wasn't his asshole what had taken Cedar's body into his own? Wasn't it how he had entered Cedar's? Could there be a closer intimacy between two men?

The thought made his cock harden even more, and he realized he didn't care who saw the rise in his sarong. *Yes*, he thought. Willed his cock to the sky and his asshole to the Earth. *Do it, Queer Ones. If you exist. Do it! Be in me. Let me be in you!*

"Feel your back, your lower back, your middle back, your upper back, feel it relaxing."

And oh, it felt good, didn't it? To let the tension and fear and yes, even suspicion and cynicism and disbelief, run right out of him as well?

If you really exist, Queer Ones, Scott challenged. *Come. Do it!*

"Feel your belly, feel your lungs, feel your heart, feel your guts, feel them relaxing....

"Feel your tits—"

Scott did just that.... Touched them. Stroked them....

"—feel your shoulders, feel them relaxing....

"Feel your upper arms.... Feel your elbows.... Feel your lower arms.... Feel your hands.... Feel them relaxing....

"Feel your neck... feel your jaws... feel your lips... your tongue... and your throat.... Feel them relaxing.

"Feel your face, feel your cheeks, feel your eyes, feel your forehead, feel your ears, feel them relaxing....

"Feel the back of your head, feel it relaxing....

"Feel the top of your head, feel it relaxing....

"Feel the bones that make up your skeleton, feel them relaxing...."

Scott felt another rush come over him... an almost high. It reminded him strangely of his mushroom trip on the first night. Not the same—but, but the same....

"Feel the skin that covers your body, feel it relaxing."

Silence.

Why.... Why, he was in a trance!

"You realize that you are totally relaxed."

Once more Donald settled into silence, and just when Scott had almost drifted off, his voice came back, full and strong and soft all at the same time.

"You are lying on a bench. Feel its hard, cool surface. It may be marble. It may be granite. It may be redwood. You sit up and look around...."

I do?

But then he did. He imagined it. In for a penny.... In his mind he sat up and looked around him, and there was only the light of torches. Scott found himself in a huge field, the grass perhaps six to eight inches high. There was a gentle breeze stirring that grass. Scott saw he was hard as stone beneath the sarong and pulled it open and let it feel the night air. Warm tonight, but a break in the heat at last—not hot.

It felt good.

Then he heard Donald's voice. He knew Donald was there. If he tried, he could see him.

But suddenly Scott didn't want to see him. He wanted to be right where he was.

"You see a path.... You get up. You walk down the path to the gate. You pause. You open the gate, and you walk through."

Scott obeyed.

"You enter a garden of beautiful red, red zinnias, beautiful blood red zinnias as far as your eyes can see."

He let Donald's world in and saw them. Saw the red zinnias going all out and around him—far, far and far.

"See the Red, Scott."

What? Donald was saying his *name?*

"Smell the Red. Taste the Red. Hear the Red. Feel the Red."

And Scott did. It smelled like cinnamon. Tasted as hot as the Hot Tamales candy he used to get when he went to the movies as a kid. The red was a gentle roar in his ears. It felt so warm….

"And the path goes on," Donald said.

"You follow it through the garden of red, red zinnias to a gentle knoll. You follow the path up and over the knoll into a field of orange poppies, wonderful, magical, orange, orange poppies…."

"Poppies" came the voice of the Wicked Witch from *The Wizard of Oz*. Scott laughed aloud.

"See the Orange. Smell the Orange. Taste the Orange. Hear the Orange. *Feel* the Orange."

Scott did. He smelled oranges; his nostrils flared at it. He could taste the Florida Sunshine Tree. It sounded like a crowd in an auditorium waiting for a concert to begin. Felt like fire that did not quite burn….

Wait! This is weird. What's happening?

For a moment Scott almost fought his way out of what was happening. It *was* weird! It *was* witchy-woo-woo! He didn't want *this!*

But then he felt Cedar's gentle touch, knuckles touching his, and that voice came back. *Do this. If only once. If only once in your life!*

My miserable life?

No! And then he heard joyous laughter! *No! Your* perfect *life!*

Scott trembled. *What—what was that?*

"And the path goes on…," Donald said. "You follow it through the field of orange poppies to a stony hill. You follow the path around the hill into drifts of yellow daffodils, bright yellow, yellow daffodils dancing in the breeze.

"See the Yellow. Smell the Yellow. Taste the Yellow—"

"Hear the yellow," Scott whispered.

Yes! Hear it!

"Hear the Yellow," Donald said. "*Feel* the Yellow."

"Feel the yellow," Scott echoed.

It smelled like the lemons in furniture polish, and tasted like lemon cake, sounded like the wind, felt blazing—raging heat, but again, somehow, he didn't burn!

"And the path goes on…. You follow it through the drifts of yellow daffodils to a forest of green ferns. You walk down the path into the forest of green, green ferns. Their quiet greenness surrounds you…."

Yes….

"See the Green."

So lush! So fertile.

Fertile. Scott smiled and his cock throbbed.

"Smell the Green." *Like the Earth in the woods.* "Taste the Green." *Like basil and thyme....* "Hear the Green." *Like birds singing in the trees.* "Feel the Green." *So luxurious. Cool, thick, dark soil running through his fingers!*

And then Scott saw something.

Someone.

Some... thing.

In his mind it looked like a man. A man who was tall and very, very dark. Muscles like coils of steel covered his body. His skin was all brown and dark green, and his legs—they looked... like bark? And his shoulders.... A thick mane of black and forest green fell from his head and yes, over his shoulders and down to the middle of his back. It wasn't just hair though. It was leaves and Spanish moss.

He—no, it. It turned its head, a huge head adorned with branches...? Horns? Were they horns? A great rack of antlers? Antlers?

And its face!

Its face was all in shadow—dark, dark shadow—its features invisible except....

Except for the eyes that glowed like deep emeralds lit from within! And was it looking at him?

"And the path goes on...."

And the figure was gone. That fast. Yes.

Because I'm.... I'm not ready for that!

A trance. I'm just in a trance.

Then relax.

Do it.

Feel this.

When in Rome....

"You follow it through the forest of green ferns to a bridge. You cross to the middle of the bridge, and you look out over a lake, a lake of brilliant blue water-lilies. These blue, blue water-lilies sing in the sunlight."

And Scott saw the Blue. He smelled it and tasted it and heard it and felt it. And the path went on. He walked over the bridge and over the lake and into a bog of indigo iris. They were iridescent, rich, and shimmering indigo. He saw the Indigo. He smelled it and tasted it and heard it and felt it. Left the bog and went to a hedge of ancient trees and beyond that to an expanse of purple violets. He experienced them on every level before finding himself in... where?

"Someone waits for you there," Donald told him. And for just one blinding, frightening moment Scott thought it was the tall green man...

The Green Man!

Scott. Don't be afraid of the Green Man!

But it wasn't the green man.

No.

"The Queer gods beckon to you. They call to you. What gift have They for you?"

Gift? There was a gift? Scott looked. *Gift?* And then he saw just what the gift was…

It was Cedar….

"SCOTT?"

He opened his eyes, and the bonfire was blazing and people were dancing around it to the beating of drums.

"I-I…. What happened?"

Cedar smiled. "I think maybe you fell asleep."

"I did?"

Cedar nodded.

"I—I guess I did."

It certainly made more sense than being greeted by a "Green Man."

"Gosh." He started to sit up. A wave of dizziness swept over him. "W-whoa…."

"It's okay, baby. Lay back."

"Oh, Cedar! I…. Oh no!"

"What, baby?"

Oh, no! No no no! "I missed the Ritual. I missed your ritual."

"Oh, Scott. It's okay."

Scott sat up, slowly this time. "I'm so embarrassed."

Cedar laughed. "Why?"

"I fell asleep!" He looked around and… saw two other men lying back… asleep?

"Want to dance?" Cedar asked him.

"D-dance?"

Cedar stood up and helped Scott to his feet. Pointed.

Scott looked and saw it. Saw men dancing around the fire.

"Dance with me?"

A voice….

Voices echoed up from his memories…

Him saying, "Hmph, I've heard you talk all about it. Magic circles and lots of dancing naked around the bonfire."

And Wyatt's reply. "Maybe you should give it a try. Go with me this year."

And his answer. "No way. None of that witchy-woo-woo for me. Way too weird. I am not running around naked for a week letting my dingle dangle."

"I don't believe it," said Scott.

"Believe what?" Cedar asked.

Scott sighed. Then smiled. "That I am actually going to do this! Okay. But I don't guarantee for one minute I'll do it naked."

"Who's asking?" Cedar asked him.

Who indeed?

He looked. Men. Dancing. Joyously dancing. Dancing naked!

Scott didn't know what to think.

But try as he might, Scott couldn't deny it. Something had happened.

And even if it was a dream, he suddenly realized it didn't matter. Not one damned bit.

He was buzzing.

His skin was buzzing.

His ears were buzzing.

He felt high, and he had not had so much as one drink.

Cedar took him by the hand, and they made their way back to Scott's tent and made love with a passion Scott could not begin to understand.

And then...

Why, the men! They were *still* dancing!

So he joined them.

Scott danced naked.

CHAPTER THIRTY-FOUR

"WANT TO do something really, really crazy?" Cedar asked him.

Scott laughed. Was almost taken over by a fit of giggles. Like he hadn't done a *lot* of crazy shit lately!

"Why not?" he said, his voice squeaking.

"Trust me?"

Scott smiled. "Yes." *I do.*

"What if I got you arrested?"

"Are you planning on it?"

"Planning on what?"

"Getting me arrested." He almost started giggling again. He couldn't help it.

"No. But it's always a danger."

Scott shrugged. He didn't care. He did not give a shit! Tonight he thought he'd seen Wyatt's Green Man. Thought there just might be "Queer Ones" and that they had given him Cedar as a gift. Ha! Why not get arrested? Hey, he worked for a law office, right? He'd get out of it.

"Come on."

They used their flashlights. It wasn't so much because of copperheads as it was that with no moon, it was as dark as a motherfucker.

It turned out they were going to Cedar's motorcycle. Now this he wasn't expecting.

"Get on," Cedar said after climbing on first.

"Won't we wake people up?"

"This, my love, is a Harley-Davidson FLHX Street Glide—"

Scott didn't even hear the name of the bike. *My love?*

"—and there's hardly a more silent bike on the road."

So with a shrug Scott did as Cedar asked. He climbed on, and Cedar started the bike, and except for an initial roar, it was damned quiet for a motorcycle, and in less than no time they were at the front gate.

"Where are we going?"

Cedar grabbed him and kissed him. Hard.

Cedar released him just as his heart was pounding so furiously he wondered, *Is this what a heart attack feels like?*

Then Cedar opened the combination lock on the front gate—

Damn! Is there a combination this man doesn't know?

—and opened it. He walked the bike through the gate and left it open.

"Shouldn't we close that?" Scott asked.

"It's after two in the morning," said Cedar. "We're okay. 'Sides. We might need to get back fast."

Scott giggled. "What are we doing?"

"Take off your sarong."

"Huh?"

"Get naked."

Scott laughed again. "You want to play here?"

"Do it."

Scott shrugged. "Okay." He reached to his hip, fumbled for a second with a knot or two, and was naked. "Now what."

Of course, he was almost blind it was so dark—no moon and they were in the tunnel through the trees that went from camp to the two mile gravel road—but apparently Cedar was getting back on his bike. "Get on," Cedar said.

No. It was a command.

"Naked?" Scott asked.

"Yes."

Scott's heart started to pound. "What are you doing?"

"Please, baby. Just do it."

So he did. It felt weird. Sexy, but weird. His legs were spread pretty far apart and that made *everything* touch the leather of the motorcycle's seat. His balls. Even his asshole.

Sexy.

But weird.

"Here," Cedar said, and Scott felt the helmet pushed against his bare chest.

What the fuck?

"Put it on."

This was kinky. But why not? He'd fuck Cedar in the dark over a bike with a helmet on if that is what the man wanted.

"Put your arms around me," Cedar said. "And keep your legs wide—"

Scott grinned. Sure. He'd keep his legs wide for Cedar.

"—open. I don't want you to burn your legs on the tailpipe."

Burn my legs on...?

"Put your arms around me!"

"No problem!" Scott leaned against Cedar, and the slope of the backseat put his crotch right there against Cedar's lower back. His *very* lower back.

He felt the stirring. *Gonna get hard!*

Because he could feel that Cedar wasn't wearing his jockstrap.

Then Cedar started the bike again.

"Wha…?"

They were moving. Not fast, but gliding down the tunnel in the trees, and then they were out under the open sky, the stars ablaze over them. Cedar did something and there was a purple glow all around them.

"Wow," said Scott.

"I wouldn't use these normally, but damn it *is* dark!"

"W-what… Cedar… what are you…?"

Cedar gently gunned the engine. "Hang on tight, baby."

And they were off.

Cedar turned the bike to the right. It took them down, down, and then up— !—and they were moving fast down a little country road and they were naked!

"Cedar!" he cried.

There was a slight revving sound, but that was all. The bike was remarkably quiet.

Scott could see very little. It was terrifying.

Terrifying.

But exhilarating.

They were flying through the night and they were naked!

They could be stopped! They could be arrested!

Then… the craziness took over. Scott clamped his thighs and knees hard against Cedar and let go of him and held his arms out to the side.

He half raised himself up—not all the way, he wasn't totally crazy—and the night flew, flew, *flew* past him and…

"I'm King of the World!" he shouted and Cedar laughed and Scott joined him and…

THEN THEY were back in Scott's tent.

They didn't waste a lot of time.

Cedar sucked on Scott's hard—raging hard—cock and then pushed him back on the mattress and straddled him like he was a Harley-Davidson FLHX Street Glide.

Before Scott knew what was happening he was sliding deep and bare into Cedar, and the feeling was so dazzling, so miraculous, so *intense*, he knew in a fraction of an instant why men took chances and had sex bareback.

Having sex with a condom really *was* like wearing a raincoat in the shower.

No wonder men begged him to let them bareback him.

There was nothing like this.

Nothing!

It was like wet velvet and—oh, so tight and wet and warm and slick and…

"Fuck!" he shouted, and who cared who heard?

He came deep and hard inside his lover and then felt the jets of hot cum splashing against his chest and neck and cheek.

It was the most incredible experience of his life.

The last thing Scott remembered was thinking *I'm King of the World,* and…

THEN CEDAR spent the night.

CHAPTER THIRTY-FIVE

CEDAR WOKE curled up behind Scott, his front to Scott's back, his arms around the man, his morning hard-on pressed against the cleft of Scott's ass.

It didn't hit him at first. Sunlight came not only through the orange fabric of the tent, but also through the open windows. Cedar had insisted on that. He didn't care if anyone heard them, for after all how much was the thin material going to hide the sounds of their loving?

Loving?

That was the first thing to make Cedar's eyes fly open.

The second was the sunlight.

He froze.

He had spent the night with Scott.

"Scott?" he croaked.

There was no answer.

"Scott?" he said, dread filling his every vein.

No answer.

A panic so *huge* it was like a whale bursting through the surface of Cedar's heart sent him flinging himself back and away from Scott and off the side of the mattress and onto the hard ground. It all but knocked the wind from him.

Cedar lay on the ground and found himself shaking. Trembling. Near pissing himself.

Then he heard the snore. Quiet at first. Then drawing out into a long rattle.

The relief was enough to make Cedar sob.

He pulled himself to his hands and knees and peered over the top of the mattress. Scott was wiggling, and now rolling over onto his back. He rubbed at his face and swatted absently at a fly and went back to sleep with another soft snore.

Cedar dropped his head down between his knees and fought to keep the tears at bay. It wasn't easy. Gods. Gods! *Oh, gods!* he cried inwardly.

He crawled to the door of the tent, unzipped it enough to crawl out, and zipped it closed.

Then he cried. He didn't let all the tears out. He knew if he did they might not stop. He'd pulled himself out of that abyss years before, and he would not return to its depth. *Oh, no.*

But some of the tears came anyway. Some of them. Like a burst of steam escaping before the teakettle was removed from the flames.

When Cedar finally gained a modicum of control, he staggered to his feet and then made his way as quickly as he could back to his camp—naked, not daring to go back for his jockstrap or even his bag (there was nothing in there that could not easily be replaced).

It didn't take him long to strike camp. He was used to packing things up fast. It's why he camped like he did. Cedar was a gypsy, after all, and a gypsy was always on the move.

Luckily, his bike didn't make much noise. Wasn't that one of the reasons he'd picked it out in the first place? Fuck that shit about how noisy bikes save lives. He needed to be able to pass through the night without disturbing anyone except maybe an owl (who pays attention to owls hooting in the dark?) or a dog on a porch (and with any luck, Cedar would have come and gone before it could decide whether to bark). He needed to be able to strike camp fast when things went bad or before the owner of a property he had chosen for his overnight stay called the police. He needed to leave early—like he did every year at Festival—before he had to say good-bye.

He hated good-byes.

Cedar made only two stops. The first was the Festival shipping container where he dropped off his tub, his hammock, chairs, and other things that just didn't travel comfortably on the back of a motorcycle, even one custom built like his own. The second was to fill his canteen with Gatorade from one of the big jug coolers in the dining hall. There was hardly anyone up, just a few early risers. He'd left early enough that the yoga people hadn't even seen him go.

The front gate was locked but everyone knew the combination. 9-8-7-6....

What the fuck have I done? he screamed inside.

A moment later he was on the gravel road and then the small county road, and he was on I-70 before he even knew where he was going.

CHAPTER THIRTY-SIX

SCOTT CAME awake to an empty bed.

He'd waked a few times in the night, surprised and so happy to find Cedar still with him. They had apparently crossed some divide, some line, because Cedar had broken his rule.

Cedar was spending the night.

But then Scott woke to that empty bed.

It made him sad—*but hey!*—Cedar had spent *part* of the night! Most of it, in fact. That was saying something, right?

So he'd crawled out of bed and gone down to the shower house and cleaned off and soaped up Bunny Penrith's back, and Bunny soaped up his and it was fun and he *knew* Cedar would be fine with it. Drake too, who was still mostly asleep. After all—there was no crack soaping or pucker cleaning. It was strictly sweet brotherly fun.

How cool was that?

There was *no* way he would have been able to wash the back of some near stranger in the shower room at the gym back in Terra's Gate. Or had that hard-to-reach spot washed on his own back. He would have had his lights punched out.

What a weird world this was.

And as each day had passed, Scott had found he liked Festival more and more. There was no understanding it. It made no sense. It represented so many things he didn't like. Or thought he didn't like. Could it be he'd been wrong?

This morning there were waffles. With blackberries! Blackberries picked the morning before up beyond the plateau in the Elysium Fields—three huge fields left to go wild and named for "a state of perfect happiness," not a meadow in Hades. And hadn't Cedar said waffles were his favorite thing in the world?

Cedar had even said it was chicken and waffles, and while that sounded way too weird to comprehend, Scott could bring him some waffles. After all, unless there was one of those People Eating Tasty Animal circles, Scott wasn't going to be able to bring Cedar the chicken part.

So after scarfing down a couple for himself, Scott prepared a plate for Cedar, piled it high with blackberries, grabbed some syrup in a cup (homemade! imagine!) and took off to Cedar's camp.

What he saw shocked him so badly he almost dropped the plate of waffles. Scott stumbled, tripped, fell back onto a log, and this time *did* spill the plate.

Cedar was gone.

The tent, the hammock, his chairs, his torches, the tub of clothes and faerie garb—everything—gone.

Scott tried to rise and found he couldn't. He almost fell when he tried. He let himself slide to the ground instead, sarong piled around him like a tablecloth.

Not happening. Not happening! This has not *happened again!*

It. Has. Not!

Knottie was the one who found him.

"Scott! Are you okay?"

He wasn't, of course.

Knottie went to him and helped him back on the log and asked him if he wanted something to drink.

"Got a beer?" Scott asked.

Knottie gave him a long look and then, apparently deciding not to argue with him, told him he would be right back. He was. With a beer. It was PBR— only the *second* worst beer made in the entire history of beer, but fuck a duck, beggars certainly couldn't be choosers, could they?

The beer went down surprisingly fast and easy, so fast that Knottie gave him a second long and weird look.

"Scott. Come on, man. Tell me. Are you okay? Do I need to call 911 or something?"

"No." He took a deep breath and fought back the tsunami of tears that wanted to come.

Again.

It had happened again.

Except I don't even have a phone number. I can't call him and have him tell me to stop calling and that he was throwing his phone away.

"Tell me how I can help."

Scott looked into Knottie's eyes (Knottie *Scottie's* eyes—he's another Scott!) and they were so blue. And kind. So kind. When had he seen such kind eyes?

Why, all around you, he realized.

He had experienced nothing but kindness. Except for maybe Ferret. *And he only wanted the same damned thing I wanted. A little love.*

"Ummm… Knottie. I…"

Wyatt.

"… would you find Little Bear for me?" he asked, and felt a burst of pride that he was calling Wyatt by the name he should be using in this place. "I bet he's at his camp."

Knottie nodded. "Sure. I can do that. You'll be okay?"

Scott nodded. It was a lie, but he nodded.

"Hey!" he cried after the retreating man.

Knottie was back in a second.

"How about a hit or two of that killer weed."

Knottie smiled. "Sure. You want that first or second?"

"First," he said.

So Knottie did just that. He brought back the most lovely orange glass pipe filled to overflowing with a nice stinky greenness, and Scott puffed away while he waited for Knottie to get Wyatt.

It didn't take long. Wyatt was back *tout de suite*, or at least it seemed that way. To tell the truth, Scott wasn't sure how much time had passed. He knew he was in some kind of shock and that it was probably Wyatt-style dramatics for him to be in such a state, and part of him was shaking a finger and saying, *"Didn't I tell you?"*

Danger! Danger, Scott Aberdeen!

"You okay?" Wyatt sat down next to Scott on the log. He glanced around in that silly-oblivious way of his and then stiffened, eyes widening, apparently noticing the lack of Jockster's camp. Scott saw all of this as if he were watching a television show on his big flat screen—everything looking real and unreal at the same time. It was almost as if he could reach out and, instead of touching his flesh and blood friend, his fingertips would touch a cold, hard plastic surface.

"Oh fucking shit," said Wyatt.

"He's gone," Scott managed.

"Oh."

That was it. *Oh.* And what was that supposed to mean?

A few hours later—no, it was probably less than a minute—Wyatt followed his "Oh" with a "Fuck, Scott. I'm sorry."

"He said he always stays the *whole* ten days," Scott said and even his voice sounded funny, like it was coming from very far away. "He said he *always* stays the *whole* ten days." This time, his voice was a growl; it sounded closer. Like the words might really be coming from his own mouth. "Wyatt…. He said he always stays the *whole* ten days."

Scott burst into tears and fell on Wyatt's shoulder, and Wyatt wrapped his arms around him—rocking him—"Sssshhhhh"-ing him and telling him it would be "all right, it really will" and that "I'm here for you, Scott."

The unreality set in again as Scott opened his eyes and looked down through his tears at Wyatt's bare chest—*At least he's not naked—he's got a sarong on*—hairy, *so* hairy, where Cedar was smooth as marble; Wyatt soft and padded where… well, Cedar was hard as marble; a little round belly where Cedar had tight abs like a washboard. There was a musk too. Scott could smell his friend, sweetly sour—he hadn't showered yet, or he had, but even though it was early in the day (what time it was, Scott had no idea), it must have been at least eighty degrees already. Cedar's smell reminded him more of amber, but not that sweet, and—*Whose idea was it to hold this festival in fucking July?* he asked. Or did he? Wyatt wasn't answering.

He looked at his friend, who had a dark shadow covering his cheeks and jaw.

"Your beard's coming back in," he said dumbly, his voice dead and neutral.

"Wow" came Wyatt's voice, and once more things sounded like they were coming from very far away. "You didn't care too much for the waffles, did you?"

That crazy comment somehow made the world become real again. It was in the singing of the cardinals and the high metallic whirring of the cicadas. In the annoying little swarm of gnats whirling around his face, the buzz of a mosquito in his ear. The tickle of his own sweat running from his right pit and down his ribs. The ache of his ass on the hard, rough tree bark. The hot air going in and out of his lungs.

At some point—Scott wasn't sure entirely when (*the pot, it was the pot, and Jesus it was good, wasn't it?*)—he went with Wyatt (*No! Little Bear!*) back to his camper and got comfortable, more or less, under the big screened-in sunshade. Scott took Howard's chair (after draping it with one of his huge towels) and sat Indian style and let time pass.

He's gone.

Very suddenly Scott wasn't sure he wanted to be at Festival any longer. It would be one thing if he and Cedar hadn't hooked up. But they had. They'd done more than hook up. They'd left the land! Cedar said he *never* left the land once he got there. They'd gone to Scott's apartment and picked out jockstraps so they could have some kinky fun together.

Not gonna do that now.

In fact, he wasn't sure he ever wanted to wear a jockstrap again.

They'd put on clothes—

(and wasn't it weird that he hadn't wanted to? Clothes were his defense and armor against the world—the one thing he could control about his appearance, the way he looked)

—and had gone to a wake together. Scott had introduced Cedar to his friends!

Goddammit, they had gotten tested together!

And everyone had seen that they'd hooked up! How would he face people? They'd be curious. Scott didn't like that. They'd ask him all kinds of questions. They'd want to know if he ran Cedar off.

Did I? Did I run him off? What did I do wrong?

"I love you, Scott," Wyatt said.

The comment startled Scott out of his reverie. "I love you too, Little Bear," Scott replied and realized he meant it. He loved Wyatt. A lot. And Wyatt loved him, although he wasn't sure why. "I'm an asshole."

"No, you're not," Wyatt said.

Scott turned to him, raised an eyebrow.

"*Well*... maybe *sometimes*," Wyatt admitted. "But who isn't?"

"Is that why he left?" Not bothering to say who "he" was. Wyatt knew.

"No, that's not why he left."

"Did he say something to you? Did you see him leave my tent?"

"Last night? *Honey!* I was cosmo'ed to the *gills*."

"No—not last night. This morning."

Wyatt gave him a look. "Honey, Jockster don't spend the night with *any*body."

"N-no. Really," Scott insisted. "I woke up a couple of times. Last time I got up to pee and I saw the sky was *just* beginning to lighten up in the east, and I was looking up at the stars and thinking how I'd never seen them like I do out here at camp. Then when I went back to bed, he was still there, and God—I can't remember being so happy as I was when I climbed in with him."

"Are you sure you weren't dreaming, darlin'?"

"I'm sure. I got in and he snuggled right up to me, and I asked him if he wanted to fuck me again, but he was already fast asleep." He sighed. "It was real. I was so happy."

Wyatt's eyes went bug wide, then went quiet. Finally, he said, "This is my fault." Wyatt's voice was clear and sharp as broken crystal. "I thought I warned you about this... how it could happen...."

Scott barely mustered a "Huh?"

"Festival romances." Wyatt sighed. "It happens every year. It's the magic of this place, all the gay men.... I'm sure the nakedness greases the wheel too, so to speak." He sighed again. "Two guys hook up and fuck like bunnies and think it's love. Festival is over and they have to go home, and they pine away for each other, and then one of them—a week, a month after Festival—moves lock, stock, and barrel hundreds of miles away to live with his Prince Charming, and a month after that they're throwing vases at each other. *Then* one or both of them starts posting *horrible* things on the Yahoo! Group and it's *so* depressing...."

"Hey!" Scott cried. "*Hello!* This is you trying to cheer me up?" For a moment Scott was actually stunned out of his fog.

"I'm sorry. But.... It's this place, you know? The energy. People *think* they're in love—"

"I am," said Scott, and then froze.

Holy shit. I'm in love.

It was stupid. Ridiculous. He'd known Cedar for only a handful of days. You couldn't fall in love that fast.

Except he had fallen in love with Sloan that fast, hadn't he?

But then he was *still* in love with him, wasn't he? More or less. Or was it. No. That love he felt for his friend was finally fading—

(*God! Cedar had helped with that, hadn't he?*)

—but it had taken ten years.

And those men online? Scott knew most of the time that he wasn't in love. That he was so desperate he was simply *pretending* he was. Lying to himself so hard that, for a very short while, he could allow himself to believe it. It had felt something like love. He'd wanted to be in love so badly, and…

Jeeze. Did it take falling in love with one man to help me finally stop loving another?

Wow. "Now I'm in love with Jockster." *Wow.* "Wow." *Wow*….

"Scott," Wyatt said. "You're not in love. It *feels* like love, I know, but—"

"Wyatt," Scott said, cutting him off. "Little Bear. Aren't *you* the one who believes in magic?"

"I-I…. Well…. Yes."

"Aren't *you* the one who's been telling me for *years* that this place is magic?"

"I-I…. Well…. Yes."

"All right then. Stop." He let out a long sigh of air. "*I* believe in this. It's real to me. I know it doesn't make sense, but I know it's real. I know that it's crazy to fall this fast. I mean, I don't even know his last name—"

"It's Carrington!" Wyatt rolled his eyes. "I mean, like—*duh!*"

"—and *maybe* you're right. Maybe once we leave this place—this *magic* place—maybe if I spent a week with him after we get home to the real world? Maybe that would be enough to make me want to throw vases at him. But maybe not. I fell in love with Sloan that fast."

"You did?" Wyatt asked, eyes wide.

"And stayed in love with him for ten fricking years."

"You're in love with *Sloan?*" Wyatt's eyes got wider.

Now it was Scott's turn to give Wyatt "the look."

"Oh." Wyatt cleared his throat. "Okay. I guess maybe I did know that…"

"And I know with my history of online romances…"

"… or I suspected you were anyway."

"… why you would doubt me, why you would think it was just old Scott falling in love again at the drop of a jock, but—"

"Romeo fell in love with Juliet at first sight," said Wyatt.

"Huh?" Scott asked.

Wyatt nodded, his voice full of sincerity. "Romeo. And Juliet."

"They aren't real," said Scott.

"Okay, Johnny Depp and Vanessa Paradis then."

"Ah…."

"Oh, wait. Skip them. Johnny ditched her for Amber Heard, didn't he? So Channing Tatum and Jenna Dewan then. That was supposed to be love at first sight. Although that should be against the law. I mean, Channing with a *woman*." Wyatt tsked. "What a waste!"

"Yeah, well…. I'm sure Jenna and a lot of women would disagree with you."

"And how about Michael Douglas and Catherine Zeta-Jones?" Wyatt exclaimed as if he hadn't heard Scott. "Oh." He grimaced. "Except look how *that* turned out. Cancer of the tongue or something like that? And was there ever a better warning about why you shouldn't perform cunnilingus?"

"Wyatt! That's terrible!"

"Tell me about it!"

Scott shook his head. "How would your boss feel if she heard you say something like that?"

"Okay. How about Tom Ford and Richard Buckley? Two men!"

"I don't even know who they are."

"You don't know who Tom Ford is?" Wyatt put his hands on his hips. "What kind of fag are you?"

Scott suddenly sat up in his chair. "Wait. Are you saying you believe me?"

"About what?"

"That I'm in love."

"I would certainly say it might be why Jockster hightailed it out of here!"

Scott heart crashed. "You mean because he knew I fell in love with him?" he cried.

"Or that maybe he was falling back…."

"Huh?"

Scott gaped at Wyatt. His heart started to pound.

"I am telling you. Jockster does *not* spend the night. Not. With. Anyone. I've never gotten the story. I don't know anyone who has." Wyatt sat down. "Jockster says there *isn't* a story. But there's gotta be one. You want a cocktail?"

"Story?" Scott shook his head. "What are you talking about? Wait. A cocktail? It's not even nine in the morning, is it?"

Wyatt raised an eyebrow. "Look, girlfriend. You've already had a beer—"

Scott jumped. *He knows I had a beer?*

"—and some doobie, so don't you preach to me about not drinking in the morning. Besides, why do you think God made Bloody Marys? I could make Bloody Marys. And besides, are you working today or are you on vacation?"

Scott jerked. *Work?*

Shit!

Didn't he have a shift at the front gate?

Scott turned to Wyatt. "What's today?"

Wyatt smiled. "See? Ain't it great? To not even know what day it is?"

"I think I have a shift this morning doing registration at the front gate!"

"Oh good! That's one of the *best* community services you can do!" Wyatt nodded enthusiastically. "It's pleasant down there in the shade, and you can relax and you get to see everyone who's coming in."

"The point is I think I'm supposed to be down there!" He couldn't go home when he had agreed to do a community service, could he? He had an obligation, and Scott always fulfilled his obligations. *Always*.

"Oh, gosh," said Wyatt. "I see your point. And I think this is Saturday. A lot of people show up on Saturday."

"Can I do it wearing something besides a negligee or a big pink hat?"

"That's your choice and… well, Scott. Can you?"

"Do it without the hat? I sure as hell say I can!"

Wyatt laughed. "No. I meant do it at all. You're pretty wrecked right now, and I would be too in your shoes. Sandals. But you're everyone's first impression of this place. You have the power to shape their whole Festival. Their experience registering, even though it might only take five minutes, can shape their whole week. Are you in the headspace to do it?"

Scott took a deep breath. Was he? Was he done crying? He couldn't say for sure he was. "What if I run behind Iggy if I need to cry?"

Wyatt nodded. "That could work." He stepped up to Scott and laid a hand on his shoulder. "Want me to come with?"

Scott thought about it all of ten seconds. "Please?"

Wyatt smiled. "You got it, baby cakes."

Scott would do his shift at registration. Then he could decide if he was going to leave.

CHAPTER THIRTY-SEVEN

WHEN SCOTT and Wyatt got to the dining hall, Scott discovered that—yes—he was late for his shift at the gate. By nearly an hour. Part of the "problem" was that it wasn't easy to check the time at camp. No one carried a watch at Festival. Wyatt had even let his cell phone die, despite the fact that he had electricity. That was *part* of what made Festival so magical—Wyatt and a half dozen others had explained to Scott over the last few days—the *not* knowing the time. If there was a meal or circle or some other event going on, then someone would ring a big old-fashioned school bell to let you know that it was time to show up. It sat atop a small tower, about ten feet tall, and when its cord was yanked appropriately, its ringing could be heard all over camp—nearly as far as the Elysium Fields.

And Scott thought not knowing the time was all fine and dandy. As long as you weren't *supposed* to be some place at a certain time. He wanted to curse Wyatt for not knowing the time when something important happened. Then Scott had a realization.

It's not Wyatt's responsibility to make sure I get to the gate on time.

It wasn't Wyatt's responsibility to have his cell phone charged.

Hadn't Scott let his own phone die?

Didn't *he* have electricity?

The thoughts brought him to a halt. It was so simple. So basic.

For someone as smart as you're supposed to be, you're just now figuring this out?

He had to sit down, late for his gate duty or not.

"You okay, Scott?" Wyatt asked.

Scott held up a hand—a *give-me-a-minute.*

Fuck me.

How much of his life had he spent blaming other people for something that was his to deal with?

The thought was so profound he could hardly move. He felt foolish.

My God…, he thought.

I'm fucked up because my parents kicked me out. I'm late because Wyatt forgot to charge his cell phone. I'm a mess because nobody loves me. I'd be happy if Sloan was my lover.

How many things had he blamed on someone else?

And where the fuck had this realization come from?

"Scott?" Wyatt asked.

It was a train of thought that was going to have to wait, wasn't it? He had to get down to registration.

Who was at the gate? Was the poor guy alone? *Shit!*

Scott did linger just a few more minutes. Enough to get some coffee. And enough time to find out that no one knew where Jockster had gone.

Leadfoot (aka Sister Hateful Heinous Bitch from Madison, Wisconsin) thought he had seen him getting some fruit from the dining hall. It hadn't occurred to him to say a word. Why should he? Sure, yes, he was on his bike. But what else was new? Jockster loved to ride his bike.

And you didn't think it was weird that he was leaving? Scott wanted to scream.

But how fair was that? Leadfoot had no clue Cedar was going anywhere.

It's not Leadfoot's fault!

Gate. Get to the gate!

When he and Wyatt got there, sure enough only one person was sitting at the front gate, alone, looking forlorn.

And who the hell should it be but Blue?

Scott felt his stomach flip. He looked at Wyatt, looked at Blue, looked back at Wyatt. Shit. Suddenly all he could do was picture Blue on his back getting reamed from both ends. He looked back at Wyatt. *Shit.*

"Sorry we're late," Wyatt was saying to Blue. "Well! *He's* late." He cocked a thumb in Scott's direction. "We had a little disaster this morning." He paused. "Well, *he* had a little disaster this morning."

"Okay, Wy—Little Bear," Scott said. "Sorry, Blue."

"No," said Blue, "it's okay. Nobody's come through. I'm glad too because I don't have a clue what I'm doing."

As if on cue they all heard the sound of tires driving over gravel and turned as one to see a big white pickup come through the gate. Wyatt walked over holding out his hand in the universal "Stop" sign, and the man pulled over into the grass.

Now what was he supposed to say, Scott wondered? Oh. Make sure they're here for Festival and not just wanting to hang out on the beach. Or cruise for sex, isn't that what Asher had said? Scott joined Wyatt and said, "Good morning, are you here for Heartland Men's Festival?" He knew he should have said *Queer* Men's Festival but he wasn't quite there yet. Maybe the next time?

"Hodor," said the big man with the muttonchops, stepping out of the truck.

Hoe-door? Is that what he said? And, oh! Damn! He was a *big* man! He had to be over six foot tall easy, with huge wide shoulders and thick in the middle, although not what Scott would have thought of as grossly overweight.

"Hey, Hodor," Wyatt said and waved him over to the table where the notebooks were. Scott stood and watched as Wyatt helped the guy, just as he had been helped when he arrived. It went fast—the guy had to write a check and sign a sheet of paper, and before Scott could even take in all that had happened, the man was climbing back in his truck. And the only word he'd said was "Hoe-door."

Hoe-door?

And remembering the speech about being a first impression of Festival he said, "Ummm… I hope you have a great festival."

"Hodor," said the man and started the truck and pulled back onto the road and went up the hill.

"What the hell?" Scott asked.

"Gods, he is so hot," Wyatt said. "And a sweetie!"

"How can you tell?" Scott asked. "All he ever says is—"

"Hodor," squealed Blue.

Scott shook his head. "I don't get it. Is that some 'faerie word' or something?"

Blue laughed and Wyatt rolled his eyes. "Sometimes I think you live under a rock. Haven't you ever seen *Game of Thrones*?"

"I don't even know what you're talking about," Scott said.

"HBO? Based on the books by George R.R. Martin? Fantasy series?"

"I don't like fantasy."

"Of course you don't," said Wyatt. "Never mind. Let me show you how to do the registration stuff…."

After that he sat down and carefully showed Scott and Blue all about the books. How the pages at the beginning were the registration sheets for the men who hadn't arrived yet and how they should be moved to the back of the notebook when they did, and the on-site registrar would take care of the rest later. How they needed to look at the sheets, which were very carefully marked and highlighted if the attendees owed any money or not, and where to sign and to make sure they wrote down the make of their cars and license plate numbers. "And oh, if they have a dog, they need to sign here." Wyatt pointed at another set of papers. "So Festival isn't liable if someone gets bitten."

It seemed easy enough.

Wyatt waited about twenty or so minutes more and then, luckily, another attendee showed up, and Scott and Blue whisked the man through everything and were sure to give him hugs and smiles and lots of welcomes.

"That was excellent!" exclaimed Wyatt as the car pulled off down the road. "We'll make a faerie of you yet!"

Scott just smiled. It was a small smile, but it was a smile nonetheless.

"Do you want me to stick around?"

Scott shook his head. "That's not fair to you, Little Bear."

Wyatt smiled beatifically. "I love it when you call me Little Bear."

The little smile tried to come back to Scott's face. "You go on back. I'll do my shift. It's not even three hours now. I can do that."

"And when you're done?"

"What about it?" Scott looked away—

"Will you be staying?"

—and there was Yggdrasil. Iggy. One of the most remarkable trees he'd ever seen. It really was huge. Someone had told him it was a cottonwood, easily eighty feet tall. He looked to the right and saw the sunflowers growing all over the earthen dam and knew that just on the other side was Lake Serenity. He cocked his head and saw the road that wound out of sight but which he knew climbed and climbed until it reached the plateau, where all the men he'd met this week, or most of them, were camped. He had met some pretty wonderful men.

Yes, the man who had most enchanted him was Cedar. Yes, his heart was aching that Cedar had left. He knew if he thought too much about that, he might start crying again right now. What he had shared with Cedar had seemed so real. More real than anything he had ever experienced with any man in his life.

Facing the rest of Festival without Cedar would be tough. Everything would remind him of the man he'd fallen in love with.

But on the other hand… did he really want to go home? Back to Terra's Gate? His empty apartment? His empty life? His job working in a law office as a glorified secretary?

Did he want to do that when not far from where he was standing there were over a hundred men who were making him a part of their family?

"I don't have to decide that right now, do I?" he asked.

"Nopers," Wyatt said.

And then, surprisingly, from seemingly out of nowhere, Scott heard Cedar's voice singing, "So every single moment I am left with the choice to stay in separation or listen to that Voice…."

"How about if I decide later," he said.

Wyatt nodded.

"And if I decide I want to leave?"

"I'll take you home. Just give me enough notice so I can get back in time for the Know Talent Show tonight."

Scott's eyebrows shot up.

Wyatt grinned. "Yeah. Remember? I told you that. Know Talent Show with a 'K.' As in 'know' we've got talent."

Scott laughed. "Oh, right. A *Know* Talent Show!"

Wyatt nodded enthusiastically.

"Well, shit. Do I want to miss that?" Scott exclaimed.

"I wouldn't advise it."

Well what the fuck. "I guess if I want, I can always leave tomorrow."

"Just make sure I have enough time—"

"—so that you don't miss something else, right?"

"Right," said Wyatt, his grin even bigger.

Scott sighed. *Oh, Wyatt.* "Okay. You got it."

After another moment, and one big hug, Wyatt turned and headed back up the hill. And Scott went back to the registration table and a young man named Blue.

FOR THE next half hour, Scott sat and listened to Blue rattle on about *Game of Thrones*. It took him that long to describe the first episode, and just as he had when Scott first met him on the Fourth of July, Blue spoke with such rapidity and excitement that there was no way for Scott to get a word in edgewise. There was barely room for him to say, "Hmmmm."

He got a break when he needed to pee, and for a moment he thought Blue was going to follow him. As he shuddered in relief from the pleasure of release of the pressure in his bladder, he gazed out at Iggy the tree, still hearing Blue rambling on in the background.

Oh, Blue, he thought—and remembered the sight of the kid at Green Man's Grove. The kid seemed to be all right. He didn't *sound* hurt. He didn't sound like anything was wrong. He seemed as animated as a little finch.

But…. In that moment Scott made a decision unlike many in his life.

"Blue?" he called out.

The nonstop talking continued.

"Blue!"

The Kajagoogoo boy went quiet. Then: "Yes?"

Scott flipped his sarong closed—*God, why do women hate skirts. It is so much easier to pee this way. No unzipping and unbuckling and pushing down and pulling up. Just pee. And how nice to have everything just hanging free and not all bound up! Hell, it's enough to make me think of giving up jockstraps…. Nah… no it isn't!*—and walked back to the registration table.

"I need to ask you something."

"Well sure! You can ask me anything you want. I am an *open* book and anytime anyone asks me a question I am more than happy to answer and—"

"*Blue.*"

Blue stopped. "Y-yes?"

Scott sat down next to him. "I need you to know that the other day, I… accidentally stumbled on you and Howard and some other man… well… ah…."

"Oh," said Blue so quietly that Scott almost didn't hear him.

Shit. I am handling this all wrong! "Look, it's none of my business, and far be it from me to criticize anyone's sexual… tastes."

Blue looked away—which wasn't normal. Blue always looked you right in the face.

"Look, I'm sorry. Maybe I should just mind my own business but... I just wanted to make sure you're okay."

Blue still didn't look him in the face. In fact, he was looking down between his feet.

"Blue?"

Blue finally looked up. Were his eyes wet?

"If you're into that, it's okay. I'm not judging you."

Those big eyes got wetter.

"I'm into jockstraps," Scott blurted before he could stop himself.

"I... you're... what?"

Scott blushed furiously. "They turn me on like a motherfucker. So if you're into rough sex, I'm not judg—"

"I'm *not,*" Blue cried. He dropped his face into his hand and started crying.

Oh, fuck me...!

Scott leaned in and put a hand on Blue's knee. To his distress, Blue flinched. "Blue."

"He called me a bitch!" Blue wept.

Before he even knew what he was doing, Scott stood up, then dropped to one knee. "Blue?"

Blue fell forward and threw his arms around Scott.

Scott stiffened for a moment, and then quite suddenly he remembered that not much more than an hour or two before, he'd cried on Wyatt's shoulder.

When in Rome?

He wrapped his arms around Blue, only to have the kid bury his face in his neck.

So it was true. Howard had taken advantage of this kid.

Shit. Asher had sex with this kid. Was that consensual? Surely Asher wouldn't do something that his partner didn't want to have done to him, would he? Blue had seemed pretty eager that day at Peter's—

"He *came* in me, Scott! He didn't wear a condom."

Scott froze, then pulled Blue closer. *Shit! Oh, God.*

God? Did I just say "God?"

"He *came* in me!"

What am I going to do?

"He didn't wear a condom," Blue whispered. "I didn't want him to do it bare! He wouldn't stop. It all sounded so hot when he was growling it in my ear at the beach. Men having sex in Green Man's Grove. I keep running it through my head. I *did* go with them. I knew what we were going to do. I guess I thought it was—I don't know—a game. Role-playing or something, you know? But then he got so mean, and I couldn't get him to stop!"

So Howard had all but raped Blue. Wyatt's Howard.

Fuck!

What am I going to do?

"Scott—he called me a *cum dump!*"

Scott let out a long sigh, and pulled Blue even closer.

CHAPTER THIRTY-EIGHT

AFTER HIS shift with Blue was over at the gate, Scott felt it was wrong to abandon the boy—

Man! He's a man. He acts like a kid, but he's—what did he say at the Fourth of July party? Twenty-one or twenty-two? Asher met him in a bar.

Blue is a man.

But still. Scott looked at the Kajagoogoo wannabe and realized he couldn't leave him on his own.

And that surprised him. *Why aren't I worrying about myself? Here I've just been dumped for the one-thousandth time and I'm worried about this kid.*

The thought brought a strange little smile to his face.

My God. I'm worried about someone else beside myself.

Then he shrugged off the thought and asked Blue if he wanted to do something, and the look of gratitude on the boy-man's face clenched it. It turned out what he wanted to do was go to the beach.

So they went to the beach.

The problem was Howard was there. And to Scott's shock, all the man did was grin. Give Blue a lascivious look and say, "*Grrrrr....*" Follow it up with a "Woof!"

He was oblivious. The man was totally and completely oblivious. He had no idea at all that anything was wrong!

When Scott turned to Blue, he saw the kid squirming.

"Want to go somewhere else?" Scott asked.

"Yes," Blue whispered.

Somewhere else turned out to be the hall where the Festival altar lay.

They walked to it, and once they got there, Scott remembered to kick off his shoes without even thinking about it. They looked at the statues, the pictures, the dozens of eclectic objects.

"These are mine," Blue said, pointing. He touched a harmonica. Battered, but lovely. Obviously not just a kid's toy.

"You can play?" Scott asked, somewhat startled. *Why, though? Why am I—*

"No. But I want to learn. Thought I'd charge it with some Festival magic, you know? Maybe the Queer Ones will help...."

"Maybe they will," Scott said and then marveled once more. *A week ago I would have snorted at that.*

"And this," Blue said and picked up a candle that looked like a penis.

Looks like? It is *a cock!*

"I collect them. I get guys to let me cast their cocks. The thing is you have to make sure they stay hard enough for the plaster to set." Blue said all this with a faraway look on his face. Like he wasn't quite there. "So I do sexy things. So they stay hard long enough—"

That was when he started to cry again. Not great heaving sobs like at the front gate. But tears all the same. "I-I'm j-just a s-slut!" Blue trembled. "Of course B-Big Sir thought I w-wanted it. I'd already f-fuck-fucking asked him if he'd p-pose for a c-candle!" More tears. Huge drops ran down Blue's face.

What to do? What to do? *Do I hug him?*

Blue turned to Scott, took a step, gave him a look with those Disney eyes, and Scott pulled him close. The way Blue melted against him, he knew he'd done the right thing.

Then once more words were out before Scott could stop them. "Did you tell him to stop, Blue? Did you tell him to stop?"

It took a thousand years for the kid—the *man*—to answer.

"No...."

"No?" Scott squeaked.

"How could I? The other guy was fucking my face. I couldn't say anything. Scott! I never should have gone with them. It's my fault!"

God. He'd heard about this. A victim thinking they'd brought it on. Was that what this was?

"I knew better," Blue whispered against Scott's wet neck. Wet with tears. "I should have had a safe word...."

But a safe word wouldn't have been much use, would it? Not when Blue couldn't speak.

Blue taking all the blame on himself didn't seem right. But was it the mature thing to do? He had gone with Howard and the other guy—whoever the other guy fucking was! He'd known they were going to get kinky. He hadn't told Howard to stop earlier, when Howard started slapping his ass.

But am I justifying this because of how big this could all be? Scott didn't know what to say to Blue, so he just held on and let Blue cry.

After that Blue wanted to be alone.

And Scott let him go.

"WHAT THE fuck do I do?"

Scott was sitting on the mats, looking at the altar, thinking. At best, the sex between Blue and Howard—Wyatt's lover—hadn't been fully consensual. He couldn't just ignore it, but he didn't know how to deal with it, either. He needed to talk to someone, but who?

He couldn't talk to Wyatt! He couldn't talk to Sloan or Asher. Cell phone reception was hell out here, and besides, he needed to look someone in the eye to talk about this. But he was stuck out here without his car. Which was his own damned fault. He could have gotten it when he and Cedar went to Terra's Gate. He'd thought about it. But he'd so wanted to ride on the back of that motorcycle, holding Cedar, that he'd given up his chance of independence. Hell! He hadn't even thought about it. Hadn't considered it.

I was too fucking afraid I'd get a nick in my perfect paint job!

Plus Sloan and Asher wouldn't know what to do. This was personal. So he couldn't talk to Wyatt, and he certainly couldn't talk to Cedar, could he? Cedar had hit the trail.

And I don't even fucking know why!

But what difference would it make if he did? He—Scott—made the decision to be intimate with Cedar. *Just* when he'd discovered he was HIV negative and that it was pretty damned likely he had dodged the bullet (a six-month test would pretty much seal the deal), he went ahead and had bareback sex again. And why? For what? A man who had vanished on him the morning after?

I let people use me! No one forced me. There were no chains, no shackles. I am the one who did it. I believed in a man once more when I shouldn't have. No one forced me. I did what I did.

Just like I have for most of my life.

So Scott couldn't talk to Wyatt—how could he?—and he couldn't talk to Cedar.

What do I do?

Who did he talk to?

He hadn't really made any other Festival friends. Not *really*.

Well, there were Super Gem and Silvercrow….

But somehow that didn't seem right. They were on their honeymoon!

Scott saw he was a *living* example of being trapped between a rock and a hard place.

If he told Wyatt that his lover had virtually raped Blue, Wyatt could very well shut Scott out of his life. And had it been rape? The line blurred. Rape was a very serious accusation. You did that kind of thing and there were consequences. Besides, it wasn't Scott's accusation to make, was it? Blue had made it clear he didn't want to pursue it since he was convinced he was to blame, that he shouldn't have gone along with the scene, or should at least have had a safe word.

Safe word! *Aarrghh!* See what happened when you pursued such craziness?

But what it really came down to for Scott was whether he should share what he knew with Wyatt. Of course Wyatt wouldn't want to hear it. The information would hurt him. And sometimes it was the messenger who got shot.

And does worrying about that make me a selfish asshole?

Fuck! Things were so much easier before I came here!

Until the last few days, Scott hadn't realized just how very much he loved Wyatt. He'd thought the member of the Fabulous Four he loved was Sloan. He thought he could tell Asher to fuck off. But then something strange happened in the last several days. He discovered that silly, goofy, crazy, flamboyant pink-shirt-wearing Wyatt…

… was the best friend he'd ever had.

I am the antithesis of everything he is and believes, and he loves *me.*

So what the hell was he going to do?

Wyatt loved Howard. Howard was the center of his life. If Scott told Wyatt the truth, chances were Wyatt would end their friendship forever.

But if he *didn't* tell Wyatt and Wyatt found out he knew…?

Well, there was a very good chance that Wyatt would end their friendship forever!

What do I do?

What do I do what do I do what do I do?

Then finally….

Oh, what the hell?

What can it hurt?

"DEAR GOD," he prayed silently, "please help me figure out what to do."

It wasn't as hard as he thought….

CHAPTER THIRTY-NINE

SCOTT ABERDEEN did not convert that day.
  He wouldn't have known what to convert *to*.
  He wasn't even sure whom he had *prayed* to.
  But he laid it on the altar of love.

CHAPTER FORTY

ONE THING Cedar did have was a cell phone. It was his one concession to being a part of the electronic world. He didn't pay it any attention when he was at Festival, but he made posts with it now and again on Facebook so his mother would be assured he hadn't been kidnapped or run over by a semi on an empty highway somewhere or murdered by a serial killer. And it wasn't even like he had to pay for it—his mother did, *And thanks, Mom.*

Today was one of those days he realized it was a good thing he did have one; otherwise he would never be able to find her. It wasn't until he reached St. Charles—just out and over the river from St. Louis—that he realized he was on his way to see his mother and that he didn't even know where she was performing.

He checked the time (something he didn't do at camp unless he had some community service or other to perform). She wouldn't be doing sound checks so early, would she? And shit. He didn't even know what hotel she was staying at. He hadn't planned on leaving Festival, so he hadn't asked her.

Why did *you leave Festival?*

It wasn't working out.

It hadn't been since the beginning. He hadn't been... well, *The Jockster!* He hadn't let Ferret fuck him. And why? Because he was feeling guilty about Scott! Why? What had he felt guilty about? They weren't a couple, for the gods' sake!

I am a free soul! I don't tie myself down. I don't want a lover. I like the road. I like the freedom to be with and have sex with anyone I want.

And then a pool man named Sam shrugged in Cedar's mind. "Excuse me for saying so, but that sounds a little shallow to me."

Sam had called him shallow? "I'm not shallow," he mumbled, sitting there on his motorcycle on the shoulder of the road. "I just can't. Not after Julian...."

He closed his eyes, clenched his jaw. Willed away any thoughts of Julian. It would only lead to pain. Boundless pain.

Cedar pulled out the phone and quickly found his mother on the contact list, pressed the little button.

She won't answer.

But she did.

SHE WAS staying at the Moonrise Hotel on the Loop, which wasn't huge but was a place where many a famous musician had stayed through the years. How perfect was that? Right up his mother's alley. And she wasn't heading over to the Verizon Wireless Amphitheater for a few hours yet. She'd been thrilled to hear from him, and he'd no sooner knocked on her hotel door when it flew open and there she was. With shawls and rings and bells on.

"Oh, Cedar," she said and took him into her arms and squeezed him tight. When she pulled back, her eyes were wet with tears. "I can't believe you're here!"

Cedar gave her his best smile—his posing for photographs with his mom smile—his best Festival-nothing-ever-gets-to-The-Jockster smile. "Well, Mom, I couldn't miss your concert!"

Her big blue eyes went wide and she motioned for him to come in. "We don't need to be doing all our hugging in the hall, now do we?"

Cedar came in and put down his bags and guitar on the bar.

Angela was there, of course, wearing her pseudo-Cyan Carrington clothes, which meant they looked nice but didn't outshine the star. The boots weren't quite as high, the jewelry not quite as fancy, and her hair was toned down a level or two. That made sense, though, didn't it? Cedar couldn't blame his mom. The people running the concert wouldn't even want that. They would want Cyan to shine like the star she was.

"Sit down, darling! Sit down. We are having sandwiches and Perrier."

Cucumber? he wondered.

But it turned out it was swiss and fresh basil, tomato, and thin slices of prosciutto on almost as thin pieces of focaccia bread, with a side of wonton wraps, and that meant it was the first meat he'd had in about a week, but what the hell? He was hungry. All he'd taken with him was some fruit.

"I just can't believe you're here," his mother said. "I know how important your gay festival is to you. And Saturday is the big day. Won't you miss something tonight?"

"It's okay," he lied. "Your event thing sounded really important to you, so I thought, what the fuck?"

She nodded, gave him a look akin to scrutinization, but he kept his poise, and after a moment she passed him the platter and told him to "Eat! Eat!" as if she were a Jewish grandmother or something.

So he took another sandwich and munched away and listened to her talk about how the evening was going to go. She would start with "Dark Witch," one of her most haunting songs, and then launch right into a few pieces from her new album. "People won't care about those, of course. I haven't had a real hit in a decade, but I must promote, right? Even if this is a big charity gig?"

"Sure, Mom," he said. "Why wouldn't you?"

Then she would do a bunch of the classics from her days with Rumors. "Otherwise I'll be lynched."

"And of course that'll be a burden," he teased. "You *hate* those songs so."

She rolled her eyes. "What can I say?" She took a bite of sandwich. "I was hoping your father would come. He said he might. Then he called this morning to let me know he wouldn't be in." She looked away, out the window. "This *morning*," she said with a sigh. "Can you imagine? This morning? Like he was going to fly in today and perform with me? We're not twenty any more. Hell, we were *never* twenty. By then we were on the road all the time...." Her voice faded away again.

Laird. Disappointing people again. So what else was fucking new?

"He's getting married," she said suddenly—and try as she might, she couldn't disguise the pain in her voice.

Gods.

"What does this make? His fourth?"

"That depends on if you count the years he and I were together but *not* married. I mean, *I* think we were, even without the paper." Once again—quiet.

"Mom, are you okay?"

She turned to him and her dazzling smile spread across her face, her eyes blazed like only Cyan Carrington's could, and she laughed. High and delightful and reminding him of Domi Dearest. Too bad Cedar didn't believe it. "Of course I am. *You're* here! I am on top of the world."

Laird. You fuck.

"So I take it you'll be heading out early in the morning to get back to camp? I was going to go ahead and stay in St. Louis for a few days." She waved out the window. "Do you know I've never been to the top of the Arch?"

"Maybe I'll go with you," he said, the words out of his mouth before he'd even thought about them.

She stopped. "Really? I thought you'd want to be getting back."

His throat froze and for a moment he couldn't even swallow. *Relax.* Cedar took a breath. "No. No, I don't think I'll be going back, Mom."

She leaned forward, and this time she *was* scrutinizing him. "Honey?"

"Yes, Mother?" He took a swig of Perrier.

She waited, as she was wont to do, and he tried to wait her out. He failed of course.

"It's a good idea, Mom."

"Why?"

None of your business, he wanted to say. But he didn't. Why would he do that? Wasn't she already hurting?

"Mom, something happened, and I just suddenly realized I needed to get out of there." *Now, leave it at that? Please?*

She stood up and came over and sat beside him. "Tell me, baby. Please?"

But I don't fucking know what to say!

"I—I…." What did he say? "I met someone."

"Really?" One of her lovely arched brows shot up, all but vanishing under her bangs. "A man?"

Cedar rolled his eyes. "Yes, Mother. A man. It's a men's festival, it's going to be a man."

She nodded. "Yes."

She waited again.

Dammit, Mother!

"That's it," he finally said. "I met a guy. It went sour, and I decided to leave."

"I see," she said. She pursed her lips. Nodded. Looked away. "Did he do something? Hurt you?"

"No!" he cried. Cedar closed his eyes, took a deep breath, and when he opened them he saw the usually quiet Angela had left the room. Thank the gods for small favors. He didn't know why he didn't care for the woman. She seemed to make his mother happy.

"No, he didn't hurt me." *Although I've hurt him. I am sure I have.*

"Then why leave? You're an adult. I am sure he's an adult. You could have only met him a few days ago. How sour could it go? And even if it went *very* sour indeed, that doesn't mean you should have left. You *love* that festival. How many times have you told me your whole year revolves around it?"

You don't understand.

"Then tell me," she said, as if she had read his mind. Sometimes he wondered if she could.

"Mom, I…. He didn't hurt me." Then admitting it. "But I suppose I've hurt him by running out like I did. I didn't even say good-bye."

"Well, surely you had your reasons," she said with a nod.

"Yeah, Mom!" He leapt to his feet. "Scott scared the fucking shit out of me!" He walked over to the bar. Perrier wasn't going to do it. He didn't ask her if she had any grass. He hoped she didn't.

"He scared you how?" she asked as he poured himself a stiff whiskey.

"I don't know, Mom." He took a swig of his drink, felt it burn its way down and explode in his stomach. Not a very *good* whiskey. "He…."

"You like him."

He spun to face her, eyes wide.

She nodded again. "Yes. You like him a lot, don't you?"

"No! Are you *kidding?* Mom! He's…. He's *impossible!* He…. He's a flat-earther. He doesn't believe in *any*thing. He thinks people who believe like we do…." He looked at her, waved his hand to indicate the both of them. "He thinks we're nuts. And he's bitter. He's angry. He's *impossible!*"

Except Scott wasn't those things. Not really. In just the last few days, Cedar had seen the magic happen. The *magick*, even. Because unlike Scott, he *did* believe in "those things." Not only that, but once again he'd seen the magic of Festival. He'd seen Scott transform. He'd seen him dance in the shower and beg for a faerie name. He'd seen him buy not one, but two, sarongs—dresses he'd called them! And then Scott had proceeded to wear them everywhere. He'd seen Scott wear a necklace he'd made from beads and nuts. He'd seen him cry in a Heart Circle.

And oh, the way he made love!

"That good, huh?"

His head snapped back in her direction. *Had* she read his mind? Did he say something out loud? What?

"Tell me something you *like* about him."

Cedar stood there for a moment, trembling, stunned that he *was* trembling. *What the fuck?* He finished the whiskey with one slam back of his head.

"He's so *injured*" came the words. Cedar couldn't stop them. "He's beautiful and doesn't know it. He thinks he's *ugly*, and oh, Mother, he's so beautiful. He reminds me of an elf. He's slim and muscular—although he doesn't think so. His eyes are amazing! He cares *deeply* about things. He's passionate about them, even when he's *being* negative. The world has hurt him so, especially his fucking religious parents. He's afraid of being hurt again, and gods dammit, now *I've* hurt him!"

He ran fingers through the long hair on top of his head, grabbed a handful, squeezed his eyes shut again. "I don't *know* why I left. I freaked. I panicked. *Mom!* I spent the night with him!"

And then she was standing next to him and pulling him close, and he dropped his head on her shoulder and damned if he didn't cry.

After a moment she pulled back and made him another drink, this one not even half as big. "Drink," she all but commanded.

He did.

The shaking stopped. Cedar took another long breath. Then he turned to his mother again.

Time to get a hold of himself! He smiled his paparazzi smile. "Now, what song are we going to sing?"

ANGELA BROUGHT in Cyan's guitar. Cedar knew it, of course. It was her favorite. Sometimes he wondered why his mother took it on the road—took such chances with it.

His mother, meanwhile, was laying out some music on the coffee table. "It's new," she said.

"So I won't be singing the chorus to one of our standards?" He smiled at his mother. "No, 'Don't look back, don't look back?'" he sang to the tune he'd heard thousands of times.

"No," she said with a twinkle in her eyes.

He glanced down at the music.

"As a matter of fact, this will be its premiere. No one's heard it. Except for Angela, of course."

"Of course." He smiled, then looked more closely.

"Open Road," it said across the top of the first page, written in his mother's lovely handwriting.

Cyan was tuning her instrument, strumming a few chords, and then humming a note.

She nodded. "I'll start and then you join in?"

"Sure," he said.

And then she began.

It had a very country sound at the beginning—unusual for his mother. She was rock and roll all the way. But by the time she started singing, he saw it was Cyan Carrington to the core, though. Of course it was.

> *Stuck out on the open road*
> *I don't know which way I'm supposed to go*
> *Guess I'll have to settle for my instincts*
> *The sky is clear there's no one near, I've nothing left to keep me here*
> *So I'll step on the gas and wipe all my tears away*
>
> *I'm listening to an old song, but I'm singing a new one*
> *I'm thinking about where I came from, and where I'm going*
> *I'm looking for a place where I belong, I know it's coming*
> *I'm listening to an old song, but I'm singing a new one."*

Cedar had it now—it wasn't that difficult. It was catchy, like all his mother's songs. He started singing. To his surprise, she let him sing the verse—

> *I see mountains on my left, ocean on my right,*
> *Will I drive another night*
> *Before I reach my destination?*
> *I don't know why, I don't know how, all I know is I feel better now*
> *Closer to a celebration.*

—and then his mother was joining in with her powerful and haunting voice. The voice that had made her so famous. How could she be anything else…?

> *I'm listening to an old song, but I'm singing a new one*
> *I'm thinking about where I came from, and where I'm going*
> *I'm looking for a place where I belong, I know it's coming*
> *I'm listening to an old song, but I'm singing a new one.*

Cedar trembled—the words!—fumbled, and lost his place on the page. His eyes were getting blurry, dammit, and then she stepped in with the bridge.

> *Oh, the sun is setting now*
> *I see my future written in the clouds*
> *And I am unafraid—of the decisions I have to make*
> *I have already paid for the mistakes I've made.*

Then he found his voice again, wiped his eyes, located the place again, And they finished the song together…

> *I'm listening to an old song, but I'm singing a new one*
> *I'm thinking about where I came from, and where I'm going*
> *I'm looking for a place where I belong, I know it's coming*
> *I'm listening to an old song, but I'm singing a new one*
> *I'm listening to an old song, but I'm singing a new one.*

There was a long silence, broken finally by Angela's soft applause. Cedar found it hard to meet his mother's eyes. For some reason he wanted to cry again.

"I wrote it for you, darling," his mother said.

Cedar swallowed hard. Of course she had. Was there any doubt? And she wrote lyrics that were perfect. Like she knew he would meet Scott, and that was just plain impossible. "I… I don't know what to say. It's… it's beautiful."

She smiled and his heart fluttered in his chest.

"Could mayhap it have been prophetic?" she asked. "Maybe you could be closer, finally, to a celebration?"

"I—I…." Sometimes he wondered if she were a real witch. Like from the movies and the old stories. From her songs. There was power in her songs. Was it real power? Her power? Could she be?

"Haven't you paid for any mistakes you may have made by now? Any mistakes you *thought* you made?"

"Mom!" He let out a sob, tried to fight it, felt the tears ready again. "It was my mistake. If I had paid better attention…. Maybe he'd be alive today."

She shook her head. "No, my darling boy. Julian made his choice. Maybe he thought he was doing it right, being with someone he loved and trusted when he did what he did. We will never know what was going on in his head and his heart. But I think what he did was selfish. He didn't think of what he was doing to you."

"Mother…."

"This Scott…. I've not seen you like this in years, baby. Something tells me you are about to make a serious mistake if you stay here. I think you need to get back on that motorcycle of yours and fly like my ravens are your wings."

"M-mom?" he wept.

"Something tells me he could be it. The one you need. You need to go back, at least to see. Don't let this chance slip between your fingers."

She was sending him away?

"B-but what about your song? Us singing together? You wanted me to sing with you."

She smiled.

"Oh, my darling. You just did."

CHAPTER FORTY-ONE

SCOTT WENT to the Know Talent Show surrounded by friends.

The day had been rough. He still hadn't figured out what to do about Wyatt and Howard. He'd been reduced to prayer. Him! And how funny was that? *Shit.* He'd even prayed about Cedar.

At first he begged for—what? God? The Universe? The Queer Ones?—to return Cedar to him. But then—right in the midst of a begging spell—he found he couldn't. Wouldn't. It wasn't pride exactly. It was something else.

It almost made him laugh. There was an old, old saying. Something about if you loved someone, you should let them go. And if it was meant to be, they would come back. His prayer quite suddenly evolved. From begging to... possibility?

After lunch, which had tasted good despite his worries and his grief, he went to the lake. He'd dropped his sarong on the beach and gone swimming—naked—and then floated on a raft where he'd been treated to another of Super Gem's awesome massages. This time it was nearly his whole body and not just his feet, and he found himself projected to some other world. It was like he was floating in the clouds along with those big birds he kept seeing high above—were they hawks?

Then he sat on the beach and listened to stories of Festivals past, heard jokes, and found himself telling one or two himself. They weren't very good. Wyatt was the joke teller. But there was laughter, and if it was only polite, Scott couldn't tell.

He decided to go for a walk then and—surprise!—that walk took him to the sarong shop. Gentle Ben's lover was there, and Scott paid for the one he'd picked out the other day. Then he chose a new one, this one all golds and oranges and reds, a tie-dyed feast for the eyes. Maybe he could make another necklace? It needed accessorizing, right?

Then he went to Domi's, and Greg made him a couple of gin and tonics, and my, weren't they good? It was a buzzed Scott who went down to dinner. That meal was something called "Dress-Up Night," and oh, the costumes!

Look there—Super Gem was wearing a Superman costume. *But holy shit!*—it wasn't a costume. It was paint. He was naked as the day he was born!

There was Wyatt. No! Stop calling him that. It was Little Bear. And he was dressed as Tinky Winky, the Teletubby. Howard, of course, was in full leather. *Sans* a codpiece.

Blind me, please. Please! Poke my eyes out.

And especially when he knew what the fucker had done with his swinging dick.

Here came Hodor (*that was his name, right?*) wearing long johns? Long johns unbuttoned almost all the way. One more button and it would have been pubic hair on show. The guy looked sexy, though, somehow, even with a bit of gray and those muttonchops. *Wow! Would I have ever thought a man like him was sexy a week ago?* Scott smiled, and so did the big giant, and when Scott said, "Nice look," he only got "Hodor!" as a response. Weird.

Domi Dearest was in camo, of course—camo underwear, sneakers, and hat, and he'd even painted his beard to match. Now that was original! How had he done that?

Rat Bastard was naked, naturally, and had a new hat, this one even wider and bigger than the one he'd worn the day Scott met him. It was a huge silver UFO, complete with flashing lights along the edge.

Scott couldn't help but wonder what Cedar would have been wearing. Considering the jocks he wore on just any day, it would have been scandalous.

Where are you, Cedar? What's more, was he okay? *Why did you leave me? No. I will not go there!*

Dolce and Gabbana were dressed as M&Ms, Gabbana in the green high heels, which made him tower over his lover even more.

Here came Hound Dog and Bean, with the latter dressed as a huge coffee cup (complete with his café's dancing goat painted on the side) and leading the former by a leash. *Oh no!* Hound Dog had a tail and…. Scott blushed and tried not to look where that tail was coming from. He couldn't help it, though. *Oh my!* Would he be able to sit down?

Little Bearded Girl was dressed as a baby, including a diaper, and carrying a huge teddy bear.

Lula Belle was wearing a full-hoop Southern Belle dress, and why not?

Two men he'd yet to meet, Lynx and Lady Bug, were dressed appropriately as their namesakes. Lynx wore a wonderful mask, and Lady Bug's red outfit with black polka dots included a matching bag.

Gentle Ben was wearing a butterfly muumuu, and his husband looked terribly sexy as a Roman Centurion.

Hey, thought Scott. *Too bad I don't have something like that! After all, when in Rome.*

Here came Silvercrow in a rainbow tutu and combat boots. Scott couldn't help but laugh in delight. In fact, it was then he realized he'd been laughing for the past half hour.

How nicely unexpected was that?

Wait. Was that…? Yes. Oh! Snowflake in a huge and fabulous white and blue ball gown with their little gray poodle in a close to matching outfit!

And there was Sundog in nothing but a white jockstrap and matching white wings.

Of course, once more, Scott couldn't help but think about Cedar—The Jockster.

Should he be surprised Knottie was in black and yellow leather? He still wasn't asking about that yellow color choice either!

And here I am in just a sarong.

It was then he felt a tug at his elbow. He turned to see Leadfoot (aka Sister Hateful Heinous Bitch from Madison, Wisconsin) dressed in nothing much more than boots and a leather mini-skirt. "Come here," he hissed and dragged Scott to the shower house. "We've got something for you."

Scott could only go along, confused and wondering. When he got there, his eyes flew wide in surprise. There was Daddy Dean—holding out the poodle skirt. "We saved it for you," said Leadfoot's lover.

Scott was stunned. "B-but I can't wear *that!*"

"Of course you can," they chorused, and they had Scott naked and then into the skirt before he could argue. They were big men!

"B-but I can't!"

"Oh, yes you can!"

They dragged him over to the full-length mirror, and the image looking back made Scott burst into laughter. But still…. "I can't wear this!"

"Yes, you *can,*" said Daddy Dean, and they presented him with huge and ridiculous cat's-eye glasses and a purse made to look like a poodle.

Scott laughed again. "Where did you find this?"

"We went into town the other day on a shopping run and stopped by this secondhand store. We saw this and knew it had to be yours!"

"B-but… I c-can't!"

"Here," said Leadfoot and handed him a huge joint.

Scott stared at it and finally thought, *Oh, what the fuck!*

A few hits later and he was ready to join the others.

The only response was a burst of applause. Scott couldn't decide if he was pleased or embarrassed. Maybe a little of both?

Dinner was wonderful. The meal was dubbed "White Trash Dinner" and was absolutely the tastiest meal of the week. It began with iceberg wedges with creamy blue cheese. And then what a shock it was to discover that the chicken-fried steaks with mushroom gravy were made from tofu! They tasted *so* good. They even had a meaty texture. And of course there were biscuits, garlic mashed "taters," and corn on the cob! Delicious! Completely and wonderfully delicious.

And once again, Scott couldn't help but wonder what Cedar would think of the meal.

But no. He wasn't going there. There was still half of Festival ahead, and he was damned if he wasn't going to enjoy it. That was about the point he realized where his train of thought was going.

The rest of Festival.

He was staying.

Scott stopped by his tent before the show, trying to decide whether to change or just what-the-hell-it and wear the damned (fun) poodle skirt all night, and as he was digging through his things he found the lights that Wyatt had given him on the first day of Festival. He opened the box to discover something that made him throw back his head and laugh. They were shaped like little green and pink and orange margarita glasses!

"They are to *live* for!" he cried.

Setting them around the tent was the last thing he did before running off to the pavilion to see the show.

CHAPTER FORTY-TWO

SCOTT WAS still wearing the poodle skirt when the Know Talent Show started.

And it was the truth. "No-Talent Show" would not have been the right title. These men, these brothers, these *faeries*, knew how to have fun. Even if some of them couldn't really sing or dance, it made no difference. Together they were wonderful.

The show started on the right note. Lady Bug, Lynx, and someone else named Precious came out, and with the song "Finally" by Ce Ce Peniston blaring, did a fun number right out of *The Adventures Of Priscilla, Queen Of The Desert*, complete with huge flat-bottomed bell-shaped pants. The three of them were in perfect synchronization and it was that bit alone that convinced Scott he wanted to come back next year.

It was Super Gem and Silvercrow at the soundboard and the infamous Snakebite, along with his lover, running the equipment that kept the show going strong, and thank goodness—they were great!

After that a cute balding man came out with a ukulele and sang a little song. He was really quite good. Made Scott wonder if he could learn. Then the man, whose name, it turned out, was Aurora, asked Gentle Ben to come out on stage. They sang a rendition of "Georgie Girl" that had almost everyone in the audience singing along.

There was quite a bit of singing, in fact. Lula Belle stunned Scott with Sondheim's "No One is Alone" ballad, sung in a deep, rich baritone.

Their act was followed by Borealis (Aurora's partner, appropriately enough), who did a very fun act. He had big fake plastic breasts tied on his chest and sang a song called "Woman With A *Y*." It was the very opposite of politically correct, poking fun at the women's separatist movement.

One of the acts that moved Scott was by a faerie who called himself Harper Bear. He came out on stage with a huge harp. It looked a lot like a classic concert harp, but was more. Something gorgeous and fantastical. He was a big man with a thick white beard, and the songs he played stirred Scott in ways he never expected.

Wyatt pretty much stole the show. He came out on stage wearing a pink outfit (and should Scott have been surprised?) consisting of a tutu, a P!nk concert T-shirt (of course!), pink lace wings, and a huge pink hat made of lace, ribbons, and Scott didn't know what else. Enormous pink sunglasses and tall pink furry boots completed the outfit. Where the hell did he find boots like that? Scott wondered.

"Hello, everybody!" Wyatt cried in a high squeaky voice. "You can just call me Pink." He giggled and everyone laughed. "I am going to sing you a little song—but first!—Aurora, would you come out on stage?

To applause, Aurora complied. He'd changed, though. He was wearing pink too. A little pink vest and a pink sarong.

Oh no! Scott grinned. Too much! This was too much.

"Aurora has graciously agreed to accompany me on his wondrous little uke. It's a damned good thing too, 'cause I can't play shit!"

Sing? Wyatt can sing?

And then Wyatt did just that.

Wyatt can sing!

> *Dr. Bronner's makes your Hoo Hoo tingle.*
> *Brothers, you know what I mean.*
> *You can always tell the folks that use it.*
> *There's a smile on their face and they always smell clean.*

> *Don't let 'em tell you that it's not okay.*
> *It's personal hygiene and oh, by the way...*
> *Dr. Bronner's makes your Hoo Hoo tingle.*
> *Brothers, you know what I mean.*

Scott exploded into laughter. How could he help it? He'd experienced Dr. Bronner's soap on his "Hoo Hoo" and tingle is just what it had done. He had tingled for a good hour!

But Wyatt wasn't done...

"Doo Doo Doo Doo...," he sang.

> *Dr. Bronner's makes your Hoo Hoo tingle.*
> *Fellas you know what I mean.*
> *Dr. Bronner's makes your Hoo Hoo tingle.*
> *It feels like your Hoo Hoo just swished Listerine.*

> *Don't let 'em tell you that it's not okay.*
> *It's personal hygiene and oh, by the way...*
> *Dr. Bronner's makes your Hoo Hoo tingle.*
> *Brothers, you know what I mean.*

> *Doo Doo Doo Doo Doo....*

Dr. Bronner's makes your Hoo Hoo tingle.
I use it every time I get the chance.
Dr. Bronner's makes your Hoo Hoo tingle.
It feels like a Peppermint Patty in your pants.

By the time Wyatt got to the next "Doo Doo Doo Doo," the whole audience had joined in.

Dr. Bronner's makes your Hoo Hoo tingle.
It's a zero calorie snack.
Dr. Bronner's makes your Hoo Hoo tingle.
It feels like your Hoo Hoo just sucked a Tic Tac.

Don't let 'em tell you that it's not okay.
It's personal hygiene and oh, by the way...
Dr. Bronner's makes your Hoo Hoo tingle.
Brothers, you know what I mean.

"Doo Doo Doo Doo," chorused Scott with the others, tears of laughter rolling down his face.

Dr. Bronner's makes your Hoo Hoo tingle.
I hope you're not getting annoyed.
Dr. Bronner's makes your Hoo Hoo tingle.
It feels like your Hoo Hoo just popped an Altoid.

Don't let 'em tell you that it's not okay.
It's personal hygiene and oh, by the way...
Dr. Bronner's makes your Hoo Hoo tingle.
Fellas it's curiously strong!

And finally, after doing a few twirls, Wyatt ended his number...

GOP you keep your laws off my Hoo Hoo
Fellers you know what I mean.
What happens with my Hoo Hoo's between me and my Hoo Hoo
You dirty old man keep your Rushes and your Ricks and your Mitts
    offa me!

Don't let 'em tell you what to do or say.

Hoo Hoos unite, stand up and say "Nay."

  ("Nay!" shouted the entire audience)

GOP you keep your laws off our Hoo Hoos

Fellas, you know what I mean!

The house exploded into applause and Scott could only lay back in his chair laughing. Laugh and be happy he was there, despite it all, despite it all.

It was then the house lights went low.

"Faeries and Gentlemen" came Super Gem's voice. "We now present a very special act...."

Better than that? Scott wondered. *There is no way that is going to happen!*

But he couldn't have been more wrong.

CHAPTER FORTY-THREE

THE HOUSE lights went out…

… and when they came back up, Cedar was on the stage, wearing his khaki shorts and a white T-shirt. He'd decided that, somehow, it was the thing to do.

He was shaking inside, unsure if what he was about to do was the right thing or not. He could only go with his gut. He looked out at the audience. Almost everyone was here and…. *Oh gods.* His heart sped up. There he was, front row…

Scott.

He smiled inside. It almost made it to the outside.

Scott was wearing a poodle skirt.

He gave his lover a small nod—*is he my lover?*—and saw the look of shock on Scott's face.

Shit. Should I have warned him?

Too late now. It's all or nothing.

"Hey, everybody," Cedar said. He trembled. Gods. Should he have asked somebody for a hit of something? *You can do this.* He looked down again at Scott. *For you, baby.*

"For those of you who don't know, I'm the Jockster."

Someone let out a catcall.

Cedar smiled again. It failed. He took a deep breath. "For years I've shared nearly nothing with you. I participate." He nodded. "But… I keep Cedar Carrington, son of famous rock stars, all to myself."

Scott gaped up at him.

You didn't know? Cedar froze for a second. *You didn't know?*

But wasn't that half the reason men around here wanted him? He looked around the house and, to his surprise, saw Scott was not the only one with a look of confusion on his face. People knew that, didn't they? Surely they did?

"Anyway," Cedar continued. "That has got to stop. There is something I need to share, especially with you, Scott."

Scott, who had been whispering something to his neighbor, snapped around and looked back to the stage.

Oh gods! Cedar gulped. *I can do this….* "You know I've lived a great deal of my life on the road. The first half was because of my mother, always on tour, always traveling, shows, personal appearances. Mom has a home—I lived there. But we were on the road far more than we were ever under that roof. At least it feels that way. Somehow that turned me into a gypsy. I decided that I didn't want to 'live' anywhere. That the road *was* my home.

"But then…. Then I met someone. A *wonderful* someone." Tears battled to the surface of his eyes. *God! I can't cry already.* But when the vision of Julian came to his mind, he couldn't fight them. So beautiful. Slim, big eyes, dark hair, smooth skin. *Oh, help!*

Cedar took another deep breath. "His name was Julian, and I fell in love. I wanted to be with him, and he wanted me to stay with him. So I did. I settled down. We bought a house, got a big golden lab, and lived what I thought was going to be happily ever after. *I* was happy. I thought Julian was."

He closed his eyes. *Tell it all.* "Sure, he suffered from depression. But we'd go somewhere, do something fun, and he would pull out of it." Cedar's voice wavered. Quivered.

"I guess I wasn't paying close enough attention." Cedar trembled again. He tried to look at everyone, but his eyes kept going back to Scott. Beautiful Scott.

"I woke up one morning… and… J-Julian…."

Cedar closed his eyes, covered them, and let out a sob. "Ju-Julian…."

He cleared his throat and shifted on his stool. "Julian was dead."

Cedar opened his eyes and saw the look of complete distress on Scott's face. *Fuck! Should I have done this in private?*

Too late now. Go on. Finish it!

"At first I just thought he was asleep. But then I couldn't get him to wake up, and by the time I figured it out… it was too late." Cedar's voice caught and another sob escaped him. "Everyone tells me it was too late already. That-that he'd been dead for hours. B-but how does that make it better? How did I *not* know?"

Cedar let out a long sigh. Tears had begun to run down his cheeks.

And, oh gods. Was Scott crying? Yes. He was….

"It got worse when the ambulance came and they told me that Julian had killed himself."

With those words, Cedar couldn't help it any more. The tears were flowing freely, and hell, could he cry any more today? How was he going to finish this if he was crying? "C-could someone get me some water?" he asked and several people leapt to their feet. It was Blue—that poor kid from Green Man's Grove—who made it to the stage. He climbed the steps and came to Cedar's side and handed him an open canteen. "T-thanks," he said and took a big gulp and handed it back.

"You want it?" Blue asked.

Cedar shook his head and Blue looked at him, started to move away, then closed the canteen and laid it at Cedar's feet before walking backstage.

Thank you, my friend. I owe you.

And he did, didn't he?

But first. Scott.

"It was a rough time," Cedar continued. "Julian never even left a note. Just swallowed a bottle of pills and spooned up to me and died." He shook his head. "Ever since then…. Well. I've not let myself get close to anyone. That was eight years ago. Somewhere along the line, the Jockster was born. And that's who I've been.

"But now…? Now maybe it's time for me to be a little more."

He sighed. Laid his fingers on the strings of his guitar. Closed his eyes. And began to sing.

> *There you are, head always hanging low*
> *So confused, you don't know which way to go*
> *I see you wishing you were somebody else, not like yourself*
> *Watching the world pass you by*
> *Watching the world pass you by*
>
> *You want to get out, you want to get in*
> *But you don't know where to begin*
> *So much time wasted on another*
> *You forgot about your own life*
> *Every day it's a new struggle, and you don't think you're gonna win*
> *Always feel like you're running for cover*
> *Like you'll never see the sun again*
>
> *But it's your time to shine, oh you've gotta let your light shine*
> *It's your time to shine, oh you've gotta let it shine.*

Cedar opened his eyes and looked down at Scott. *This is for me. This is for you. Can you hear me, my love?* He shivered. *Don't stop. Finish!*

> *If you could learn to see the world with new eyes*
> *Then you would find it's cloaked in a disguise*
> *Of reality made by somebody else, much like yourself*
> *It can be changed anytime*
> *Yes, it can be changed anytime*
>
> *You want to get out, you want to get in*
> *But you don't know where to begin*
> *So much time wasted on another*
> *You forgot about your own life*

Every day it's a new struggle, and you don't think you're gonna win
Always feel like you're running for cover
Like you'll never see the sun again
Baby, you're gonna see the sun again

But it's your time to shine, oh you've gotta let your light shine
It's your time to shine, oh you've gotta let it shine."

Then, before he could stop himself, "I love you, Scott."

And to Cedar's utter joy, he saw, rather than heard, Scott say it too. "I love you."

The room exploded into applause.

CHAPTER FORTY-FOUR

"CAN YOU forgive me?" Cedar asked him, and Scott didn't know how to respond.

They had left the pavilion, and as they walked across the grassy plateau, they could hear P!nk's "Perfect" filling the night behind them.

"Forgive you?" Scott asked.

"Y-yes. I shouldn't have left."

No. You shouldn't have. But somehow he wasn't even tempted to say it out loud. "Did you mean it, Cedar? *Do* you love me?" He closed his eyes, afraid of the answer—but needing to know. No games. *No more fooling myself.*

"With all my heart. Gods. I do love you."

Scott almost cried. Opened his eyes and looked at Cedar. *He loves me? He really does?* And from the look on Cedar's face, he could see he did. The impossible had finally happened. Someone loved him! Scott stopped Cedar and stepped into his arms, pulled him tight, and kissed his cheek. "I can't believe this."

"I know. It's crazy, right?"

"Crazy," Scott said. "Totally. No one will believe it. They'll say it's just crazy old Scott again."

"Again?"

Tell him about all his online love affairs? No. Not today. "They'll say I'm crazy when I tell them I fell in love with you so fast."

"Me too. Crazy me. But Scott, I can't help it. I know I only met you a few days ago, but from the first minute I saw you... something happened to me."

"Me too," Scott cried. "But I just thought.... Well, I thought it was just me being foolish again. I can't love you that fast, can I?"

"I don't know," Cedar replied.

"Wyatt says this happens all the time. Two men fall under the spell of this place and *think* they're in love, but a week after Festival they're throwing vases at each other."

"I promise not to throw a vase."

Does that mean I will see you next week? Scott wondered. "Good. The only vase I have is worth a fortune. I found it for a steal at an estate sale."

"You and your expensive tastes."

Scott shrugged. "I can't help it."

"You know all that stuff is just... *stuff*, right?" Cedar asked him. "Your Ralph Lauren bag, your Versace glasses...."

My Cartier ice bucket. My Lacoste towels....

"Just stuff, my love."

My love?

"You are the worth. *You* are what's valuable."

Scott's heart raced. No one had ever said things like this to him before.

"Take it from someone who grew up rich...."

Grew up rich. It reminded Scott of something Cedar had said. "Wait." He shook his head. "What was that stuff about famous rock stars?"

"You—you really don't know?" Cedar asked. "Most people do."

"No," Scott said. *Not a clue.* "Tell me."

"Scott.... My parents are Cyan Carrington and Laird Addington."

Cyan Carr— His eyes went wild. "*The* Cyan Carrington? You mean... Cyan and Laird from Rumors? The rock band?"

"Yes," Cedar whispered.

"The 'don't look back, don't look back' Rumors? 'And she looked back and turned into a pillar of salt' Rumors?"

Cedar nodded. "Yes."

"Holy shit." Scott couldn't believe it. "I fucked the ass of a rock star's kid?"

Cedar laughed. "And came up my ass, yes. The rock star police are coming to get you."

Scott's eyes went wilder.

"You know I'm kidding right? About the rock star police."

Scott shook his head. "I just can't believe it."

"It's not something I broadcast. People treat me different when they know. Give me things. Treat me like I'm some kind of god or something. Wait on me hand and foot."

"Well, I'm not going to wait on you hand and foot," Scott said.

"How about if I wait on you instead."

Scott smiled.

"Do I have to wait?"

"Wait for what?"

"To make love to you?"

"No way," said Scott.

They all but ran to his tent.

THE LOVING was good. They'd fucked each other, each going just until they thought they would cum, and then they would switch places. Sometimes one would push the other's legs back and take the other that way, sometimes one would just climb on top.

They fucked until they couldn't take it anymore, and then they rode the wave, finishing inside each other. Claiming each other.

They rested on their sides, Cedar behind, pulling Scott tight against him.

"That's why I don't sleep with anyone," Cedar whispered. "I was so afraid I would wake up and…."

"Sssshhhhh…," Scott said.

"May I spend the night with you?"

Scott's heart took wing. "Yes, you may."

Just as Scott started to drift off, Cedar snuggled closer and whispered in his ear. "I want to spend more than tonight with you."

Scott bit his lip. Dare he even hope? "We have all week," he said.

"I want *more* than that. I want to spend every night with you."

"And if Wyatt's right? If a week from now we can't stand each other?"

"I promise, no vase throwing."

Scott giggled and they snuggled even tighter and fell fast asleep in each other's arms.

CHAPTER FORTY-FIVE

THE NEXT day Scott went out in a jockstrap. He left the sarong behind.

He was as nervous as shit. No one had ever seen him in one of his jocks before—not one that wasn't a classic boring brand, that is. But Cedar was with him.

He found out why it was that Cedar—back when they were at Scott's apartment—wanted him to bring one of them. It turned out they had matching ones. And that's how they went out. Matching.

The pouches were black with a gray-bordered blue stripe down the middle. The leg straps were black and the waistband was royal blue with a black band in the middle and the logo "Cellblock 13" in bold white letters in front. Not one of Scott's more nondescript pairs.

"Are you sure?" Scott asked. "I'm not too fucking skinny?"

"Baby, you look so hot it's going to be all I can do to keep the men from trying to grab that beautiful butt of yours."

Scott blushed. "Walk close behind me?"

Cedar waggled his eyebrows. "You bet."

The outfits went over well. Scott got so many hoots and hollers and catcalls, he stayed almost permanently red all morning.

Of course they were naked on the beach.

Dolce and Gabbana loaned them their huge inflatable raft, and they floated off together across the lake, holding each other, kissing, dozing. They would have done more, but Scott wasn't quite ready to take the chance someone would see them, even when they'd taken the raft to the far south of the lake and away from prying eyes.

They were greeted warmly everywhere they went. People complimented Cedar on his performance the night before, and his bravery. And so many told them how cute they looked together.

It was in midafternoon, when Scott saw Blue sitting alone on the swing under the big oak tree, that his mood shifted.

He stopped and turned to Cedar.

"You okay?" Cedar asked.

"I-I've got a problem."

"What's that?"

Scott's stomach twisted.

"It's got to do with Blue over there." He nodded toward the young man, his legs swinging, feet not quite touching the ground.

Cedar sighed. "Yeah."

"Cedar—I talked to him the other day. What happened, what we saw? It wasn't quite consensual. Sure, he went with them—with that ass Howard...."

"Howard?" Cedar asked.

"Big *Sir*." Scott groaned inside. He swore he wasn't going to call the man that.

"Of course. I knew that."

"The point is that, at the worst, he practically raped the kid—and at best it was dubious consent. It's so fucking confusing, and I don't know what to do."

"Shit," said Cedar, and he took Scott's hand and pulled him back around the dining hall and sat him on a pretty little bench that someone had thoughtfully decorated with a rainbow boa.

"Shit is right." Scott leaned a head on Cedar's shoulder. He wanted to close his eyes. He wanted to do what the old Scott would have done. Nothing. But that really wasn't an option anymore. So instead, quietly, he told Cedar the whole story.

"Does he want to call the cops?" Cedar asked when Scott was done.

Scott sighed. "No. He doesn't want to do that. He says he went with them willingly enough. He just didn't like the way they treated him. He admits that they should have had a safe word. He says they were slapping his ass on the way, and he thinks he might have given them the wrong impression. He blames himself, Cedar."

"Fuck." Cedar let out a long sigh. "Classic sexual abuse behavior."

Scott thought of Blue and the trauma that could ride him for the rest of his life. "Gods, Cedar! I don't know. There's so much I don't know. Blue.... He acts like such a kid. But he's a man. Maybe he needs to take responsibility before he hooks up with someone, especially *two* someones! But is that just blaming the victim? Is there something I should be doing for him?"

Cedar shook his head. "There isn't anything you can do if he doesn't want it. Except be his friend. Let him know you'll be there for him if he needs it. Sounds to me like you've done that already."

Scott nodded doubtfully. Cedar was probably right, even if it didn't *feel* right. But then all of his other fears and worries came back in a rush.

"What am I going to do about Wyatt?" Scott cried.

"What about Wyatt, baby?"

"If he finds out that I knew and didn't say anything...."

"Are you afraid that Wyatt won't want to be your friend anymore?"

That was what he was afraid of, wasn't it?

I should be ashamed of myself.

And then Scott realized he *was* ashamed.

"No matter what I do, I could lose."

There was a long pause. "If every choice you have could end with you losing, then I think the obvious choice is that you do the right thing."

For a moment there was total and perfect silence. Not a single sound. No voices from the dining hall. No wind. Even the birds had stopped singing, the cicadas gone mute.

All Scott could hear was…

"If every choice you have could end with you losing, then I think the obvious choice is that you do the right thing."

That and…

"He *came* in me, Scott! He didn't wear a *condom*."

Cedar broke the silence. "You think Wyatt needs to know."

Oh fuck. Of course Wyatt needed to know. And not just because Howard may or may not have raped Blue. But because if he'd had sex with Blue without a condom, then who else had he had sex with without one? "Oh God, oh God." Why hadn't he even thought of that? Howard was not only menacing others, but he was taking Wyatt's life in his hands. That fucker! That son of a goddammed bitch!

"I'll tell him, baby."

"What?" *What?* What had Cedar said?

"I'll go tell Little Bear for you. I hardly know him. Maybe it would be best from me. Lets you off the hook."

Lets me off the hook.

"If I tell him and he doesn't want anything to do with me again, that's okay. You two are best friends."

Best friends.

"So I'll do it." Cedar stood up. "I'll do it now. I'll bet Little Bear is at his camp."

"He's setting up for another salon tonight," Scott said. He was all excited about it too. He was going to be serving one of his favorite shots. "Cocksucking Cowboys."

"What?" Cedar asked.

"He's going to be serving Cocksucking Cowboys."

"Oh." Cedar shrugged. "Okay… whatever. Why don't you go keep Blue company, and I'll go talk to Wyatt."

You would do that for me, thought Scott with wonder as Cedar turned and started walking away.

Scott jumped to his feet and rushed to Cedar, reached out and took his shoulder. "No," he said, "I'll do it."

Cedar looked at him, eyes swimming with questions.

"What are friends for?" Scott asked.

Cedar let out a long sigh. "My gods, I love you."

Scott didn't know whether to laugh in joy or cry at the words. He did neither.

He said, "I love you too."

CHAPTER FORTY-SIX

SCOTT FOUND Wyatt right where he thought he would: inside his camper getting ready for his little party. He'd knocked on the door, and Wyatt let him in, flush and excited. On the little counter, Scott saw Wyatt had filled his sink with ice, and there were a couple of liqueur bottles chilling. Butterscotch schnapps and Bailey's Irish cream.

"Hey, Scott! I have a great new joke for tonight."

Joke? "Oh?"

"Yeah. How do we know that Michelangelo was gay?" As usual, Wyatt was thrumming with excitement.

"I-I don't know. How *do* we know that Michelangelo was gay?"

"Because if he'd been straight, he would have painted the ceiling of the Sistine Chapel with a roller!" Wyatt fell back against the pop-up's little table he was laughing so hard.

It was a funny joke. Any other time he would have laughed.

"Oh, come on, Scott! Now *that* one was funny. You *gotta* laugh at that one."

Scott didn't say anything.

"Scott…. Are you okay?"

Again, Scott didn't say anything. He was frozen in place, trying to figure out how to lead into what he had to say. Should he just spit it out?

"Baby cakes, *you* needs to sit down," Wyatt said in his most queenie voice. "And what's more, I think *you* needs a Cocksucking Cowboy!"

"Yeah," Scott managed. "That sounds perfect."

So Wyatt opened his bottles and took a small glass, poured in the schnapps and topped it with a little of the Bailey's, and handed it to Scott. "Bottom's up, darlin'."

"Kinda big, isn't it? Don't you need this for tonight?"

"Scott. I gots me *plenty* for tonight. Drink. I can't put it back in the bottles now."

So Scott drank. He threw it back—for courage—and even popped it a couple times on the countertop's surface. Just like you were supposed to.

Wyatt sat down across from him. "Now tell Little Bear what's wrong."

Scott stared at his friend. His wonderful, goofy, adorable friend. Scott wanted to cry. But no. None of that. *Tell him.* "Howard had sex with Blue."

Wyatt cocked his head, got a curious look on his face, then asked, "What?"

Scott took a breath and wished for another big shot. "Howard had sex with Blue and...."

Before he could finish, Wyatt shook his head. "No, Scott. I don't know who told you this, but I know that didn't happen. I vetoed that shit."

Vetoed? "V-vetoed?"

"Yes," Wyatt said, nodding. "Night we were all at Peter Wagner's. The way he was pawing at the boy burned my ass. I vetoed that right away."

"Vetoed?"

"Yes, Scott. When you have an open relationship, you have rules to make sure it works. And one of our rules is that we can veto a play partner. Howard vetoes me now and again, and sometimes—not often—I veto him. And I told him no on Little Boy Blue."

Oh fuck me, thought Scott. Things had just gotten worse.

"I feel kinda bad about it. I know Howard likes his twinks, and the last thing I am is a twink. I should just let him do the kid. I guess I was just jealous—"

"Wyatt. I *saw* it." It was out of Scott's mouth before he could stop it.

Wyatt stiffened. There was a long pause. Then: "When?"

"The other morning." Scott swallowed hard. "The day I was making the necklace. The morning you didn't know where Howard was." Was that yesterday? The day before? Time ran all together here in Shangri-La. "A few hours later Cedar and I—Jockster—we went to Green Man's Grove... to have sex. But Howard was there already. With Blue and somebody else. I don't know who. They were fucking Blue over this big rock."

God! There. He had said it.

There was a long pause. Scott could see the hurt and confusion on his friend's face. *I did that. I made my best friend hurt.*

"I... I see." Wyatt shook. "Well.... I guess he and I will have to talk tonight. I'll wait until after the salon, of course. I don't want to ruin the party." He smiled a wavering smile, then stood up and took Scott's glass. "I should rinse this out. It'll attract flies."

He turned away and Scott said, "There's more."

"My own fault really," Wyatt said as if he hadn't heard. "I shouldn't have vetoed Blue. It wasn't fair. I'm a chubby cub. Blue is a pretty boy. How could I be that for Howard? If you're going to be in an open relationship, and I *am*, then I have to be mature about this kind of stuff and—"

"Wyatt, Howard barebacked Blue."

Wyatt froze. Another long pause. "What?"

Scott let out a long sigh. "He fucked Blue without a condom. Blue was really upset too. He cried on my shoulder for—"

Wyatt spun around. "Lied. The little fucker must have lied!" He nodded, eyes wide. "Little drama queen just wanted attention. I know Howard. He wouldn't play unsafe. I *know* it."

But Scott saw it in his eyes.

Oh shit, thought Scott.

There was a knowing in those eyes.

"I'm worried about you, Wyatt," Scott said. "I would have kept my mouth shut. I almost did. It's not my place to judge your relationship—" *My God! Did I just say that?* He took a breath. *Howard, you fucker. It's bad enough that you all but raped a man, but...* "—but I thought that if Howard would fuck Blue without a condom, then who else—"

"Scott!" Wyatt made a strange little strangled sound. "I-I gotta get ready for tonight. You should go."

Oh no....

"And aren't you having a little soiree too? Your 'famous' and *wildly* original Bucket-*O*-Ritas?"

Wow. That was kind of mean. Wyatt. Mean. Shit. Scott bit his lip. Hard.

"You should be getting ready. I know it's hard to make those things. Remember. I'm supposed to send people down your way once I've got them cocktailed. Gotta celebrate you and Jockster getting together. *Right?*"

The last word was almost a shout.

Scott's heart broke. He nodded. "Okay," he managed.

(*"If every choice you have could end with you losing, then I think the obvious choice is that you do the right thing."*)

And it looked like he had lost.

Scott left the little trailer, and as he stepped down onto the grass, he realized something else.

He wasn't the only one to lose tonight, was he?

Great friend I am.

CHAPTER FORTY-SEVEN

CEDAR AND Scott didn't say much while they got ready for their event. Blue was there, and he was helping. Well, he was running back and forth from the pavilion getting about a dozen chairs. Scott had only brought two with him from home. He hadn't thought he'd need more than that.

Scott had tried not to cry, but he did. When Cedar showed up at Scott's camp with Blue, he'd fought the tears back valiantly. But as soon as the kid ran off to get the first of the chairs, Cedar took him in his arms and Scott cried. He made it quick, though. He let it out in a rush and then pulled it in before Blue got back.

Blue. Looking at him only made it worse.

He was tempted to blame Blue. *If you hadn't gone off with Howard then none of this would have happened.*

But that would have been the old Scott. And he was beginning to think he liked this new Scott. This new Scott aborning. Like a Phoenix?

"Hey," Scott said as they arranged chairs. "What do you think of Phoenix as a faerie name? For me?"

"Well…," Cedar said.

"I like it!" Blue exclaimed.

"It fits…."

"Why do I hear a 'but'?" Scott asked.

"It's just that there must be a million Phoenixes out there." Cedar pursed his lips. "And Griffons. And Ravens. Storms, Angels, Rains…. Lots of Cats, too, but that's mostly women. "

"Well, I don't want to be a frigging cliché," Scott said, feeling defeated for some reason. *Of course, losing one of the best friends you ever had could have something to do with it!*

"It'll come," Cedar said.

"I don't think I really need one," Blue said. "My name's fucking weird enough."

They decided to delay their little "*soiree*" awhile. Super Gem had planned a dance at the pavilion, and Scott had come to adore the man. Look at him as a… well, a guide of sorts. He'd really helped Scott the day he thought he'd lost Cedar. Helped him without hardly saying a word.

Scott chose a combination of his new orange and gold sarong with his orange PPU jockstrap with its unique black-bordered leg straps. He loved that jock. And as far as he knew, the color didn't mean a damn thing. He didn't know if he'd dance in nothing but the athletic supporter—*Athletic? Hah! Him! Right!*—but hey, if the sarong swirled and gave a peek, why not? Hadn't he walked around most of the day in a jockstrap?

Hell. I ruined my friendship wearing nothing but a jock.

Cedar went with a jock sans sarong, and why not? Cedar Carrington he may have admitted he was to Scott and all of the attendees of the Heartland Queer Men's Festival, but he was also The Jockster, and Scott would have it no other way. Cedar wore something totally unlike any Scott had ever seen before, though, and he fell in love with it. It was white with a brown leather band in front and it had white ropes instead of elastic leg straps. Even the pouch was fabric instead of the classic supporting woven mesh.

"Wow," said Scott. "I've never seen anything like it…. I mean—*wow!*"

"It's from some company called Modus Vivendi. I think this was inspired by that sequel to *The 300.*"

"Which was wretched," Scott said.

"I missed it," Cedar said. "But I liked this."

"Hell yes!" Scott exclaimed. It was damned sexy. Made Scott want to make love. But it was a little difficult to get it up when you've lost your best friend.

The house lights were off when they got to the pavilion, but Dale must have brought his laser show because the ceiling and stage were awash with a zillion green and red swirling stars.

Super Gem and his husband—*Husband! Imagine!*—were at their station at Snakebite's soundboard and the house was a rockin'.

Madonna was followed by Katy Perry's "Roar," which led into Kylie Minogue singing the highly sexy "Can't Get You Out Of My Head."

Gentle Ben and his husband were serving wine off to the side—apparently the pavilion itself was an alcohol- and chemical-free zone—and who cared that it was wine in a box? And wasn't it ironic that Scott didn't care. He. Scott. The snob. But then hadn't he heard that some boxed wine or other had won some huge award in France—to the horror of the French? Scott and Cedar had a glass themselves, and hell, it was delicious!

But then Lady Gaga's "Born This Way" came on, and dammit, Scott couldn't resist. He let a smiling (beautiful) Cedar pull him up on the stage. The lyrics had taken on a whole new meaning to him this week. He danced through P!nk's "Raise Your Glass" as well and even Whitney Houston's "I Want to Dance with Somebody."

After that it was time to leave. It wouldn't be a good thing for people to show up at Scott's first "salon" ever and there not be anyone there.

Scott switched on his (Wyatt's) margarita party lights while Cedar dashed down those damned sixty steps to the dining hall and got the bucket of frozen party goodness out of the kitchen freezer.

To Scott's surprise and happiness, they had quite a few visitors, and the frozen margaritas were all used up. Precious brought some booze he needed to get rid of (sadly, he had to leave on Monday) and the party was able to go on long past the time Donna Summer's "Last Dance" drifted down to them from the pavilion on the summer breeze.

Just as things were wrapping up, Wyatt arrived. Only a few people were left by then: Hound Dog and Bean (their normally boisterous dogs asleep beneath their chairs), Lorax, Bobcat, and Hodor—he of only one word. A lightning bug flashed a margarita green. It was the first lightning bug he'd seen the whole week, and wasn't it funny it was even occurring to him at a time like this? "Any margaritas left?" Wyatt asked. "I hear they're a hit."

Scott stiffened. He couldn't move.

"Sorry," Cedar piped in. "They've been gone for a couple hours."

"Ah well," Wyatt said.

"We've got a *little* more raspberry vodka though," Cedar said.

"What'cha got to mix it with?"

"Some lemonade?"

Wyatt smiled. "Why that would be most satisfactory, kind sir," he said and settled into one of the wooden pavilion chairs.

Cedar made him a drink and then settled down next to Scott, laying a hand on his bare thigh. After a few drinks he'd gotten ballsy enough to cast off the sarong. It was a very warm night, and he didn't need it.

"The lights look good," Wyatt said.

"T-thank you." Scott sat down next to his friend. "They're your lights."

"Nonsense. I gave them to you. The cocktail is quite good too."

Scott shrugged. "Precious brought the vodka."

"How fortuitous," Wyatt replied. "You have good friends."

"I…." Scott's voice caught. "The best."

There was a long pause. Wyatt looked up. "Wow," he said. "Look at that. Have you ever seen so many stars?"

Scott looked, and it was indeed beautiful. Over and over he was amazed at the sky here at camp, so very far from Kansas City. The stars were so vibrant— so alive. Oh! And look there. Another firefly.

Then he got an idea.

Scott got up and went and turned off the margarita party lights. Suddenly they were plunged into complete darkness. There was no moon, and the stars were like diamonds and sugar cast over black satin. They could even see a path of light across the sky that was the disk of the Milky Way.

And lightning bugs. Here. There. And over there. Where had they come from? It was like strange little green stars had dropped down from the sky to join them.

"Wow," Scott gasped. He had never seen anything more beautiful in his life. "You don't even see this in Terra's Gate, even though we're such a small city. I thought the sky was beautiful the first night. But wow. You take this for granted living in a city."

"You take a lot for granted," replied Wyatt quietly.

Scott felt the words like a knife to the heart. He glanced around him, but no one was saying a word. Without the lights he could hardly even see them. It was almost like they weren't there.

"No," Wyatt said with a sigh. "Not you. *We* do. We all take a lot for granted."

"Tell me about it," said Hound Dog.

"I do," said Lorax. "That's why I come back here every year. To be reminded. To get me back on track."

Scott swallowed a sob. *I won't cry.*

An infinite time passed then, while no one said a word.

"I love you, Scott," Wyatt said. "You know that, right?"

The sob escaped. "I— You do?"

"I do."

There was a long silence.

Then: "Aren't you going to say, 'I love you too, Wyatt'?"

Scott almost laughed. "I do," he whispered. "I do."

Another pause.

"That took a lot of guts, Scott."

Scott let out a strangled cry.

"I don't know how you did it."

"I—I…." Scott stopped. He didn't know what to say.

"Howard and I… talked. Well. Screamed, really. I'm sure everyone heard."

"N-no," said Scott.

"We were at the dance," Cedar said. "It was loud."

Wyatt laughed. "We were pretty loud too. But I'm glad the music drowned us out."

"Maybe we should go," said Bean.

"No," Wyatt said. "Stay. Please. All of you."

Silence filled the night again.

"We're okay," Wyatt said.

"You and Howard?"

"Yeah, me and Howard…."

Scott's stomach clenched. He couldn't help but wish for a different outcome.

Really? What did you want? For them to break up?

And quite suddenly he realized that *is* what he wanted. Wyatt deserved so much better than Howard. And goddammit all, Howard was getting off lightly!

"But that's not what I meant," Wyatt said.

"Huh?"

"I meant *you* and *me*."

You and me? There is *a you and me?* Now the tears were flowing. Again. *I've never cried so much in my life*, Scott thought.

"We're okay? Right?" Wyatt asked.

"Yes," said Scott. "We are."

"Good."

Silence.

"You look hot in that jockstrap, by the by."

Scott burst into laughter. It was a weird feeling, laughing and crying at the same time.

"I can't believe you had the balls to do it. Prance around all day like that. Kudos, my friend."

My friend...! "Well, you know what they say," Scott replied. "When in Rome."

"Yeah. When in...." Wyatt sat up. "Hey!" he exclaimed. "*That's it!*"

"What?" Scott asked.

"Your faerie name! What do you think of... Roman?"

"I—I...." *Roman.* Then, "Roman," he said aloud, trying it out for size.

"I like it," said Cedar.

"You do?"

"Me too," Lorax said.

"Yeah," Bobcat added.

Hound Dog and Bean agreed. And he thought that Hodor giving a mighty "Hodor!" meant he agreed as well.

"Roman," Scott said and felt a little burst of excitement.

"Shall we make it official?" Wyatt asked.

"Yes," everyone chorused.

"All right then! On three! One.... Two.... Three...!"

And as one, the small group shouted into the night: "Roman! Roman! Roman!"

Sarah Jane and Rammstein jumped up and barked, as if joining in. And who knew, perhaps they were.

Hell. Even Hodor said his name!

A chill passed through Scott, and goose bumps shivered all down his arms and back and even his ass. Cedar pulled him to his feet. Kissed him. Everyone rose and kissed him as well.

"Welcome, Roman," Wyatt said. "It's official and said three times. Welcome to the Faerie."

CHAPTER FORTY-EIGHT

IT WAS the first Saturday of the month, and that meant it was Porch Night, the must-not-miss evening for the F.F., aka the Fabulous Four. Since it was August, it was Wyatt's turn to host, and it was no surprise that he had made Aviation Cocktails. At least no surprise to Scott (known in some secret circles as Roman).

"And gods, do you *know* how hard it was to find crème de violette? And all for a few dashes? I almost skipped it. Harry Craddock just omitted the stuff in his *very* influential *Savoy Cocktail Book*, published in 1930 I might add. I thought about it. I really did. But I know the sweet, sexy man who gave me the recipe would *never* have approved. Besides this *is* Porch Night, right?"

And I would have made a bucket of frozen margaritas, thought Scott.

"And are you guys sure you don't mind me being here?" Cedar asked. "I know this is supposed to be just you four. Isn't that the rule?"

"You know," said Wyatt. "I don't ever remember that actually *being* a *rule*."

"But...." Scott shut his mouth. He had almost said, "But we've never allowed Howard to join us," but chose to leave it unsaid instead. Howard was out for the evening. Gods knew where.

"I think the rule was more that someone you're casually dating shouldn't come," Wyatt added, passing out the purpleish cocktails. He smiled at Cedar as he handed him his drink. "I don't think you two are casually dating."

"Not throwing vases yet," Scott said, and Cedar and Wyatt laughed.

"I don't get it," said Asher, trying his cocktail. "Gosh. This is *nice*."

Wyatt all but glowed with pride. "Score! Asher likes a cocktail that *I* brought to the table!"

Scott looked around at his friends. He knew they were suspicious. He *knew* what they were thinking. At least what Sloan and Asher were thinking. *That I've done it again. That Cedar is boyfriend de jour.*

But no one was saying that.

Not even Asher.

Then Scott thought of something. "Then what about Max?" he asked.

And to Scott's surprise, the very mention of Max's name made something magical happen. A feeling washed over him, a light-headedness that made him stumble.

"Babe? Are you okay," Cedar asked, rising to steady him.

"Y-yes," he somehow said. "I am."

He looked at Sloan and once more wanted to cry. *So much crying lately!*

I've released you, Sloan, he thought. *I have finally and at last let you go.* He smiled. His heart fluttered. "I think you should call Max," Scott said. "I don't think the rule of 'casually dating' applies for you two either."

"I—are you sure?" Sloan asked.

"I'm sure," Scott said and Wyatt agreed and Asher—well, he was too busy studying his cocktail to say anything.

Sloan smiled that smile where his dimples sank in deep, especially the right one. It was a beautiful smile. Scott had been in love with that smile for so many years. But now? He looked into Cedar's beautiful face. Looked at *his* smile. His heart began to speed up and damned if his cock didn't shift in his pants. *Oh, those eyes!*

Scott turned back to Sloan. *I release you.* Then, aloud, "Yes. He needs to be here."

Sloan jumped from the porch swing and grinned like a little boy, practically prancing. "I'm going to call him. His son isn't back from France yet. And I don't think Max has any studying to do." He bounced. He actually bounced, and then pulling his cell phone from his pants, dashed down the steps and out to the sidewalk.

Scott felt his heart skip a beat. *Felt* it happen.

It was nice.

"Where's the bathroom?" Cedar asked.

"I'll show you," Wyatt said. "I gotta get the whores de ovaries anyway."

They went into the house.

Scott turned back to Asher and saw him eyeing Cedar as he left.

Don't approve? he wondered.

But then Asher looked up at him. He shook his head. "I have to tell you, Scott. I'm impressed. I mean. *Wow*. He's *hot*."

Too hot for me, motherfucker?

Asher smiled. "And he's a nice guy. It's about time. I knew you could do it."

Scott's mouth fell open.

"Could do what?" Wyatt asked, coming out onto the porch holding a baking pan with a ludicrous furry bear-paw oven mitt.

"The Heimlich maneuver," Asher said, taking one of the proffered mini quiches.

"The Heimlich maneuver?" Wyatt exclaimed. "No! You can do the Heimlich maneuver, Scott?" He held out the pan to Scott. "I do know you look *smokin'* in a Cellblock 13 jockstrap."

"He sure does," said Cedar, joining them. He was a fast pisser. "Turned me into a top!" He grabbed a couple quiches and kissed Scott. "Well, no. Not a complete top."

Scott blushed and Cedar grabbed his ass.

Asher leaned back in the porch swing just as Sloan rushed back up the steps. "Max is coming!"

"Just make him clean up before he gets here," said Wyatt, and they all began to laugh.

Scott caught Asher staring at Cedar again. He shook his head, then turned to Scott. "So tell me about this witchy-woo-woo camp," Asher said.

"It's *not* witchy-woo-woo," Scott snapped, and then almost laughed at himself. "It's the Heartland Queer Men's Festival. And it's miraculous. It's going to be what my whole year revolves around."

"Oh, really?"

"Really," Scott said.

The last days of Festival had been wonderful, if not quite as explosive as the weekend had been. Things calmed down after Sunday night. By Monday morning the number of attendees had dropped by more than half, bringing it from 136 to 59. By Tuesday they lost another dozen. It was a law of the world: most people had to work, and for some, other things had greater precedent on their limited vacation days than ten days of Festival.

Not for Scott, though. It would be the entire ten days or nothing from now on as far as he was concerned.

He had cried and laughed a lot those last four days. And Thursday didn't really count. Festival turned the land back over to the general public at noon. There had even been a bell.

The last of the last gathered together for a group photograph just before that bell was rung. Then the hugs and kissed commenced, and oh, how his heart had ached. He didn't want to go home.

Funny, he thought and laughed. *I didn't want to go to Festival in the first place!*

Wil Cooper, his boss, had come to him toward the end of Scott's first day back to work (and oh, how hard it had been to leave Cedar at home). "You're floating," he said.

"I am not!" Scott snapped, then blushed, then grinned.

Wil raised an eyebrow. "Wow. You *did* have a good time."

"I-I did," Scott told him. "Thank you. If you hadn't made me go...."

I don't know where I would be today, Scott realized.

Scott looked at Wyatt, and before he knew he was going to do it, he was hugging him tight and kissing his cheek.

"Watch the hot pan," Wyatt exclaimed.

"Watch who you're kissing!" Cedar said and pulled Scott into his arms and laid a kiss on him that made him want to leave Wyatt's and take Cedar home to bed.

"Wow," said Asher. "Just... *wow*."

But no, thought Scott. *Not right now*. They had time.

From the way Cedar was looking at him, he knew they had lots of time.

Magic.

It was magic.

His thoughts went back, and he heard the song his fellow faeries all sang together at that last Circle. *Dear friends, queer friends.*

The thought brought tears to his eyes.

Then he looked at the men sitting around him. Sloan. Wyatt. Cedar—oh Cedar! And yes, even Asher. *Dear friends. Queer friends.*

He almost wanted to sing.

Let me tell you how I am feeling...

In fact, he'd opened his mouth when Wyatt rescued him.

"Hey!" Wyatt all but shouted. "Stop me if you heard this one, but—"

As if there were any stopping Wyatt!

"—what's the difference between a bitchy queen and an evil queen?"

No one had an answer, of course. Not even Max, who was stepping up onto the porch at that very moment. After all, Terra's Gate wasn't a very big town. It hadn't taken him long to get there. But then, he had motivation.

Wyatt pumped himself up and then cried. "A bitchy queen takes one look at the outfit you're planning on wearing that night and says, 'You're not going out in *that*, are you?' And the evil queen says, 'Darling! You look *fab*-ulous!'"

Their laughter filled the night.

NOTES FROM THE AUTHOR— MUSIC AND MORE

From the very beginning, I realized that music was going to be a very important part of this book. But that can be difficult. Books are a written medium and unless the reader is familiar with the songs, lyrics on a page aren't necessarily meaningful. Nevertheless, I knew there had to be both songs and lyrics in this book.

So….

First of all, I want to send out a very special thanks to Heather Thornton for letting me pretend that her songs were written and recorded by Cyan Carrington. I know how to tell stories, but a poet or lyricist I most assuredly am not. Heather is a most remarkable songwriter and vocalist, however, and hey! Now you can look her up and actually *hear* some of the songs in my novel. I hope you will. You'll be glad you did. You can find her song "Open Road" on YouTube. Here is the link:

https://www.youtube.com/watch?v=xc6x9CenQjU

You might even support an artist. It's not just us writers who are starving! Find Heather at http://www.heatherthorntonmusic.com/.

The song "Dear Friends, Queer Friends" is a very old Radical Faerie song that has been sung for more years than I will ever know. I got a surprise recently and found out that it is a reworking of a very, very old Quaker song, although the lyrics herein are quite a bit… ah, different! LOL! Jon Watts, a Quaker and songwriter and recorder, did a wonderfully haunting version you can find on YouTube. If you want to hear it, check it out, and imagine the "Queer" lyrics I use in this book, here's a link: Enjoy! http://www.youtube.com/watch?v=0i0a76cFkso

The "Dear Friends, Queer Friends" lyrics were by Donald Engstrom, who gave me permission to use them here in my book. He is a good friend of the famous Starhawk. If you know who she is, you will gasp like I did! Imagine! Being friends with *the* Starhawk!

Donald also created the Queer God Ritual, which he kindly gave me permission to use. I did take a few liberties with it, but he has always said that is exactly what people should do. Thank you, my dear brother!

If you have a chance, *please* (pretty please?) check out the song "Altar of Love" by Karen Drucker and David Ault. It is *wonderful*! I would also highly recommend you check out their websites at http://www.karendrucker.com/ and http://www.davidault.com/.

And as far as the hilarious "Hoo Hoo Song," well, that one is by the amazingly talented Celia. I've seen her in concert and I am a big, big fan. She's a singer, songwriter, and hilarious comedienne. Her CDs are incredible and her Trestle Foote Faerie character is sidesplitting.

Find her at www.celiaonline.com.

And you can also hear the "Hoo Hoo Song" if you go to YouTube (you'll be glad you did):

https://www.youtube.com/watch?v=P2vP1jbvu9E

RECIPES:

I am surprised by how many e-mails I get telling me how good the food in my stories sounds, and do I have the recipes? No—LOL!—I usually don't. I either made them up off the top of my head because they sounded good or saw things online while researching. In my book *Spring Affair*, I simply used the menu of a local vegan restaurant to make the menu for Café Namasté.

So I began to think…. Should I start including recipes? After all, the wonderful writer EM Lynley includes them in her Delectable series (you should check them out, by the way; they are wonderful!).

Well, then I met her and she enchanted me (we got drunk together), and I mentioned the above, and she encouraged me to do just that—include recipes! Said she wouldn't consider me copying her at all.

So here it is, folks. Some recipes. I've tasted all of these and love them. Let me know if you do!

Bon appetit!

COCKTAILS:

Cocksucking Cowboy

2/3 ounce butterscotch schnapps
1/3 ounce Bailey's Irish cream (or appropriate knockoff)

Pour butterscotch schnapps into a shot glass. Very carefully add the Bailey's so that it floats on top, making a lovely little two-layer drinkie. Serve.

Aviation Cocktail

1-1/2 ounces quality gin
3/4 ounce lemon juice
2 dashes maraschino liqueur
2 dashes crème de violette

Mix together in a cocktail shaker with ice. Serve in cocktail/martini glasses with a cherry and maybe a twist of lemon peel to make it especially *fab*-ulous. Chilling the glasses makes it faerie perfection.

ENTREES:

Caribbean Black Beans
Serves: 4

1/4 cup olive oil
1 onion, chopped
2 cloves garlic, chopped
1-1/2 teaspoons chili powder
4 cups cooked black beans
3 cups water
1 bay leaf

1 tablespoon red wine vinegar
1/2 tablespoon Tabasco pepper sauce
1 pinch sugar
1 cup long grain enriched white rice
1/2 teaspoon turmeric
3/4 cup red onion, chopped
2 jalapenos, minced
1/2 7-ounce jar roasted red peppers

Heat oil in heavy large saucepan over medium heat. Add onion and cook until beginning to soften, about 5 minutes. Add garlic and chili powder and cook 1 minute, stirring constantly. Add beans, 1 cup water, and bay leaf. Simmer until reduced to thick soup consistency, about 20 minutes. Remove bay leaf. Add vinegar, pepper sauce, and sugar. Season beans with salt and pepper.

Meanwhile, bring remaining 2 cups of water to boil in heavy medium saucepan. Add rice, turmeric, and a pinch of salt and stir. Cover and cook over low heat until rice is tender and all liquid is absorbed, about 20 minutes.

Mix chopped onions and chilies in small bowl.

Mound rice in center of platter. Spoon beans around rice. Arrange roasted pepper slices atop beans.

Pass red onion relish separately if desired.

Cold Cucumber Sauce
Serves: 4

1/2 pound cucumbers (about 2 small), peeled, seeded, and halved lengthwise
1/2 teaspoon kosher salt
1/4 cup red onion, minced
1/4 cup yogurt, drained of excess liquid for about 30 minutes (or use Greek yogurt)
1/4 cup sour cream
1 tablespoon fresh herbs, minced (dill, mint, cilantro, parsley and/or chives—you can pick and choose which of the herbs you want to use, 1 tablespoon total. The ones listed are suggestions.)
1 tablespoon jalapeño, minced (or more if you like it hot)

1 tablespoon lemon juice, or more to taste
black pepper to taste

Cut the cucumbers into 1/8-inch dice. Place the cucumbers in a large colander, set in the sink or a large bowl, sprinkle them with salt, and let them drain for 30 minutes.

Meanwhile, place the onion in a bowl, cover with cold water, and let stand for 30 minutes.

Transfer the cucumbers to a large bowl, squeezing the last bit of excess moisture out of them with your hands before you place them in the bowl. Drain the onion thoroughly and add to the cucumbers. Add the yogurt, sour cream, herbs, and jalapeño. Mix gently and add the lemon juice. Season with black pepper (you shouldn't need any salt) to taste and add more lemon juice, if you wish. Refrigerate for at least 1 hour before serving.

Chicken-Fried Tofu

This is a surprisingly delicious meal. I was stunned while eating it. The frozen and then thawed tofu mocks the texture of meat. Really! Make sure you freeze the tofu solid and then let it thaw before making this meal. No shortcuts!

1 pound extra-firm tofu (it comes in a brick-like shape), frozen, thawed, patted dry, and sliced into 1/2-inch thick slices. This makes three to four slices.
Flour for dredging
1 whole egg
1/4 cup soy sauce
1/4 cup water
1 teaspoon black pepper
1 teaspoon ground cumin
2 teaspoons ground coriander
1/16 box Whole Wheat Ritz Crackers (about 1/2 a sleeve from one of the large boxes)

Gravy
1-1/2 teaspoons olive oil

1 whole Portobello mushroom, cap only, chopped 3/4 inch thick
1/2 teaspoon black pepper
1 heaping tablespoon flour
1/2 teaspoon ground cumin
1/2 teaspoon ground coriander
1-1/4 tablespoons soy sauce
1 cup water

Preheat oven to 400 degrees F.

Freezing the tofu first is very important; it alters the texture and makes the tofu chewier.

Wring or press tofu until dry after thawing. (You can expedite thawing by placing tofu under cold running water.) Arrange four shallow pans or bowls for dipping. The first has a mixture of the soy sauce, water, and spices. The next is for flour. The next is beaten eggs. The last is cracker crumbs. Roll the tofu slices in each and place on a lightly greased baking sheet. Bake for 15 minutes.

Meanwhile, make the gravy. Heat oil over medium heat. Add the chopped mushrooms and sauté until they release their juices and the liquid evaporates. Add flour and spices and stir until lightly browned. Add soy sauce and water and continue to cook until thickened. (I'd substitute milk for some of the water.) Serve over tofu.

B.G. THOMAS lives in Kansas City with his husband of more than a decade and their fabulous little dog. He is lucky enough to have a lovely daughter as well as many extraordinary friends. He has a great passion for life.

B.G. loves romance, comedies, fantasy, science fiction, and even horror—as far as he is concerned, as long as the stories are character driven and entertaining, it doesn't matter the genre. He has gone to literature conventions his entire adult life, where he's been lucky enough to meet many of his favorite writers. He has made up stories since he was child; it is where he finds his joy.

In the nineties, he wrote for gay magazines but stopped because the editors wanted all sex without plot. "The sex is never as important as the characters," he says. "Who cares what they are doing if we don't care about them?" Excited about the growing male/male romance market, he began writing again. Gay men are what he knows best, after all—since he grew out of being a "practicing" homosexual long ago. He submitted a story and was thrilled when it was accepted in four days.

"Leap, and the net will appear" is his personal philosophy and his message to all. "It is never too late," he states. "Pursue your dreams. They will come true!"

Visit his website and blog at http://bthomaswriter.wordpress.com/ or contact him directly at bgthomaswriter@aol.com.

Seasons of Love Series

http://www.dreamspinnerpress.com

Don't miss

Don't miss

THE BOY WHO
CAME IN FROM
THE COLD

B.G. THOMAS

http://www.dreamspinnerpress.com

Also from this author

All
ALONE
in a Sea of
ROMANCE

B.G. Thomas

http://www.dreamspinnerpress.com

Also from this author

ANYTHING
COULD
HAPPEN

B.G. THOMAS

http://www.dreamspinnerpress.com

Also from this author

Grumble Monkey & the Department Store Elf

B.G. THOMAS

http://www.dreamspinnerpress.com

More from this author

http://www.dreamspinnerpress.com

More from this author

http://www.dreamspinnerpress.com

More from this author

How Could Love
Be Wrong?

B.G. Thomas

http://www.dreamspinnerpress.com

More from this author

http://www.dreamspinnerpress.com

DESERT crossing

B.G. THOMAS

More from this author

http://www.dreamspinnerpress.com

More from this author

http://www.dreamspinnerpress.com

www.ingramcontent.com/pod-product-compliance
Lightning Source LLC
Chambersburg PA
CBHW050033030726
47506CB00001B/250